Evelyn Hood was born and raised in Paisley. An ex-journalist. she has been a full time writer for several ... talents to plays, short stories, child ... novels that have earned her widespr ... increasing readership.

For more information about Evelyn and her books, visit www.evelynhood.co.uk

PEBBLES ON THE BEACH

Evelyn Hood

sphere

SPHERE

First published in Great Britain in 1995 by Little, Brown and Company
This edition published in 1996 by Warner Books
Reprinted 1996 (twice), 1998, 1999
Reprinted by Time Warner Paperbacks in 2004
Reissued in 2010 by Sphere

A CIP catalogue record for this book
is available from the British Library.

ISBN 978-0-7515-4521-0

Printed and bound in Great Britain by
Clays Ltd, St Ives plc

Papers used by Sphere are natural, renewable and
recyclable products sourced from well-managed forests and certified
in accordance with the rules of the Forest Stewardship Council.

Mixed Sources

Product group from well-managed
forests and other controlled sources
www.fsc.org Cert no. SGS-COC-004081
© 1996 Forest Stewardship Council

Sphere
An imprint of
Little, Brown Book Group
100 Victoria Embankment
London EC4Y 0DY

An Hachette UK Company
www.hachette.co.uk

www.littlebrown.co.uk

To Una and Malcolm,
for putting up with me through thick and thin

1

'Lachlan!'

Trace horses dragging a loaded cart up Mearns Street from the docks to the nearby sugar refinery clattered by just as Elspeth shouted her cousin's name across the width of the playground, ironbound wheels and hooves rumbling and sparking over the cobblestones.

The figure leaning against a tenement wall opposite the school gates, studying a newspaper, didn't move. Frustrated, Elspeth put two fingers to her lips in the way Thomas and Lachlan had taught her years before, and blew a piercing whistle that cut through the chill autumn air.

This time Lachlan looked up at once, his young face splitting into a huge grin as he saw her at the bottom of the school steps. He wasn't the only one to look in her direction; all through the playground and in the street beyond the railings heads turned. Women gossiping to each other from the tenement windows opposite the school, most of them with their arms comfortably folded on cushions or blankets protecting them from the stone sills, gaped and craned to see where the noise had come from.

'Elspeth Bremner! Kindly remember that you're a young lady and not a steam whistle down at the shipyards!' snapped the teacher who had just emerged on to the steps, and Elspeth whirled guiltily, the movement whipping her skirt against her long thin legs.

1

'Yes, Miss Scott, sorry, Miss Scott. It's just th-that—' She was stammering in her excitement at seeing Lachlan right there in Greenock, when she had thought him to be in some army barracks in England, '—that's our Lachlan over there. He m-must have come home on leave and I didn't know about it—'

The woman's face softened. 'In that case, run along – but don't you ever let out that dreadful noise in my hearing again.'

'Yes, Miss Scott, thank you, Miss Scott.' Elspeth set off at a run across the playground, weaving around the loitering groups. Her schoolbooks, held together by an old belt, were clutched to her chest, and the thick brown plait that hung down her back bounced against her spine with every step.

The headlong rush didn't stop until she was through the gate and across the street, letting the bundle of books fall unheeded on the pavement, running straight into Lachlan's open arms, being swung up into the air and round in a circle.

'I didn't know you were coming home!' she said breathlessly as he put her down.

'Neither did I till yesterday. God, Ellie, ye've put on weight! Ye were just a wee scliff of a thing when I last saw ye.'

'I'm older now.' She prodded him in the stomach. 'You've got fatter yourself.'

'Och, that's the stodge they feed us in the army,' Lachlan McDonald said, then glanced over Elspeth's shoulder. 'Hello, Molly.'

'Hello.' Molly McKibbin's round face was strangely blotchy. She looked, Elspeth thought, surprised, as though she was coming down with something. 'You dropped your books, Elspeth.'

'I didn't drop them, I threw them down.'

'Without looking? They could have landed in some old man's spit,' Molly said self-righteously, turning the bundle over and examining it carefully.

'They're fine.' Elspeth knew that her voice was too sharp,

2

but with good reason. It was true that she and Molly always walked home from school together, but surely today, with Lachlan arriving so unexpectedly, Molly should have had the tact to leave the two of them on their own. Elspeth reached for the books, but Lachlan stretched a long arm out beyond hers, and got to the shabby strap first.

'I'll carry them. I'll take yours as well, if you like,' he added, and Molly promptly handed over her own armful of books, simpering foolishly.

'You've both shot up while I've been away,' he teased, and Molly's simper became a silly little giggle. Best friend or not, Elspeth could have slapped her.

'What's that on your face?' she asked instead.

Molly's hand flew up. 'Where?'

'Your cheeks are all blotchy – and your neck, too. Big red blotches all over. Have a look at yourself in that shop window there.'

'Stop teasin' the lassie,' Lachlan told her, amused. 'It's nothin', Molly, just a wee bit red – from the wind, mebbe. It's cold enough. Come on, I've only got till tomorrow and I don't want to spend my leave standin' here.'

Behind their wire-framed spectacles, Molly's eyes shot a look of pure venom at Elspeth, who gave a bland smile in return.

'Where's your uniform?' Elspeth slipped her hand possessively into Lachlan's free arm as they turned towards home, leaving Molly to trail behind them.

'Ach, I couldnae wait to get out of it and intae my own clothes. It's scratchy, and it doesnae fit me properly. They never do.' Then, squeezing her arm against his side, 'Happy birthday, Ellie.'

'You remembered?'

'Of course I remembered, that's why I'm here. I said to the Sergeant-Major, "Listen, sir," I said. "Our Ellie'll be thirteen years old next Thursday, so I'd be much obliged if ye could see yer way tae stoppin' the war for a couple of days so's I can go home and taste a bit of that dumpling my mum'll be making for her."'

'You did not!' Molly gasped from Elspeth's other side.

'Of course he didn't, don't be daft!'

'But I would have, if he hadnae come up with the idea himself before I even got a chance tae speak tae him.'

'I wish it was longer than just till tomorrow!'

'Aye, well, I've not quite managed tae see the Kaiser off yet, so they need me tae go back and finish the job properly. Then I'll be home for good. Here – try my jacket pocket.'

Elspeth slipped her hand into the nearest pocket, as she had often done on cold days in the past, before the war. The familiar warmth of his body against her fingers, the confident swing of his hip, brought back comforting memories. She had missed Thomas, the first of the two brothers to go off to war, but Lachlan had always been a special favourite. When he was called up, only weeks after his seventeenth birthday, she had cried herself to sleep for several nights after he left.

Her fingers encountered a tiny glass bottle; she drew it out and gave a gasp of delight.

'It's toilet water! Oh, Lachlan—!'

He flushed. 'Well, ye're growin' up now, aren't ye? I thought that'd please ye more than sweeties.'

Molly pushed in between them, so close that she tramped on Elspeth's heel. 'It's bonny,' she agreed, her voice hushed with awe as she peered at the pretty little bottle with a delicate spray of lavender pictured on the label. She reached out an avaricious hand, but Elspeth pulled her own hand back and opened the bottle to allow the light fragrance of lavender to tickle at her nose. She flipped the bottle deftly over then upright again, then dabbed her wet fingertip below each ear.

'Can you smell it, Lachlan?'

He sniffed, his nose cold against her earlobe. 'Aye, but I'd as soon smell dumplin'. Come on, I'm hungry!'

Ignoring the silent plea in Molly's eyes, Elspeth refastened the bottle and put it into her pocket. Tomorrow after school she would let Molly have a dab of lavender, but not today. This was her birthday, her special day, and she wanted to keep its joys to herself for a little while, at least.

The three of them reached the top of the slight hill leading up from the school, and Elspeth stopped, as she usually did, to drink in the view. So did Lachlan; she had known he would, in spite of his claim to be hungry. Like her, he loved any view of the River Clyde.

The rest of Mearns Street ran down the hill that Greenock was built on. From where they stood, the tenements on either side, dropping away below them, framed the width of the River Clyde and the soft green hills on the far side. At the bottom of the street could be seen a clutter of cranes in one of the shipyards fringing the river all along the Greenock shore.

Today, both the September sky and the river below it were grey, but that didn't bother Elspeth, nor, she knew, would it concern Lachlan. The Clyde fascinated them both in all its moods, at all times of the year.

'It's grand tae taste this air again, and see the hills,' Lachlan said after a moment. 'They don't have a lot of hills in England.'

He drew in a deep lungful of air and Molly, standing demurely on his other side, did the same. 'Wee bizzum!' Elspeth thought resentfully, for normally Molly fussed and fretted impatiently when Elspeth stopped at this point every day. Peering round Lachlan, she glared at her friend, who smiled sweetly back at her.

She got her revenge a few short minutes later, when they reached the corner of Roxburgh Street. 'See you tomorrow then, Molly.'

'Eh?'

'This is where you turn off for your own house,' Elspeth said slowly and clearly, as though talking to a small child, taking

Molly's books from Lachlan and handing them back to their owner. 'Unless you've moved and not thought to tell me?'

Embarrassment spread the blotches over poor Molly's face until they joined together to create a full blush. 'Oh. I didn't realise we were here already.'

'I'll see you tomorrow morning, then.'

As the two of them crossed Roxburgh Street, leaving the other girl behind, Elspeth took Lachlan's arm again, hugging it tightly against her side. He wasn't going to be home for long and she wanted to make the most of this short, precious moment together. In the evening the neighbours would crowd into the small flat to greet the returned warrior and hear about his experiences, which meant that there would be little enough private time to spare.

Lachlan's mother, she knew, would feel the same way. Flora McDonald, fair though she was in most things, had always favoured her sons more than her daughters.

'What's the army like, Lachlan?'

'Ach, it's OK.'

'Have you done any fighting yet?'

'We've just been trainin' so far,' he said vaguely. 'How's school?'

'It's OK,' she mimicked, and he gave her a friendly punch on the shoulder.

'Don't you be so cheeky tae one of His Majesty's brave soldiers! Just a year to go, eh?'

Elspeth hesitated, then decided to let him be the first to hear her news. 'Miss Scott said this morning that she thinks I should stay on for another year.'

'Oh? So we've got a clever-clogs in the family, have we?'

'It's not just me – Mattie's done well too, in spite of having to be off so much.' Mattie, Lachlan's sister, was in the class above Elspeth's. She suffered from asthma and was at home that day, recovering from an attack. Mattie should have left school the previous June, but her parents had agreed to let her stay on for an extra year, to make up for the time she had missed.

'Right enough, ye write a grand letter. Half the lads in the unit look forward tae your letters arrivin'.'

'You don't show them to anyone else, do you?' Elspeth asked, alarmed.

'Why not? Reading them makes me feel as if I'm back home again, and they're funny, too. The other lads enjoy them. But ye'd not want tae stay on at the school, would ye?' asked Lachlan, who had been desperate to leave school as soon as possible and join his father in one of the shipyards.

'I think I would. I like school, and Miss Scott says I could get a better job if I stayed on longer. She says that mebbe I could learn to be a teacher myself.'

'God, imagine havin' a teacher in the family! Have ye told Mam?' It would never occur to Lachlan to mention his father first. Henry McDonald was an easy-going man, happy to leave the family decisions and the family budget in his wife's capable hands.

'I've not told anyone yet, except you. D'you think Auntie would agree?'

Although Flora McDonald and her husband were the only parents Elspeth had ever known, Flora had always insisted on her calling them Auntie and Uncle.

'I don't know, Ellie. Mebbe she will. The war'll be well over by then, surely, and that means that Thomas and me'll be back home, so that'd help with the money. Mind you, I've still got my apprenticeship tae finish.'

'I thought that with Rachel earning a wage now, and Mattie out of school by then—'

Elspeth's voice trailed away. Flora and Henry McDonald had been good to her as it was, taking her in when her mother, Flora's dearest friend, died giving birth to her. But they had their own family to worry about, and they might not be prepared to support her for longer than they had to.

They were at the spot where Regent Street cut across Mearns Street now, the corner where their tenement building stood. 'I've got something else for you,' Lachlan said as they stepped into the spotless close with its tiled walls and scrubbed stone floor, edged all the way from the pavement to the top landing with white pipeclay. 'I came across it on the train and thought ye'd like it.'

'Something you found? A kitten?' Elspeth asked doubtfully, following him up the first flight of stairs. Flora refused to allow any pets in her house, not so much as a canary, on the grounds that it might aggravate Mattie's asthma. A kitten would only cause trouble.

'Wait and see.'

The tenement consisted of a ground floor with three floors above. There were six sets of stairs to climb before the flat was reached, and three half-landings where the stairs took a bend. Each half-landing was lit by a window set with a mosaic of coloured glass. Elspeth loved these windows, for on sunny days the colours spilled over the stone stairs in a fallen rainbow.

The kitchen, which also served the family as living room and dining room, was cosy and welcoming as usual, warmed by a small coal fire as well as the heat from the gas stove. Today, the whole flat was rich with the smell of the dumpling Flora always made to celebrate a family birthday. Rachel, her oldest, was setting the table, assisted by Mattie, still pale and drawn from her bout of asthma. Rachel worked as a laundrywoman and seamstress in a large estate a little further along the coast, and as luck would have it, she had that afternoon off.

Flora McDonald was in her usual place by the stove, but it was the young man busy at the sink by the window, dressed only in a pair of khaki trousers, who caught Elspeth's eye as soon as she stepped into the room.

'Thomas!' She threw herself at him, regardless of the water spraying from his face and hands as he swung round from the sink.

'Steady on, Ellie,' he spluttered, at the same time returning her hug enthusiastically, while Flora, her face flushed with heat, her hair detaching itself strand by strand from the loose bun at the back of her head, snatched up a towel and began dabbing at the two of them.

'For goodness' sake, lassie, ye'll soak the place with yer carrying on!'

'Lachlan, why didn't you tell me?'

'I wanted tae surprise ye. She thought I'd brought her a kitten, Tom.'

'It's as well ye didnae, for it'd have gone straight out again,' his mother told him. 'Take this towel, Thomas, and let me get back tae my stove.'

'Mebbe ye'd've preferred a kitten, Ellie.' Thomas towelled himself vigorously.

'I'd rather have you two home any day of the week!'

'That reminds me—' He hung the towel up by the sink and fumbled at the khaki tunic hanging over the back of a chair, finally withdrawing a small cardboard box, slightly squashed. 'Happy birthday, Ellie.'

Inside the box, pinned to a small square of card, was an oval brooch made of polished pebbles. The centre and largest stone was dark and glossy, while those set around it were red and green, pale blue and the soft pearly grey of the sky and the River Clyde on a still, mild autumn day.

'As soon as I saw it, I was minded of the times we've collected pebbles along the beach,' Thomas explained as Elspeth stared in silence at the brooch. Then diffidently, 'D'ye like it?'

She found her voice, though it was only a whisper at first. 'Oh, Thomas, it's beautiful!'

'It is that,' Rachel agreed as she and Mattie came to look. Then she sniffed at the air. 'What's that smell? It's like – flowers.'

'Don't be daft,' Lachlan said swiftly as Elspeth, suddenly remembering the toilet water, cast a guilty look at Flora, who didn't approve of lip colours, perfume, powder or scented soap. 'How could ye have flowers at the top of a tenement?'

He glared at his sister, who grasped the message in his brown eyes and sniffed again, loudly. 'It's gone now – my nose must've gone funny for a minute.'

'Pin it on for me, Thomas.'

He did as he was bid, his fingers damp and cool against Elspeth's chin. 'There. It looks nice.'

She reached a hand up to caress the little brooch. It was the first piece of jewellery she had ever owned. And Lachlan's gift was the first scent she had ever had, apart from the illicit bottles of rose-water she and Mattie sometimes made from crushed rose petals in the washhouse during the summer.

Looking from Thomas to Lachlan, she loved the two of them with all her heart, for today, her thirteenth birthday, they had combined to remind her that from that day on, she was grown-up.

2

'So neither of ye knew that the other was comin' home on leave?' Henry McDonald pushed his empty plate away an hour later and leaned back in his chair, stretching strong, sinewy arms above his head. After a thorough wash in the sink to remove the grime of the shipyard, he smelled of carbolic soap, and his greying curly hair, still damp, stood up in a spiky halo round his broad moustached face. His two sons and two daughters had all inherited his curls instead of their mother's straight hair.

'Not a bit of it. The first I knew was when Lachlan here got out of the next carriage when we reached Glasgow.'

'Does a twenty-four-hour leave not mean they're going to send you abroad?' Rachel wondered aloud. Her brothers exchanged brief looks, and for a moment a chill seemed to threaten the room's warmth before Lachlan said casually, 'Mebbe it does, and mebbe it doesnae. They never tell us much about their plans.'

'That's what happened when they let Bob Cochran home for twenty-four hours,' Rachel persisted.

'How's Bob doin' these days?' Thomas wanted to know.

'Fine, the last letter I got.'

'It must be serious if ye're writin' tae each other,' Lachlan said.

'She sleeps with his letters under her pillow,' Elspeth said.

11

Unlike the house servants on the estate, Rachel didn't live in. The three girls shared one tiny bedroom, Rachel with a cot of her own, the two younger girls squeezed into a bed little larger than a single, but not as broad as a double bed.

'Does she now?'

Rachel's pretty round face went pink. 'I do not! Don't listen to her, Thomas, Ellie's just a wee liar,' she flared, but Mattie came to Elspeth's rescue.

'You do so. And you keep his photograph under the mattress'

'Here, here – no fightin' when we're all together at last,' Flora ordered. 'Clear the plates, Elspeth.' She waited until fresh plates, spoons and a large jug of custard were on the table before carefully bringing the rich, round, steaming birthday dumpling to the table. Amid a murmur of anticipation, she picked up a long sharp knife and cut into it, releasing a further gout of steam and the mouth-watering aroma of currants and raisins and treacle.

A second cut parted the first generous soft slice from the dumpling, and as it was skilfully flipped on to a plate Elspeth's heart quickened as she noticed the gleam of white paper against the moist brown interior. It was the custom, on special occasions like birthdays and Christmas and Hogmanay, to wrap silver threepenny bits in paper and bake them in the dumpling.

Normally the first slice would have gone to Elspeth, since it was her special day, but instead Flora laid the plate before Thomas, her first-born and favourite.

He immediately handed it across the table. 'Here ye are, Ellie – it's your birthday after all.'

With the tip of a spoon she dug into the slice, withdrew the tiny bundle, and opened it, the paper hot against her finger tips, to disclose a shining silver threepenny piece.

'Lucky you,' Mattie said. 'Think of the sweeties you can buy with that.'

'Or a nice bit of ribbon,' Rachel suggested.

'Far better tae put it away – the time might well come when ye'll be glad of it,' Flora put in, but Elspeth shook her head to all the suggestions.

'Uncle Henry, could you drill a wee hole in it for me, so that I can hang it on a bit of wool round my neck?'

'If ye want, hen,' her uncle agreed amiably, ignoring his wife's scandalised tutting.

'Ye're never goin' tae spoil a good thrup'ny piece by turnin' it intae a necklace, lassie!'

'It won't be spoiled. I'm going to keep it always, to remind me of today, with all of us together again.'

'Ye'll forget all about that the minute ye go intae the corner shop and see those jars of raspberry balls and liquorice straps,' Thomas told her.

'I won't.' She looked round the table at the only family she knew, and contentment surged through her. At that moment, life was perfect, she thought – then happened to meet Flora's eye.

In the older woman's glance she saw, not for the first time, a distant expression that made her feel that she was being singled out, set aside from the others round the table. Elspeth had seen that look several times during the past thirteen years; when she was a small child, it had set her off into inexplicable bouts of frightened tears which Flora, all at once her usual motherly self again, had soothed away. Now there were never tears, just a numbing, bewildering sense of being different, a chill reminder that she didn't really belong to the only family she had ever known.

'The army cooks can't cook as well as you do, Mum,' Thomas said just then, and Lachlan, his mouth full of warm, spicy dumpling, mumbled enthusiastic agreement.

Flora smiled, and the moment of uncertainty was gone as though it had never existed.

Elspeth could think of no reason for her aunt's flashes of hidden resentment. But she knew, from experience, that they would come again; always, like today, when she least expected them.

'It's not fair!'

'It's perfectly fair – and don't use that tone of voice tae me, lady,' Flora snapped, hanging Mattie's school blouse on the clothes horse to air and lifting the next garment from the pile waiting to be ironed. 'Ye've already had an extra year at the school tae set ye up for the future.'

'Mattie's had two extra years!'

'Mattie's already missed out on a lot because of her bad chest, and she's just as clever as you. Ye're not the only one with brains in this house, remember that. When she came this afternoon tae speak tae me about it all, Miss Scott could dae no more than agree with me. We cannae afford tae keep two of ye – d'ye not think Mattie deserves her chance just as much as you dae?'

'Y-yes, but—'

'There ye are, then.' Flora thumped the iron down on its end. 'We can just about manage with one of ye stayin' on, but not both. Anyway, fluff an' dust bothers Mattie's lungs, and it'd be more difficult tae find work for her than for you. So – it's only right that she's the one who gets tae stay on at the school.'

Tears crowded behind Elspeth's eyes, and she had to blink hard to hold them back. She had dreamed of becoming a teacher, had let herself believe during that extra year of schooling that it was going to happen. The sudden shock of hearing that her dream had crumbled to dust was more than she could bear. She made one last appeal. 'Uncle Henry—?'

'Now don't go encouragin' the lassie, Henry,' Flora warned at once. 'Ye know as well as I dae that one of them'll have tae go out tae work.'

Henry McDonald shifted uncomfortably in his chair, lowering the newspaper he had been holding before his face. 'I'm sorry, lass, yer auntie's right. We cannae afford tae keep the two of ye on at the school, with the lads both still away.'

'I know,' Elspeth said wretchedly, 'I know.'

'My heart's broken for the lassie,' Henry said when she had gone out of the room. 'Did ye see the way the light just went out of her eyes there?'

His wife smoothed the iron over his work shirt. 'She's too quick at wantin' her own way, that one. And she's old enough tae know that we all have tae deal with disappointment from time tae time.'

'I know, but—' He bit the words off, but it was too late. The iron was banged down so hard that the sturdy table shook, and Flora whirled to confront him, hands fisted on her hips.

'But what, Henry McDonald?'

He rattled the newspaper noisily, trying to find the right words. 'Sometimes I feel you're a wee bit too hard on that lassie, Flora.'

'Too hard on her? You're sayin' that tae me, who took her in when her own grandmother would have nothin' tae do with her? Me that raised her when I'd more than enough tae do carin' for my own bairns? Don't haver, man,' Flora said witheringly. 'I'm hard on them all – I have tae be. We've not got the money tae spoil any one of them, as ye well know.'

'Aye, but – it's just that sometimes I feel ye're harder on Ellie than the others, and I cannae think why, when I mind how you and her mother were closer than sisters—' His voice died away as he looked up and saw the rage in his wife's eyes and the colour rising in her face.

'Sometimes ye've got a nasty tongue on you, Henry, and a nasty mind, accusin' yer own wife like that!'

'I didnae mean anything by it,' he protested. Henry McDonald was a strong man, afraid of nothing. All the men who worked with him in Lithgow's shipyard respected him and thought highly of him. They would have been amazed if they had seen the way he seemed to shrink into his chair before his wife's anger. 'I just thought—'

'Aye, well, thinking's no' bringin' more silver intae the house, is it? If I was as soft as you are, we'd all of us be in the poors' hospital by now,' Flora said scathingly, and returned to her work, attacking the shirt with the heavy, hot iron as though Henry was inside it.

Prudently, he went back to his paper. Flora was a good wife, but he knew from experience that he'd do best to hold his tongue, rather than bring even more scalding anger down on his head.

In the privacy of the small bedroom, Elspeth sat on the edge of the bed she shared with Mattie and revelled in the luxury of a good cry for a full five minutes. Her shoulders shuddered as she gasped and sniffled and wept for the future she had wanted so much, and had lost for ever. She would have enjoyed a good loud, babyish bawl, but instead she wept quietly, determined not to let her aunt and uncle hear her grief. Fat tears poured down her face and dripped off her chin, some trickling between her lips to lie salty on her tongue.

Lachlan's comment on her thirteenth birthday kept coming back to her: 'The war'll be well over by then, surely, and that means that Thomas and me'll be back home, so that'd help with the money.'

But almost a year later the war was still going on, and Lachlan and Thomas, both over in France now, hadn't been home since her birthday. Although their mother never spoke to anyone, not even Henry, of any fears she may have harboured for them, more silver glittered through her fair hair than ever before, and her mouth had tightened.

At last the tears began to ease off and Elspeth's wet face started itching unpleasantly. She scrubbed her hands over it, smearing tears over her cheeks, then got up and washed them away, dipping a face cloth into the chipped bowl of cold water that stood on the tallboy, then drying her face on the well-worn towel drooping from a nail in the wall.

She was just in time; as she put the towel down the door to the flat opened and Mattie, who had been packed off on an errand, passed the bedroom door on her way to the kitchen.

Elspeth peered into the foggy mirror that stood on a rickety table at the window, and saw that her eyes were pink-edged. Dropping to her knees by Rachel's bed, she pulled out the cardboard box that held the older girl's good shoes, lifting them out then scooping up the sheet of cardboard below. This was where Rachel kept her secret hoard of powder, lipstick and perfume, bought out of the few pennies the girl was allocated from her weekly pay packet, and well hidden from her mother.

Elspeth opened the little box of powder with fingers that shook in their haste, and dabbed the puff round her eyes. She put it back exactly where she found it, then replaced the cardboard and the shoes before pushing the box well out of sight beneath the bed.

Referring to the mirror again, she saw to her horror that now clumps of powder stuck to her lashes, which were still damp, and that the skin round her eyes was thick with the stuff. Hurriedly, she smoothed the surplus powder away with the tips of her fingers, then used her handkerchief to wipe up the grains that had fallen on the table. Mattie came in just as she finished.

'What're you doing?'

'Nothing. Just thinking.'

Mattie's nose wrinkled. 'What's that smell?'

'What smell? '

'It's—' Mattie sniffed again. 'You've not been at Rachel's perfume, have you?'

'Of course not!'

'You know what she's like if she thinks we've touched her stuff.'

'I told you – I've not touched it!'

Mattie hesitated, then sat down on the bed she and Elspeth

17

shared, linking her fingers tightly on her lap. 'Mam says that Miss Scott came to visit her today.'

'I know. She told me.'

'Imagine, a teacher coming to the house to talk about you and me, and in the holidays too.' There was awe in Mattie's voice, and Elspeth fully understood why. Teachers belonged in school, not in houses; it had never occurred to either of them that teachers had any other kind of existence. For all the two girls knew, Miss Scott might well be hung up in the classroom cupboard out of school hours, waiting patiently with the boxes of chalk and shelves of books for the next school day to begin.

'Did Mam tell you what's been decided?'

'Yes.' They were both silent, then Elspeth went on, her voice sharp with accusation, 'I didn't know you wanted to be a teacher.'

'I didn't, till Mam said that Miss Scott said that I was clever enough. With me being off school so much, I never thought—' Mattie's voice trailed away, and her fingers writhed in her lap, getting into such a tangle that Elspeth began to wonder if the girl's hands could ever be separated again. 'Ellie, it's not fair that you have to be the one to leave.'

'Yes it is.' Hard though it was to say the words, Elspeth recognised that Aunt Flora had right on her side. Mattie was just as clever as she was, and the girl had been off so often during the past ten years that if the days at home were added up she must have missed at least a year's education. And Mattie was Aunt Flora's own daughter, while Elspeth wasn't.

'I feel terrible about it, Elspeth.'

'Aunt Flora's right, they can't pay for us both. I'll enjoy going out to work,' she lied. 'I'll try for a job in an office. Mebbe I'll learn how to typewrite, and do book-keeping.'

The thought of it cheered her up a little. She had always thought that working in an office would be interesting. She might even turn out to be good at it.

Mattie smiled at her gratefully. 'I'll tell you all about

18

everything I learn. I'll show you all the books I have to read, so that you'll know all about how to teach.'

'And I'll tell you all about my office work.' For a moment, Elspeth felt better about everything. Peering into the mirror again, she was relieved to see that the puffiness had begun to fade from around her clear blue eyes.

Then, as her aunt called the two of them through to help her with the evening meal, realisation hit her. The summer holidays would be over in another five days, and two weeks after that she would be fourteen, a birthday that marked the end of her schooldays.

Panic swept over her, and as she followed Mattie into the kitchen she felt as though she was falling, and there was nothing to hold on to.

Flora McDonald, a trained seamstress, had dressed her family almost entirely by her own efforts, using a large heavy sewing machine that was her pride and joy. She had even made most of the clothes her husband and sons wore, and had taught the three girls to sew as soon as they were old enough to be trusted with needle and scissors.

The skills Rachel had learned from her mother had led to a position with one of the wealthy families living on the hill above the town, and Elspeth, too, had shown talent. In her constant eagerness to please her aunt and justify the day Flora had taken her in, she had worked hard and learned well, and by the time she was in her teens she was making most of her own clothes. To her dismay, her own diligence turned out to be her undoing, for as the school summer holidays drew to a close, Flora announced that she had arranged an interview for Elspeth with the sewing-room supervisor at Brodie's, the town's largest department store.

Her plea to be allowed to seek work in an office had been turned down flat.

'Office work indeed! What next? Yer poor mother and me

were seamstresses, and that's what you'll be too. Brodie's is the best store in the town – ye're very lucky, gettin' an interview there. When ye've got a man and bairns of yer own tae clothe ye'll be glad of the trainin' Brodie's'll give ye,' Flora said, and would hear no more about offices.

Elspeth, who had never been inside Brodie's in her life, gazed around, fascinated, as she followed her aunt through the entrance and found herself in a world she had never known existed. Despite the hardships of the war, the counters scattered throughout the ground-floor area seemed to her to be well stocked with rolls of ribbon and lace, buttons, hooks and eyes, and banked rainbows of sewing thread in little display boxes.

'Don't dawdle, Elspeth.' Flora tossed the words over her shoulder as she hurried towards the stairs. 'We're expected, and I'll not have them thinkin' ye're a poor timekeeper.'

Up a flight of stairs they sped, to another open area, this time set out with men's and children's clothing. The third floor held women's clothes; Elspeth caught a glimpse of gloves on one counter, petticoats on another, as Flora stopped to ask directions, then the two of them went through a door and into a narrow dark corridor, quite unlike the spacious areas they had just left.

'First door on the right,' Flora muttered, fidgeting along the corridor and pausing before a door that almost vibrated with a humming sound from the other side of the panels. It sounded to Elspeth as though a lot of sewing machines were being operated within the room.

'This'll be it,' Flora muttered, tapping tentatively with her knuckles. They waited for several long minutes, but there was no answer.

'They'll not hear you for the noise,' Elspeth ventured. 'You'll just have to go in.'

'Ye don't just walk intae strange rooms – ye wait tae be told!' Flora snapped, and they waited in vain for another few minutes before, clearly remembering the passing of time, she gave an anguished little whimper and steeled herself to open the door and reveal a large, stuffy room. An enormous table holding an impressive number of sewing machines, all in use, took up most of the space. A few of the machinists flicked a brief glance at the newcomers, then returned to their work. One of them, a pretty, red-haired girl, smiled and winked at Elspeth. A tall, cold-eyed woman examining the output of one of the machines finally noticed them, and straightened up.

'Yes?'

'We've got an appointment with Miss Buchanan – about a job.' Flora, unusually nervous, stumbled over the words.

The woman surveyed them both for a moment as though amazed that two such ordinary people should dare to approach her, then said shortly, 'This way.'

They followed her in single file along the edge of the room to a doorway that led into a tiny office, with only enough room for a cluttered desk and two chairs. 'Miss Buchanan is with a client at the moment,' the woman told them. 'I'll inform her of your arrival when she's free. What name shall I say?'

'Flora Mc— I mean, Elspeth Bremner,' Flora almost whispered. Elspeth had never known her aunt to be so cowed; the woman's nervousness started to affect her, and her knees began to shake. As soon as they were alone Flora pounced on her, brushing imaginary fluff from her best woollen coat, setting her beret straight, whirling her round to tweak at the thick dark brown plait hanging down her back.

'Stand straight, for any favour! Speak out when Miss Buchanan asks ye anythin', but don't talk unless ye're invited tae. And don't fidget!'

The inspection over, Flora sat herself down on the small plain chair at their side of the desk, drumming her fingers on her knee, while Elspeth pulled her shoulders back and stared at a crack on the wall behind the desk, wishing that she hadn't turned out to be so good with a needle.

The drumming of the sewing machines on the other side of the wall reminded her of the little she had been able to glimpse of the sewing room as she and Flora were whisked through it. The only windows she had noticed were small, and ran along the upper wall area on one side of the room, so that the girls working at the machines couldn't see out. Her heart sank, and she wanted to run from the room and from the building. Only the thought of what Aunt Flora would say and do to her kept her in her seat.

They waited in silence for a further ten minutes, both jumping when the door finally opened and Miss Buchanan arrived, small and elderly, slightly stooped and with a permanent frown tucked between eyes magnified by her spectacles.

'Mrs – er—' She fluttered a hand towards Flora in greeting, then withdrew it and edged in behind her desk, leaving Flora with her own hand outstretched. 'And – um,' she added, settling herself into her chair.

'It's about the interview,' Flora said too loudly, her cheeks pink with embarrassment as she sank back into her own seat and folded her hands together. 'You said you'd see Ellie – Elspeth – about a post.' She was speaking, Elspeth thought, surprised, as though her mouth was full of wee pebbles that slowed and restricted her speech.

'Oh yes, I did agree to consider her for employment in our workshop.' Miss Buchanan's small hands sifted through a pile of papers on the desk before emerging with a sheet of notepaper bearing Flora's careful handwriting. 'What age is she?'

'Almost fourteen,' Flora offered as Elspeth opened her mouth to reply. 'Fourteen in September. She'll be leaving school then.'

'And you want to be a seamstress?' Miss Buchanan's artificially large eyes studied Elspeth, who opened her mouth to reply, and was forestalled.

'She's very good with her needle. I taught her myself. Her mother and me were both seamstresses in Glasgow,' Flora contributed, rummaging in the depths of her worn shopping bag and bringing out a piece of snowy linen, carefully folded. She opened it to reveal two pieces of embroidery. 'These are the lassie's own work.'

Miss Buchanan opened a drawer and took out a pair of thin gloves. Slipping them on she studied the material, holding it close to her eyes to examine the fine stitching. Laying it down again, she took off her spectacles, which dangled from her neck by a ribbon. Immediately, her eyes became small and insignificant. She studied the work again, this time holding it almost at arm's-length, then, sounding surprised, she commented, 'This is quite good.'

'Oh yes.' Flora's nervousness had vanished for the moment; her voice was clear and firm and smug, for all the world, Elspeth thought, resentful at not being allowed to say a word on her own behalf, as though she had done the work herself.

'As you probably know, we now have a large ready-to-wear department, and most of our seamstresses' work involves making alterations in our ready-to-wear stock for our customers,' Miss Buchanan told Flora, as though Elspeth was invisible. 'We do a certain amount of dressmaking for our special clients, but that work, of course, is only undertaken by our most talented seamstresses. Few girls attain that standard.'

'I'm sure Elspeth'd be able to reach it, in time,' Flora snapped back, and Miss Buchanan's brows rose.

'As to that, Mrs – only time will tell.' For the first time, she looked at Elspeth studying her carefully. 'Would you like to work here?'

'I'd prefer to work in an—'

'She would.' Flora said swiftly.

'I believe that she might fit in here quite well. We'll give her a three-month trial, Mrs – er—'

Ten minutes later it had been arranged between the two women that Elspeth should start work the week after her birthday. 'What d'ye think ye were doin'?' Flora hissed in her normal, unpebbled voice as soon as they were back among the shoppers again. 'For a minute there I thought the woman was goin' tae say ye were too cheeky for the job.'

'I only wanted to ask if there was any work in the offices.'

'There isn't. It's not everyone that gets tae work at Brodie's, for they're very particular. Ye're lucky ye've been accepted as a seamstress, so let's have no more nonsense about offices. Yer mother'd be pleased,' she added as an afterthought as they descended the stairs.

'I might as well not have bothered going to the interview myself,' Elspeth wrote to Thomas that evening. 'It was a bit like being sold at a cattle market. Maybe I should be grateful that Miss Buchanan didn't insist on opening my mouth and having a look at my teeth, the way they do with horses.'

3

Elspeth's final day at school was one of the worst she had ever known. Usually, the 'leavers' lolled about on their last day, doing nothing, eyed enviously by those still bound to the classroom. But Elspeth worked hard, savouring every moment.

'This is the last time I'll walk into school – the last time I'll hang my coat up on this peg – the last time I'll sit in this seat—' The litany kept ringing through her mind, each 'last' clanging like a bell summoning mourners to a funeral.

When the real bell rang to mark the end of the day, she lingered at her desk, making a business of emptying it, until there were no more corners left to study in search of an errant eraser or a missing pencil.

'Come on,' Mattie said impatiently from the doorway.

'I'm coming.' Elspeth closed the desk – 'this is the last time I'll close this desk' – and followed her cousin from the room, her hands hanging uselessly by her sides. There were no books to carry, for they had all been handed in for some other pupil to take home and study in future.

Miss Scott stopped her in the hallway. 'Good luck, my dear. I'm sorry you weren't able to stay on any longer.'

'Yes, Miss Scott, thank you, Miss Scott,' Elspeth mumbled to the teacher's sturdy shoes, unable to meet the sympathy that she knew would be in the woman's eyes.

'Come back and see us. We'd like to know how you're getting on,' Miss Scott said, then, mercifully, she let them go, and for the last time, Elspeth walked out of the school door, down the steps, across the playground. Molly, a few months older, had left joyfully at the beginning of the summer holidays, and was working in a bakery in West Blackhall Street.

'I wish it could have been you staying on instead of me,' Mattie said by her side.

'No you don't, you want to stay as much as I do.'

'You're right. I suppose I meant that I wish we could both have stayed.'

'No, Aunt Flora's right – you've not been at school as often as me because of your chest.'

'That doesn't help to make me feel any better about it.'

'Nor me,' Elspeth thought as she walked out of the school gates for the last time.

Working in the sewing room at Brodie's wasn't as bad as Elspeth had feared. For one thing, she was allowed to pin up the long brown plait that had been a temptation all through her schooldays to boys who pulled it in the classroom and sometimes in the street. She hinted at getting it cut, but Flora wouldn't hear of it.

'Ye've got lovely hair, just like yer mother's, rest her soul. It'd be sacrilege tae cut it off. One day ye'll thank me for no' lettin' ye dae it!'

There was also the pleasure of taking a wage packet home every Friday. True, it had to be handed over to Flora unopened, just like Uncle Henry's and Rachel's wages, but at least she was earning her keep, instead of being an added burden. The fourpence handed back for her own use each week was a fortune compared with the twopence spending money she had received before.

The small, high windows in the workroom couldn't provide enough ventilation for the number of women and girls there, so the place was airless, and noisy with the continual whirring of the machines, but once the strangeness of everything and her shyness among people she didn't know wore off, Elspeth found that she was good at the work, and took pleasure in getting the occasional word of grudging praise from Miss Arnold, well known for her high standards and sharp tongue.

'If they'd left the men at home and just sent her tae fight the Jerries instead,' muttered Lena Stewart, who worked on the machine opposite Elspeth's, 'she'd've cut the legs from the lot of them with one sentence and saved us a lot of bother.'

Elspeth was surprised into a giggle, quickly disguised as a cough as Miss Arnold's cold eyes swept in her direction. Nobody was allowed to talk during working hours, but she discovered on her first day that there was always a certain amount of conversation going on, sometimes in whispers and murmurs hidden by the continual sound of the machines, sometimes by means of signals, or silent mouthing and lip-reading.

'Everyone needs tae talk,' said Lena, the redhead who had winked at her on the day of her interview. 'It's not natural tae expect women tae keep their mouths shut for hours.'

She was very pretty, with the type of looks that would have caused Flora MacDonald to tut disapprovingly. Her curly red hair continually escaped from the ribbons that were supposed to hold it back from her face, and she was well rounded, her creamy skin dusted with freckles. Her brown eyes sparkled, and even without artificial colouring her mouth was full and red.

Lena, Elspeth had quickly discovered, was a rebel, dressing in bright clothes despite Miss Buchanan's insistence on muted colours for her staff, and talking when she was expected to be quiet. She only kept her job because she was an excellent seamstress.

'Are ye stayin' in for yer dinner?' she asked when Elspeth's first morning's work ended and she was following the other girls out of the room – not through the door leading from the store, but through another, smaller door at the back of the room which led to narrow wooden stairs.

27

'I'm going home. I only live in Mearns Street.'

'Ye should bring a piece and eat with the rest of us.' As they reached the bottom of the stairs, Lena gestured towards an open door in front of them. Peeping in, Elspeth saw a large room with benches set at long tables. Men and women were settling down at the tables, unwrapping packets of sandwiches.

'The nobs have a place of their own upstairs,' Lena explained. 'Counter staff and floorwalkers and the like. This is for folk like us and the packers and carters. There's hot water and milk and mugs, and ye bring yer own tea and sugar in wee screws of paper.'

Elspeth, hurrying home through a drizzle of rain, liked the idea of sharing her midday break with Lena and the other girls, but when she suggested it to Flora, her aunt was horrified.

'Eating down in the basement with the carters and all? Ye don't know what ye might catch! Ye're better off with a good hot dinner here.'

'But I don't have much time – it would surely be better for me to eat something at the store instead of running home and running back and mebbe being late.'

Flora put a bowl of soup before her. 'I ate my dinner with Mattie. I can see tae it that ye're not late back.'

'That's another thing – I get out later than Mattie, and that means you've got two dinners to see to. If I stayed at work there'd only be hers.' A fresh shower, hurling itself against the window, gave Elspeth further ammunition. 'And winter's coming in, Auntie Flora. I might catch cold running to Mearns Street then back, and if I did I'd have to stay home, for Miss Buchanan and Miss Arnold would never let me cough and sneeze over the customers' clothes.'

'Aye, well, there is that,' Flora said slowly. 'But I hope I'd not be expected tae make up pieces for yer dinner – I've got enough tae see tae in the mornings as it is.'

'I'll do my own. I'll get up earlier.'

To her joy, Flora gave in, and Elspeth spent her midday

breaks in the canteen, drinking scalding-hot tea out of a tin mug that would have sent her aunt running for the disinfectant if she had known of it, and eating her sandwiches at a wooden table. At last, she began to feel like one of the crowd.

It was during those midday breaks that she discovered that Lena was a singer. Every time a music-hall company came to Greenock Lena was in the audience, treating her fellow workers the following dinner-time to an impromptu concert of every song in the programme. She had a good memory, and only needed to hear a song once to recall tune and lyrics.

Her voice was lovely, strong and confident when the song required it, or so sweet and pure that even the gruff carters could be seen to buff a tear away with the back of a hand when she sang a ballad or lullaby.

'It's what I like doin' best,' she confided to Elspeth. 'I sing in our local pub on a Saturday night, and at gatherin's.' Then, her eyes glowing, 'One day I'm goin' tae sing on a proper stage, like the Hippodrome or the King's Theatre. D'ye go there?'

Her eyes widened when Elspeth admitted that she had never been inside a theatre. 'But they're so bonny, with crimson velvet curtains tied back with gold ropes, and pillars right up tae the ceilings, and folk on the stage with beautiful clothes. There's lovely scenery on the stage too – come tae the Hippodrome with me on Saturday night.'

'I can't. My Aunt Flora doesn't like theatres.'

'I'm no askin' yer Aunt Flora,' Lena pointed out. 'I'm askin' you.'

'But I'd have to ask her, and she'd say no.'

'Don't tell her, then. Say ye're goin' out with a friend – it wouldnae be a lie.'

'She'd find out anyway,' Elspeth said, but finally agreed, after much coaxing, to ask her aunt's permission.

Flora's reaction was just as she had predicted. 'The theatre? Indeed you'll go tae no such place, milady.'

29

'But it's with one of the girls at the store.'

'I don't know what her mother's thinking of, lettin' her watch folk cavorting about on a stage.'

'Her mother's dead. She lives with her father.'

'There ye are, then – there's no woman in the house tae guide her. No wonder the poor lassie's goin' wrong. That'll no' happen tae you – ye're just out of the school and still a bairn.'

The unfairness of it stung Elspeth. 'How can I still be a bairn when I'm old enough to earn my own keep?'

Her aunt's head snapped up, eyes blazing. 'I'll tell ye how – while ye behave like a bairn ye'll be treated like one. The very idea,' she clucked like an agitated hen, 'answerin' me back after all me and yer Uncle Henry've done for ye!'

'I didn't ask you to take me in!'

Flora's patience snapped. 'Ye cheeky besom, ye!' she railed. 'Times like this I think we should have left ye tae yer Grandma Bremner. She'd've packed ye off tae the orphanage, and I don't see *them* lettin' ye stay on at the school for another year!'

No matter how hard Elspeth worked at holding her tongue and keeping the peace, Flora managed time and time again to overturn her attempts to be a dutiful foster daughter. The argument raged on, ending, as sometimes happened, with Flora ordering her out of her sight, and Elspeth running off to Granjan's tiny kitchen, tears of frustrated anger running down her cheeks.

'I never mean to upset her, but I keep doing it!' she sobbed, and Janet Docherty, Flora's mother, hauled herself out of her chair and crossed the faded rag rug to pat her bowed head.

'Yer Auntie Flora's awful hard tae please at times. It's just her nature, she doesnae mean tae sound as hard as she does.'

'I know, but I don't make things any better when I answer back. Why can't I stop myself?' Tears dripped from Elspeth's chin and made damp circles on her woollen skirt. She was huddled into a chair with her knees drawn up to her chin and her arms wrapped around them.

'If it was that easy for folk tae hold their tongues, there wouldnae have been any wars,' Janet pointed out, then, as the sobbing eased to a sniffing, hiccuping stop, 'Feelin' better now? Here—' A clean dishtowel was thrust into Elspeth's hands. 'Dry yer face, pet, an' I'll put the griddle on. Pancakes and a cup of hot tea'll make the world look better.'

Janet Docherty never threw anything away if she could get some use out of it. Greaseproof papers that had wrapped squares of butter were neatly folded and stored in a drawer once the butter was finished; now she produced one and ran it over the large black iron griddle to grease it. A paper spill from a vase on the mantelshelf was lit at the fire and used to light a ring on her small gas cooker, then she lifted the griddle by its hooped handle on to the ring to heat.

'You're awful good to me, Granjan,' Elspeth said gratefully, scrubbing at her eyes with the dishcloth.

'Ye're a good, obedient lassie and we all need a bit of comfortin' now and again.' Janet took a bowl down from a shelf and collected flour and an egg and milk.

'If I was good I wouldn't anger Aunt Flora so much.'

'Ach, Flora gets het up too quickly. She always did, even as a wean,' said Flora's mother cheerfully, measuring flour into the basin. 'Wash yer face at the jawbox now, and fill the kettle for me.'

After obediently splashing her face with cold water at the tiny sink set below the window, Elspeth dried it before filling the kettle, while Janet whipped the contents of the mixing bowl into a creamy, pale golden liquid. Scooping a spoonful up, she dropped it on to the heated griddle, which started to sizzle. The soft dough spread to just the right size, then halted, bubbles forming on its surface, as Janet dotted the large griddle with more spoonfuls. Then she started flipping them over deftly with a fish slice, disclosing the golden-brown cooked side of each.

Nobody could make pancakes as swiftly or as well as

31

Granjan, Elspeth thought contentedly, setting the table and opening the window to fetch a pat of butter from the larder, a small wooden box with a mesh door to let air in, fastened to the windowsill to keep any meat and milk and butter stored inside it fresh and cool. Her stomach gave an unladylike rumble as she turned back into the room and smelled the delicious aroma of fresh-made pancakes.

Although her own children had been raised to call Janet Gran, Flora had tried hard to make little Elspeth address her mother as Auntie Janet. 'She's got a gran of her own, it would-nae be right tae let her call you gran too,' she had said when Janet protested.

'Ach, away wi' ye – there's nothin' wrong with her havin' two grans, like most bairns. Yours'd have two if Henry's mother was still livin', God rest her.'

'It's not right,' Flora had insisted stubbornly. Elspeth, only just over a year old and confused by this sign, the first she received, that she wasn't one of Flora's children, had found her own compromise and began calling Janet Granjan, to the old woman's secret delight. Flora, frustrated in the face of the child's determination, had given in and let the name remain.

Now, while they ate, Elspeth told Granjan about Lena. 'She's a good seamstress, but she's awful casual about her work.' She bit into a pancake, and Janet clucked, shaking her head.

'I hope she's not leadin' ye intae bad ways, lassie.'

'Oh no, I'm doing well. Miss Arnold set me to sewing some lace on a petticoat yesterday, and it's not everyone that's given work like that. She says I've got a deft touch. It's lovely material, Granjan – so soft and silky. Wearing it must be like wearing a sunbeam.' She stopped to wipe melted butter from her chin, then giggled. 'Imagine walking round all day wearing a sunbeam under your clothes.'

'Ye're awful like yer mother,' Janet said without thinking. 'She could jump from sorrow tae laughter in the blink of an eye too. Not that she was often sad, even when things were goin' against her. Maisie always saw the good side of life – and of folk.'

'Am I really like her?' Elspeth was greedy for all that she could glean about her mother.

'I've told ye often enough. Ye've got her hair, and her bonny face.'

'But not her eyes.'

'Did Flora say that?' Janet asked, taken by surprise.

'She's like Grandmother – neither of them ever tells me about my mother. I wouldn't know anything about her if it wasn't for you, but you never say I've got her eyes, Granjan.'

'Ye're gettin' altogether too sharp for yer own good, young lady. Watch out ye don't cut yerself.'

Elspeth nibbled at her pancake, then said, 'I've got his eyes, haven't I?'

'Whose?'

'My father's.'

Janet poured a second cup of strong tea for herself. 'I never saw him, so I cannae tell,' she said shortly, her discomfort so obvious that Elspeth, much as she longed to ask more questions, changed the subject.

'Thomas thinks I should take evening lessons in typewriting and shorthand.'

Janet set the teapot down with a thump and stared at her. 'What on earth for?'

'Because I want to work in an office, only Aunt Flora won't let me. Thomas said in his last letter that there's no reason why I shouldn't try to learn office skills, so that I could mebbe use them one day.'

'Don't you let him unsettle you, pet.' Janet Docherty's voice was uneasy. 'Ye're a seamstress, and that's an end of it.'

'He's not unsettling me, he's just saying that one day I might decide to do something else. He's learned to drive in the army, did you know that? He says he didn't realise how interesting engines were. He might be thinking of a change himself one day.'

'Thomas is doin' very well as a gardener. And anyway, who's tae pay for those evening lessons he's got ye talkin' about? Not Master Thomas, I'll be bound.'

'I'd pay for them myself. I'm saving up already, for I like the idea,' Elspeth said eagerly. 'I'll mebbe learn book-keeping as well, if I can afford it.'

'Now don't go rushin' intae anythin',' Janet warned. 'Here – have another pancake.'

'I wish Grandmother was more like you,' Elspeth said, doing as she was bid.

'Tuts, lassie, it'd be a dull world if we were all alike.'

'But I should be closer to Grandmother than I am. After all, she's my real mother's mother. D'you think she'd really have sent me to the poors' hospital if Aunt Flora hadn't taken me in?'

Janet, about to sip her tea, spluttered into the cup and almost choked. Elspeth hurried out of her chair and round the table to pat her on the back. 'Sit down, sit down, I'm fine,' Janet gasped when the coughing fit was over. 'God save us, child, what gave ye an idea like that?'

'Aunt Flora says that's what Grandmother would have done. That's why I was crying so hard when I got here.' Elspeth, who had gone back to her pancake, put it down again, her appetite fading as she remembered the anger in her aunt's face, the pain of the words she had hurled.

'What a thing tae say tae a bairn!'

'I'm not a bairn any more, Granjan, I'm a working woman, old enough to know the truth.'

'And how can Flora have any notion of what Celia Bremner would've done?'

'She didn't take me in when my mother died. Surely that shows that she didn't want me,' Elspeth said round a lump in her throat that wasn't for her, but for the helpless baby she had once been.

'Only because Flora wouldnae hear of anyone but herself takin' ye in. Wasn't she yer poor ma's best friend? Does that not show ye how much she wanted ye?'

'Yes, but – Grandmother doesn't have any photographs of my mother in her house, nor anything that belonged to her. I don't think she'd have taken me if Aunt Flora hadn't wanted me.'

'Now ye're just haverin',' Janet said sharply. 'And we'll have no more of it. Eat up that pancake, and stop fiddling with it. It's time ye were getting back home.'

4

A large red hand suddenly imposed itself between Elspeth's eyes and the table, whipping her exercise book away before she could do more than give a squeak of surprise at the interruption. She had been so involved in writing the letter that she hadn't noticed anyone approaching.

'What's this ye're scribblin' at – a letter tae yer sweetheart?' The ginger-haired messenger boy danced round to the opposite side of the table, waving the book.

'Give it back – please.'

'In a minute. Let's see, now. "Dear – er – dear L-lachlan,"' he read aloud, struggling over the words like a small child learning to read. 'Who's Lachlan, yer fancy man?'

'My brother.' Elspeth stood up and reached for the book, her face burning with embarrassment as a few people sitting at the long table looked on, laughing. 'Give it back.'

The boy pursed his lips. 'If this Lachlan's yer brother, what's yer sweetheart's name, then?'

'I don't have a sweetheart.' Elspeth, unused to being the centre of attention, felt humiliating tears stabbing at her eyelids, and wished that she could just crawl under the table and hide.

'A bonny lassie wi' no young man of her own? Tell ye what, I'll give it back if ye'll promise tae come tae the pictures with me tonight,' the lad suggested, smirking.

'Just give it back.'

'Aw, come on – a wee visit tae the—' he began, then it was his turn to yelp with shock as a hand skelped lightly across his ear, while at the same time its partner whipped the book away from him.

'Stop yer nonsense, Johnny Crawford, and leave the lassie alone,' Lena Stewart ordered, handing the exercise book back to Elspeth.

'What d'ye think ye're doin', you? That was sore!'

'Ach, away ye go, I scarce touched ye. Ye'll get a lot worse than that from the Boche if ye're ever old enough tae go and bother them,' Lena teased. 'Away and play with yer pals, and stop pretending tae be a man when ye're nothin' but a wee laddie.'

The boy's face went scarlet as an elderly carter shouted from further down the table, 'Ye're right there, Lena hen – he's that young he's still walkin' all bandy-legged!'

'Bitch!'

'Here, here – another word out of ye and I'll learn ye what a proper slap feels like,' Lena told him sharply, and he subsided, slinking away, crimson to the tips of his ears. 'Don't let the likes of him bother ye, he's just tryin' it on. He's fancied ye ever since ye started workin' here.'

'Lena!'

'Have ye never noticed the wee glances and the wee smiles? Ach, there's no harm in him, but ye could do better for yerself. Why not come tae the dancin' tomorrow night?' Lena coaxed, not for the first time. 'There'll be plenty of men there, and there's somethin' about a uniform and a foreign accent that can set a lassie's heart racin'.'

The deep-water area off Greenock, known as the Tail o' the Bank because it marked the end of a vast mudbank, was always busy with warships these days, and the townsfolk had become used to sharing their streets with foreign seamen in unfamiliar uniforms, speaking different tongues. The local people held concerts and dances for these young men so far from home, and in turn they provided plenty of company for local girls with sweethearts in the services. Lena and most of the others who worked in the sewing room attended the dances.

'You know Aunt Flora won't let me.'

'Why not?'

'She says I'm too young.'

'Ye're old enough tae earn a wage,' Lena pointed

'That doesn't make any difference to her. I don't really want to go to dances anyway.'

She was grateful when Lena shrugged and accepted her decision without any further attempt to get her to change her mind. She had no wish to cause further trouble with Auntie Flora by sneaking out behind her back. One way or another she was certain to be found out, and then there would be another row. In any case, she was intent on saving every penny she could so that she could pay for evening classes.

Although she spent very little on herself, the tiny hoard of coins kept in an old tobacco tin in her bedroom never seemed to grow. She had borrowed a book on book-keeping from the lending library and worked on it in her spare time, but it was difficult, on her own, to grasp the finer points of crediting and debiting and cross-referencing.

Once, sent along to the accounts office to deliver a note from Miss Buchanan, she had looked enviously at the confident young woman sitting at a desk before a large, solid typewriter, tapping briskly on the keys. She longed to try her hand at typewriting.

Reaching the bottom of the page, she awoke from her daydream to find that her pencil had written, 'Yesterday when I was typewriting to Mattie' instead of 'talking to Mattie'. Vexed, she began to tear the sheet out neatly.

'What's wrong?' Lena wanted to know.

'I wrote the wrong word.'

'Scribble it out, then. I've tae dae that all the time when I'm writin' tae George.' Lena's young man was in the navy.

'I don't like pages with mistakes scribbled out, it looks untidy. I'll do it over again at home.' A glance at the large clock on the wall showed that it was almost time for the loud bell that summoned the sewing girls and the carters and cleaners and packers and messenger boys back to work. The counter and office staff ate their sandwiches upstairs, in a room next to the offices.

'Ye're awful fussy,' chimed in one of the other seamstresses, leaning on Elspeth's shoulder so that she could have an upside-down look at the unwanted page. 'Ye should see the letters I write tae my young man – they're that untidy, he sometimes says he cannae make out what I'm sayin' tae him.' She hesitated, then asked diffidently, 'Would ye mebbe write tae him for me, Ellie? It'd please him tae see a tidy letter for once.'

'I couldn't do that.' Elspeth was shocked at the idea. 'It wouldn't be your letter then, and that's what he'll want more than anything.'

'What he wants is tae be able tae read what I'm tellin' him. He says that when ye're in a shell hole with all that mud, and the bullets flying around, ye don't want tae have tae keep peerin' at a piece of paper, tryin' tae make out what it's sayin'. Anyway, I'd tell ye what tae write. I just want it put down nice. Ye could do it in the dinner hour tomorrow,' the girl added eagerly.

'I don't know—'

'If she writes a letter for anyb'dy, Cora Simpson, she'll write one for me,' Lena broke in jealously. 'She's my friend more than yours, and I don't like writin' either. I only do it because George is desperate for letters.'

'I'd pay ye, Ellie,' Cora said at once. 'I'd give ye a penny tae dae it for me.'

Lena knocked the girl's arm off Elspeth's shoulder. 'And I'd pay her tuppence, so there!'

'I haven't said I'll do it yet,' Elspeth protested as the two girls glared at each other. She couldn't believe that anyone would be silly enough to pay to have something done when they were perfectly able to do it themselves.

'If ye do, it'll be for me, because I'm yer friend.'

'But I asked first!'

As they wrangled, Elspeth put aside the absurdity of writing other people's letters, and started to consider the benefits. If she wrote the two letters, she would be able to add thruppence to the money she was putting by to pay for her evening classes.

'I'll do them both,' she announced, 'for a penny halfpenny each. One tomorrow and one the day after – you can toss a coin to pick which one I write first.'

And to her astonishment, both girls agreed.

Cora won the toss. It was strange, writing someone else's letter at their dictation. At first, Elspeth, who had done well in grammar at school, found herself wanting to make corrections, much to Cora's indignation.

'Listen, it's my letter tae my lad,' she snapped. 'Just write what yer told – and I'll have an extra page of that book when ye're finished, so's I can write my own wee private bit tae him. He'll just have tae put up with my own scribbling for that bit.'

Once Elspeth settled to writing down the dictation, the way her class had been taught in school, the work came easily, and two days later the tobacco tin in her drawer at home was richer by three pennies. To her astonishment, once the others who ate their midday meal in the basement room caught on to what she was doing, a few more girls asked her to write letters for sweethearts and fathers and brothers away at the war. Then one of the carters asked if she would write to his daughter, married and living in Stirling.

'Her mother was the one that always wrote tae her, once a week without fail.' He took off his cap and scratched his bald head. 'Since the wife died our Betty expects me tae keep up with the letters, but I was never a letter-writer, and it comes awful hard.'

'She just wants to know what's been happening to you and the neighbours, now that she's not here to find out for herself,' Elspeth suggested, and he nodded.

'I know that, lass, and that's the sort of things I talk about all day tae my horse. It's easy with the horse, but when it comes tae puttin' it all down on paper for our Betty I'm tongue-tied. Ye'd be daein' me a right favour if ye'd see tae it for me.'

Then an elderly cleaner timidly asked her to write a letter to the factor about rainwater pouring in through her kitchen window.

'When I'm in front of them, all they see's an auld woman no worth botherin' about, but a letter in a nice hand's different. It's more—' She searched for a word, and beamed when Elspeth suggested, 'More businesslike?'

'That's it, hen – ye've the right way with the words. Will ye dae it for me?'

'Tell me what you want to say.' Elspeth drew the exercise book towards her. 'I'll write it down, then I'll do a proper letter tonight and give it to you tomorrow.'

When word that the factor's men had repaired the window went round the store, Elspeth was inundated with requests. She spent her evenings writing letters, and once or twice had to call on Mattie for assistance in return for helping her cousin with her homework.

'Imagine people paying to have letters written for them, when they could manage for themselves,' she wrote to Lachlan and Thomas. 'I'm getting to know as much about this town as the journalists who write in the *Greenock Telegraph*. Only they know about the important things, while I know about varicose veins and who's had a baby and how someone's Uncle William's come down with the bronchitis again. It's just as well that I can keep secrets.'

'It'll bring you out of your shell, and high time too,' Lachlan wrote back, while Thomas's letter said, 'You're discovering that everyone has some talent that's needed by others, Ellie. It's called supply and demand, and if you're wondering how I know such high-flown things, it's because I've learned a lot myself, mixing with so many different folk. That side of the war's interesting, but I'd give anything to be back home, waking in the morning and knowing that I'm going to be working in the Bruces' nice garden without having to duck every time a Boche shell comes screaming past. They don't have gardens here, only mud.'

'It's a lot of nonsense,' Flora announced when she discovered what was going on. 'Folk should see tae their own letter-writin'.'

'You rely on Ellie to do most of the writing to Thomas and Lachlan,' Mattie pointed out, and earned a cuff on the ear for her disrespect.

'That's different, milady, and well ye know it. I've got more than enough tae see tae as it is. I'd certainly not go askin' a stranger tae write letters for me. And I'm not so sure that it's right for ye tae take money for doin' it, Elspeth.'

'They want to pay their way,' Elspeth explained hurriedly, anxious in case her aunt put a stop to the letter-writing and the money she was earning towards night school. 'I don't ask to be paid.'

'Ye should be proud of the lass, Flora.' Henry's voice came from behind his newspaper. 'She works all hours at that writin' she's daein', and she surely deserves tae be paid for it.'

Flora frowned and muttered, but to Elspeth's relief she raised no further objections. Sometimes, but only sometimes, Flora McDonald listened when her husband spoke.

By January 1918 Elspeth had saved up enough money to start evening classes twice a week in typewriting, shorthand and book-keeping at Greenock Higher Grade School.

On the other three evenings and at weekends she was kept busy coping with the demand for letters, which grew until she had to rise half an hour earlier in the mornings to fit them all in.

Typing and shorthand and book-keeping satisfied her love of order and neatness, and from the start she enjoyed evening classes, getting even more pleasure out of them than she had done from day school.

She quickly realised, too, that office work brought far more satisfaction than machining a neat hem on a skirt, or even stitching the pretty petticoat Miss Arnold entrusted to her one day with the comment, 'You're one of our more careful seam-stresses, Elspeth. I can trust you not to make a mess of this.' Sewing had always been part of her life, but office skills brought a fresh challenge, one that she took on with enthusiasm.

Shorthand, a written language that could never be spoken, fascinated her. She took great pleasure in her newfound ability to cover a page with its crisp, swift hooks and strokes and curls, then translate the symbols back into real words. In book-keeping, she loved to see lists of figures growing on the pages of her cash-book, each amount neatly ranged beneath the figure above, each corresponding with a figure on another column, another page.

She particularly enjoyed sitting at a typewriter, tapping on the keys and watching the letters forming on the paper that moved regally upwards, line by line, from the carriage. Sometimes the teacher tapped out the alphabet on the blackboard with a cane, and the whole class was supposed to hit the correct keys to the rhythm she was setting. When the exercise worked, the sound of the keys all crashing together to the beat of the cane was music to Elspeth's ears, and it set her teeth on edge when slower girls missed the beat and threw the rhythm out.

Most of all, she treasured the knowledge that her precious evening classes were being paid for by money she herself had earned. She was doing what she had always wanted to do, and she hadn't had to turn to anyone else for help.

She envied those classmates who had already gained entrance into offices, and had been sent to night school by their employers.

'One day,' she told Mattie, her only confidante apart from her letters to Thomas and Lachlan, 'I'm going to work in an office. If you're determined enough, you can do anything.'

5

When Elspeth first started her evening classes, she didn't say a word about them to Grandmother Bremner, in case they turned out to be a mistake and she had to accept failure and give up. But by May they were going so well that she felt free to talk about them on her monthly visit to the old lady. Grandmother, she felt sure, would be pleased to hear that she had even managed to pay for them herself, and was beholden to nobody.

Celia Bremner lived near Bogstone railway station in Port Glasgow, a shipbuilding town adjacent to Greenock. The tenants in the row of tenements in which she lived were envied by others, because the railway line, which the tenement faced, had been built above the shore road to Greenock. The line was flanked on one side by a sheer drop of at least thirty feet to the shore road, and on the other side by Grandmother's street, which ran parallel to the line, but a little above it. This meant that the tenement windows had an excellent view of the Clyde, looking right over the railway line and even over the shipyards beyond to the open stretch of water and the soft green hills on the opposite shore.

The Bremners were, as Grandmother often told Elspeth, of good stock. Looking at Celia Bremner, erect as a soldier on parade, pride stamped into the hard lines of her face, Elspeth had no reason to doubt her words. During her regular visits to the house, which had started after Celia Bremner was widowed, the old woman always sat in an upright, heavily carved chair, her lower arms laid along the wooden armrests, her hands, twisted with rheumatism, curving precisely over the polished knobs at the ends. She and the chair fitted each other so well that as a child Elspeth had wondered if the chair had been specially made to her grandmother's measurements, and had supposed that somewhere in the house stood a series of identical chairs, starting with a small one made for her grandmother when she was a child, then ranging in size to the imposing adult chair standing now by the fireplace.

Grandfather Bremner, who had, as far as Elspeth knew, never set eyes on her, had been paymaster in one of the sugar refineries; a man, according to his widow, who had been looked up to by his staff and highly regarded by his employers.

Elspeth's secret hope was that if she did well enough at night school, her grandmother might be willing to put in a good word for her at the office where her grandfather had once worked.

She began by talking about the letters she was writing for other people, and was interrupted before she could get to the part about the night school classes.

'I trust you're not asked to write anything vulgar or sensational in those letters?'

'Oh no, Grandmother. Just news of what's happening in the town and with the soldiers' families.'

'In that case I believe your grandfather would have approved,' Celia Bremner said in her dry, flat voice. 'We should all use our God-given talents, and your ability to write comes from him. He himself wrote excellent letters.' Her glance travelled briefly to the mantelpiece, where a photograph of herself and her late husband stood in an elaborate carved wooden frame.

Every item of furniture in Celia Bremner's three-roomed house was carved. Wherever the eye landed it was met by a profusion of balls and claws, bunches of grapes, climbing vines, and formal flowers, all in a state of suspended animation, as though some wicked witch had cast a spell over them and stopped the flowers just at the point of opening, the leaves when they were about to toss in the wind, the grapes at the moment before they were plucked.

Even the photograph of Grandmother and Grandfather Bremner looked as though it had been frozen in time, Elspeth thought, following the old lady's gaze. He, richly moustached but balding, his eyes staring coldly through the glass, sat in a chair – surely a photographer's chair, since it was plain, with no sign of any carvings – his wife on her feet, slightly behind him, one hand firmly planted on his shoulder as if to show that he was hers and nobody else's, her sculpted hair glimpsed beneath a feathered hat.

Studying the photograph, Elspeth found it hard to imagine her grandparents in any other, less formal pose, sitting eating their dinners, for instance, or sleeping in the large carved bed in the bedroom. It was certainly impossible to imagine them talking, laughing, moving freely.

She wondered what it must have been like for her mother to grow up with these two people. From what Granjan said, Maisie Bremner had been a happy young girl, full of fun. Perhaps, thought Elspeth, feeling an itch on her calf and unable to scratch it in front of Grandmother Bremner, that was why there were no photographs of Maisie on the mantelpiece. Even a pictured image of her might hint at too much movement, too much liveliness, in this immaculate flat where the only thing allowed to move was the pendulum of the grandmother clock in the corner of the living room. Even that was strictly regulated to make sure that it didn't recklessly drop or add a second.

Deciding that a respectable interval of time had been given over to contemplation of her grandparents' portrait, she moved tentatively towards the core of her news. 'I enjoy writing letters. I'd like to work in an office one day – like Grandfather.'

To her surprise, her grandmother's nostrils flared and her already stiff back stiffened further. Her large-knuckled hands gripped at the armrests.

'Offices are not suitable workplaces for respectable women!'

'But a lot of women work in offices now, Grandmother.'

'That's between them and their consciences,' the old woman rapped out, eyes flashing. 'If this letter-writing is going to lead to such foolishness on your part, Elspeth, I trust that your Aunt Flora has the sense to put a stop to it at once. You're fortunate in having found a good position as a seamstress with a reputable firm, and with diligence, you may do very well for yourself there. I'll not have any more talk of office work from a granddaughter of mine, d'you hear me?'

Elspeth was completely taken aback. She had no idea what she had done to deserve this outburst, but instinct told her that retreat was the safest option. 'Yes, Grandmother.' The itch was worse now, nagging and niggling, demanding to be scratched. She shifted slightly in her chair in an attempt to relieve it.

'Don't twitch, child, it's unladylike. I expect it means that you want your tea,' Celia said reprovingly. 'Very well, you may go to the kitchen and fetch the tray.'

Elspeth, disturbed by her grandmother's sudden change of mood, was only too happy to leave the room. Clearly, there was no question of talking about her night classes now. She felt sure that if the old woman knew about them, she would put a stop to them.

Despite her rheumatism, Grandmother Bremner kept her kitchen, like the rest of the house, spotless, with never a thing out of place. The kitchen was actually a scullery, a walk-in cupboard barely large enough for the gas cooker, sink, and closet it held. The kettle, sitting over what Granjan called 'a wee peep of gas', was ready, pluming subdued little puffs of steam into the air.

With some difficulty, for the scullery was so small that

there wasn't room for even one person to bend down when the door was closed, Elspeth indulged in the luxury of clawing at her calf until the itch was subdued, tears of relief coming to her eyes. She was sure that another minute of sitting in the living room while the itch grew to monstrous proportions would have set her screaming.

The itch finally gone, she warmed the teapot then emptied it into the sink before, mindful of her grandmother's wishes, measuring a precise half-spoonful of tea into the pot from the elaborately painted caddy with its picture of Queen Victoria. After pouring boiling water into the pot she refilled the kettle from the kitchen tap.

A tray had already been set with cups and saucers, plates, milk jug and sugar bowl. Elspeth added the teapot, covered it with the knitted cosy Grandmother always used, and took four biscuits from the biscuit barrel on the shelf, laying them neatly on the blue leaf-shaped plate already on the tray. Back in the living room she put the tray down on the small table between their two chairs and poured tea, first putting in the correct amounts of milk and sugar.

They had their tea in silence, because Grandmother didn't believe in talking while taking refreshments. Sipping at the pale liquid, which she found tasteless compared to the sturdy, strong brew she was used to at home, Elspeth wished that she was back there, practising her shorthand and book-keeping, and perhaps writing two letters that she had promised for Monday morning.

She wished, too, and with all her heart, that Grandmother Bremner was more like Granjan. The two women were like chalk and cheese. Both had given birth to one child, a daughter, and both were widowed, but that was as far as any resemblance went. Granjan was small and plump and cosy, with twinkling grey eyes and a ready sense of humour, while Grandmother was tall and bony, with a long unsmiling face and cold blue eyes. Both wore their hair in a bun, but there again, they were quite unlike each other. Granjan's hair was grey, and always making attempts to escape from captivity; Grandmother's was pure white and drawn back tightly, enhancing the skull-like look of her face. Grandmother spoke very properly, articulating each word clearly, while Granjan chattered on in the local dialect, saying 'tae' and 'ye' instead of 'to' and 'you' and scarcely bothering with word endings like 'th' and 'ing'.

On leaving school, Granjan had worked in Boag's factory, where the bags from the many sugar refineries in Greenock were washed and prepared for re-use, while Grandmother had obtained a position as lady's maid in one of the big houses in Largs, a residential town further along the coast, where many of the wealthy manufacturers from Glasgow had built seaside homes.

Both women had given up work when they got married, Granjan to a labourer at Caird's shipyard, Grandmother to an ambitious wages clerk in one of Greenock's sugar refineries.

Granjan, forced to become the breadwinner within two years of her marriage, when her husband, still in his twenties, was crippled in an accident at the yard, had taken work wherever she could find it, as a cleaner and washerwoman. Widowed in her mid-thirties, she still paid her way by washing for women who could afford to pay someone else to see to their laundry.

Grandmother's husband had achieved the position of paymaster before his death, leaving his widow with enough money to continue living in the comfortable flat they had shared, and to cover her frugal lifestyle. It was once she was on her own that Celia Bremner had acknowledged the existence of her dead daughter's illegitimate child, insisting on monthly visits. Flora had taken Elspeth to Port Glasgow in the early days, leaving her at the door and waiting for her in the street an hour later. As soon as Elspeth was old enough, she started making the visits on her own, although as far as she could tell, her grandmother didn't derive any more pleasure from their meetings than she herself did.

When they had finished tea Elspeth removed the tray and carefully washed and dried the fragile fluted cups, then put them away in the cupboard. As always, her grandmother took advantage of her absence to visit the lavatory.

Unlike most residents in the three towns – Port Glasgow, Greenock and Gourock – strung together along the banks of the Clyde, Grandmother was fortunate enough to have an indoor lavatory. While this was a blessing to be envied, Elspeth was aware that as far as Grandmother was concerned it was more of a curse if anyone else happened to be in the flat, as it meant that they could hear the cistern flushing.

She had learned early in her visits to remain quietly in the scullery until the noisy rush of water had ceased and the old woman had had enough time to settle herself carefully back in her chair, as though she hadn't moved from it at all. Celia Bremner hated to let anyone know that she did anything as common as using a lavatory.

Elspeth often wondered how her grandmother would have managed in the Mearns Street tenement, where all the tenants on one landing shared the privy on the half-landing below, and the folk on the ground floor had their privy in the back yard. She was sure that Grandmother Bremner would rather have burst than admit that she was prey to the same physical actions as other human beings.

Waiting in the scullery until it was time to return to the living room, Elspeth recalled her own sense of shock on hearing from Molly McKibbin, one of a large family, about how men and women made babies. It had been then, and still was, very difficult to think of Auntie Flora and Uncle Henry indulging in such goings-on in the large kitchen wall-bed they shared, but quite impossible to fathom out how the couple in the photograph on Grandmother's mantelpiece could ever have conceived her mother.

Even now that she was older and had had Molly's scarlet-faced, giggling whispers confirmed by some of the girls in the sewing room, she couldn't believe it of her grandmother. Surely a woman who hated to have it known that she had to answer calls of nature like everyone else would never have permitted herself to get involved in that way with a man!

'I hope you've not chipped any of my china.' Celia's cold, creaky voice brought her back to the present just when her thoughts were threatening to get completely out of control.

'No, Grandmother.' She returned to the living room, hoping that her expression carried no hint of the impure thoughts she had been having. 'I was just dusting the biscuit barrel.'

'And how is everything in the sewing room?' Celia Bremner asked when they were facing each other across the fireplace again.

'Very well, thank you, Grandmother. Miss Arnold allowed me to hand-stitch a hem on a petticoat last Thursday, and she was pleased with it when I'd finished.' In her enthusiasm at the memory of Miss Arnold's grudging praise, Elspeth hitched herself slightly forward in her chair. 'It was beautiful material, lovely to touch—'

'Sit up, girl, you're slouching. I'm glad to hear that you're giving satisfaction. You get your sewing ability from me, of course – when I attended Miss Hope Childes, I was well known for my delicate stitching,' Celia said firmly, giving no credit at all to the hours of hard work Flora McDonald had put into teaching Elspeth and her own two daughters how to sew.

'Miss Arnold says that she might let me do some more work for clients who have their clothes made for them.'

Her grandmother inclined her head. 'You could do well for yourself, then.'

The clock in the corner gently chimed the half-hour, and Elspeth sighed inwardly. Thirty more minutes must pass before she was free to make her excuses and go.

'Thomas wrote to me last week,' she volunteered. 'He's in Belgium now. Lachlan's still in France, and we don't hear so much from him just now. I hope he's all right. Thomas says things are just as bad as ever before.' She looked down at her hands, and tried hard not to let her voice shake as she went on, 'I'm so worried about the two of them. I couldn't bear it if they didn't come back home.'

'They're doing their duty by their king and country,' Celia Bremner said implacably. 'You must fix your mind on that, and accept whatever the Lord may choose to send.'

Elspeth was startled by the sudden jolt of anger that ran through her. She longed to ask why anyone should accept without protest a war that was killing hundreds and thousands of ordinary young men like Thomas and Lachlan, but she didn't dare. Instead, she folded her lips together to contain her fury, and waited for the clock to chime four times and release her.

When it finally, grudgingly, did so, she held back until she had rounded the street corner and was well out of sight before starting to run, rejoicing in her freedom and the pleasure of stretching her limbs after having to sit so still in the claustrophobic room she had just left.

6

Spring made little impact on the cobbles and slabs of Greenock's streets and back yards, though flowers and trees and bushes could be seen stirring with life in the town's parks and in the wealthier townsfolk's gardens and the countryside beyond. Most of the residents, though, marked the arrival of the spring season by the soft green shading on the hills at the other side of the Clyde.

In the battlegrounds of France and Belgium there was even less indication of the release from a long, cold, wet winter. Elspeth gathered from Thomas's letters that the rain had eased somewhat, and smoke from the guns drifted across blue skies, but the mud was still there. In one letter he wrote about spending a night in the ruins of a big house, similar to the house his employers, the Bruce family, had in Gourock, describing graphically the glassless windows, the odd scrap of wallpaper still clinging here and there to what remained of a wall, a door hanging askew on one twisted hinge.

'It was hard to believe that it had once been a cosy home where a family had lived,' he wrote. 'I wonder where they are now, and what's become of them? We thought we were in clover when we arrived, because almost one entire room was left standing, complete with a fireplace and a bonny ceiling, with carving all round. We gathered up wood and lit a fire, only to discover that the chimney had fallen in, so we were driven out of the place by clouds of smoke. We were so pleased at being able to sit at a real fire in a real fireplace that we hung on for as long as we could, until we were all wheezing and coughing, the tears running down our faces.

'I managed to find time to go out into the grounds before we left. It reminded me a lot of the Bruces', for this place had a kitchen garden and a rose garden and once it had had some bonny box hedging and statues on the terracing, all broken and destroyed now. All the glass was gone in their greenhouses, of course, but I did find a pot with a hyacinth blossoming in it, a lovely deep blue flower. I cleared the broken glass from it and moved it to a sheltered spot. Maybe after the fighting is over and the folk come back to rebuild their house, the hyacinth will still be there, waiting for them. It was good to think that all this destruction can't entirely kill Nature off.'

As Elspeth had told her grandmother, Lachlan's letters to her and to his parents had become sporadic. When he did write, his letters were short, and tended to be filled with memories of the past: 'Do you remember that day we all walked over the hills to Loch Thom and had a picnic?' or, 'I was thinking this morning about the time Thomas and me went to Gourock and hired a boat and rowed out into the river so far that we thought we weren't going to get back before the hire time was up.'

She knew from what the other girls in the sewing room said that men on active duty often clung to thoughts of home. One of the carters who had fought in the Boer War in South Africa told her that it was important to soldiers to know that everything was the same at home, just waiting for them to return and slip back into the place they had left.

'Not that anything's ever the same,' he said, scratching his bristly chin, 'for the man himself's bound tae be changed by the things he's seen an' heard an' done. But even so, he needs tae believe that his real life's still waitin' for him back home. That's what keeps him goin'.'

*

In the summer, as the tide of battle slowly began to turn in the Allies' favour at last, a War Office telegram arrived at the McDonalds' flat. Lachlan had been wounded, and was in hospital in France.

To Elspeth, who had become increasingly superstitious about both Thomas and Lachlan, and had taken to lying awake night after night, fretting over them, the news was welcome. The war had dragged on far longer than anyone had at first believed possible, and by now almost every family she knew had lost a young man in the fighting, or had had word of wounds received in battle.

So far this hadn't happened to the McDonalds, and she had got it into her head that Thomas and Lachlan had escaped harm for too long while men were injured and killed all around them. Some form of blood sacrifice, she had begun to believe during those long dark sleepless nights, might have to be made before they could be truly safe.

Now she saw Lachlan's wound as just such a sacrifice, an omen that both he and Thomas would survive and return home safely when the war was finally over. She was even relieved for Lachlan's sake, happy to know that for a little while, at least, he was distanced from the fighting and able to rest in safety and without fear.

But when she tried to express these thoughts to Flora, who had almost fainted away at the sight of the War Office envelope, her outraged aunt was in no mood to listen.

'All I know is that my poor laddie's lyin' hurt and in pain in some foreign hospital, with none of his own there tae see tae him,' she snapped. 'I see nothing tae be happy about – and neither would you, if ye'd the sense God gave ye!'

Once again, Elspeth thought in despair, biting her tongue to prevent herself from trying to explain and thus annoying Flora even further, she had caused trouble without meaning to. Would she never learn to keep her opinions to herself?

She was already feeling low that summer. The evening

classes had ended, and wouldn't begin again until September, and as Mattie's school was also closed there was no homework to study with her.

More orders for letters were coming in, and her savings for the next evening-school session were growing, but she missed working on the typewriter, and found a sewing machine a poor substitute. She begged a large sheet of cardboard from a local shopkeeper, and carefully, working from memory, drew out on it a typewriter keyboard. Working on it helped to keep her fingers supple, but at the same time she missed the crisp tapping of a real typewriter's keys.

August brought some excitement to the sewing room. Catherine Bruce, the elder daughter of the family for whom Thomas worked in peacetime, was engaged to a young captain in the Scottish Rifles, and when he was sent home to recuperate from wounds, the couple decided to marry before he went back on duty. The bride's mother, Mrs Lorrimer Bruce, was insistent on a proper church wedding complete with bridesmaids. There was also to be a full trousseau for her daughter's honeymoon, brief though it must be, as the groom was to rejoin his unit by mid-September.

Because the war and the lack of time made it difficult for the trousseau to be made in Glasgow, as would have happened in peacetime, Brodie's store was pressed into service. The sewing room suddenly became a whirl of activity, with all the seamstresses enlisted to help meet the deadline. Even the 'plain' sewing women, who normally only dealt with alterations to ready-made clothes, were given something to do for the wedding.

Miss Buchanan rushed about like a dandelion ball caught up in a whirlwind, her arms filled with sketches and patterns and materials, and Miss Arnold, two bright spots of colour high on her normally pale cheekbones, seemed to be everywhere at once, instructing, checking, criticising, while at the same time soothing her near-hysterical superior.

'This is a great honour for the department,' she told the staff at least once every day. 'We must show Mrs Bruce that we can do as well as any big Glasgow store.'

'The gentry won't even let a war deprive them of their bit of show,' Lena said with a sniff as they all stitched and cut and trimmed.

'What's wrong with a nice dress and jacket?' one of the other women wanted to know. 'That's what my sister wore when she married her sweetheart a few months ago. It's the marryin' that counts, not the show.'

'When ye're a nob, it's the show that counts more than the marryin',' Lena retorted disparagingly. 'What I'd like tae know is, where did they get all this lovely material? It's hard tae find stuff like that nowadays.'

'I heard that a lot of it comes from Mrs Bruce herself,' one of the other girls ventured. 'She put it by before the war began, just in case it was needed for somethin' like this.'

'God! The rest of us makin' do with what we can find, and the likes of the Bruces even hidin' away good cloth!' For a moment Elspeth thought that Lena was going to explode. Her face went red and her hair seemed to give off flashes of light. She opened her mouth to speak, then bent over her work, almost choking with suppressed anger, as the door opened and Miss Arnold swept back in to urge her staff to further efforts.

Elspeth didn't object at all to the hustle and bustle, because the hard work gave her something to do and took her mind off the loss of the evening classes. She enjoyed handling the beautiful materials chosen for the trousseau, and loved the sight of all the colours spilling across the worktables, brightening the drab room.

Once, when she was sent to the fitting rooms with a lawn petticoat she had just finished, a beautiful garment trimmed with pink ribbons and lace, she caught a glimpse of the two Bruce sisters.

Catherine Bruce, the bride-to-be, was a pretty young woman with soft dark hair framing a round face. She was standing before a full-length mirror, garbed in a crimson silk underdress beneath a sequined net overdress in the same colour. Two of the seamstresses were on their knees beside her, working on the hem, while Miss Arnold watched critically, her back to Elspeth, who hesitated at the door, unwilling to interrupt.

She had never seen a more beautiful dress, but the wearer's brows were drawn together above dark-lashed green eyes, her full small mouth turned down at the corners in a sulky pout.

'I still don't like the neckline. It doesn't look right.'

'I think it very flattering, Miss Bruce.' Elspeth had never heard Miss Arnold speak in that soft, soothing voice before. 'Just your style.'

'That's very well, but you're not the one who has to wear it, are you?' the girl snapped without taking her eyes off her own reflection. Elspeth saw Miss Arnold's back stiffen, but when the woman replied it was in the same quiet, reasonable voice.

'If we change the neckline, we change the entire style of the dress, madam.'

'For goodness' sake, Kate, stop fussing. It's lovely, and you know it,' a new voice cut in, and for the first time Elspeth, spellbound up to now by the beauty of the dress, noticed the girl sitting in the corner. Clearly this was Catherine Bruce's sister, for there was a strong family resemblance; but while the bride was pretty, the other girl was breathtakingly beautiful. Her hair was hidden beneath a turban striped in two shades of green, the darker shade an exact match for her wide, clear eyes, and a dark green feather swept up from it. Her silk suit, also in dark green with a lighter shade picking out the lapels, cuffs, and facing, was cut in a severe military style, and her small, narrow feet wore soft green kid button boots. Her face was less rounded than her sister's, almost angular, with a small yet soft mouth.

'It's all right for you, Aileen, all you need is one

bridesmaid's dress. I wish Mother had come with me,' Catherine Bruce fretted, turning back to the mirror.

'So do I,' her sister agreed, then the lovely green eyes discovered Elspeth. 'Someone's waiting to speak to you, Miss Arnold,' she said, and the supervisor turned.

'What do you want, Elspeth?'

'You asked for this, Miss Arnold.'

'Yes, I did. Run along now,' Miss Arnold said briefly, taking the petticoat and turning back at once to her client.

The bridesmaids' dresses, Elspeth knew, were to be in pale yellow muslin, cut straight across from shoulder to shoulder and trimmed with silver and yellow roses. Aileen Bruce would look beautiful in hers, she thought, hurrying back to her work.

As the wedding date approached, Miss Buchanan, clearly convinced that the clothes would never be ready in time, worked herself into a frenzy.

'If she's not careful, one of these days she'll go whizzin' out the door and bump intae hersel' coming back,' Lena remarked during a midday break in the basement. 'Either that, or she'll run right up her own arse by accident. We used tae have a dog that was forever chasin' its own tail – it never did catch it, but she's in danger of catchin' hers.'

'I wish she'd just keep out of the way and stop telling us to leave what we're doing and go on to something else,' Elspeth complained. She was working on another petticoat, one with a lot of tucking in the bodice that required careful and time-consuming work, and twice that morning Miss Buchanan had tried to make her stop what she was doing and turn to another garment.

If it hadn't been for Miss Arnold's cool efficiency, Miss Buchanan would have got the entire sewing room into such a tizzy that work on the wedding clothes could well have descended into chaos. She took to following Miss Buchanan around, calmly and quietly countermanding her superior's conflicting orders and ensuring that one garment was finished before work started on the next.

'It's Miss Bruce that's the real problem.' Lily, one of the women who had been in the fitting room the day Elspeth took the petticoat in, leaned across the table. 'Talk about fussy – she doesnae like any of the things she ordered. Keeps wanting them all tae be changed, and she should know better than anyb'dy how little time we've got left. She's spoiled rotten, that one, thinks money's all that matters. Thank goodness her man comes from Perth – the folk up there are welcome tae her.'

'Remember that she's tae stay with her mother till the war's over,' someone else cautioned. 'We'll not get rid of her until her husband's back home for good, so let's hope nothing happens tae him.'

'I can see the day he'll wish something had,' Lily sniffed. 'Courtin''s one thing, marryin''s another. I should know – it wasn't until my man went off to the fighting that I realised what a pain in the neck he is. Once Miss Catherine's new husband's got her all the time he might wish he'd never proposed.'

'The sister seems to be quite nice,' Elspeth offered, and Lily shrugged.

'She's decent enough. Mind you, she's been away at some posh boarding school, so she's mebbe learned a few manners there. Once she's been under her ma's wing for a year or two she might be just as bad,' she said, then, coaxingly, 'Elspeth, ye wouldnae have the time tae write me a wee letter tae the factor, would ye? He's tryin' tae tell me I'm still owing my share of those roof repairs, and I know I'm not. But I cannae seem tae put the words down the right way.'

Preparing the trousseau in time for the wedding date began to resemble being in a locked room with the walls slowly moving in to crush the life out of its occupants. As the wedding day approached, the seamstresses worked almost every evening until quite late. Miss Buchanan tottered continually on the verge of apoplexy, while Miss Arnold's controlled serenity was magnificent to see.

It was just as well that there were no evening classes, for Elspeth would have had to miss them. She had been put almost entirely on to fine work that couldn't be done on a machine, and her fingers were red and stiff, the skin rough from plying a needle, her back aching with tension after long hours bent over the worktable. At home, she had to work into the night and get up early in the morning to keep up with her letter-writing as well, but she was determined not to let it fall behind, for it had turned out to be a lucrative sideline.

Between the letters and overtime in the sewing room, her savings had grown considerably and she now had enough to ensure another year at night school, even though she had given a percentage of her overtime earnings to Flora.

To her surprise, her aunt was reluctant to take it. 'Ye've been workin' hard, lassie, with never a word of complaint. Ye deserve tae keep it,' she said, but Elspeth insisted, constantly aware of the debt she owed Flora and Henry McDonald, and anxious to do what she could to repay them.

Secretly, she dreamed of buying them a nice house one day, and furnishing it throughout, to show them how grateful she was for all they had done for her, and to make up for all those occasions when she had inadvertently annoyed Aunt Flora.

One evening when the seamstresses were working late on the last part of the wedding trousseau, a list of the clothes completed went missing, together with two essential patterns. Everyone stopped work and the sewing room was searched, but it was nowhere to be found. Miss Buchanan had had to go home at dinner-time with a severe headache, and as it was her habit to scoop up every piece of paper she could find during her dashes into the sewing room to interrupt and harangue her long-suffering workers, Miss Arnold searched her tiny cubby-hole, but came back empty-handed.

Elspeth and Lena, who had both just finished the work they had been doing, were despatched to the main office, where a copy of the list was kept in case of emergencies, while the overseer continued to hunt for the patterns.

'Mr James Brodie's still on the premises, so he'll be in his room, off the accounts office. He'll know where the list is. Remember to speak clearly, don't gabble, and don't stare at the floor when he speaks to you. I don't want him to think that we employ mindless idiots in the sewing room. And remember that the staff call Mr James "sir",' Miss Arnold cautioned, and the girls, their minds seething with instructions, obediently scurried off up the narrow stairs to the top floor, where the main office and accounts department were housed.

'Why send two of us?' Elspeth wondered as they went.

'So that we can keep each other out of mischief.' Lena was bounding ahead. 'It's great tae get out for a few minutes, isn't it?'

There was no reply when they tapped at the door of the main office. After waiting for a moment or two, Lena nudged Elspeth in. The room was empty, and so, they realised after tapping at the inner door, was the small office belonging to Mr James Brodie, manager of the store, and son of the owner, who had retired.

'Now what do we do?'

'Wait here. There's no sense in goin' back empty-handed,' Lena advised. 'The lights are on and the door's not been locked, so he can't be far away. He'll have gone tae the privy.' She stood in the middle of the main office, turning slowly, taking everything in. 'It's awful tidy, isn't it?'

'That's because they don't have patterns and cloth everywhere.' The office's neatness delighted Elspeth. The high desk along one wall was swept clear of books and papers, pens were laid in the grooves provided and the inkwells were free of stains. All the drawers and cupboard doors were closed, and neat rows of files filled the shelves that lined another wall.

'It's brighter here during the day than it is in the sewing room.' Lena indicated the skylights let into the ceiling. 'I wish we'd some daylight, I hate workin' under the electric light all the time.'

Elspeth didn't hear her. Her eye had fallen on the small table in the corner, with the unmistakable shape of a typewriter filling out its protective dust cover. Envy and longing flooded her mind and her fingers started to itch. She edged over to the table to run her fingertips over the cover, then, after a quick look at the door leading to the corridor, she whipped it off to reveal the typewriter itself.

'Here – what're ye doin'?'

'Just looking.' Her eyes devoured the machine greedily; it was high and shining and solid, the round keys, each with its letter or number clearly stamped on it, as mouthwatering to her as a glossy heap of liquorice allsorts would have been to a hungry child staring in through a sweetshop window.

Her fingers yearned to touch those keys, her ears longed to hear them at work. Several sheets of paper lay by the machine, white and untouched as a fresh snowfall, waiting for letters to be tapped briskly across their pristine surfaces. It was almost too much to bear, being so near a typewriter again and not being able to touch it.

'Mr James can't be at the privy,' she said without taking her eyes from the machine. 'He'd have been back by now.'

'My dad can spend hours in our privy,' Lena said from behind her. 'He suffers terrible from constipation, and when he manages tae go it takes a while. The neighbours have tae pee intae buckets when that happens. Here, what're ye doin' now?' she added in alarm as Elspeth drew out the chair tucked in beneath the desk.

'Just looking.' Elspeth sat down and let her fingers rest on the keys. A shiver of pure pleasure ran through her, and she knew that she couldn't leave things at that. She had to try the typewriter, to find out whether, during the summer, she had lost her recently learned skills.

'Keep an eye on the corridor,' she said, reaching for a sheet of paper and rolling it into the machine.

'Elspeth Bremner! You'll get us both the sack!' Although she could be a rebel in the sewing room, Lena was intimidated by the office, a room she had never been in before.

'I'll not be a minute. Just watch the corridor and tell me if you hear him coming.'

Beneath her fingers the keys leapt into life. 'The cat sat on the mat,' she typed, then ran the carriage back to start a new line. 'The quick brown fox jumped over the lazy dog' was followed by a swift, sure alphabet, every stroke true and clear like a run of notes on a piano.

'That's clever! Where did ye learn tae dae that?' Lena asked in wonder, coming to lean over the desk.

'I've been going to evening classes.' Elspeth hadn't told any of her workmates about her studies for fear of being laughed at, but now, with her ability clear for all to see, she didn't mind talking about it. She ran off another alphabet, her wrists at just the right angle, her fingers skimming over the keys, her eyes fixed on the paper and not the keyboard. Her teacher would have been proud of her, she thought, tossing the carriage back with a flick of the wrist to begin a new line.

She was so taken up with the joy of touching a typewriter again that she didn't even register the fact that Lena, who was supposed to be keeping watch, was in fact standing beside her, equally entranced. Neither of them heard the footsteps in the corridor, or the door opening behind them. When someone suddenly stepped into their line of vision and a male voice, as crisp and sharp as the tap of the keys on the paper, asked, 'Just what do you think you're doing?' the two girls jumped and squealed.

7

James Brodie's long, handsome face was grim, his brows drawn into a frown as he surveyed the two young women trembling before him. 'Well?'

Lena, gasping like a landed fish, her hand pressed tightly to her heart, was for once lost for words. Elspeth, suddenly aware of the enormity of her actions, stood up slowly.

'I – we – Miss Arnold sent us for a copy of Miss Bruce's wedding list, Mr – s-sir.' The words stuck in her throat, on her tongue, behind her front teeth, and it was difficult to get them out. Mindful of Miss Arnold's orders, she lifted her chin when all she really wanted to do was to hide her face against the linoleum on the floor.

The eyes surveying her were frosty, and so was his voice when he said, 'Did she ask you to fetch the list, or to type it out?'

'You werenae here, sir.' Lena finally found her voice, and her wits. 'We were waitin' for ye.'

'You were doing more than waiting.'

Elspeth swallowed hard. 'I – I was just trying out the type-writer – sir.'

'But you're a seamstress, not a typist.'

'She goes tae the night school,' Lena said eagerly. 'She knows how tae work it.'

'Then she'll know how to leave it as she found it, won't she?

And while you're doing that, I'll find this list you're supposed to be fetching.'

Silently, cheeks burning and mouth trembling, Elspeth rolled the sullied sheet of paper from the machine and laid it down on the desk before lining the carriage up properly. In a futile attempt to erase her crime, she used her clean handkerchief to wipe the surface of the keys before replacing the dust cover. By the time she had finished, Mr James had returned from his own small office. He handed the list to Lena.

'Take that to Miss Arnold, and tell her—' He stopped, looking from one flushed face to the other, then said ominously, 'Never mind, I'll tell her myself. I'll have that, young woman, it's my property.'

Elspeth had picked up the used sheet with some idea of removing all traces of the sacrilege she had just committed. Scarlet with mortification, she laid it in the outstretched hand.

'Now you can go back to where you belong,' the manager said dismissively, and the two of them crept out and along the corridor, running down the stairs as though the devil was at their heels, not stopping until they were back on the level where the sewing rooms were situated.

'Sweet Jesus, I near died when I saw him standing there,' Lena gasped, clutching at the banisters with her free hand.

'You were supposed to keep watch for him!' Elspeth blazed at her, fighting back tears of humiliation. It had been the worst moment of her whole life.

'I wouldnae have heard him even if I'd been at the door. It's unnatural for a grown man tae be so light on his feet. Anyway, it's all your fault for touchin' the thing in the first place. I wasnae doing anything wrong – it was you,' Lena said virtuously. 'D'you think he'll tell Miss Arnold?'

'He's sure tae. Did ye see the look on his face? He was ready for throwing us out of the place there and then.'

'What'll we do?' Elspeth wailed. 'What'll Aunt Flora say if I'm turned off?'

Her distress cooled the older girl's anger. 'Ye'll get another position, surely.'

'But it was her that got me this one! She'll say I've let her down again – I'm always doing it! Oh, why couldn't I have kept my hands to myself?' Elspeth wrung the offending hands, in such a state that Lena put an arm about her.

'Don't fret, hen, it'll all work out somehow. Come on, we'll have tae get back tae Miss Arnold, she'll be in a state about this precious list of hers. Don't say anything tae her, what she doesnae know won't hurt her – and no doubt she'll hear about it soon enough. There's one thing,' she added consolingly as they went along the corridor, 'at least yer typewritin' was nice and neat. He cannae accuse ye of doin' it badly.'

Fortunately, Miss Arnold, who had found the missing patterns just before they returned, was less harassed by the time they arrived back in the sewing room. She took the list from Lena, then looked from one to the other. 'You took a long time.'

'Mr James was in the – wasnae there,' Lena said smoothly. 'We had tae wait for him tae came back.'

The supervisor peered more closely at them. 'You're both looking flushed. What have you been up to?'

Elspeth, in the grip of her own private terror, stared dumbly back at her, but Lena was ready with another glib answer. 'We ran down the stairs, 'cos we knew you'd be waiting.'

'Well, you've wasted enough time away from your work. Elspeth, I want that skirt I left by your machine hemmed, and Lena, you can stitch the ribbons on to that camisole,' the supervisor ordered, and bustled off to the cutting room.

Elspeth sank thankfully into her chair and picked up the skirt. It was just as well that she had to machine instead of sew by hand, for she was shaking so much that she couldn't have threaded a needle. As it was, it took all her concentration to guide the material through the machine in a straight line.

*

Normally, when she got home from working overtime, she was as hungry as a horse, but that night she couldn't touch her supper.

'I hope ye're not sickening for something,' Flora fretted. 'I've got enough on my mind worryin' about our Lachlan without you falling ill as well.'

'I'm fine.'

'You don't look it,' Rachel said, eyeing her.

'I've got a sore head. It's all that sewing. I'll go to my bed early.'

'I'll be glad when this wedding's by.' Flora removed her untouched plate and covered it with a clean cloth. 'I'll put this in the oven, mebbe yer uncle'll be glad of it when he gets back from his meetin'.'

Elspeth lay sleepless, racked by guilt and wishing that she had never gone near the typewriter. When Mattie came to bed, tiptoeing about in the dark, trying not to waken her, she pretended she was asleep. A little later, Rachel came in with a candle and was about to light the gas mantle when Mattie hissed. 'Leave it, you'll wake Elspeth.'

Rachel sighed gustily, but did as she was told, though she would have been better to light the mantle, as she kept falling over things in the candle's weak light, yelping and muttering and loudly hissing, 'Shush yourself!' each time Mattie tried to quiet her.

At last she settled down, and soon both she and Mattie were breathing slowly and evenly, with the occasional fluttering snore. Elspeth lay awake, listening to the movements of her aunt and uncle, and the sounds of the tenement – the faint gurgle of water in the pipes, the clump of heavy footsteps on the stairs, the wailing of a child startled awake by a nightmare. She heard Mr McAllister from the flat below returning late from the pub, raising his voice in song then shouting at his wife and being shouted at in return.

Gradually, all the noises eased off as the tenement settled

down for the night. Then there was only the occasional plaintive toot from one of the many ships out on the river, or the melodious sound of a church clock striking the hours and half-hours.

Elspeth was still awake, feverishly going over and over those few moments of temptation in the office, wishing that she had pushed her hands into her pockets, or even cut them off, rather than allow them to touch that typewriter. One hand sought the little silver threepenny bit she had found in her birthday dumpling more than a year earlier, clutching it tightly. True to his word, Uncle Henry had drilled a hole in it for her, and she had worn it round her neck ever since, day and night. One of the first things she had bought with her earnings had been a fine chain to replace the piece of wool it had hung from. It had helped her in moments of stress, but tonight, not even the feel of it biting into her palm could comfort her.

The thought of having to tell her aunt that she had been turned away from the good, respectable job that had been found for her set her moving restlessly in the bed. Mattie, sound asleep, gave a moan of protest as an elbow jabbed into her back, and Elspeth made herself lie still, picturing the look on Flora's face when she heard the dreadful news.

The next two days, busy as they were, dragged by. Every time Miss Arnold or Miss Buchanan came into the sewing room Elspeth cringed, her heart thumping so hard that it was like a drum beating in her ears. She scarcely ate a thing, and it was all she could do to concentrate on her work, and on the letters she wrote during the midday meal break.

Lena, on the other hand, behaved as though nothing had happened, talking when she was supposed to be concentrating on her work, chattering like a budgie during their breaks, laughing and joking with the carters and the errand boys.

'Ach, he'll have forgotten all about it,' she said airily when

Elspeth wondered aloud when retribution was going to fall on them both. 'If he'd meant tae tell on us he'd have done it right away. Besides, we didnae steal anythin', or break anythin', did we?'

'I touched the typewriter, and spoiled a sheet of paper.'

'With the money he has, he can afford tae lose a hundred sheets of paper. And it'll teach you tae keep your hands tae yourself in future, miss. Now stop worryin' about it,' Lena ordered. 'Ye're like a wee ghost. Ye'll make yerself ill if ye don't watch out.'

Flora already thought that Elspeth was sickening for something, and had made her take a spoonful of her favourite cure-all, brimstone and treacle. For once, Elspeth had swallowed it down without protest, for she knew that she wouldn't feel better until she had received some form of punishment for what she had done, and if Mr James Brodie had indeed decided to let them off this time, the nasty-tasting medicine would do instead.

When nothing had been said after three days, she allowed herself to relax, trying to push the shameful episode to the back of her mind so that she could concentrate on the last frantic whirl of getting the trousseau finished.

To everyone's surprise, they managed it. Mrs Bruce and her daughter gave their grudging approval to the garments that had been made in a very short time, Miss Buchanan stopped behaving like a whirling dervish and Miss Arnold permitted herself a slight smile as she congratulated the seamstresses on their hard work.

There was even a small bonus payment made to each of the women. Elspeth used hers to buy a little brooch for Aunt Flora, some tobacco for Uncle Henry, ribbons for Rachel, and a new pen for Mattie.

'Ye should have spent it on yerself, lassie,' Flora said, surprisingly, when the gifts were handed out. 'Ye've worked hard and almost made yerself ill intae the bargain.'

But Elspeth, still suffering from guilt over what she had done in Mr James Brodie's office, had no desire to spend a penny of the money on herself, or even to put it into her savings. As she saw it, she was buying back a clear conscience by spending her bonus on others. She bought a small poke of raspberry balls for Granjan, who doted on them, and since she couldn't think of a gift for Grandmother, she went out into the countryside on her way to visit the old lady and picked a bunch of flowers.

Celia Bremner's eyebrows shot up at the sight of the pale pink wild roses and red campion. 'What's this?'

'I thought you'd like them, Grandmother. The fields are looking pretty just now, and I wanted you to see what's growing there.'

'Unexpected gifts,' said Grandmother shrewdly, 'are usually the sign of a guilty conscience. Have you been up to something, child?'

Elspeth's mouth dropped open, and she felt the beginnings of a blush warm her face. 'No, Grandmother.'

'I hope not. Very well, you may put them in the small glass vase you'll find at the back of the middle shelf above the sink. And bring a tray cloth with you, to put under the vase. Flowers drop petals and make a mess. It'll be easier to gather it all up if it falls on the cloth.'

Filling the vase and drying it carefully before arranging the flowers in it, Elspeth wished that she hadn't bothered picking them. She was sure that under Grandmother's baleful stare the poor things would wilt and die earlier than they might have in anyone else's house. She wondered if this was the way her grandmother had treated her mother, and if so, how Maisie had managed to be as bright and happy as Granjan said she was. Elspeth was sure that if she herself had had to grow up in Grandmother's house she would have wilted away very quickly.

Carrying the vase carefully back into the living room, a

clean tray cloth draped over one arm, she was grateful to Aunt Flora for having taken her in, instead of leaving her to her grandmother's tender mercies.

On the day of the Bruce wedding, the last Saturday in August, Mattie, Lena, Elspeth and Rachel walked to Gourock to see the bridal party emerge from the church. It was a beautiful day – 'It wouldnae dare tae be anythin' else, for the Bruces,' Lena said scornfully – and the bride's white satin dress, embroidered with silver threads, shimmered in the sunshine as she and her groom emerged from the church's cool darkness and paused on the top step.

An awed murmur rose from the women clustered round the gate. Many of them were pale and thin, grey-faced from over-work and worry and lack of nourishment. In the main, the clothes they wore were shabby, and most of them carried small children and had toddlers whining impatiently round their skirts. Marriage had done little for them, and yet, Elspeth thought, taking a moment to note the way their tired, dull eyes brightened and softened at the sight of the newly married couple, they still loved to see a wedding; and still clung to the hope that for someone else it would turn out to be the roman-tic, happy-ever-after story they had dreamed of for themselves as young girls.

'Would you look at that dress,' Rachel sighed, eyeing the panels of embroidered lace draping into points at each side of the mid-calf-length skirt.

'And the veil,' Mattie marvelled, as a light breeze caught the fragile lace, causing it to drift round the bride's head. 'Isn't it bonny? Was it made at Brodie's too?'

'I heard it was her mother's,' Lena informed her. 'Italian lace. It must've cost a fortune just on its own.'

As the rest of the wedding party came out to join the bride and groom, the women at the gate crowded closer, peering through the bars at the beautiful clothes, the smart hats, the jewellery sparkling at the women's throats and ears and wrists and fingers.

The precious stones were no doubt real and very beautiful, but Elspeth, putting her hand up to caress the pebble brooch Thomas had given her, wouldn't have exchanged it for all the diamonds and rubies and pearls and sapphires adorning the Bruce women and their guests. The minister, moving here and there among the guests in his sober black robes, looked like a crow socialising with a flock of peacocks.

The five bridesmaids were as pretty as a bunch of daffodils as they grouped together in their yellow muslin gowns. Wide-brimmed straw hats in the same shade as the dresses were tied under their chins with long pale gold ribbons.

As one of them stepped aside from the rest to talk to a tall young man in naval uniform, she took her hat off to reveal the pale gold rose nestling against the crown. She turned to smile at the women clustering round the gate, and Elspeth recognised her as Aileen Bruce, the girl she had seen in the fitting room. Her hair, black as ebony, was cut short and clung to her small, neat skull.

Lena's eyes were on the naval officer. 'Ooh, he's a bit of all right! Lucky her, with him for a sweetheart!'

One of the women standing beside them let out a cackle of amusement. 'That's not her sweetheart, that's Ian, her brother. I should know, 'cos I used to work in Mrs Bruce's kitchens before I got married.'

'Which of them's *his* sweetheart, then?' Lena wanted to know, and the woman shrugged.

'Don't ask me. When I worked there he was only a lad at school, but even so, every girl who came tae the house made eyes at him.'

'I'm not surprised.' Lena clutched at the railings, almost forcing her body through them in her attempt to watch Ian Bruce as he moved with his sister through the throng on the gravel sweep before the church. 'He's lovely!'

'I wouldnae mind a few hours alone with him,' one of the other women said, and there was a squeal of laughter when Lena wriggled her shoulders and retorted, 'You're slow – I'd only need a few minutes!'

Hooves clattered on the road behind them as the carriages that had been waiting a short distance away came up to form a line at the gates. The elderly horses that drew them – all the young, fit horses had been commandeered for the war effort – had been groomed until their coats shone, and flowers had been pleated into their manes and tails. Ushers crunched down the gravel drive to open the gates, and the onlookers fell back to form a guard of honour on the pavement as the wedding party prepared to leave for the reception at the Bruces' large house.

Elspeth raised herself on tiptoe and craned her neck to take in everything she could. Seen close to, the wedding dress and veil were the loveliest, most fragile things she had ever seen. A thousand points of light blazed from the small tiara on the bride's dark head, and the cloudy veil was so fine that it surely must have been spun by angels from happy dreams, she thought, lifted into a rare and unexpected transport of poetic fantasy by the colour and excitement of the occasion.

The bridegroom, a thin-faced young man smart in the uniform of an army captain, walked with a very slight limp, a relic from the wound which had sent him home from France for a few months and made this summer wedding possible. The limp and the uniform added to the romance of the occasion, and a faint sigh of sympathy rippled across the onlookers as he handed his bride into their carriage. Its seats were covered with white satin, and flowers were scattered here and there among the rich snowy folds.

Aileen Bruce dipped a slim hand into her brother's pocket and brought out a small paper bag. Hurrying after the newly-wed couple, she sprayed a fountain of rice over them just as they were getting into their carriage. The women crowding the pavement on both sides of the open gates squealed and laughed as stinging pellets of rice fell among them, and Aileen laughed back at them before gathering up her skirt and springing nimbly into the second carriage, followed by the other bridesmaids.

Mr and Mrs Bruce, he in top hat and tails, she in powder-blue silk with a cluster of deep blue feathers pinned to the brim of her hat, were ushered into their carriage by their son, who then stepped up to sit beside them, looking neither to right nor to left. Viewed from close quarters, he was the handsomest man Elspeth had ever seen, even on the cinema screen. Lena clutched at her wrist as he passed by, her nails digging into the skin, and hissed dramatically, 'I'd die for a man like that, so I would!'

After the guests had swept away in their carriages, a small group of men and women who had followed the others out of the church and had hung back during the general movement to the carriages, came down the drive, accompanied by the minister. The four women were in nursing uniforms, and some of the men also wore uniform – the dark blue of the navy, or army khaki, with two in the lighter blue of the air force. Others were in civilian clothing. Some wore slings, some had crutches, one was missing an arm, his empty sleeve neatly pinned up.

One or two members of the small group bore no outward sign of wounds, but like many of the women on the pavement, they were gaunt and stamped with the marks of suffering. One young man, who had a tearing, rasping cough that sounded as though he was shredding his lungs, pressed a large handkerchief to his mouth every time an attack started, as though ashamed to be associated with such a harsh sound.

The onlookers fell silent, knowing that these were some of the men living at the Bruces' big house, part of which had been turned into a convalescent home for wounded military. Some of the women on the pavement reached out to touch a shoulder or a hand, or called, 'Good luck tae ye, laddies,' or

'Bless ye,' as, with the help of the nurses, the men boarded a wagon that had halted at the church gate.

When the wagon had departed and the church gates were closed the girls strolled silently back to Greenock, each caught up in her own thoughts. Glancing at them, reading their expressions, Elspeth was certain that Rachel was thinking longingly of the bride's clothes, and Lena of the bride's brother. Mattie looked as though she was musing over the pleasure of being involved, even briefly and from the sidelines, in something out of the ordinary.

Elspeth herself, as they walked home, started composing her next letter to Thomas, who, as he worked for the Bruce family and hoped to continue working for them when he was finally free of his war duties, would surely want to know all about the wedding. She was also thinking of the convalescent men she had just seen, and about Lachlan.

8

Although at first it was understood that Lachlan's arm wound was not serious, he was still in a French hospital at the end of August. His letters, dictated to one of the nurses there, were very brief, merely informing his worried parents that he was recovering and being well looked after. There were no letters for Elspeth, nor did she expect any under the circumstances.

She herself wrote to him every week, as usual, making her own letters as cheerful and amusing as she could, avoiding any reference to his wound, or to the likelihood of him being sent back to his battalion when he was fit again.

Flora continued to fret about her younger son. 'If it's takin' so long for him tae get better, how can it only be a mild wound?' she repeatedly asked her family, who knew no more than she herself did. 'It must be worse than they're lettin' on. It's gone gangrenous, that's what's happened. He'll have tae have it cut off, and what'll become of him then? How can he work in the shipyards with only one arm, tell me that? Or mebbe they'll not cut it off in time, and he'll die, out there in that hospital where he doesnae know anyone, and they don't even talk the same language as he does—'

'Come on now, lass,' Henry would interrupt at this point, his voice rough with his own worry. 'If he was as bad as that they'd tell us. Anyway, there'll be army nurses and doctors there, as British as he is. Who d'ye think writes his letters for him? A Frenchie nurse couldnae do that, now, could she? He'll be fine, you wait and see.'

Thomas, still in Belgium, did his best to find someone who knew about his brother's battalion and could tell him what might be happening to Lachlan, but with no luck. There was nothing to do but wait and worry and hope.

By the end of September the tide of war had firmly turned in the Allies' favour. The Germans were being swept back all along the Western Front, yielding yard by yard at first, then mile by mile. This meant that Thomas, in Belgium, was now in the thick of it all, and between fretting about him at war and Lachlan in hospital, Flora, weakened by worry, fell victim to the Spanish 'flu that swept across Europe, killing hundreds of people already battered by years of deprivation and suffering because of the war.

In Flora's case, it was so bad that she had to be taken into the Greenock and District Combination Hospital. Without her, the small flat immediately began to resemble a yacht at sea, suddenly deprived of sails and keel and tossing helplessly on the waves. The three girls did their best to keep things going, but without Flora at her usual place in the kitchen, there was a frightening sense of uncertainty about the place.

Nobody was allowed to visit the ward where Flora lay with other 'flu victims, in case the visitors themselves caught the infection. The nurses and doctors, it was said, were going down like flies themselves.

Henry, a strong and confident man in the shipyard, collapsed like a deflated ball, and spent all his time at home sitting gazing into the fire, scarcely hearing a word that was said to him, his pipe, usually puffing tobacco smoke into the air, empty and clenched between his teeth.

'It's like looking at a whipped dog,' Mattie said nervously one evening as the three girls sat in their tiny bedroom. They had taken to spending most of their time there, because they felt like interlopers, sitting in the kitchen with Henry and his silent grief.

'He's hurting, and he doesn't know what to do about it. If he could just see her it might help him.'

'It wouldnae do her any good, though, would it?' Rachel said. 'It'd only make her feel worse, that long face of his hanging over her bed. She'd be certain that she wasn't going to survive.'

When Granjan moved in and took over her daughter's responsibilities, things became a little easier. No matter how worried she herself might have felt about Flora, she didn't show it in the slightest. Instead, she bustled round the kitchen, cooking delicious meals, chattering cheerfully, bullying Henry out of his trance and on to his feet.

She found all sorts of odd jobs for him to do, fastening down a corner of linoleum in the hall that had been threatening for months to trip up unwary feet, tightening drawer handles, whitewashing the kitchen ceiling.

'Now's yer chance tae get things done,' she would say, almost forcing a brush or a hammer or a screwdriver into his hand, nagging him to his feet when all he wanted to do was sit and stare into the fire. 'Think how pleased Flora'll be when she comes home tae find everythin' done. Ye know how much she hates a mess – best see tae it all while she's tucked up in her hospital bed, not knowin' a thing about it.'

She made him paint the woodwork throughout the small flat and re-paper the kitchen, searching Greenock and Port Glasgow herself for paint and paper, scarce commodities. With the help of the three girls she herself scrubbed the rugs and polished the linoleum and washed the curtains and cleaned the windows.

'We've got tae get it all done before Flora comes home,' she kept saying, and gradually, in the face of her persistence, Henry and the girls began to think of the time when Flora was well again, instead of wondering if that day would ever come.

At night, Elspeth lay in bed long after Mattie and Rachel

had drifted off to sleep, praying for Flora's recovery, suffering agonies of guilt over the number of times she had upset and annoyed the older woman, wishing that she could have been a model foster daughter, worthy of all that had been done for her, and that she herself had been struck down instead of Flora.

She even promised herself that she would never again upset Flora, if only she could recover and come home. Knowing all too well from bitter experience how easy it was to do or say the wrong thing without even knowing that in Flora's eyes it was wrong, she was uncomfortably aware that she would prob-ably not be able to keep those promises.

It was so difficult, she thought, to live by other people's standards.

When she woke up one morning with a sore throat and aching joints, she was convinced that her prayers had been answered, and that she had been given the chance to bear Flora's illness in her place. But it turned out to be ordinary influenza, and after a few days of Granjan's nursing, she was up and about again, though pale and shaky.

By that time, Flora was on the mend, and had been moved into an open ward. Elspeth had to stay behind when the others visited her, in case, in her own enfeebled state, she re-infected herself or her aunt. Mattie and Rachel were awed by their mother's fragility.

'I've never seen her like that before, all pale and thin and just lying there, with her hair down in two plaits,' said Mattie.

'I have,' Rachel told her. 'When you were born.'

Henry, who stayed on by his wife's side when the others left, looked more like his old self when he got back. 'She gave me dog's abuse when I told her we'd been paintin' and paperin' the place. Said I should've waited until she was home tae see what I was up tae. That's your fault,' he accused his mother-in-law.

'Indeed it is not, it's yours for waggin' yer silly tongue,' she snapped back, a gleam in her eyes. 'She's quite right when she says ye should've known better – better than tae go tellin' her!'

'Ach, she got it out of me. I was never good at keepin' anythin' from Flora.'

'That's the best way for a married man tae be,' his mother-in-law told him drily. ''Specially if it includes his wages. It saves a lot of quarrelling.'

'It didnae save me from a tellin'-off. The whole ward was listenin', tae. I didnae know where tae put my face.'

'That shows she's getting better.' Janet, who only reached halfway up Henry's waistcoat but matched him in width, craned up towards his chin, sniffing loudly. 'I didnae know they sold beer in the hospital.'

He reddened and retreated to his usual armchair, picking up his pipe and reaching for his tobacco pouch.

'Ach, I met some o' the lads on my way home and went for a wee drink with them.'

'That's another thing ye don't want tae go tellin' Flora when ye visit her tomorrow night,' Janet said, grinning at the girls, who beamed back. After almost two weeks of sucking at an empty bowl, the man of the house was filling his pipe again. Flora McDonald was going to recover, and all was well with her household.

A few days later Elspeth returned to the sewing room, which was almost empty because many of the women, including Miss Buchanan, were off with 'flu.

'But not Miss Arnold,' Lena said sadly after getting a lecture from the overseer for chattering when she should have been working. 'There's not an influenza germ that'd dare tae touch her.'

'I notice you didn't get it,' Elspeth pointed out, and her friend grinned.

'The devil looks after his own. Any word about your Lachlan?'

'He's been moved to a hospital in England.'

Lena's brows rose. 'What for?'

'I don't know. The letter just said that he'd been moved, and they'd let us know when he was coming home.'

'That means he's finished with the fightin'. My dad says it'll all be over soon, so they'll surely not send him back now.'

'I suppose not.' Elspeth knew that she should be happy for Lachlan, safe in Britain and away from the front line. Wasn't this what she had wanted for him? But as she settled some material beneath the sewing machine, she wondered, as they were all wondering at home, why Lachlan was still in hospital, and why they hadn't been told more about his condition.

Flora, who firmly refused to go to a convalescent home, returned to her family, pale, thin, still weak, but determined to take up her usual everyday life as quickly as possible. She inspected the decorating that had been done during her absence, and grudgingly admitted that it 'wasn't too bad'.

'It was mebbe as well tae get it seen tae, with our Lachlan comin' home soon,' she decided, sinking into a fireside chair. 'Mattie, put the kettle on, I've been parched for a decent cup of tea these last few weeks. I cannae be doin' with being ill. It's all a nonsense.'

A nonsense that had claimed victims throughout the town, including two in their tenement, an elderly woman who lived alone on the ground floor, and a three-month-old baby, the first child of a couple on the second floor, conceived during her father's last leave from the Royal Navy.

Flora had fully recovered her strength by the time the war finally came to an end in November. That evening, Greenock held one big street party, and Elspeth, Rachel and Mattie wandered round the packed town, enjoying a sense of freedom that they had never known before. Hundreds of thousands of men and women on both sides had lost their lives during the struggle, and proper mourning for them would come later, but for that evening, all people wanted was a chance to mark the end of the conflict.

From the shipyards and from the vessels moored at the Tail o' the Bank came the clamour of sirens, and in the town itself everyone who could play a fiddle or an accordion or even a penny whistle had brought it along. Cars and buses and tram-cars, nudging their way slowly and patiently along the streets, tooted their horns or clanged their bells, while those hanging out of the windows had plenty of time to shake hands with the people all around before passing on their way.

Groups of women and children and old men leaned on every tenement windowsill, calling down to the crowds below. Folk were hugging and kissing total strangers, talking and laughing with them like old friends, drinking and dancing together. Here and there, couples had opted out of the crush and could be seen closely entwined in shop doorways and close-mouths, oblivious to everyone else.

They met Lena and some of the other girls from the sewing room, arm in arm with a group of foreign seamen, most of the men clutching bottles of beer. When they were introduced, Lena's escort, a young giant of a man with a thatch of black curly hair, insisted on kissing all three of them. His mouth was wet and rubbery, and tasted of drink, and it was a relief when he and Lena moved on and Rachel, Mattie and Elspeth were able to scrub at their mouths with handkerchiefs.

'I don't know how Lena can enjoy kissing the likes of him.' Mattie's face was wrinkled with distaste. 'It was terrible! I think he tried to put his tongue in my mouth, too.'

'He did not!' Elspeth was scandalised at the very thought.

'Either that, or he'd three lips. If that's what kissing's like, I'm not going to bother getting myself a boyfriend.'

'Bob doesn't kiss like that at all,' Rachel put in quickly. 'It must be because that man's foreign.'

'Oh, so Bob's kissed you, then?' Mattie winked at Elspeth as her sister blushed deeply. Until now, Rachel had refused to admit that she and Bob were anything but good friends.

'If you must know, he kissed me goodbye the last time he was home on leave. And he's asked me to marry him.'

'Rachel!' The two younger girls stopped and eyed her with a new respect.

Rachel preened and simpered, enjoying her moment in the limelight. 'I haven't said I will, so don't you go telling Mam when there's nothing at all to tell.'

'But you'll say yes, won't you? When he comes home from the army?' Elspeth thought it was all very romantic.

'I might – and I might not, so not a word,' Rachel cautioned, and they both crossed their hearts, then Elspeth, looking beyond Rachel, said in astonishment, 'Granjan! What are you doing here?'

'Celebratin' the end o' the fightin', same as you.' Janet Docherty was bright-eyed and flushed with excitement. One arm was closely linked to her neighbour, Mrs Begg, and from the elbow of the other dangled the shiny black leather handbag only brought out on special occasions. It was bulging, as usual, because Janet made a point of taking everything of importance with her when she went out, just in case she got knocked down and taken to hospital, and needed her personal papers. 'Bein' old doesnae mean we cannae have a celebration, does it, Teenie?'

'I'm just glad I lived tae see the day,' Mrs Begg confirmed, dipping her head up and down energetically. With her small sharp eyes and her long thin nose, the gesture made her look like a bird drinking from a puddle. 'Though we'll no' be out too long. The town's too crowded for my liking.'

'Ach away wi' ye, it's just grand tae see all the folk so happy,' Janet chided her. 'How's Flora? Are Henry and her not out in the streets too?'

'My dad went to have a drink with his mates, but Mam's at home,' Rachel explained. 'She says she's happy just sitting on her own, thinking about Thomas and Lachlan coming home soon.'

'Aye, right enough, it's grand tae think that we'll get them back again,' Janet agreed. 'Come on now, Teenie, we'd best be off an' let the lassies enjoy themselves,' and the two elderly women forged on through the crowds.

A group of people were dancing in Cathcart Square; for a while the girls stood and watched, then they too were pulled into the dance. Elspeth's partner was a burly man in civilian clothes, probably a shipworker who, like Uncle Henry, had been excused military service because he was needed in the yards. As they revolved under a streetlamp, she saw that beneath a bushy moustache his grinning mouth revealed tobacco-stained teeth. His hands were hot and damp as they clasped hers, spinning her round and round until her feet were almost lifted from the cobbles.

'Don't worry, hen, I'll no' let ye fall,' he bellowed, seeing the panic in her face. It was a relief when the music ended and she was able to stop, one arm looped about a lamp standard because the square was still whirling about her head.

'Here – this'll steady ye,' the man said, pushing an opened bottle under her nose.

'No – no thank you.' She tried to pull back, but the bottle followed, nuzzling insistently against her mouth.

'Go on, a wee drop'll no' hurt ye.'

'I don't want it.'

'Let's have another dance, then,' he wheedled as the accordionist started up again. He tried to draw her back on to the cobbles, a hand about her waist, but she clung to the lamppost, shaking her head.

'It's time I was getting home.'

'On a night like this? The war doesnae end every day, hen. We'll dance the night away an' have somethin' tae tell our grandweans, eh?'

'I have to go,' Elspeth insisted, breaking free, backing away from his clutching hands. There were so many people about that it was easy to plunge back into the crowd, away from him. That same crush, however, made it impossible for her to find Mattie and Rachel. She worked her way round the square in search of them, then, deciding that the task was impossible, she began to struggle out of the square, along Hamilton Street. There was no fun in being out on her own; she might as well make for Mearns Street and home.

It had been possible to walk along the crowded streets when there were three of them linked together, forging a path through the crush. Alone, Elspeth found, it was a different matter. She kept getting forced back by the sheer numbers moving towards Cathcart Square, drawn by the jaunty music. It seemed to be a matter, as Flora McDonald tended to say on a busy day, of one step forward and two steps back all the time.

Once, when a drunken French sailor unexpectedly scooped her up and whirled her round above the heads of the passers-by, she thought that she glimpsed Rachel on the other side of the road.

''Ello, pretty mademoiselle,' the young man yelled above the general noise as he set her down again. He attempted a gallant bow, but his feet betrayed him, sending him stumbling sideways. His friends, roaring with laughter, caught him before he landed among a sea of feet, and carried him off with them, while Elspeth, beginning to lose her nerve now that she was on her own, launched herself off the edge of the pavement and across the road.

9

When she got to the opposite pavement Rachel was nowhere to be seen. Elspeth struggled on in the direction of home, then realised after a few stumbling steps that she had turned round without being aware of it and was heading back to Cathcart Square. She started to retrace her steps, only to run into the man who had danced with her earlier.

'There ye are, hen, I've been lookin' for ye. Come on, just a wee dance—'

He got a firm grip on her wrist this time, and started towing her back in the direction of the accordion music, pushing his way through the crowds. Elspeth pulled back, but couldn't break his grip. A gap cleared to one side of her, and she wrenched herself towards it in the hope that her change of direction would catch him by surprise, only to find that she had made a mistake. Her sudden sideways lunge had taken them to the inside of the pavement, and instead of pulling her onwards, he now crowded her against the wall of a tenement building.

'D'ye no' want tae dance?'

'I want to go home!'

'A wee kiss first, eh? A wee kiss tae celebrate a great day—'

'No!' She tried to wriggle away, but she was pinned between his large body and the wall. He clamped his arms round her, at the same time shuffling along sideways like the crabs she had sometimes seen on the shore when she played there as a child. Elspeth couldn't understand what he was doing until the wall suddenly dipped away from behind her and she staggered back a step or two before coming up against another solid obstruction. He had eased her into the doorway of a shop, out of the way of the people flocking past.

Elspeth, panicking, kicked out at him and tried to push him away. He laughed at her, crowding her more closely against the shop door.

'I like a lassie wi' spirit,' he said, then kissed her hard, pushing her lips against her teeth, forcing her head back until it was jammed against the door. It was as though he was trying to force his own face right through hers. She was sure that he was going to succeed, and the bones of her face were going to give way. Mattie had been right about Lena's boyfriend kissing her with his tongue as well as his mouth. This man was doing the same, and disgust and revulsion almost choked her.

One of his hands managed to insert itself between their bodies, crawling like a spider over her until it reached her breast, where it fastened hungrily. A year earlier, he would have had nothing to clutch, but since the summer her body had fleshed out, maturing at what seemed to Elspeth to be an incredible and embarrassing speed. Before then her measurements had been more or less the same from shoulder to thigh, but now her waist had slimmed down, while her breasts and hips had rounded out.

She tried to scream, but he was pinioning her mouth with his own, and it was difficult enough to breathe, let alone shout. Even if she had been able to make any sound it was unlikely that anybody would have heeded; there was so much noise in the street that even a loud yell could have gone unnoticed.

He was pushing himself against her now in short, rhythmic thrusts, while one knee tried to intrude between her legs.

The separate, onlooking part of her mind suddenly fled, unable to tolerate what was happening, and sheer terror gripped Elspeth. She couldn't breathe, she was at the mercy of this man she had never met or seen before. She was going to die, her mind screamed at her. She was going to die, either of suffocation or from what he was about to do to her.

Her understanding of the sexual act had always been sketchy, made up as it was by only half-believed information from her schoolfriend Molly, giggling comments overheard in the sewing room, and magazines and novelettes she and Mattie had smuggled into their bedroom. The foster-sisters had mulled over what they knew of the subject frequently, and between them had tended towards the romantic side, with the men always honourable and respectful towards their women-folk.

Now, as the stranger's knee managed to prise her legs apart and his hand tightened painfully on her left breast, Elspeth knew that she and Mattie had been wrong in their assumptions. Love wasn't as essential as they had thought – there was a physical relationship too, one that had nothing to do with tenderness or respect, but everything to do with hurting and perhaps even killing.

The noise that had been beating in her ears since she had ventured on to the streets began to fade, the glow of the gas streetlights to dim. She closed her eyes tightly to shut out the face pressing against hers, and flashing lights seared the inside of her lids.

The man lurched back slightly, releasing her mouth and breast, moving his hand downwards. She felt his knuckles pushing painfully into her stomach as he apparently fumbled with his belt. Sucking air into her starving lungs, Elspeth made one last bid for freedom, lurching towards the pavement with its continual flow of passers-by. He reached out a long arm and wrapped it about her, hauling her back against the door, moving his body so that it formed a blockade between her and the people only a matter of a yard away in the street.

'Hold still, ye stupid bi—' he started to say, then suddenly grunted, lurching hard against her so that the air she had managed to drag into her lungs was forced out again by the weight of his body.

'Ye dirty midden, ye,' a familiar voice yelled. 'I'll teach ye tae put yer mucky hands on my grandwean, Johnny Lafferty!'

The man pulled back, spinning to face the street. 'Ow!' she heard him yelp as a well-aimed blow from Janet Docherty's best handbag landed on his nose. He tried to retreat sideways along the shopfront, hands thrown up before his face to protect it from the blows raining on him. 'For God's sake, missus!'

'Keep God out o' it, foul-tongued blasphemer that ye are!' Janet was smaller than he was, but she managed to keep aiming blows at his face by bouncing like a rubber ball with each swing of the bag. Mrs Begg, bleating, 'Oh dear, lassie, oh dear!' put her arms about Elspeth, who was sagging at the knees.

Despite the noise in the street, Janet's outraged yells and the howls of the man now cowering against the shop front attracted attention. A small crowd gathered to watch and laugh, their backs forming a wall around which the rest of the revellers flowed.

'The dirty bastard was tryin' tae attack my grandwean,' Janet informed them between blows. 'And her only a wee bit of a lassie!'

'I didnae ken she was yer grandwean,' the man wailed, then, appealing to the onlookers, 'I didnae ken!'

'Mebbe no', but ye must've kent she was someone's grandwean, ye filthy pig, ye! An' you a grown man wi' a wife, God help her, an' six weans of yer ain!' said Janet, and aimed another blow at him. Because he had lowered his arms in order to appeal to the crowd, her best handbag landed fairly on his nose, and he yelped like a beaten dog.

The onlookers were all on Janet's side. 'That's right, missus, you show him,' a man shouted, while others jeered at the drunk, and a woman screeched, 'I ken him tae – a worthless piece o' scum that's nae use tae his wife except for fatherin' more and more bairns on the poor sowl!'

'Mercy me,' said Mrs Begg in distress, doing her best to cover Elspeth's ears.

'Here's a polisman, missus,' someone called out. 'Hand the rascal over tae him.'

Janet stood back, the first white-hot rush of anger spent. 'Ach, let him run tae his hole, stinkin' rat that he is,' she said with sudden dignity, and the crowd, respecting her right to decide, stood back to let the man go, then melted away as the policeman approached.

'Are ye all right, pet?' Janet asked anxiously, gathering Elspeth from Mrs Begg's arms, then, as Elspeth nodded, beyond speech for the moment, 'Here, Teenie, you take her on that side and I'll take her on this, and we'll get her out of here.'

'Are ye taking her home tae her mammy?' Mrs Begg asked above Elspeth's bowed head as the three of them struggled along towards Nicolson Street.

'Have ye lost the wits God gave ye, woman? Can ye see our Flora's face if we take the bairn back lookin' like this? We'll take her tae my house and get her tidied up first.'

Back in Granjan's cosy little flat in Nicolson Street, Mrs Begg made tea while Janet washed Elspeth's face and hands and combed her hair, talking soothingly as she worked.

'Thank goodness I caught a sight of ye when ye were tryin' tae get away from that drunken lout. No sense frettin' over what didnae happen, is there? Ye've got a split lip on ye, hen.' She dabbed gently at Elspeth's mouth. 'But that's easy explained tae yer Auntie Flora – ye'll no' be the only one in Greenock tonight tae walk intae a lamppost in all that crush.'

'I've got a wee bit of whisky in my kitchen cupboard. Will I fetch it and we can put some in her tea tae help her get over

92

the shock?' suggested Mrs Begg, who lived across the landing.

'And take her back tae Flora smellin' of drink? For goodness' sake, Teenie! She'll be fine, won't ye, pet? All she needs is a good strong cup of tea with plenty of sugar in it.'

She was right. By the time the cup was half empty Elspeth was feeling more like herself, though Granjan was still seething.

'That Johnny Lafferty's always been a midden, so he has.'

'He was drunk, he didn't know what he was doing.' Now that the nightmare was over Elspeth felt a shred of pity for the man who had so quickly turned into a whining child under her grandmother's relentless attack.

'The man's never sober. That poor wife of his has a lot tae put up with!'

'Where d'you know him from, Granjan?'

'From here. He lives up above.' Janet Docherty glared up at the ceiling. 'I should push the handle of my broom clean through right now an' hope it'd come out right where he's standing. I'd do it too, if it wasnae that I feel so sorry for Liza. She's got no chance of a decent life with him, and most of her bairns'll probably grow up tae be like their wastrel of a faither, then she'll have even more heartbreak.'

She shook her head in sorrow, then went on briskly, with a change of tone 'Now – finish yer tea, and Teenie and me'll see ye back home. Flora'll be frettin' about ye, specially if Rachel and Mattie are home already. Mind, now, all ye need tae tell her is that ye met up with some friends, then got pushed intae a lamppost by accident in the crush. And put that man out of yer mind, hen. There's plenty of fools like him in the world, but with any luck ye'll never meet up with another of them. If ye do, and yer as close tae him as ye were tae Johnny, take my advice and bring yer knee up like this – see? It fair takes their mind off any further ill-doin'.'

'Janet!' Mrs Begg screeched as Granjan demonstrated by lifting one plump knee up sharply, almost overbalancing.

'Ach, stop yer scrakin', Teenie Begg. Lassies should know these things. That's what saved me more than once in my own young days. Come on, then, pet, time you were home. And I'd be grateful,' Janet added as she helped Elspeth on with her coat, 'if ye'd no' let on tae yer Auntie Flora that I used the word "bastard" in front of ye. It was all said in the heat of the moment, hen.'

Elspeth had always thought that once the war was over, everything would get back to normal, but instead, life went on as usual for several months. There was still a shortage of food and clothing, and most of the men were still away from home. Women still did men's work in the factories and shipyards, and on the buses and trams as clippies and drivers.

Round about Christmas time the foreign ships began to depart from the river and the first of the Greenock men returned home. Among them was Bob Cochran, Rachel's sweetheart. Rachel went about with a permanent smile on her face, but Bob, never a chatterbox, had become even more morose during his time away. When he did speak it was usually to complain about the way the soldiers had been treated by officers who knew nothing, but thought they were superior just because they had been brought up in posh houses and went to posh schools.

His other complaint was about conditions in the shipyard where he had taken up his former job.

'What did we fight for, tell me that?' he would demand, sitting opposite Henry in the McDonalds' kitchen, his booted feet sprawled across the rag rug. 'What did we risk our lives for, and live in muddy water up to our knees for? Tae build a better world, they told us.' A contemptuous jerk of his close-cropped head towards the hall door indicated that 'they', the officers and shipyard owners and others of their ilk, existed somewhere outside the tenement. 'But what's better about it, tell me that? I'm no' paid any more than I was before I went away. I'm no' treated any better. A land fit for heroes? That's not what I'd call it!'

'He's an awful moaner, isn't he?' Mattie said in disgust when she and Elspeth had escaped to the bedroom, Elspeth to write letters, Mattie to do her homework. 'I don't remember him making such a fuss about everything before. He was quite nice then.'

'He's got a right to be angry, I suppose.' Elspeth was curled up at the head of the bed, trying to get as close as she could to the gas mantle, which didn't give out much light. Mattie was sitting on Rachel's bed, beneath the other mantle. 'He must've had a hard time of it, and then he comes home to find that things are no better than they were before.'

'I'd think more of him if he made the best of it,' Mattie said flatly. 'I don't know what Rachel still sees in him. He looks so – hard, doesn't he? Mebbe he'll look better when his hair grows back.'

They collapsed in giggles, remembering Bob's first visit to the flat after leaving the army. Before going off to war, he had had a fine head of light brown hair, thick and soft, but to Rachel's dismay he had come home for good with his hair cropped even more ruthlessly than army regulations demanded, so close to his scalp that the skin shone through. The shaven head, accentuated by his thick, short neck and powerful shoulders, gave him a menacing look.

'Och, Bob, why did you let them cut your nice hair so short?' Rachel had asked, running her hand over the stubble. Then she pulled her fingers back sharply as her beloved said, 'Nits.'

'Nits?' Rachel almost screamed the word, wiping her hand hurriedly on her skirt, while Henry stopped in the act of knocking out his pipe, and Flora gasped. Head lice were common in the Greenock tenements, but Flora had worked hard to keep her own children's heads clean, combing their hair with a special close-toothed comb every day, washing their heads with strong-smelling coal-tar soap that they all hated. To the McDonald household, nits meant dirt and squalor.

'We was alive with the wee bu—' Bob shot a look at Flora and suddenly remembered where he was, '—blighters in the trenches. If we hadnae had our heads shaved we'd've been too busy clawin' at ourselves tae shoot back at the Jerries.' Then, as Rachel moaned softly, 'Ach, don't make such a fuss. I've been well scrubbed wi' disinfectant since then. They're all gone – and the body lice tae. What else can ye expect?' he went on as Rachel retreated from the arm of his chair, shuddering. 'We was crowded together for weeks on end in these trenches, never findin' the time tae change our clothes, let alone clean them.'

A sneer brushed across his mouth as he surveyed the horror in the faces around him. 'Ye know a pal's really a pal when ye've shared nits an' fleas with him,' he said, then the sneer changed to a hoot of derisive laughter.

'D'you think Thomas and Lachlan'll have their hair all cut off too?' Mattie said when the girls' giggles had died down. Without being aware of her actions she ran a pencil through her own brown curls, using it to scratch at the scalp beneath.

'How should I know?'

'You write to them both.'

'Nits aren't the sort of thing you ask about in letters. I see that Aunt Flora's bought in some extra-strong soap, and another bottle of Jeyes fluid,' Elspeth said, then she and Mattie shuddered in unison.

10

Thomas arrived home in the middle of February, a week after his twenty-third birthday. His brown hair had been cut short, but not nearly as short as Bob's. It clung round his scalp in curls, and his boyish body had filled out, not with fat, but with muscle. There was a new awareness in his eyes, too, but apart from that he was the Thomas they all knew well, still cheerful, happy to be back, with none of Bob's bitter resentment at the war that had torn him from home and family.

'It wasnae a picnic, and I'd not want tae go through it again,' he said as he enjoyed his first home-cooked meal, 'but a lot more had it worse than me, losing their lives or bits of their bodies, or their homes and everything they had in life. And I'm talking about civilians too, not just soldiers. Those poor souls in France and Belgium that saw their towns and villages turned into battlefields – it'll take them a long time tae get back to a normal life.'

He waited until the meal was over, and the neighbours who had crowded into the flat to welcome him back had eventually returned to their own homes, before telling his family that he had visited Lachlan on his way home.

Flora was overjoyed. 'How is he? How's his arm?'

'It's fine, Mam, all mended, and only a wee scar to show where the bullet went in. Lucky for him it didnae do any permanent damage. His arm'll mebbe never be as strong as it used tae be, but there won't be much difference.'

'Than why isn't he home? He'll do far better here than in any hospital where there's nobody of his own blood tae comfort him. I would've gone tae visit the laddie, but what with the influenza and yer dad needin' me here tae see tae his meals for him when he comes in from—'

'Mam, will ye just wheesht a minute and listen tae me?' Thomas asked quietly, but with a gravity in his voice that brought all their heads swivelling round in his direction.

'There's more tae it than they said, isn't there?' Flora's clenched fist went up to her mouth. Above it, her eyes were anguished. 'I knew they werenae tellin' us the truth of it!'

'Flora—' Henry reached across from his own chair to put a large hand on his wife's knee. 'Just dae as the laddie asks, and give him the chance tae tell us what's amiss wi' Lachlan.'

Thomas looked from one face to the other. 'He's fine, in his body,' he said at last, carefully. 'But in his head—'

'He was wounded in the head as well?' Rachel asked sharply, while Flora whimpered into her fist, her free hand finding and clutching Henry's fingers.

'Just in the arm, and I've already said that that's fine. It's inside his head I'm talking about. He'd a hard time of it in France, with all the noise and the business of seeing laddies he knew and fought beside being injured or killed. It's all been too much for him.'

'Shell shock.' Elspeth didn't know she had spoken until they all looked at her.

'That's what the hospital folk said. It's somethin' that can happen tae a soldier.'

'How did you know what it was called, Elspeth?' Henry asked.

'One of the girls I write letters for, her lad's cousin had it. He'd to come home early from the war. He's getting better now,' Elspeth added swiftly to her aunt.

'I don't understand.' Mattie's thin face was puzzled. 'How can he be shell-shocked if a shell didn't hit him?'

'It's the noise,' Thomas explained. 'The noise all the time of those big shells screamin' past day and night, sometimes for days on end without any stop tae it. Ye've no idea of the noise unless ye've lived through it.' He paused for a moment, then said, 'It's a wee bit like standin' in a very big railway station, with trains runnin' through every platform, one after another, never stopping, never givin' yer ears a rest, even when they're dingin' wi' the noise and ye'd give anythin' ye had tae get a bit of peace and quiet, only nothing'll make it stop.'

He paused, looked at his family's perplexed faces, and shrugged. 'I don't have the words tae explain it any better. It's like something in a nightmare. The place where Lachlan was based was very bad for the shellin'. If he hadnae been shot in the arm, I don't know what would've happened tae him. He'd mebbe have gone mad, poor soul.'

'By the sound of it, he has.'

The words were no sooner out of Rachel's mouth than Thomas rounded on her, jumping up from his chair to grab her shoulders. 'Our Lachlan's not mad,' he said vehemently into his sister's startled face. 'And don't ever let me hear ye say that about him again!'

'Here—' Henry cut in sharply, getting to his feet. 'No need for that!'

As they all stared at Thomas in astonishment, his hands fell away from his sister's shoulders, and he stepped back, his Adam's apple lurching visibly in his throat as he gave another gulping swallow.

'I'm sorry, Rachel. I – I didnae—'

'You frighted me!' Rachel's pretty face was red with shock and embarrassment.

'I'm sorry,' Thomas said again. 'It's just that – Lachlan's not mad, and I'll not hear anyone sayin' it. Nobody.'

Henry took his son by the arm, drawing him to his own armchair. 'Sit down here, lad, by the fire, and tell us more about what's ailin' him.'

Thomas resisted the hand on his arm, moving back to the table, where he sat down. 'You sit in yer own chair, Da, I'm fine here.'

'What's wrong with Lachlan?' Flora had scarcely noticed the interruption.

'He's a wee bit confused, Mam. He's spent so much time under fire that he can't grasp the fact that it's all over and he's safe. He jumps at the slightest noise. He – he cries a lot,' Thomas said, and Mattie and Elspeth stared at each other. Men didn't cry. Crying was for bairns and small children. They couldn't imagine Lachlan, who found a laugh in everything that happened to him, even the bad things, in tears.

'He'll get better, though?' Mattie's voice was very small, and Thomas reached across the table to give her hand a reassuring squeeze.

'Of course he'll get better, given time. The nurses and doctors are working with him. They're very kind tae him, you need have nae fear about that. He's well looked after.'

'Not as well as he would be in his own home. I want him back here,' Flora said firmly.

'When he's a bit better I'll—'

'Never mind when he's a bit better, I want him home now. He's my son, and I want tae look after him myself!'

'Mam—' Thomas began, but she ignored him.

'Are ye tryin' tae tell me they won't let him out? Is it a hospital or a prison he's in – tell me that?'

'It's a hospital, and of course they'll let him out, but should we not give them a wee while longer with him?'

'We've been without the two of ye for near enough four years, and we want ye both back here, where ye belong!' Flora insisted.

She was adamant, refusing to settle for anything less than a firm promise that Thomas would write to the hospital the next day, and travel back down to England within the week to bring Lachlan home. At last, worn out from a long day of travelling and talking, he gave her that promise, and the family all went to bed.

In the narrow lobby Elspeth asked fearfully, 'Thomas, is Lachlan going to be all right?'

'Of course he will, but it might take longer than Mam thinks.' There was no gas lighting in the boys' tiny room, and in the glow of the candle he carried, Thomas's face was drawn with tiredness, his eyes deep black pits. 'We'll all have tae be very understandin' with him.'

'We will be. Get a good night's sleep, you look as if you need it.'

He smiled slightly. 'I've learned tae sleep in all sorts of places at all sorts of times. Don't you worry about me, I'll be snoring as soon as my head touches that pillow.'

On the following day Flora made Thomas write to the English hospital. He posted the letter on his way to Gourock to see Mr Bruce, his former employer, about getting his old job back.

All that day in the sewing room Elspeth fretted about him. The men working in factories and shipyards had been assured of their own jobs back when the fighting was over, which meant that Lachlan would be able to return to the shipyard. But Thomas, employed by one man instead of a company, couldn't be so sure of returning to his old employment. He might have to seek work elsewhere, in a job market in turmoil, with returning servicemen expecting to be reinstated at once, to the resentment of some of the women who had kept the shipyards and factories and shops going by taking over men's work. They had worked on the buses and trams, even carrying sacks of coal on their backs, and had enjoyed being independent at last, and earning decent wages.

Now many of them were rebelling against a return to their kitchen sinks and dependency once again on their menfolk. Many women whose men either didn't return or were too badly wounded to work were terrified of losing the wages they had become accustomed to, and ending up with their children in the poors' hospital.

As Miss Buchanan refused to allow what she called 'unnecessary adornments' among her workforce, Elspeth couldn't wear Thomas's little pebble brooch at work. She kept the silver threepenny bit hidden beneath her blouse, and several times that day she felt for its outline, wishing on it for Thomas.

When she got home that evening he was in the kitchen, peeling potatoes for his mother and grinning from ear to ear.

'He's not only willin' tae have me back, he's goin' tae buy himself a motorcar, and I'll have the job of looking after it and driving him and his family around as well as helping in the gardens,' he announced proudly. 'It's a good thing I learned tae drive in the army.'

'Here, give that knife tae Elspeth, now she's home, and let her see tae the potatoes,' Flora fussed, but Thomas shook his head.

'Elspeth's been workin' hard all day while I've been enjoying myself, getting to know Greenock again. I can see tae them.'

'It's not seemly, a grown man doing a woman's work!'

'Mam, in the army we'd tae turn our hands tae everything. If I'd a pound for every potato I've peeled in the past four years I'd not need to work ever again. Imagine,' he exulted, wielding the knife so vigorously that peelings flew all over the kitchen and Flora, always a thrifty housewife, was driven to the point of apoplexy, 'me, drivin' a fine car and gettin' paid for it!'

Two days later a letter arrived from the English hospital, advising against taking Lachlan away so soon. Flora's mouth tightened as she read it. 'He's been in hospitals quite long enough. It's time he was with his own folk.'

'Mam, the doctor's working with Lachlan just now, and if we give him a wee while longer—'

But Flora would have none of it. 'Write back, Thomas, and

tell them ye're on yer way there and they've tae let our Lachlan go.'

Thomas's eyes met Elspeth's, and his shoulders lifted in a faint shrug. 'Aye, Mam, if that's what ye want.'

As he didn't have to start working for Mr Bruce until the following Monday, he left for England early the next day, taking with him money that Flora had somehow managed to scrape together to pay for the train fares. That day and all during the next, as her sons travelled homewards, Flora worked on their room, hauling the narrow beds out from the walls, scrubbing the floor, polishing the small window and washing down the woodwork. She even managed to whitewash the ceiling and put some cream paint on the walls.

They were due home on Saturday, which meant that all the members of the family would be free to greet them. When Elspeth got back from the department store, breathless and red in the face from running all the way, Mattie was pacing the pavement outside the close, so wrapped up against the chill February air that only her red nose could be seen peeping from the scarves wound round her head. Elspeth could hear the breath whistling in the other girl's lungs.

'What are you doing out on a cold day like this?'

Mattie coughed wheezily into a mittened hand. 'Mam's been beating every cushion in the house, and my chest got so bad with the dust I had to get out of the place.'

'But she knows you can't take the dust! She shouldn't be beating cushions while you're home.'

'She can't see past Lachlan just now. She's so desperate to get things nice for him that everything else's gone clean out of her head. Go on up and see if the place is clear.'

Elspeth could smell the dust in the air as soon as she walked into the flat. Flora, down on her knees, giving the shining brass tongs and poker and hearthbrush an unnecessary final polish, looked as though she hadn't stopped working all morning.

'There ye are, at last. Put the kettle on, will ye? My throat's dry. Did ye see our Mattie on yer way home? I was wantin' her tae give me a hand, but she's been out half the morning.'

'She's outside in the cold wind, because the dust from the cushions brought her asthma on again.'

For a moment, Flora had the grace to look slightly ashamed, then she rallied. 'I couldnae have the place lookin' like a midden when Lachlan's coming home after all these years!'

'Aunt Flora, this house is never a midden, it's as clean and as neat as a palace.' Elspeth lit the gas ring under the kettle, then took a cup and saucer out of the cupboard.

'Ye can cut some bread and bring out the cheese, and we'll have somethin' tae keep us going.' Flora glanced at the clock and sucked her breath in. 'Would ye look at the time! Yer uncle and Rachel'll be home any minute. Fetch Mattie up and she can give ye a hand gettin' things ready for them.'

'She can't come up yet, Aunt Flora. I can still smell the dust in the air, it'll only make her chest worse.'

'Of course it won't – she's growin' out of the asthma, she's not as bad as all that,' Flora snapped. She had always gone out of her way to help Mattie during her bouts of asthma, sitting up at nights with the girl without a word of complaint, boiling kettles to create steam and making bread poultices to ease her daughter's chest. Now, guilt at having made Mattie ill in her eagerness to get everything ready for Lachlan brought a sharp note into her voice. 'Go down and fetch her.'

'She'll only start wheezing again as soon as she comes in. You'll need to wait until the dust—'

'That's enough, miss!' Flora McDonald snapped, her cheeks, already flushed with activity, flaring with added colour. 'Do as I say!'

Arguing would only have added fuel to her anger and precipitated yet another row between them, so Elspeth held her tongue and did as she was told. On the first landing she stopped and unbuttoned her coat so that she could fumble in her skirt pocket. She brought out some coins she had been paid that morning for writing two letters, balancing them thoughtfully on her outspread palm. They had been intended for the old tobacco tin used for saving money to pay for her evening classes, but today Mattie's need was greater than her own.

With a small, regretful sigh she slipped the coins into her coat pocket and continued on down the stairs.

Mattie was still pacing, her nose redder than before. 'Can I go up?' she asked eagerly when Elspeth appeared.

'The dust's still in the air. Aunt Flora says we're to buy three meat pies and have our dinner at Granjan's,' Elspeth lied, drawing the coins from her pocket. 'She gave me the money for them.'

Mattie's eyes brightened. 'I'm starving,' she admitted. 'And freezing.'

'Come on, then.' Elspeth linked arms with her and the two of them set off, walking as quickly as Mattie's breathing would allow. Aunt Flora was going to be awful angry, Elspeth thought as they went. The trouble she would get into when they returned would be well deserved for deceiving both her aunt and her cousin. But on the other hand, she couldn't have let Mattie go back up into the dusty air of the flat, or hang about any longer on the windy pavement.

11

For once, the angels were on her side. When she and Mattie, the latter breathing more easily now, returned to Mearns Street later that afternoon, Granjan was with them.

'Ye don't think I'm goin' tae let our Lachlan come back home from the war without his granny there tae greet him,' she had insisted, and Elspeth was happy to agree, knowing that Flora wouldn't make a fuss about her deception in front of Granjan.

The place was spick and span and dust-free, and Bob Cochran was waiting in the kitchen with the rest of the family, dressed, as they all were, in his Sunday best. He got up to let Granjan have his seat by the fire.

'Where have you two been?' Flora wanted to know.

'At Gran's,' Mattie answered cheerfully. 'We bought meat pies and had our dinner with her.'

'It was a kind thought, Flora hen,' Janet Docherty chimed in. 'The three of us had a good gossip, and all the dust's cleared out of the lassie's lungs now.'

Flora's eyes narrowed as they met Elspeth's. She opened her mouth to speak, but just then Mattie, at the window, shrieked, 'I see them – I see them!'

'Where?' There was a rush to the small window, and Mattie narrowly escaped being knocked into the sink by the crush of bodies at her back.

'There, look, coming up the hill.'

'It's them all right.' Bob's height gave him the advantage of being able to see over everyone else's heads. 'That's Thomas, carrying the suitcase, and the other—' He paused, then said, his voice puzzled, 'The other's surely Lachlan.'

'Now sit down, the lot of ye, and I'll go tae the door on my lone.' Flora's voice, trembling with anticipation, rang out over the excited chatter. 'Mind that the laddie's no' been well, and don't all rush at him at the one time.'

As the others did as they were bid, almost falling over each other in their haste to take their places, Elspeth craned across the small sink to look down at the street. She saw Thomas walking slowly towards the tenement building, a suitcase in one hand, the other holding the arm of the man who walked by his side, head bent, huddled into his coat.

Often in the past she had waited at this same window, watching for Lachlan returning from the shipyard. Despite the hard day's work he had just finished, he always ran up the hill effortlessly, craning to look up at the kitchen window, waving to her with both arms sawing through the air above his head. It had become a ritual for the two of them.

But if Lachlan was indeed Thomas's companion today, he was walking like a feeble old man. Some of the joy of seeing him again began to seep away, to be replaced by anxiety, and an eerie sense of dread.

It seemed a long time, long enough for them to exchange puzzled glances before they heard Flora opening the door and saying tremulously, 'Oh, Lachlan!'

When she finally came into the kitchen tears were trickling unashamedly down her face, and her smile was almost a grimace. 'Here he is, at last!' she announced, then, turning back to the door, 'Come on in, son. Everything'll be all right now ye're home.'

Lachlan came in hesitantly, stopping in the doorway as he took in the crowd waiting for him in the small kitchen. For a moment Elspeth thought that he was going to turn and go out again, then she heard Thomas say, low-voiced, 'Go on, you're doing fine,' and Lachlan McDonald, home from the war at last, stepped into the kitchen.

The greetings died in their throats. His head was down, his eyes fixed on the floor or on his hat, which was clutched between hands that turned it round and round unceasingly. His light brown hair was much longer than Thomas's, and untidy, as Lachlan's soft fine hair had always been, but the shine had gone from it and it hung lank and lifeless.

'Well, well.' Henry McDonald, swallowing back his shock at first sight of his younger son, got to his feet and moved to clap the young man's shoulder. Normally his large, strong hand landed on backs and shoulders heartily, but this time it paused for a fraction of a second in mid-air as Lachlan flinched, then landed gently, more of a caress than a clap. 'Welcome home, son,' Henry said, his voice gruff. 'Come on in and sit down – here, sit in my chair, near the fire.'

'He'd be best at the table, Da,' Thomas said swiftly, managing to reach round his brother's painfully thin figure to pull a chair out for him. He eased Lachlan out of his coat and into the chair, talking cheerfully all the time, his eyes, moving from one person to the next, carrying clear warning that Lachlan must be treated gently.

They all understood. One by one, they offered a few words, a touch of the hand. As Lachlan's pale, drawn face bobbed up at each of them through a ragged fringe of hair, his lips curved in a forced smile and he spoke their names – 'Mattie . . . Rachel . . . Elspeth . . . Gran' – in a slow, puzzled way, as though surprised to see them there. After each naming he ducked his head down again, pushing his chin against his chest as if he was afraid of drawing too much attention to himself.

Thomas stood behind and slightly to one side of him, his hand on Lachlan's stooped shoulder; now and again a quiver ran through Lachlan, and each time that happened Elspeth saw his brother's hold on his shoulder tighten very slightly in reassurance.

When they settled themselves round the table to eat, Thomas, beside Lachlan, talked cheerfully and continuously, though he himself looked exhausted, his face grey and his eyes heavy with strain. Every now and again he sprinkled his chatter with, 'Isn't that so, Lachlan?' or, 'Didn't we, Lachlan?' And each time Lachlan gave a quick, shy nod, and a muttered 'Aye.'

'We thought we'd never get here, didn't we, Lachlan? The train was busy, and it crawled all the way. I think myself it was an English train, with no liking for coming over the border, for it seemed tae get even slower after that. We were luckier than some, though, weren't we, Lachlan, for we found seats beside each other, and the hospital had given us a packet of sandwiches, so we didnae starve.'

It was painful to watch Lachlan's terror and the efforts he made to keep it under control. It was as though he was with hostile strangers, Elspeth thought, rather than his own blood-kin, the people he had grown up with. She wanted desperately to put her arms around him and hold him close, safe from the world. But she sensed that even a touch of her hand might send him into a panic.

Watching the way he pushed the food around his plate, it was clear to her that he should have stayed in the hospital until he was more able to face the world. She looked round the table, seeing the tears in Mattie's and Rachel's and Granjan's eyes, the stunned horror on Henry's face, and, even worse, the mingled incredulity and distaste on Bob Cochran's coarsely handsome features, and experienced a rush of anger at Flora for having insisted on dragging her son home with no thought to how he might feel about it.

Flora herself was clearly determined to make the most of the situation. Like Thomas, she talked cheerfully, pretending that everything was all right, even laughing now and again, a harsh, forced laugh that made Lachlan jump.

'D'ye not want yer nice mince?' she asked him, as though he was a child, when every other plate had been emptied and Lachlan's reduced to an unappetising congealing mush of meat, gravy and mashed potatoes. 'I made it specially for ye. It was always your favourite – mind how much ye liked it?'

'I think he got enough to eat on the train, Mam.' Thomas picked up the cold plate and handed it to her. 'They gave us a lot of sandwiches, didn't they, Lachlan?'

It was the same with the dumpling and custard. Scarcely a spoonful went into Lachlan's mouth, although Granjan and Elspeth, in an attempt to draw attention away from him, started up a conversation about nothing in particular, glaring at the others until they took the hint and joined in.

A few minutes later, glancing back at Lachlan, Elspeth was horrified to see a large tear drop from his lowered face into the yellow and brown soup he had made of his pudding. It was followed by another, then another.

'Thomas—' she began, just as Lachlan's shoulders began to shake and a muffled whimper escaped from his throat.

'I think it's time we went tae our beds,' said Thomas swiftly, getting to his feet. 'It's been a long day, and I'm tired out. You must be too, eh, Lachlan? Come on, old son,' he added gently, and his brother allowed himself to be eased to his feet and turned towards the door.

'I'll help ye,' Flora and Henry said at the same time, but Thomas shook his head.

'We'll be fine. We'll see ye in the mornin', eh?'

When the door had closed behind them, the people left at the table stared at each other blankly. Mattie began to weep, and Elspeth felt the tears she herself refused to shed forming a solid ball of grief in her throat.

'Mattie, stop behavin' like a daft wean!' Flora's voice was over-loud. 'We're all home together at last, and there's nothin' tae cry about! Ye'll take a cup of tea now, Mam?'

But Granjan excused herself, saying that it was time she was off home. Bob immediately offered to walk back to Nicolson Street with her, and Rachel said that she'd go too. Elspeth got the impression that Bob couldn't wait to get away from the flat.

Once the three of them had gone, Flora sent Mattie and Elspeth off to bed, announcing that she would wash the dishes herself. Although it was still early they went without argument.

'That's not our Lachlan at all,' Mattie burst out as soon as they were alone in the bedroom. 'What's happened to him?'

'I don't know.' Elspeth spoke with difficulty round the great lump of tears in her throat. 'But whatever it was, it must have been terrible.'

'Bringin' him home was a nightmare,' Thomas admitted to his family the following morning. Lachlan was still asleep, and the rest of them had gathered in the kitchen. 'It was hard for him tae be outside the hospital, with crowds of folk in the streets and the railway station, and in the train. Times I'd tae coax him every step of the way, and once when a train whistle blew he threw himself under a bench and I'd the devil's own job getting him tae come out again. We nearly missed our train over the head of it.'

His lips twisted in the ghost of a grin. 'I've never seen our Lachlan move as fast as that in my life. It gave one or two other folk a shock, too. The rest of the time he was clutching my arm so tight it felt as though it had been caught in a vice.' He rolled up his shirtsleeve to reveal the bruises made by Lachlan's fingers on his muscular, hairy arm.

He himself still showed some of the previous day's exhaustion, having had his sleep interrupted each time Lachlan awoke and cried out in terror at finding himself in unfamiliar surroundings.

'But he doesnae need tae be scared of anything now,' Flora fretted. 'He's home, in that room he's slept in ever since he was old enough tae spend a night away from my side.'

111

'I know, Mam, but Lachlan's not the laddie he used tae be,' Thomas tried to explain patiently. 'The things that happened tae him in the war have changed him. He's coming tae folk and things he used tae know like a stranger, seein' them for the first time. We must give him time tae get used tae being home again. The Sister at the hospital told me he took time tae settle in there, and the same'll have tae happen here.'

'But you haven't changed, Thomas, and Bob didn't change.' Rachel's pretty face was twisted with the effort of trying to understand. 'Why should Lachlan?'

'I've seen it happen tae more than one poor soul. Mebbe it's because they're more sensitive than the rest of us, mebbe it's because they were in the worst of the fighting, or mebbe a mixture of the two. There's no discredit tae them, for at times we all saw things that no human being should have tae see.' Thomas paused, his warm brown eyes darkening with bleak memories. Then he blinked, shrugging himself back to the present.

'It was easier for me, for we were moving on, over the French border and through Belgium, fightin' as we went. We'd a job tae do and we were able tae get on with it. But there was a time when Lachlan's unit was pinned down under fire for days on end, then more time spent advancing a wee bit, then being driven back again, then tryin' tae advance again. And they suffered heavy losses.'

'What can we do for him?' Flora wanted to know.

'Just – accept him, Mam. Don't try tae push him intae gettin' better. The doctor I saw says it's best just tae treat him gently. Let him know he's not on his lone, and leave him tae work things out in his own time.'

'I don't know how long the shipyard'll keep his job open for him,' Henry said doubtfully.

There was a note of suppressed irritation in Thomas's voice when he answered. 'Then he'll have tae find a new job when he's able, Da.'

'Will he ever get back to himself?' Mattie asked.

'Of course he will, given time.'

Elspeth, glancing at Thomas, saw the flicker of doubt that crossed his face as he spoke, and a shiver ran through her.

As Thomas had said, the Lachlan who had come back to them after the army finished with him wasn't the Lachlan they had known. It was as though some stranger had put on Lachlan's body as he might have shrugged on his jacket. It didn't quite fit, it didn't look right, and yet in some eerie way it was still undeniably Lachlan.

It was hard for them, but hardest of all for Lachlan. He spent most of his time huddled in Flora's armchair by the fire, or in his tiny bedroom, occasionally with a newspaper in his lap, though he rarely read it. He jumped at sudden noises or movements, and responded timidly and haltingly when spoken to, searching for the right words, his voice often tailing away in mid-sentence. At night, in the grip of nightmares, his screams frequently woke the entire household, and the neighbours too.

Used to working in the constant din and clatter of machinery in the shipyard, Henry McDonald tended as a result to speak loudly at all times, and to move about noisily at home. After startling Lachlan into a fit of hysteria when he barged noisily into the kitchen on his return from work on the day after the boy's arrival home, he had to work hard at learning to change his ways.

That first day alone in the house with Lachlan was bad for Flora. He panicked when he saw her getting ready to go to the shops, and was equally panic-stricken when she suggested that if he didn't want to be left alone, he could go with her. Finally she had to take her coat off, and stay at home. As it was her custom to shop each day, there was nothing in the house for that night's dinner. When Mattie arrived home from school she was sent back out again to buy pieces of fried fish for the

113

evening meal, and Flora suffered the humiliation of seeing her family eat their first shop-cooked meal.

After that, Janet Docherty came every morning to sit with her grandson while Flora went to the shops. The old woman's placid nature was good for Lachlan; when she was there he relaxed more than he could with his mother, who watched him anxiously all the time, trying to anticipate his every need.

'Ye don't need tae treat the laddie as if he's made of fine china, Flora,' Janet tried to explain to her daughter. 'He'll no' break. It's just as if he's had a blow tae the head—'

'It's nothin' like that at all, Mam!' Flora swatted the words aside impatiently. 'It wasnae his head that got hurt, it was his arm – and what I'm sayin' is, how can a bullet in anyone's arm make them go the way our Lachlan's gone? Tell me that.'

'I didnae say he'd been hit on the head,' Janet said patiently. 'I'm just sayin' it's like a blow tae the head, and – wheesht for a minute, will ye, and let me explain,' she added as Flora opened her mouth to protest. 'If ye get a hard knock on the skull, ye feel all dazed and out of place for a minute, don't ye? Mind that time ye fell off the wash-house roof that ye'd no right tae be on in the first place, and ye felt dizzy for a whole day after it? That's the way poor Lachlan's feeling right now, with all that's been happenin' tae him.'

'But he's not just been like that for a day, has he? It's been months, from what we've heard, and there's no betterment.'

'Aye, well, as far as he's concerned, the fallin' off the wash-house roof business must've happened tae him time after time, day after day, and nob'dy knew, so it just kept gettin' worse and worse. The longer it went on and the worse it got, the longer it'll take him tae get over it,' Janet ended triumphantly. 'D'ye see?'

Flora sniffed. 'There's a queer difference between fallin' from a wash-house roof and bein' in a war,' she said, and Janet, realising that she wasn't going to best her daughter, held her peace and went back to her knitting.

Elspeth, who had come home for her midday meal, as she now did two or three times a week to see how Lachlan was, had been listening to the exchange, but for once she had the sense to keep out of it and avoid bringing Flora's wrath down on her head. But she was impressed by the old woman's grasp of the situation.

'How did you manage to work out all that about the wash-house roof, Granjan?' she wanted to know as the two of them went out of the close together, Janet heading back to her own home and Elspeth bound for the sewing room.

'Ach, there's nothin' tae it, hen. Christ did that sort of thing all the time in the New Testament tae explain things tae the folk, and if it's good enough for Him it's good enough for me,' Janet said breezily, adding, 'Mind you, I don't know if He'd've managed with his wee stories so well if a lot of the folk listenin' tae Him had been like our Flora.'

12

It was difficult to explain to friends and neighbours just what had happened to Lachlan. Normally when a soldier returned from the war, everyone in the tenement where his family lived, and sometimes everyone in the entire street, flocked to welcome him back and hear about his experiences. Lachlan had always been popular with young and old alike, and quite a few people were offended when asked not to come to the house on his return.

'Their experience of men getting hurt in the war's kept to bullet wounds or sword slashes, or coughing their lungs up from the gas,' Thomas explained to Elspeth. 'They can understand amputation and death, but not someone being hurt in the head without anything actually smashing through his skull.'

'You said there were a lot of soldiers hurt like Lachlan.'

'Aye, but some of them are still in hospitals, where Lachlan should still be, and there were some poor devils couldn't take it any more and took their own lives, while others' – Thomas stopped short, then went on cautiously, watching her from the corner of his eye – 'others were killed for it.'

'What d'you mean?'

'Shot as cowards, or as deserters.' Thomas's voice was so matter-of-fact that for a moment she couldn't take in what he was telling her. When she did, she gaped at him in horror.

'Killed by their own side, you mean?' There was something about the unexpected sight of blood and flesh normally kept

116

tidily where it should be, beneath intact skin, that made the onlookers' stomachs twist and knot in sudden revulsion. Elspeth had experienced it at school more than once, when a child tripped and cut its head open, or someone tore an arm on one of the spiked railings that surrounded the playground. She felt it now.

'That couldn't happen!'

'I've seen it, Ellie.' The bleak, dark look was in his eyes again. 'There was one in our own unit, a decent enough laddie, just seventeen years old. We could all see that it was gettin' tae him, but the officers wouldnae listen when some of us tried tae tell them. The way they saw things, a soldier had tae be brave all the time, else he was lettin' his king and country down. I sometimes wondered how the King himself would've managed if he'd been there instead of safe at home. Anyway, one day this poor lad couldnae take any more. We were goin' intae battle, and he threw his rifle away and started crying like a bairn. Crying for his mam, he was, with his eyes squeezed shut and his mouth open and the tears and the snot runnin' down his face.'

'What happened?'

'They arrested him, and held a court martial as soon as they could. Then they found a bit of wall that was still standing and they stood him up against it with a blindfold round his eyes, and they shot him. He wasnae the only one it happened tae, but he was the only one I knew as a comrade.'

Elspeth felt sick. 'Did his parents know?'

Thomas's shoulders had hunched as he relived the experience. Now they straightened, and he went on polishing his shoes for work the next day. They got muddy, working in the Bruce gardens, but Thomas liked to start the day with clean shoes, and he always scraped off all the mud and polished them every evening.

'They were told he died in the line of duty. At least they never knew the truth of it, and there's not one man in the unit that'd tell them different if he was tae meet up with them. So now ye know why our Lachlan's one of the lucky ones, in spite of what he's goin' through just now. That's why I'll do anything I must tae get him better. I'm not lettin' the army destroy my brother the way they destroyed that laddie and all the others, pushing them intae a hell they couldnae handle, then punishing them for allowin' it tae get tae them.'

It was difficult for Elspeth to explain about Lachlan to the girls at work. They all knew that her foster brothers had come back safely from the war, but nobody could understand why, with his arm wound fully healed, Lachlan showed no signs of returning to the shipyard.

Lena, who had an eye for the opposite sex and had tried on several occasions to coax Elspeth to agree to a visit to the local Hippodrome in a foursome – the two of them, Thomas, and Lachlan – couldn't understand it at all. 'If he's got the right number of arms and legs and he's not even lost his sight like some poor buggers have, why's he ill?' she wanted to know. 'What else can be wrong with him?'

'It's his head—' Elspeth began, then, realising that they would all think she was talking about a head wound, she amended it to, 'I mean, inside his head.'

'Ye mean he's a daftie?' one of the girls suggested, and Elspeth rounded on her.

'I do not! Our Lachlan's a clever lad – everyone knows that!'

'Aye – clever enough tae pretend that there's somethin' wrong with him when there's nothin' at all,' Betty Jardine sneered. 'If you ask me, he's just swinging the lead.' Betty's brother and one of her cousins and the young man she had been walking out with had all been killed during the war. She and her family had suffered badly, and because of this she was treated more gently than usual by the rest of the girls, though she was sharp-tongued and carping by nature, and before her tragic losses she had been thoroughly disliked.

'He's not! How dare you say such a thing about our Lachlan!' Elspeth was furious, and close to tears with frustration.

'What else is there tae say?' Betty shot back, and there was a murmur of agreement round the large table. Elspeth stopped her sewing machine and half rose from her seat, sheer rage closing her mind to everything but the need to punish Betty for the terrible things she was saying about gentle, suffering Lachlan. Just then Miss Arnold walked in, her presence putting a stop to what might have become a nasty confrontation, and the girl sitting next to Elspeth grabbed her skirt and hauled her back down to her chair.

'Just as well,' Lena said during the midday break. 'That Betty's got sharp fingernails on her, hen. Ye might've got the worst of it – and lost yer job, too.'

'I'll not have her saying such things about our Lachlan,' Elspeth muttered sullenly, but she was secretly relieved that the overseer had arrived when she did.

She had only once in her life been involved in a fight, and that had been a shoving and hair-pulling playground clash with another six-year-old who had tried to steal her new pencil-case. Even now the memory of it made her face burn with shame. She vividly recalled the humiliation of being made to stand in front of the entire class afterwards, the shocked outrage in her teacher's voice as she said, 'Elspeth Bremner, I never thought I'd see you behaving like a guttersnipe!' The final word, spoken with the utmost contempt, had hurt her far more than the two strokes of the belt the teacher had then delivered on her small, wincing palm.

A month after she started work, two of the women from the packing department had come to blows in the basement room during the midday break, kicking and clawing, dragging at each other's hair, screeching like harlots, and eventually rolling on the ground, with a crowd gathered round them, yelling encouragement. Elspeth had stayed well back, the sound of the fight stirring unpleasant memories of her own single lapse.

Both women, eventually separated by a floorwalker drawn to the scene by the noise, had been dismissed on the spot. The very thought that the same thing could have happened to her if Miss Arnold hadn't come in when she did made her cringe, and resolve to say nothing in future about her home life, or Lachlan.

He had been damaged as cruelly as any man blinded or crippled in the war. The real tragedy of it was that in Lachlan's case, nobody could see the wounds.

Although it was only April, the sun was warm on Thomas McDonald's back as he raked and smoothed the gravel of the long curving driveway leading to Overton, the Bruces' house. Occasionally he stopped to stretch and ease stiffened muscles, leaning on the long-handled rake and taking a moment to look about him.

One side of the drive was bordered by a wall of rhododendrons a good twelve feet high. In a month's time they would be studded with crimson and pink and white flowers, each as large as a dinner plate. Where Thomas stood, almost at the top of the drive and near the point where the gravel opened out into a great forecourt in front of the graceful grey-stone mansion, the opposite side of the drive was a smooth grassy bank topped by a row of peony bushes. They had already started blooming, each individual blossom made up of hundreds of tight-packed velvety crimson petals. Beyond, in flowerbeds dotted over the smooth green lawns, the last of the daffodils and tulips could still be seen, and in the woods edging the estate, where he had been working the day before, he had seen stretches of bluebells beneath the trees. Thomas loved this place, and had clung to the memory of it during the war. To him, the gardens of Overton represented peace and serenity and an assurance that while they were there, nothing totally evil could happen.

Returning to his work, he thought of Lachlan, sitting at

home day after day, and longed to bring him to this place with its wide sweeps of smooth green lawn, the walled kitchen and rose gardens, and the lily pond. Surely in gardens like these, with grassed paths leading between flowering bushes to secret little glades, each holding a surprise – a sundial, a huge stone urn filled with flowers, a statue, a graceful gazebo to rest in – his brother's troubled mind would mend.

Thomas believed in the healing power of the open sky and the sight and smell and touch of growing things. He had tried to persuade Lachlan to walk with him to the open land behind Greenock, where they had once played as boys, but Lachlan had lost his nerve once he got to the street, and bolted back to the flat.

It would help if Lachlan could be transported most of the way in the handsome dark blue car now standing in a former carriage-house at the rear of the Bruce house. But Mr Bruce wasn't the kind of man to permit his car to be used for the benefit of his chauffeur-cum-gardener's brother.

Thomas's mouth was dry; he looked up at the sun, and estimated that soon it would be time to go round to the kitchen for a cool glass of lemonade, unless Ina brought one out to him before then.

Ina, one of the Bruces' housemaids, had shown her interest in him from his first day back after the war. She was a pretty girl, with large blue eyes and fair curly hair, and Thomas had been happy to start walking out with her.

Hooves crunched along the drive from the double gate and Thomas moved to the verge and kept working. To his surprise the horse stopped instead of passing by.

'Hello. I thought you were the chauffeur now.'

Startled, he looked up at the girl sitting straight-backed in the saddle.

'I'm a gardener as well, Miss Aileen, when the motorcar's not needed.' The smart grey chauffeur's uniform, complete with gloves and peaked cap, was kept in a small room off the kitchen, so that he could change into it when the car was required.

'Isn't gardening a comedown after driving the car?'

'Not for me, I like working in the garden just as much as I like driving.'

'D'you like horses too?'

Thomas glanced at the handsome chestnut she rode. 'Yes, miss.'

'In that case,' Aileen Bruce said hopefully, 'would you mind very much taking Cavalier round to the stables for me? I should do it myself, but I've stayed out too long and we have guests arriving soon. I must go and change or my mother'll be furious.'

'Of course, miss.' Thomas laid the rake down carefully on the grass verge and went to the handsome chestnut cob, taking the reins in one hand and running the other down the animal's soft nose. The girl slipped from the saddle with ease to stand beside him, her own hand caressing the horse's neck. The other took off her brown leather peaked cap to reveal sleek black hair cut close to her neat skull.

'He's beautiful, isn't he?' She spoke easily, as though Thomas was a friend rather than one of her father's employees. 'I should stay with him until he's been unsaddled and rubbed down and settled into his stall – it's a poor rider who doesn't look after her mount, you know – but I daren't upset Mother. Give my abject apologies to Alfred, and tell him I promise it'll never ever happen again.'

'Yes, miss.' Thomas glanced down at the girl, a good head smaller than he was, and suddenly the world shifted abruptly on its axis. He had often seen her in the gardens, a pigtailed schoolgirl, but while he was away she had become a beautiful woman, and this was the first time he had ever been so close to her. He stared, unable to help himself, at her perfect face, the vivid green, thick-lashed eyes looking up into his.

She blinked, then glanced away from him and back at the

horse. 'Thanks,' she said, then, as though she could no more help it than he could, she looked into Thomas's eyes again.

They might have stood there forever, if a voice hadn't called her name. Wrenching his eyes from her, looking over her head, Thomas saw his employer's wife standing at the top of the steps.

'I'd better go – thanks again,' Aileen Bruce said, and set off at a run across the great sweep of gravel to the house. The scarlet jersey she wore with fawn riding breeches made an exotic splash of colour against the grey walls, and a shaft of sunlight on her black hair made it gleam like a blackbird's wing as she followed her mother into the house.

Thomas watched until she had disappeared, then ran his free hand through his own hair, which had grown longer since he came home from the army, and had fallen into its usual casual waves. He clicked his tongue at the horse and gave its warm silky neck a final caress before leading it round the side of the house, towards the stables.

'We'll never manage it!'

'We will, Aunt Flora.' Elspeth put another pin into the paper pattern, and slid the muslin cloth carefully along the table so that she could reach the next stretch of pattern.

'We'll have to manage, for I'm not letting Annie Cochran outdo me.' Rachel emphasised her words by stabbing at the air with a large pair of scissors.

'I don't know why ye didnae just insist on waitin' till the end of the year, like we agreed,' her mother lamented, pushing back a strand of hair that had come loose from the bun at the back of her head.

'Because I want to get married, and it's a long time till the end of the year.'

'Aye, well, ye'll find that marriage lasts a long time too,' Flora muttered. Her face was red and shiny, for it was a lovely day outside, and the kitchen was hot. They had tried opening the window, only to close it again because the refreshing breeze had riffled the cream-coloured muslin Rachel had chosen for her wedding dress, making it impossible for them to cut it out.

Rachel paid no heed to her mother. 'Anyway, it means that we'll have a nice wedding breakfast in a hotel, instead of all crowding in here.'

'Da's not pleased about that – there's no drink sold in the Anderson Waverley Temperance Hotel,' Mattie put in from the window, where she was perched on the draining board, stitching a broad brown ribbon round a straw hat.

'It'll not do him any harm tae drink lemonade for once,' Flora told her, adding, 'If we ever get there.'

Bits of ribbon and material lay all over the kitchen. It was as bad, Elspeth thought, pinning another section of pattern and material together, as the time the sewing room at Brodie's were all trying to get Catherine Bruce's wedding trousseau ready.

Ever since Bob Cochran had come home from the war he and Rachel had been saving and planning for their wedding on New Year's Eve, the traditional date for Scottish marriages since it enabled the happy couple to start both a new year and a new life together. But at the end of April Bob's parents had suggested that since his sister Annie was marrying in May, there should be a double wedding, followed by a joint reception in the back hall of the Anderson Waverley Temperance Hotel in West Blackhall Street. The booking was made possible because Archie Cochran, Bob's father, was a leading member of the local temperance movement.

With very little time in which to prepare for the wedding, life in the McDonald household had become chaotic. By some miracle, Bob had managed to find a two-roomed flat to rent down by the river, and he and a band of helpers, including Thomas and Henry, were working there at that moment in an effort to make the place habitable in time.

'Where's the light brown thread?' Flora asked, and they all stopped what they were doing to hunt for the elusive bobbin.

When it was finally located under a pile of ribbons, she dislodged Mattie from the draining board so that she could get enough light to see as she threaded her needle.

'I'm tellin' ye,' she said again, her eyes crossing as she tried to fix them on the thread wavering close to the needle's eye, 'we'll never manage it.'

'We will so, Mam.' Now that she was almost a married woman, Rachel felt bold enough to defy her mother. 'We will.'

They did. And, thought Elspeth as she stood in the hotel's back hall watching Rachel dance past on Bob's arm, her pretty face glowing with happiness and excitement beneath the bell-shaped brim of her straw hat, it had been worth it. It was a lovely wedding, marred only by Lachlan's absence. Thomas had volunteered to stay at home with him, but Flora wouldn't hear of it.

'Ina'll be expecting you to take her, and Mam's already said she'll keep Lachlan company, so that's that decided.'

'Of course, we all know why the Cochrans were so eager,' Elspeth heard Flora murmur now as the other happy couple whirled past on the small dance floor. 'They had tae get their Annie married off quickly. Would ye look at the size of her?'

'Ach, Annie was always a plump lassie,' Henry said placatingly. Seeing him glance at the glass of lemonade in his hand before taking a tentative sip, Elspeth nudged Mattie's elbow and both girls stifled giggles. Clearly, Henry McDonald was missing his usual glass of beer, and wishing that his daughter's new in-laws weren't in the temperance movement.

'Don't talk nonsense, Henry – Annie Cochran was solid all over before, not just in front.' Flora tugged at her new gloves. 'She's either gone too far too soon with that young man of hers, or the fat's slipped.'

She brushed a piece of thread from the skirt of the dark green suit she had bought just before the war. It was a bit tight for her now, and as it was a heavy winter suit she was hot, but she couldn't bring herself to take the long jacket off, for she was tormented by the suspicion that the skirt fastenings, unable to hold her in place any longer, might give way, treating the wedding guests to a glimpse of her petticoated hip bulging through the gap.

'It'll mebbe be our Thomas's turn next, him and Ina,' she added, spotting her elder son's fair head among the dancers. 'If they get married, mebbe Mr Bruce'll give them a nice house on the estate.'

13

'Which of you,' Miss Arnold asked from the door of the sewing room, her voice so cold that the words might have been carved from ice, 'is the girl who apparently had the audacity to touch the typewriting machine in the accounts office?'

Elspeth felt as though someone had hit her hard and unexpectedly in the stomach with a rolling pin. The material she was holding dropped from her fingers; her mouth dried and her face flamed as a shockwave ran through her entire body.

Lena, too, was stunned into blushing confusion by the question, coming as it did so long after the crime had been committed. Before she could prevent herself she turned and looked at Elspeth, but even if she had been able to hide her reaction, it would have made no difference, since the culprit's guilt was so obvious that every eye in the room, including Miss Arnold's, was on her.

'I—' Elspeth started to speak, but no sound came out. She cleared her throat and tried again. 'It was me, Miss Arnold.'

'And when was this?'

'When we were working late on Miss Bruce's wedding clothes. You sent me to the office—'

'I sent— I did no such thing!'

'Yes you did.' Elspeth was too caught up in the need to explain to realise that she was not only contradicting Miss Arnold, but implicating her. 'It was when we were busy with

127

Miss Bruce's trousseau, and you sent me to ask Mr James for a list.'

The woman's face crimsoned. 'For a list – not to make free of the office and touch things!'

'She didnae dae any harm.' Lena rushed to defend her friend. 'You sent me as well, Miss Arnold, and I saw what happened. She just touched the machine, then Mr James came in and—'

'That's enough! Get on with your work. As for you, Elspeth Bremner, you're to go at once to Mr James's office!'

Elspeth's knees were so weak that she could scarcely walk along the corridor. She swallowed convulsively several times, blinking hard to clear her sight, which had misted over. How could Mr James do this to her? How could he be so cruel, waiting for months before deciding to punish her for her lapse?

Then a far more frightening question crowded into her head, obliterating her anguish over James Brodie's betrayal. What was Aunt Flora going to say?

By the time she reached the accounts office she had made up her mind that when the ordeal to come was over she would walk out of the department store with her head high – then run away somewhere, anywhere. She couldn't face Flora and tell her that she had been dismissed for bad conduct, with no reference to show to a future employer.

In the accounts office the typewriting machine, the cause of Elspeth's shameful downfall, sat smugly on its table in the corner, shrouded by its dust cover. A young man and an older woman were sitting on tall stools at the high sloping desk running along the opposite wall, each writing in large ledgers.

The woman twisted her head over her shoulder. 'Yes?'

'I'm—' Elspeth swallowed hard, then tried again. 'I'm to see Mr James. I was sent from the sewing room.'

The young man looked up, his gaze sweeping her from top to toe.

'Oh, yes,' the woman said, and to Elspeth, the words had an

ominous sound. Everyone, it seemed, knew about her crime. 'He's expecting you.' She nodded at the closed door leading to the inner office. 'Knock on the door first, and wait till he tells you to go in.'

Wiping her palms nervously down the sides of her serviceable blue skirt, Elspeth approached the door, knocked tentatively, waited for a moment, then knocked again.

'It's all right, he only bites on Wednesdays,' the young man said. She turned, surprised, to be met by a wide grin.

'You've got enough to do without poking your nose in where it isn't wanted, Graham Adams!' the woman snapped, just as a voice shouted, 'Come in!' from the office.

Elspeth, faced with the choice of confronting James Brodie again or showing abject cowardice and running away, grappled with the door handle and almost plunged forward into the lion's den without giving herself further time to think.

'Yes?' The man who had caught her tampering with the office typewriter looked up from his crowded desk.

'You wanted to see me, Mr James? Elspeth Bremner,' she added as he stared blankly at her.

'And what did I want to see you ab—?' he began, then recognition came into his eyes. 'You're the one I found typewriting that night.'

'Yes, sir.'

'Your friend said you went to night school?'

'Yes, sir. I've been studying for eighteen months. Typewriting and shorthand, and book-keeping,' she added, since he seemed to be expecting her to go into detail.

'And what does a seamstress want with book-keeping and all the rest of it?'

'I – I want to work in an office one day,' she said, then shied back nervously as he got up and surged round the desk towards her, dislodging a pile of papers as he went. He and Elspeth both caught at it as it prepared to launch itself into space, then Mr Brodie took a sheet from the top.

'This'll do.' He opened the office door. 'Follow me, Elspeth Bremner.'

She did, and together they surveyed the covered typewriting machine, until Mr James said impatiently, 'Well? It's a good machine but it hasn't learned to uncover itself yet, so take the cover off, sit down and put some paper into it. Now,' he went on when she had done as she was told, 'make it type something.'

'What, sir?'

'Anything – I just want to see if you know what you're doing.'

'The cat sat on the nat,' Elspeth typed, then, professional pride overcoming fear, she pushed the carriage back and corrected her mistake. 'The cat sat on the mat,' the second line said, with confidence. As her fingers recognised the familiar, pleasant sensation of keys yielding beneath them, the third line appeared. 'Peter Piper picked a peck of pickled peppers.'

'Now try copying that.' The paper he had brought with him was thumped down beside the typewriter. Elspeth picked it up and looked at it, appalled. It was a long handwritten list of materials, complete with measurements and prices which would, she knew, have to be laid out in neatly spaced columns.

'What's the matter?' James Brodie asked from above her head. 'Do they only teach you quotations and nursery rhymes at the night school?'

'No, sir, but – I'll need more paper.'

'Then take that one out, and put another one in,' he said, exasperated.

'Excuse me, Mr James, I think the lassie would do better on her own, without anyone standing over her,' the woman at the desk suggested.

'Hmmpphh. Very well, Elspeth Bremner, bring the copy to me when you've finished it – and I'll expect to see it before the sun sets and the moon comes up,' the manager said, and stamped back into his small office, shutting the door noisily behind him.

When a fresh sheet had been rolled into the machine, Elspeth, grateful that she had reached tabulating in her studies, set up the machine, and began to type.

Ten minutes later she laid the typed sheet on James Brodie's desk, with the original list beside it. He picked them both up, comparing them line by line, while she waited, hands linked. In spite of her confusion and bewilderment, she had enjoyed typing again, and the need for concentration had soothed her.

'Very good,' he said at last. 'Go back to the sewing room now, and tell Miss Arnold that I'd be grateful if she would allow you to begin tomorrow morning at half past eight sharp.'

'Begin?'

'Begin,' he repeated, then, eyebrows raised, 'Did she not tell you?'

'Tell me what – Mr James,' she added hurriedly.

He laid the papers down. 'What d'you think you're here for?'

'To be dismissed, because I typed on the typewriter that time.'

'Well, well,' James Brodie said thoughtfully. 'Isn't that a bit of malice?' Then, just as Elspeth opened her mouth to assure him that she had intended no malice at all, but had only wanted to try the typewriter, he returned to the business in hand. 'The fact of the matter is, Miss Bremner, my typist has fallen ill and I need someone to take her place until she comes back. I recalled being told that you were taking lessons, and so I asked Miss Arnold to send you along. You may go now – and remember, half past eight, and not a minute later. There's a lot to be done.'

She ran all the way home from work that afternoon, bursting into the flat to announce that she was to leave the sewing room and work in the department store office and be a real typewriter, for a little while, at least. Mattie and Rachel were delighted for her, and when he came home, Thomas picked her up and swung her about the room.

'Good for you, Ellie!'

Uncle Henry joked about Elspeth running her own office next, and Auntie Flora said that Elspeth had done well – then launched into a lecture about the need for her to mind her manners and do as she was told and not make a nuisance of herself in the accounts office.

'She's not going tae make a nuisance of herself, Mam.' Thomas was brushing his shoes, and preparing to meet Ina on her evening off. 'They need our Ellie's talents – she'll do well for herself, just wait and see.' Even Lachlan smiled and hugged her and said how pleased he was. Then, putting the tip of a finger against the little silver threepenny piece at her throat, 'It's brought you luck right enough.'

'It has,' she agreed, and wished that she could find some way of bringing a little luck to Lachlan, who sorely needed it.

It wasn't until that night that she remembered Mr James's comment about malice, and told Mattie.

'I thought he meant me, touching the typewriter when I shouldn't have, but now I'm thinking it was Miss Arnold he was talking about, not telling me why he wanted to see me.'

'Jealous old cat,' Mattie said absently, peering at a textbook. The single cot had been taken out of their room when Rachel married, giving them a bit more space. Mattie was studying, sitting on her haunches at the end of the double bed, while Elspeth herself, leaning against a pillow propped against the bedhead, was writing letters, using her drawn-up knees as a desk.

'It's all water under the bridge now. No harm was done, after all.' Elspeth put the writing pad aside and eased herself on to her knees, her face alight. 'The important thing – the wonderful thing – is that I'm going to get to work in an office!'

'Until the real girl comes back, just,' Mattie cautioned.

'Even so, I'm going to be able to type all day long.'

'And this time,' Mattie cast her work aside too and bounced

up on her own knees, taking Elspeth's hands in hers, 'you're going to get paid for it!'

It had been cloudy all day, threatening rain, but not following the threat through until early afternoon, when Thomas, giving a final trim to the box hedging round some herbaceous borders, felt the first drops on the back of his neck. He ignored them, and worked on, but within minutes the rain was falling hard and fast, soaking him, and there was no sense in continuing.

The nearest shelter was a small hexagonal summerhouse in the nearby rose garden; Thomas pulled up the collar of his thick working shirt, and ran, skidding slightly on the wet paving stones between the rose beds. He cleared the three steps up to the summerhouse in one stride, threw open the double doors with their diamond-shaped panes of coloured glass set into the top sections, and catapulted into the little building.

Something already inhabiting the space within moved and gave a shriek of fright. Before he could stop himself, Thomas, too, gave out a sharp, startled cry, then felt like a complete fool as he saw Aileen Bruce crouched against the opposite wall, green eyes wide, one hand pressed to her mouth and the other to her heart, a handful of rosebuds scattered on the floor round her feet.

For a moment he stared at her dumbly, unable to believe that she was really there. Ever since the day he had spoken to her in the drive, Thomas had been unable to get the girl out of his mind. He saw her occasionally, on the tennis court, or out riding, or sitting a short distance behind him as he drove her and her parents. He had developed a strange sixth sense where she was concerned – when she was nearby he knew it, even before he actually saw her.

Once, when she was gathering flowers for the house, he had cut off a spray of lilac that was difficult for her to reach. He would never forget the light, sweet touch of her hand against his as she took the spray, the wide smile as she thanked him.

'Thomas! I thought – you came barging in like—' She gave a nervous giggle. 'I feel such a fool.'

'So do I.' In his dreams over the past months he had rescued her several times from runaway horses, or saved her from drowning. In reality, he thought grimly, sick with humiliation, he had gone crashing into the summerhouse and scared the life out of her. Desperate to get out of the confined space and go somewhere where he could slam his fist, or at least his stupid head, against the good solid trunk of a tree, he muttered an apology and turned to the door, just as the shower settled in and rain started drumming hard on the wooden roof just above their heads.

'Wait – you'll get soaked out there. There's room for us both.' She moved forward to stop him, then gave an exclamation and bent to pick up a rosebud. 'Oh, the poor thing, I've stepped on it.'

'Let me, miss, some of those thorns are wicked.'

'They can draw your blood just as easily as mine,' she objected as he knelt to gather the roses.

'I'm used to thorns.' He picked the flowers up and laid them carefully in the trug she held out to him.

'You must think I'm empty-headed, screaming and giggling like that,' she said, sitting down on the bench and settling the trug by her side.

He wanted to tell her that he thought she was the most beautiful, most wonderful woman he had ever met. Instead, he cleared his throat and said, 'Not at all, Miss Aileen. I've seen plenty of men during the war yelling because they thought a shell was going to get them, then laughing like idiots with the relief when it didn't. I've done it myself.'

'You were in the war? So was my brother. He enjoyed it.'

No doubt he had, Thomas thought grimly. Ian Bruce, an arrogant, handsome young man with never a glance or a word for the servants, was employed by a firm of lawyers in Glasgow, and lived in the city, driving to Gourock most weekends in his own smart two-seater car. When he was at home during the summer there were tennis parties, either on the Bruce court, which was kept in immaculate condition for them, or at friends' courts.

Ian Bruce, Thomas thought, would have been an officer. True, some of the officers had suffered just as much as their men, but others – and he had a feeling that Bruce was one of them – had never really had to face the realities. Aloud, he said bluntly, 'There's not much pleasure in killing and being killed.'

'Tell me about your war.'

He could have told her about the mud and the misery and the naked fear. He could have talked about the helpless certainty at times that the war would never ever stop, that he and those with him would spend the rest of their lives struggling with the enemy for a few hundred square yards of ground that for some unknown reason mattered tremendously to both sides.

He could have told her about the times when all he had wanted was to feel the impact of that final, fatal bullet, and get it all over and done with; about what it was like to see close friends screaming and dying.

Instead, his words underlined by the rain hammering on the roof, he told her about Lachlan, and what the war had done to him.

She listened without interruption, her green eyes luminous in the summerhouse's dim light. 'That's – terrible,' she said, when he had finished. 'That poor young man. My brother made it all sound like a bit of a lark. I'd no idea what it was really like.'

Thomas came back to earth with a jolt, cursing himself all over again for his stupidity. Her brother had probably tried to protect her from the truth, and he had come lumbering along and told her things she should never have heard.

'It was a bit of a lark, quite a lot of the time,' he lied. 'I expect your brother made a better job of it than I did.'

'I expect,' said Aileen Bruce shrewdly, 'that his war was easier than yours. What's going to become of your brother? Will he get better?'

'I don't know,' Thomas said honestly. 'I keep telling the rest of them that he'll be fine, but it's been so long now that I'm not sure. The nightmares have almost gone, but he's not got any of his confidence back.'

'Would a doctor not be able to help?'

'No!' He spoke so fiercely that she jumped. 'He's had his fill of doctors and nursing. I should have insisted on him staying in that hospital for a while longer instead of bringing him home because my mother wanted it. They might have made a difference then. But it's too late now tae think of ifs and buts. If we were tae send him back tae hospital now it would only make him think we'd given up, or that we don't want him. Besides, it'd more likely be the asylum now than the hospital, and I'm not having our Lachlan put intae that place.'

He stared down at his hands. 'Mam – my mother – she's beginning tae treat him as if he was a bairn again, and that's not good for him. The other day I caught her running a brush through his hair. Next thing we know she'll be dusting him, as if he was part of the furn—'

He halted, realising that something was missing, and glanced up at the roof. 'The rain's stopped.'

They made for the door at the same time, reaching out for the latch simultaneously, so that his hand landed on hers.

'I think, miss—' he started, just as she began, 'Perhaps we should—' Then they both stopped, laughing. She was so close that he could smell her skin, fresh and flowery, like a summer's day. He began to remove his hand from hers, but just then Aileen turned her own hand round so that their fingers became entwined. The trug fell to the floor for the second time, and her other hand came up to touch his face lightly, then moved over his shoulder to the nape of his neck, while his arm reached around her waist, drawing her closer.

Ina kissed boldly, her mouth open and her tongue teasing his, but Aileen Bruce's kiss was chaste and innocent, and all the sweeter for that.

It was a short kiss, but long enough for Thomas's entire life to change for ever. When they separated and he looked down into her face, he saw her eyes filled with the things he himself wanted to say. He bent towards her again, then a voice calling some distance away broke the embrace and sent them springing away from each other.

'I'm – I'm sorry, Miss Aileen, I had no right—'

The hand that had cupped the nape of his neck touched his mouth, stopping the words. 'I wanted you to kiss me,' she said, then, with sudden urgency, 'You must go. I'll find you tomorrow.'

Blessed by the rain, the garden smelled fresh and faintly perfumed, like her skin. Thomas, dazed by what had just happened, and by the strength of his own reaction, blundered out of the summerhouse and through the bushes, heedless of the light sting of branches against his face, and the soaking he got from them.

He reached the place where he had been working just in time; as he retrieved the shears from under the bush where he had stored them, Aileen and her brother met at the other side of the tall beech hedge a few yards away from him.

'I've been looking for you everywhere,' Ian Bruce said irritably. 'Where have you been?'

'Picking roses. I took shelter in the summerhouse.' Her voice, Thomas thought, stirring to the memory of her mouth beneath his, was like little bells chiming.

He bent his head over his work just as the two of them turned the corner and came towards him.

'If you wanted flowers,' Ian Bruce said shortly, ignoring the figure kneeling at the side of the path, 'you should have asked one of the gardeners to get them for you. That's what they're there for.'

'I'm quite capable of doing things for myself,' she retorted, then they were past, and Thomas looked up as they went through an archway of green and out of sight, Ian Bruce carrying the basket of rosebuds, his free arm about his sister's shoulders.

The thought came to him that while Ina fitted snugly in his arms, Aileen Bruce belonged in them. He knew what his grandmother would have said if she had known what had happened in the summerhouse: 'It'll all end in tears!'

Maybe so, but he had never been happier in his entire life than he was at that moment.

14

The typewriter clacked nonstop, turning out a continuous flow of lists, letters, and memorandums to the many departments housed within Brodie's store. As the days flew past, Elspeth's confidence grew and her initial shyness eased off. James Brodie was a fair employer, a man who put in a decent day's work and expected the same of his staff. He didn't hover over them all the time as Miss Arnold and Miss Buchanan did in the sewing room, nor, if he was in a bad mood, did he vent it on them. Wilma Morgan, the older woman, was a sharp-eyed clerkess who ruled over the accounts office, but was friendly enough as long as she was given the respect she considered due to one who had worked there for ten years. Graham Adams, still serving his apprenticeship as a clerk, was a cheerful nineteen-year-old with ambition.

'If I play my cards right, I'll be the boss in here, in time,' he bragged to Elspeth when Wilma and Mr Brodie were out of the office.

She pressed the tabulating key, and the large heavy carriage sped on its way, then crashed to a standstill at the correct place. 'D'you think so?'

'The way I see it, once the old man dies and Mr James inherits the store, he won't want to be stuck here day in and day out. He's got no choice just now, for his dad expects him to do as he did. He never missed a day at his desk himself, until the bronchitis got worse and he had to stay at home.

139

Imagine owning a place like this and sitting behind a desk like one of the staff!'

He had swung round on his high stool and was leaning back against the sloping desk, his elbows hooked nonchalantly on the ridge that prevented the heavy ledgers from sliding off. 'Once Mr James owns the place, I reckon he'll want to have more time for yachting. He's got his own boat at Gourock – takes it out every Saturday afternoon, and does some racing in it, too. He'll want a second-in-command here, and that'll be me.'

He jabbed at his own chest confidently with a thumb. 'So keep in with me, Elspeth, and you could do well for yourself.'

'I'm not going to be here for long. The typist'll be back one of these days, then I'll have to go back to the sewing room.'

'I can still do you some good there, for Mr James's manager would be in charge of all the departments.'

Elspeth rolled a sheet of paper out of the typewriter and put a fresh sheet in. 'I won't be here by then. I don't want to spend the rest of my life as a seamstress. I want to work in an office.'

'I could arrange that for you, when I'm in charge.' He paused; although she was concentrating on her work, he knew that he was running his eyes over her, a habit of his that she disliked intensely. 'Have you got a sweetheart?'

'My aunt says I'm too young.'

'What age are you, then?'

Lena would have come up with a pert return, or slapped his face for his cheek. Elspeth merely answered the question. 'I'm fifteen.'

'A bit young, but still, I'm not particular,' Graham said magnanimously. 'I'll take you out tonight, if you like.'

'I'm visiting my grandmother tonight.'

'Tomorrow.'

'I'm helping my Aunt Flora to do the weekend cleaning.'

'When, then?'

He was smirking confidently, appearing to think that Elspeth would be flattered by his attentions. Instead, she merely found his persistence irritating. What with the excitement over her temporary move to the office, worry about Lachlan, and her letter-writing she had enough to think about.

'I don't know.'

Graham's eyes hardened and his mouth turned down at the corners. 'I'll not wait around for ever.'

'I'd not expect you to,' she retorted, just as Wilma's heavy tread could be heard in the corridor outside. Graham spun round to the desk, snatching up his pen.

'Damn!' he muttered, and Elspeth glanced up to see a large blot of ink, dislodged from the pen as he grabbed it, spread itself over the page he had just completed.

Then Wilma was in the room, wailing over the mess he had made, and suddenly Graham, reaching for a sheet of blotting paper, protesting that it had been an accident, seemed a far cry from being Mr James Brodie's manager, and lord of all he surveyed.

Although Elspeth, as an office employee, could have eaten her midday sandwiches in the upstairs canteen, she continued, despite Wilma's obvious disapproval, to join Lena and the others in the big basement room. For one thing, she knew that soon she would have to return to the sewing room, and she had no wish to annoy the women there by appearing 'snobby', and for another, her letter-writing was still in demand, and she depended on the money she earned from it for her night-school classes.

She had thought that once the war was over her talent for writing letters would no longer be of use, but she was wrong. As well as the usual formal letters voicing complaints or asking advice, girls who wanted to keep in touch with soldiers and sailors who had been in the town during the war sought her assistance, and once the returning brothers and cousins heard of her skills they, too, contacted her, eager to keep in touch with young women they had met elsewhere, but unable to put together the things they wanted to say.

Elspeth, who had long since passed the stage of being embarrassed at requests to write about love and longing, and had in fact become famed for her ability to write love letters, sat patiently, exercise book in one hand and pencil in the other, while her clients blushed and stammered and said, 'Ach, just tell him I love him, and I cannae wait tae cuddle him again,' or, 'Can ye put down somethin' nice about her bonny face in the moonlight, and how I'll never forget that night when we – tae hang wi' it, just say that night, she'll know what I mean.'

The pennies and halfpennies filled her tobacco tin to capacity, and were exchanged for sixpences, then shillings, then half-crowns. Only Thomas knew how much she had saved, and he advised her to keep her own business to herself.

'But it seems underhand, not letting Aunt Flora know.'

'There's nothing wrong with it. You pay your wages into the house the same as the rest of us, and anything extra's yer – your own business,' said Thomas, who had been working hard on improving his speech since donning a chauffeur's uniform. 'You might need something some time, and be glad of the money.'

He urged her to open a bank account, and after she had approached the bank door three times then turned away again, unable to walk into such a place on her own, he went with her, handsome and reassuring in his smart grey chauffeur's uniform.

As they stepped back on to the street, the bankbook clutched in Elspeth's hand, Thomas said, 'I'm fetching Mrs Bruce in ten minutes. There's time to give you a lift back to Brodie's.'

Sitting in the deep, comfortable seat beside him, gliding through the streets with the mingled smell of leather and Mr Bruce's cigars tantalising her nose, was like glimpsing heaven. She had just begun to imagine herself a titled lady, dressed in the best Brodie's had to offer, on her way to take tea with the Provost's wife, when Thomas broke the spell. 'I'm worried about our Lachlan. He's not gettin' any better, is he?'

'He still needs time,' Elspeth offered, but without much

conviction, for she knew what he meant. Lachlan, who had always had some artistic skill, had taken to drawing, first on the margin of newspapers with a stub of pencil he had found, then in a blank exercise book Mattie had given him, together with a better pencil.

At first the family had looked on his new hobby as a step forward in his recovery, but all the drawings turned out to be of men in battle, some yelling defiance at the enemy as they charged, bayonets fixed on their rifles, others screaming in agony as they writhed on the ground. They were appalled by the pictures, drawn with such ferocity that the pencil dug deep into the paper.

'Mebbe we're treatin' him the wrong way,' Thomas fretted. Glancing sideways at him, Elspeth saw that his face was bleak with worry. 'Mam treats him as though he's a bairn again, and he's content to let it happen. Mebbe he needs to be pushed into doin' more for himself, instead of havin' things done for him.' He turned the wheel, easing the big car round a corner. 'He's only just gone into his twenty-first year – his whole life's still in front of him. Times I lie awake at night worryin' that he'll spend it just the way he is now.'

'But if we try to push him, could it not make him worse?'

'Mebbe, but being kind to him isn't making him any better, is it?' Thomas said in despair as they reached the corner of the street where the department store stood. 'I'd best let you out here, so's nobody in the store sees you.'

Standing on the kerb, watching Thomas drive off, Elspeth decided that one day she would like to have her own car and her own chauffeur. Patting the pocket that held her new bankbook, she felt that by opening a bank account, she had just taken the first step to future affluence.

'I will not have it!'

Elspeth, who had just stepped into the flat, halted as she heard the words booming from the kitchen.

She recognised the voice – one she had never expected to hear in Mearns Street.

'There's nothin' wrong with the lassie workin' in an office,' Flora rapped back. 'What d'ye think she'll do, Mrs Bremner – help herself tae one of the clerks?'

Elspeth opened the door on a gasp of outrage from her grandmother to see Flora McDonald and Celia Bremner facing each other across the kitchen table. Flora was red in the face, and two bright red blotches stood out on Celia's sallow cheekbones.

'You're a bad besom, Flora Docherty,' Celia hissed, using Flora's own name, as was the custom among local women. 'I never liked our Maisie going about with you – it's no wonder she went wrong!'

'It wasnae me that did for Maisie, and well you know it,' Flora almost shrieked. 'If anythin' harmed that poor lassie, it was growin' up with all the bitterness and vindictiveness in that house of yours. Oh, she told me about it – she had tae tell someone!'

Celia gave a strangled cry, her hands forming themselves into claws. For a moment Elspeth, still transfixed in the doorway, thought that her grandmother was going to throw the table aside and launch herself on Flora, then another voice broke in, high and desperate.

'Stop it!'

She hadn't even realised that Lachlan was in the room until he cried out, for he wasn't in his usual chair by the fire. Instead, he huddled in the corner between the sink and the wall that held the curtained bed-recess, his thin body pressed against the wall as though trying to force its way through the plaster and bricks. His face was ashen, and his body shaking so much that water splashed over the edge of the cup he clutched tightly in both hands.

'Stop it,' he said again through clenched teeth, his voice thin and raw. 'Stop it, stop it, stop—'

'It's all right, Lachlan, all right.' Elspeth erupted into the room, pushing past her grandmother, and squatted down beside him, talking soothingly, trying to take the cup from him. As his fingers began to relax, a ship's siren suddenly blared out from the river below. It was too much for him. He gave a short, high, animal-like scream and his body jerked at the sudden noise. Cold water slopped over Elspeth's hands, soaking through her gloves, and Lachlan's fingers spasmed, tightening round the cup until she feared that it might break.

Then Thomas was pushing her aside, raising his brother to his feet, coaxing him away from the wall and out of the room, talking in the low, soothing voice he always used for Lachlan.

Celia Bremner watched him go, her face frozen in a grimace of astonishment and distaste. 'What in the world's wrong with the laddie?' she wanted to know when the two young men had gone from the room.

'I told you, Grandmother, it's what happened to him in the war. He can't help it.'

'He should be in the infirmary – or the asylum.'

'You hold yer tongue!' Flora almost spat the words at the old woman. 'There's nothin' wrong with my laddie that a wee bit of peace and quiet cannae cure. Ye've said yer say, Mrs Bremner – now ye can get out of my house.'

'Elspeth, you will come with me. This is no place for any granddaughter of mine.'

Elspeth felt as though the ground had been pulled from beneath her feet. Panic caught her heart and squeezed it painfully as she backed away from her grandmother, groping with one hand for the sturdiness of the wall at her back. Her fingers caught instead at the bed-curtains, gathering a handful of the material.

'I don't want to,' she heard herself saying.

'It's not a question of what you want. I'll not have my own flesh and blood living in this house.'

'Ye never wanted Ellie before, so why should ye have her now?' Flora wanted to know. 'I'll not let you waste her life the way ye wasted poor Maisie's.'

'You have the nerve to say that to me, when your own son's no better than—'

'Mam!' Thomas's voice was like the crack of a whip. He moved quickly from the door to intercept his mother, who was on her way towards Celia Bremner. 'Sit down, Mam, I'll deal with this.' His mother's body stiffened, like that of a small child unwilling to be put in a seat, but Thomas's youthful strength won, and Flora had no option but to sit down. Then he turned to Celia. 'Mrs Bremner, I think you should go home now.'

She eyed him warily, moving back a step. 'Elspeth—'

'Elspeth's staying here for the moment. If she wants to live with you, she'll make her own way.'

'She'll do as her grandmother tells her!'

Thomas's face was like stone, though his voice was still low and reasonable. 'Elspeth's old enough tae earn her keep, and she's old enough tae make up her own mind. Not one person in this house'll try tae influence her, one way or another. You have my word on that. Now – I'll walk with you down tae the tram stop, and see you on your way.'

Celia summoned up the last of her strength. 'Elspeth, I'll expect you in Port Glasgow!' With one last, scathing look at Flora, she made for the door, but by that time her fingers were trembling so hard that they fumbled helplessly with the handle.

Thomas reached round her to open the door. 'I'll not be long,' he told the others as he followed Celia out. 'Ellie, look after Lachlan.'

As the outer door closed, Flora slumped in her chair. She, too, was shaking, her face grey and old. 'Elspeth, see tae Lachlan.'

'Aunt Flora, why is my grand—'

'Do as yer told!' Flora snapped, summoning such a steely edge to her voice that Elspeth fled at once from the room.

Lachlan was sitting on his bed; when she sat down beside him, her arm against his, she could feel him trembling.

'It's all right, Lachie, it was just my grandmother in a temper.'

'I don't like folk shouting,' he whispered through white lips.

'I know. I don't either.'

'She was shouting about you, Ellie. What've ye done tae make her so angry?'

'I've not done anything. She's just awful strict, like a teacher.'

'She told Mam that ye've tae go and stay with her.'

Elspeth felt a shiver run through her at the thought of living in the cheerless house she could scarcely bear to sit in for even two hours.

'I'm not going.'

'Good.' Lachlan took her hand in his. He was like a child, Elspeth thought sadly, remembering how she had always looked up to him in her own childhood, always longed to be as grown-up as he was.

She started talking about times they'd had as children, and about her work, and gradually he relaxed. She heard Thomas return eventually, going directly to the kitchen. Then Mattie and her father came in and the small flat grew fragrant with the smell of the midday meal. And still she talked, until, at last, Thomas appeared in the doorway.

'It's dinner-time.'

Lachlan went off cheerfully enough, while Elspeth lingered to ask, 'How's Grandmother?'

'I went all the way back with her, to be on the safe side. She was in an awful state, poor old soul.' A faint smile touched the corners of his mouth. 'She wouldn't talk to me. I had to sit at the back of the tram and pay my own fare. I think she was glad enough to have someone keeping an eye on her, but she'd have died before she'd admit it. Don't say anything to the rest of them,' he added as they went through the hall. 'Mam won't want them to know what happened.'

15

Flora refused to discuss Celia Bremner's visit, and Elspeth was left puzzling about what she had overheard, and trying to make sense of it. Finally, she ventured to speak to Granjan about it.

'It's no business of yours or mine, pet.'

'But it is my business,' Elspeth said, exasperated. 'The quarrel was about me. I thought Grandmother would be pleased about me wanting to work in an office like my grandfather. But when I mentioned it she was so sharp that I didn't even dare to tell her I was going to night school. What have I done wrong?'

'Nothing at all,' Janet Docherty hastened to assure her. 'It wasnae you who did wrong.'

'Who did, then?'

Janet sighed. 'I suppose ye should know – but not a word tae anyone. If Flora knew I'd told ye she'd be ragin'.'

'Not a word, I promise.'

'It was yer grandfather.' Granjan spoke as though every word was being dragged out of her. 'It seems there was this woman worked in the same office as him, and he – liked her.'

Elspeth gaped at her. 'He fell in love with another woman while he was married to Grandmother?'

'It happens tae folk sometimes – but not often,' Granjan added hurriedly. 'Marriage is marriage, and nothin' should come between man and wife. But I'll admit that Celia Bremner was never what ye'd call a warm, lovin' sort of woman.'

'Did she find out about it?'

'If she didnae know before he went off, she must have known then,' Janet said drily. It was almost too much for Elspeth to take in.

'You mean he ran away – with this woman?' Her voice rose to a squeal, and Janet winced.

'For any favour keep yer voice down – the neighbours'll hear.'

'But Grandmother said he died.'

'So he did, as far as she was concerned.' Janet bent stiffly to pick a piece of fluff from the carpet. 'Marriage is important tae a woman, Ellie. There's a certain respect in havin' a ring on yer finger an' bein' called Missus. There's as much respect for a widow, but little for a deserted wife.'

'Folk must have known, surely.'

'Of course they did. The whole place buzzed with it, and I felt that sorry for Celia – not that she was a woman who'd let anyone sympathise with her. The gossip soon died down, the way gossip does. As tae her sayin' he died – he might well have by now, for all folk know. An' give the man his due, he saw tae it that she wasnae left destitute.'

Elspeth sat silent, trying to understand the new picture Granjan had painted of Celia Bremner. She was such a proud woman, and she must have suffered greatly over her husband's desertion.

'Was it just after that that she started wanting to see me?'

'I believe it was, hen.'

'She wants me to go and live with her,' Elspeth said, and shivered. 'But I can't. I'm sorry for what happened to her, but it doesn't make her a different person.'

'We all have our own lives, and nobody else can live them for us. You do whatever's best for you,' Janet told her. 'But whatever you do, mind what I said – not a word about this tae a soul!'

*

As the day for her usual monthly visit to Port Glasgow drew near, Elspeth was in a quandary. She had decided, after the quarrel, never to visit her grandmother again, and the decision had been a relief, for she hated the duty visits. But Granjan's story had made her feel guilty about turning her back on her maternal grandmother, who had already lost her husband and her daughter – or, rather, driven them both away from her.

She was still unsure when the day came, and was taken aback when Flora said after the midday meal, 'Is it not time ye were gettin' ready tae go tae yer grandmother's?'

'You want me to go, after what happened between the two of you?'

Flora glared. 'That has nothin' tae dae with you doin' yer duty by her. She's yer own flesh and blood.'

'I'll come with you, Ellie,' Mattie volunteered as Elspeth hesitated, and her mother rounded on her.

'Ye'll do no such thing, lady. Elspeth's old enough tae tend tae her own business.'

Apprehension settled in a solid lump behind Elspeth's ribs as she prepared for the visit. By the time she reached her grandmother's door it had become a hard, jagged boulder. She banged the polished brass doorknocker the way she had been taught, loud enough to be heard, but not loud enough to annoy Grandmother, then stepped back, hands folded protectively across the part of her stomach where the boulder lay.

After a moment she heard movement behind the door, then it opened to reveal Celia Bremner, as erect and as awesome as ever.

'It's you,' she said, as she always did. Then, moving back, 'You'd best come in.'

The visit went along its usual lines, with not a thing said about Celia's visit to Mearns Street. In the kitchen, the teatray was set out as usual, as though there had been no question of Elspeth staying away.

After tea, instead of waiting in the kitchen until

Grandmother emerged from the lavatory, Elspeth tiptoed into the living room to study the photograph more closely. Surely that balding, respectable man behind the protective glass couldn't possibly have had a sweetheart, she thought, but a more intensive study showed that in actual fact he was quite a good-looking man.

Noting afresh the possessive hold his wife had on his shoulder, Elspeth began to understand why he had felt the need to escape. Then the cistern was flushed, and she fled, mouse-like, back to the kitchen, reaching it just in time.

Flora sank into a chair by the table and fanned herself with one hand. 'That washhouse was like a furnace today,' she said, then, as she always did when she returned to the house, 'Put the kettle on, Elspeth, I could do with a cup of tea.'

Thomas, studying a book at the table, put a detaining hand on Elspeth's wrist as she moved past him to the cooker. 'Lachlan,' he said blandly, 'put the kettle on, will you?'

Lachlan, who had been idly gazing into space, stared. So did his mother.

'What?'

'Elspeth's been helping you with the washing, Mam. She's just as tired as you are, and I'm tryin' to read this book about car engines. Lachlan's not doing anything.'

'But Lachlan's—'

'—as able as any of us to make a cup of tea,' Thomas said evenly. 'It's time he was doing something round the house.'

Flora went red. 'Don't talk nonsense. Elspeth, do as you're told.'

Thomas's fingers tightened. 'Sit down, Elspeth, and let Lachlan see to it.' His brown eyes flashed a clear message at her, and she sank into a chair, her heart thumping, and her palms clammy.

'I'll make it myself,' Flora said icily, but Thomas's free hand caught at her sleeve as she started to rise.

'He can manage, Mam. He's a man, not a bairn.'

'He's not well!'

'And he'll not get well if you keep fussing over him. It's gone on long enough. You heard me, Lachlan,' Thomas told his brother, his voice suddenly hard. 'Get up and put the kettle on.'

Lachlan, who had been looking wide-eyed back and forth between his mother and brother during their argument, did as he was told. Seeing his hands shake as he filled the kettle, Elspeth longed to get up and do it for him, but didn't dare.

'Now put the cups on the table,' Thomas said, his voice crisp and hard. An officer's voice, Elspeth suddenly realised. The voice of authority, one that Lachlan had been trained in the army to obey automatically.

Step by step, keeping one hand on his mother's wrist, Thomas talked his brother through the ritual of making tea. Uncertainly, moving like an old man, Lachlan did as he was told, while Flora sat motionless, her mouth so tight that it could scarcely be seen, her eyes like icy pebbles.

When the time came for Lachlan to pour boiling water from the kettle to the large shabby tin teapot, his hands were trembling so much that Elspeth was convinced that he was going to scald himself. She half rose from the chair, then as Thomas said her name very quietly, forced herself to sit down again.

After Lachlan had placed a cup in front of each of them, he began to take his own tea back to his chair, where he took all his meals, a towel tucked into the neck of his shirt by Flora. Thomas's voice halted him. 'Sit at the table with us, Lachlan.'

The young man hesitated and half turned, his eyes pleading. 'Here, beside me,' Thomas said implacably, drawing out a chair, and Lachlan obeyed.

It was more like a funeral than four people enjoying a cup of tea. Thomas talked about car engines, while Flora stared at the table, making no attempt to drink her tea, and Lachlan, after trying to lift his cup two-handed and being forced to put it down again because his trembling hands threatened to splash hot liquid all over the table, gave up the attempt.

Elspeth, glancing over at him, saw that he was weeping silently. She put her own cup down, determined this time to do something about his misery, but just then he got to his feet and left the room, scrubbing one sleeved arm over his face in a heartbreakingly childish gesture.

'Are ye satisfied now?' Flora hissed at her first-born as soon as Lachlan had gone. 'D'ye not think the poor laddie's got enough trouble without you bullyin' him? Wait till yer father—'

'Sometimes, Mam, we have to be cruel to be kind.' Thomas got up with an abrupt movement and went to the door.

'Where d'ye think ye're goin'?'

'To Lachlan.'

'Leave him – ye've done him enough harm!'

'It's me he needs. Sit down, Mam, and drink your tea.'

'I don't want it!'

'When we behaved like that, you called it cutting off our noses to spite our faces,' Thomas said, and left the room. Flora scraped her chair back from the table, poured her tea down the sink, and began to scrub the potatoes for the evening meal, the water flying in all directions a testimony to her inner fury.

The next morning Thomas, who had until then been helping Lachlan to dress and undress, got his brother up half an hour earlier than usual, and stood over him while Lachlan laboriously dressed himself.

Flora tutted when he appeared in the kitchen with his shirt buttons in the wrong buttonholes. 'Lachlan, will ye look at yerself, laddie! Come here till I sort ye out.'

Lachlan started to move obediently towards her, but Thomas, coming into the room at his back, stopped him.

'Leave him be, Mam. Look, Lachie—' He hooked a finger into the loop of shirt on Lachlan's thin chest caused by an unused buttonhole. 'You've missed one. You'll have to undo them all and start again. From the top now, and work your way down.'

From then on, the battle for Lachlan was under way. Flora's fingers itched every time she saw her son with his braces twisted or his shoelaces untied, but Thomas continued to push his brother into looking after himself, and saw to it that Elspeth and Mattie and his father did the same.

At first, Lachlan's struggles were painful to see. Often he was in tears of helpless frustration, but gradually, the tears gave way to bouts of anger, mainly directed against Thomas, who shouted back at him, goading him on.

'He never used to lose his temper,' Elspeth said nervously after Lachlan had stormed off to bed following a particularly bad flare-up.

'It's time he learned, then.'

'Thomas, are you sure you're doing the right thing, treating him this way?'

'It's that, or seeing him turn into a helpless invalid.' Thomas pushed his thick fair hair from his face, but, as usual, it fell back across his brow as soon as it was released. 'And what'll happen to him then, Ellie? Who's going to care for him when Mam's gone? D'ye want to see him put into the asylum or the poors' hospital, or left to walk the streets because he can't fend for himself? I know I'm hurting him, but it's like thawing out someone who's been frozen. It's sore, but if he isnae thawed out he'll die. That's what's happening to Lachie.' He caught at her wrist, shook it slightly. 'And you've got to help me, for none of the rest will.'

Picking up Lachlan's discarded sketch book he leafed through the pages, then gave a short laugh. 'Take a look at that.'

The battle scenes concentrated now on one soldier. In every sketch he was injured and suffering, and in every sketch he bore a clear likeness to Thomas.

'The man's got talent,' Thomas commented drily.

He didn't let up for a moment, and as the days and weeks went by, Lachlan began to show unmistakable signs of improvement. Tormented by his brother's jibes about grown men who let their mammies look after them, he began to shrug his mother's hands away when she tried, in Thomas's absence, to do something for him.

Looking at the expression on the older woman's face each time that happened, Elspeth sympathised with her, for she was only trying to do what she saw as the best for Lachlan. She herself felt ashamed of the times she had answered Aunt Flora back and been difficult, and tried to be kinder and more understanding.

Unfortunately, Flora, wounded to the core by what she saw as Lachlan's rejection, interpreted Elspeth's overtures as pity. She became even more irritable with the girl than before, and gradually, Elspeth's good intentions flew out of the window, the two of them reverting back to the uneasy relationship they had known for years.

Flora's bitterness over Thomas and Lachlan was eased when Rachel plucked up the courage to tell her that she was expecting a child.

'There's just one thing,' the girl went on nervously. 'It's due in January.'

Flora, as used to mental mathematics as any housewife forced, week after week, to make the money available go as far as possible, did a swift calculation in her head, then glared at her daughter. 'A seven-month bairn?'

'Eight months, Mam.'

'Don't quibble with me, lady, it's still too early. Some of the neighbours might be daft, but they're no' fools. No wonder ye were so keen tae take up the Cochrans' offer of a double weddin'!'

'What with Bob coming back safe from the war, and all . . .' Rachel's words faded under her mother's look, then she made one more try, 'At least we're not as bad as Annie Cochran and her man – their bairn's born already.'

'Just because she just made it tae the kirk in time, it doesnae excuse what you did. After the way I've tried to bring you up well,' Flora foamed, 'here ye are, giving yer father and me a showin' up before the whole street.'

'It happens to other folk,' Rachel protested tremulously.

'But it's never happened to us. If this is a lassie ye're carryin', wait and see how you feel if she comes tae you with the same tale. Ye'll not be so pleased about it then.'

Tears were shimmering in Rachel's eyes now. 'Don't be like that about it, Mam, Bob's bad enough without you starting on me.'

'What d'ye mean? Is he not pleased about the bairn?'

Rachel sniffed. 'He doesnae want a family so soon. He says I should have been more careful.'

'He what?' Flora's maternal instinct flared up. 'The cheeky monkey! It takes two tae make a bairn, just you tell him that from me! And when it comes, it'll be a lot bonnier than that wee red-faced greetin' thing his sister Annie's got. All my bairns were bonny.'

'Does that mean you're not angry with me, Mam?'

Flora had gone too far to draw back now. 'Aye, well, what's done's done,' she conceded, 'and it'll be nice tae have a grand—' She broke off as the door opened and Thomas walked in.

'Thomas?' She glanced at the clock. 'What are ye doin' here at this time of the day?'

He was in his chauffeur's uniform, the peaked cap tucked beneath one arm. 'Ma – Mother, I've brought Miss Bruce to visit you,' he said awkwardly, just as Aileen Bruce, in a beige silk dress under a long deep green linen jacket, came into the kitchen at his back.

Her smile, as she advanced on Flora, a slim hand extended, was radiant. 'Mrs McDonald – I've been looking forward to meeting you.'

Flustered, Flora and Rachel scrambled to their feet.

'Where's Lachlan?' Thomas asked as Aileen's soft, cool hand met Flora's rough and reddened fingers.

'In his room. Thomas—' Flora said as he went into the hall, then belatedly remembered her manners. 'This is my eldest, Rachel. Ye'll have a wee cup of tea, Miss Bruce?'

Aileen beamed at Rachel, who smiled shyly in return, one hand trying to tidy her hair unobtrusively. 'It's very kind of you, but we're hoping to take your other son for a drive.'

'Our Lachlan?' Flora signalled to Rachel to scoop up the cups sitting on the floor by the two fireside chairs.

'I thought he might enjoy a run to Loch Thom. It's lovely up there.'

'Ye'll take a seat, at least.'

'Thank you.' Aileen Bruce sank gracefully into a chair by the table and, apparently unaware of the tension in the room, chattered easily until Thomas returned with Lachlan, who, much to his mother's relief, had put on a jacket and tie and brushed his hair. His brown eyes were wary, and he was rubbing his hands nervously down the sides of his trousers.

'Here we are.' There was a forced cheerfulness in Thomas's voice. 'Miss Bruce, this is my brother Lachlan.'

Aileen's wide smile broke over Lachlan, making him blink. 'How do you do? I'm sorry you've not been well. Thomas tells me you're feeling better, though.'

'H-how d'ye do?' He shook her hand as though it was made of porcelain.

'I hope you'll come out with us for a wee run.'

'Of course he will,' Thomas said heartily. 'We'd best be on our way – we'll not be long, Mother.'

16

Lachlan was still out when the rest of the family arrived home, and the flat was spotless, for Flora had spent the rest of the afternoon, with Rachel's help, cleaning every inch of it. But there was no evening meal waiting for them.

'I'm not havin' that Bruce lassie findin' us sittin' eatin',' Flora said firmly. 'She'll not catch me unawares twice. Ye'll have tae wait until she's been and gone before ye eat. Henry, away tae the wee room and change intae yer best clothes. I've left them out for ye.'

'Put on my good clothes on a weekday? The lassie's flesh and blood the same as the rest of us,' Henry protested, his stomach rumbling. 'She knows that we eat, there's no shame in her seein' us doin' it.'

'That's not what I think – and for goodness' sake do somethin' about that noise,' Flora snapped as his empty stomach protested again. 'D'ye want tae shame me entirely?'

Hurt and hungry, he took himself off to the pub, announcing that he would buy a pie to keep body and soul together. Flora, her mouth a thin, tight line, started to clean the spotless sink.

'D'ye think she will come back?' Mattie asked hopefully. 'I wish I'd been home earlier to see her!'

Flora, plying a washcloth energetically, sniffed. 'There was nothin' tae see, just a wealthy lassie who'd no business to be here.'

'It was nice of her to think of taking Lachlan out,' Mattie protested. 'Most posh folk are too neb-in-the-air tae come near a tenement.'

'Not Miss Aileen,' Elspeth said. She, too, was disappointed at missing the girl's visit, but at least she could claim to have seen her at close quarters before. 'She was in the fitting room at Brodie's once, when she and her sister were having clothes made for the wedding. I thought then she would be nice to know. D'you not mind, Mattie, when we went to see her sister comin' out of the church after she got married? Miss Aileen was the chief bridesmaid.'

'Oh, yes – a bonny girl, she was, with black hair and a lovely smile.'

'There's more tae folk than a nice smile and clothes that cost enough tae feed a workman's family for a week,' Flora interrupted. 'Dust that skirtin' board if ye've nothin' else tae dae, Mattie. And Elspeth, take a dry mop over the hall linoleum.'

To the girls' disappointment, Lachlan came home alone shortly afterwards, glowing with fresh air and exercise. Aileen and Thomas had taken him over the hills to Loch Thom, the town's reservoir.

'It was grand tae see the grass and the water again, and hear the birds,' he said with an enthusiasm Elspeth hadn't seen since his last war leave. 'We'd a right good walk round the water's edge, the three of us. She's kind, that Miss Aileen. Mam, Thomas says tae tell ye he'll get somethin' tae eat at the big house. He'd tae take Miss Aileen home, then tonight he's drivin' her mother and father.' His eyes swept the empty, polished table. 'Have I missed my dinner?'

Flora's dread of another visit from Aileen Bruce turned to insult because the girl hadn't returned to see the result of all her polishing and scrubbing. 'There's cold meat, and I'll fry up some cold boiled potatoes,' she said shortly. 'That'll have tae dae ye for once.'

*

Thomas didn't come home till late, tiptoeing into the dark, silent hall. When his duties as a chauffeur kept him at work in the evenings, he always went straight to bed without disturbing the sleeping household, but tonight the kitchen door opened to reveal his mother's silhouette.

'In here.'

The kitchen was dimly lit by one gas mantle, and Henry's snores wafted from behind the curtains closing off the wall-bed. Flora had changed into her long-sleeved, throat-to-ankle nightdress, with a large shawl over it. Her grey hair, released from the bun she put it up in every morning, hung down over her shoulders, giving her a vulnerable look. But there was nothing vulnerable about her voice.

'Well?' Thomas asked when they were confronting each other.

'You know fine!' his mother told him, low-voiced, mindful of her sleeping husband. 'Bringin' that lassie intae my kitchen without warning and giving me a right showin'-up!'

Thomas had changed out of his chauffeur's uniform and back into his own clothes. 'Mam, the kitchen was spotless. It always is – there was no need for you to be ashamed of it.'

'But she's used tae a lot better than this, isn't she?' Flora glanced round the small room where the entire family ate and washed and spent their spare time. Ever since Aileen Bruce had stepped into it, she had been looking at it through different eyes, seeing what she imagined Aileen had seen – a crowded little room with handmade rag rugs laid on linoleum that was kept spotlessly clean, but was also faded from all those scrubbings, and cracked in places.

'That doesnae mean that there's anything wrong with the place. She's a nice lassie, Mam, she didnae come here to look down on us.'

'Why did she come, then?'

'To take Lachlan out, and to meet you. She's heard all about you and the rest of the family from me.'

Flora pulled the shawl more tightly about her body. 'Since when does a gardener talk about himself and his family tae his employer's daughter?'

He flushed angrily, his patience almost spent. 'I'm a chauffeur as well as a gardener—'

'Fancy names don't change folk.'

'—and sometimes I've to drive Miss Aileen places,' Thomas forged on, refusing to let the jibe get to him. 'She's interested in folk – where's the harm in that?'

'There's plenty harm when a man workin' for a lassie's father looks at her the way you did today.'

His flush deepened. 'What d'you mean by that?'

Flora put her hands flat on the table, grunting a little at the pain in her stiff wrists, and looked hard at her elder son, the first-born who had always meant more to her than any of the others.

'Ye know fine what I mean. Stop yer nonsense now, Thomas, before ye make a fool of yerself.'

Their eyes met and locked, then Thomas turned and walked out of the room.

Lachlan, worn out by excitement and unaccustomed exercise, was sound asleep, and didn't stir as Thomas undressed and slipped into bed. Tired though he was himself, he lay awake in the darkness.

'Your mother doesn't like me,' Aileen had said as they drove back to Gourock after dropping Lachlan in Mearns Street. She had moved into the front seat, close enough for him to smell the scent she always wore.

'Of course she does! Who could dislike you? Lachlan thinks you're an angel come down from heaven,' he told her, grinning. They had reached a quiet stretch of road, and he drew the car in to the side and stopped. 'You'll have to get into the back now. You can't let your parents see you sitting beside the chauffeur.'

She put a hand on his arm, preventing him from getting out. 'And what do you think about me?'

'You know what I think,' Thomas said hoarsely, and as though it was the most natural thing to do in the world, she came into his arms, her mouth hungry for his. He kissed her, quickly and softly at first, then hard, with passion. She responded just as passionately, and he crushed her even closer, heat racing through his body.

Ever since that first kiss in the summerhouse they had been meeting when and where they could. At first the excitement of their secret trysts had been enough, but over the past few weeks their feelings had deepened.

Now, as they drew apart, he said, 'I can't bear the thought of you going away for a whole month.'

'Neither can I, but they wouldn't dream of letting me stay behind.' She reached up and traced his eyebrows with the tip of one finger. 'We'll write to each other, every day.'

'Where can we send the letters?' Thomas asked in despair. 'There's nobody we can trust. You'll meet someone, and fall in love and forget about me – and mebbe that'd be for the best.'

'No!' It was a soft, urgent cry, followed by a rain of butterfly-light kisses on his chin and mouth.

'That's what's going to happen sooner or later, Aileen. I don't see your parents letting you marry their chauffeur.'

'There must be some way!'

Thomas doubted it. He had known from the start that nothing could come of their feelings for each other.

'We have to go,' he said reluctantly, opening the car door. 'They'll be wondering where you are.'

After tucking her tenderly into the cool recesses of the back seat, he resumed his place behind the wheel, taking a moment to glance at the river, lazy and mirror-like beneath the blue, sunny sky. Downriver, the surface was gashed by a passing ship on its way up the Clyde to deliver its load in Glasgow, passing a trim, brightly painted passenger steamer taking day trippers round the islands scattered thickly at the mouth of the river. The disturbed water at the wake of both vessels broke into white ruffles that spread slowly, in long rolling waves. Eventually, those waves would break on the banks.

On the far side, dolls'-house-sized dwellings could be seen, the hills rising behind them soft and green and peaceful.

'I love you, Thomas,' Aileen said softly from the rear of the car as he eased it back on to the road. He smiled at her in the mirror.

'I love you too,' he said.

Now, remembering their stolen moments, Thomas tossed restlessly in the dark of the night, wishing with all his heart that he could have turned the wheel just then and taken the car safely over the surface of the river and on to the far shore, then up into the rich, placid green hills beyond, driving forever with Aileen, never to be found by anyone.

In August, Theresa McCabe, James Brodie's typist, was well enough to return to the office, and Elspeth was sent back to the sewing room.

She was apprehensive about her reception, worried in case the other seamstresses would accuse her of being 'posh', or having airs and graces after spending time as an office worker, but thanks to her decision to continue spending her midday breaks with them, and her friendship with Lena, there was no trouble from the others.

The only person who caused her grief was Miss Arnold. 'I hope this won't be beneath your dignity,' she would say scathingly when giving Elspeth work to do, or, 'You'll be sure to let me know if you think this will ruin your hands, won't you? We never know when Mr James might need your invaluable assistance again.'

'Pay no attention,' Lena advised. 'She's jealous because she cannae do anythin' but sew, and she's not all that good at it. Well, she's not,' she protested as the girls huddled round the table greeted this sacrilege with gasps. 'When does she ever do any sewin' herself?'

'She worked on Miss Bruce's trousseau last year,' one of them volunteered.

'Only plain sewin', though. She got where she is by makin' up tae Miss Buchanan. I'll grant ye she's quite good at organisin', but when it comes tae plyin' a needle or usin' a machine we're all better than her. Mebbe we have tae put up with her behaviour, but we don't have tae be frightened by it.'

'Miss Buchanan'll be getting retired in a few years,' someone pointed out. 'Then Miss Arnold'll get her job. You should try tae get Miss Arnold's place when the time comes, Lena.'

'Me? I'll be long away by then. I'll be on the halls, see if I'm not,' Lena said haughtily.

Following her friend's advice, Elspeth swallowed hard when Miss Arnold's tongue lashed at her, and trapped her own tongue between her teeth to hold back the retorts that so swiftly came to mind. Gradually, as the weeks went by, the woman grew tired of baiting her, and life settled back to normal.

Unable to believe what her casual passing glance had revealed, Elspeth spun round, almost bumping into a fat elderly man, and hurried back to the small shop window.

It badly needed cleaning, and the space beyond it was crowded with the richly varied collection to be found in any pawn shop, but the typewriter in the middle of the clutter stood out like a precious stone in a box of costume jewellery, large and black and solid, its great carriage scarcely demeaned by the bracelets and necklaces that had been looped around it.

She put down the bag containing the exercise book she used to list details of letters to be written, and cupped her hands against the glass to cut out the sun's reflection. Peer as she might, she couldn't see a price ticket.

She straightened up and turned to the shop door, then had

to lean against the window instead as her legs suddenly went weak. For a moment she doubted if she had the strength to take the few steps needed to reach the door, but as she stood there, quivering with excitement, the bell jangled as a woman went in. The thought that she might be enquiring about the typewriter, might even buy it, gave Elspeth the energy she needed, and she followed the woman in so closely that she narrowly avoided being hit in the face as the door swung back.

She trembled in the background, relaxing slightly when the woman produced a vase from her shopping bag and began to haggle with the thin, stooped man behind the counter. The two of them argued comfortably for some time while Elspeth shifted from foot to foot and tried to choke back a sneeze as dust tickled at the back of her nose.

At last, client and pawnbroker reached agreement. Money was handed over and the woman hurried out, while the pawnbroker gathered up the vase and carried it off into the back shop, tossing, 'I'll no' keep ye a minute, lass,' over his shoulder.

After a moment, the bell above the street door jangled and a young man came in, brushing past her to duck round the edge of the counter.

'Can I help you?'

'Th-that typewriter in the window – is it for sale?'

'The Underwood? Yes, it is, the man who pawned it didn't come back for it.' He pulled a ledger from beneath the counter and flipped through it. 'Nine shillings.'

Elspeth did a swift sum in her head. 'I could manage three shillings and sixpence just now, and pay the rest up, if that would be all right.'

'Is it for yourself?'

'Yes. I can type,' Elspeth said quickly in her own defence. 'I'm attending night school, but it's not on just now.'

'Have a look at it, while I ask my uncle.' He cleared a space on the narrow counter, then, after a tussle, managed to heave the typewriter out of the window. As he went into the back shop, Elspeth caressed the typewriter keys gently, dizzy with the thought of owning such a machine.

The young man returned and thrust a sheet of paper at her. 'You'll want to try it out,' he said, and watched with interest as she rolled the paper into the carriage, lined it up, and dashed off the first thing that came into her head. Rolling the paper out of the machine, she studied the result.

'The t's not working.'

He came round to her side of the counter to look over her shoulder. '"Wee sleekit cow'ring tim'rous beastie",' he translated, with some difficulty. 'You're a Burns fan?'

'It's a good poem for practising.'

He tested the keys, then announced, 'That one's sticking. I can oil it for you, and dust it.' Then, straightening up as the older man came through from the back shop, 'What d'you think, Uncle George? Can the young lady buy it in instalments?'

'Well—' The pawnbroker scratched at his chin, the rasping of fingernails against beard-stubble loud in the small claustrophobic space.

'It's been sitting in the back shop for long enough,' his nephew urged. 'Not many folk in this town are desperate to buy a typewriter.'

The pawnbroker glared. 'It's a valuable machine.'

'I'd not expect to take it away until the money's all paid up,' Elspeth put in hurriedly.

'And when'll that be?'

'I'll put something towards it every week, and it'll be paid up by the end of the year – earlier, if I can manage it.'

With almost two-thirds of the asking price still to be found, it was a reckless commitment, but she couldn't afford to ask for longer. She might lose the typewriter altogether, and when would another chance come along? She would make every saving she could, and add in the little she got back from Auntie Flora each week.

'How can I be sure ye'll no' lose interest and stop payin'?'

This is a valuable piece of machinery, ye know.'

'If I do stop you can keep what I've paid so far.'

She remembered another barrier to her ownership, and drew a deep breath. 'I've not got the three and sixpence on me, but I'll bring it in tomorrow.' Her whole body was tense with urgency; she felt her mouth trembling, and put a hand up to hide this sign of weakness.

'Come on, Uncle George, it's a fair offer,' the young man urged, and his uncle, after deliberating, nodded creakily, as though the decision he had just come to hurt physically as well as emotionally.

'As long as I get the first payment tomorrow. If I don't, or if ye miss a week, the machine goes right back into the window, mind. Kenneth, I'll hold you responsible.'

Elspeth almost wept with relief. 'I don't know how to thank you!' she said when the pawnbroker had shuffled back through the curtained doorway at the side of the counter.

'For a start, you could give me your handkerchief.'

'My – what?'

He grinned down at her. He had a nice face, round and cheerful. His hair was dark, and his brown eyes crinkled at the corners when he smiled. 'The typewriter needs cleaning – you've smeared dust all over your face.'

'Oh!' Luckily her handkerchief was still spotless and unused. She gave it to him and he wiped her chin and cheek carefully before returning it to her.

'That's better. I'll put it away in the back shop for you, and get it into working order. I'll need your name and address for our books.'

'I'll type it for you,' Elspeth said proudly. 'But you'll have to fill in the t's yourself.'

'Miss Elspeth Bremner,' he read aloud when she had finished, then, holding out his hand, 'Kenneth Monteith.'

'How do you do?' She felt colour rising to her cheeks as they shook hands.

'Are you planning to use the typewriter to start up in business for yourself?'

'Oh no, I'm a seamstress – but I'm going to work in an office one day,' she explained as he raised his eyebrows. 'I write letters for folk, sometimes business letters, so a typewriter of my own would be useful.'

He was about to say something else, but his uncle called on him from behind the curtain. 'Well,' he came round the counter to open the street door for her, 'I'll see you tomorrow, when you make your first payment. Good afternoon, Miss Bremner.'

Her feet skimmed the pavement as she went home. She couldn't believe that at last she was going to have her very own typewriter! She could write letters on it, and maybe papers for Mattie. She was on the threshold of a new life, and the possibilities ahead were endless.

17

There was very little left in her bank account once she'd taken out the deposit for the typewriter, but that couldn't be helped, she thought, hurrying to the pawn shop with the money. She peered in the window as she passed, but the typewriter had gone.

To her relief, Kenneth was behind the counter. 'It's all right, it's in the back shop,' he reassured her as soon as she went in. 'I started working on it today.'

After checking the money and entering the amount into a ledger, he wrote the date and amount on a small card and handed it over. 'This'll help you to keep the payments in order. I've put the full amount at the top,' he explained, then, diffidently, 'I was wondering – there's a good film on at the Central Picture House this week, and I don't like going on my own. Would you care to come with me?'

Elspeth, aware of a sudden warmth in her face, could have wept. Kenneth Monteith would soon begin to think that she was a red-faced clown at this rate. But this was the first time a young man had ever invited her out, apart from the Brodie's messenger boy, and Graham in the office. She hadn't taken either of them seriously, but Kenneth was different. He had been very helpful about the typewriter.

'Yes,' she heard herself say, though she was sure that she hadn't definitely made her mind up. He grinned, showing strong white teeth.

'Tomorrow night? I'll call for you at half past six.'

'I'll meet you outside the Central at quarter to seven,' she said hastily, explaining to Mattie later, in the privacy of their room, that she wasn't at all sure what Aunt Flora would have to say about a gentleman caller.

'She might not let me go at all. It's safer to let her think I'm going out with Lena and the others.' She had been permitted to attend the cinema once or twice with girls from work.

Mattie wrinkled her nose. 'I couldn't be bothered walking out with a young man just now – not when I'm getting ready to go to college.'

'We're not going to start keeping company, it's only a visit to the pictures.' There were times, Elspeth thought, when Mattie had a bit of an opinion about herself. She had left school now, and soon she would leave for Glasgow to start her teacher-training course. In the meantime she had found work during the summer months as a sales assistant in a Gourock dress shop. Since starting the job, a distinct loftiness had crept into her manner.

'He's taking me to the Central Picture House,' Elspeth told her importantly. The Central in West Blackhall Street was one of Greenock's newest and most impressive cinemas.

'D'you like him? I'd need to like someone an awful lot to let them take me to the pictures.'

'He's nice enough, but I'm only going because he's been so kind about the typewriter. Anyway,' Elspeth added honestly, 'I fancy seeing the inside of the Central.'

Fortunately, Kenneth was already waiting outside the picture house when she arrived, so she didn't have to stand around in the open, where one of the girls from the sewing room might have spotted her. To her embarrassment, he insisted on paying for both seats, and buying her a small box of liquorice allsorts.

'You're saving for that typewriter, remember?' he said as they stopped to admire the large fireplace in the foyer, a special feature of the Central.

'I know, but you'll not earn much in that wee shop.'

'I'm fine, don't worry about me. I don't work for Uncle George all the time, just in the holidays,' he said casually as they headed towards the auditorium. 'I'm going back to Glasgow in October to start my second year at the university. I'm hoping to be a doctor.'

They were going up some stairs, and Elspeth tripped over her feet and almost fell flat on her face. Wait till Mattie heard about that, she thought gleefully when she had recovered. And Aunt Flora. To think that she, Elspeth from the sewing room, was going out with a university student – and a future doctor!

She had scarcely recovered from that shock when they entered the auditorium. For a moment, she stood still, looking around. It was magnificent, with its chandeliers and decorative ceiling and plush tip-up seats and uniformed attendants. They took their seats just in time, and as the film flickered on to the screen, Elspeth, glancing round the dark auditorium, saw that some of the young men had their arms about their girls' shoulders.

She sat primly upright, wondering what she should do if Kenneth put his arm about her. He had bought her ticket, and given her sweets, so it would surely be rude to push him away. On the other hand, she wasn't certain that she wanted to be hugged. Fortunately, she didn't have to make the decision, for Kenneth was too engrossed in the film to make any overtures.

Glancing sideways at him, she decided that she liked his profile. His nose was straight and not too long, and he had quite a nice-shaped chin. She offered him a sweet, but he was so engrossed in the cowboys and Indians racing across the screen that he didn't notice, and finally she had to tap him on the elbow, making him jump.

'Liquorice allsort?'

'Oh – thanks.' He fumbled in the box, found a sweet, and turned back to the screen.

Elspeth relaxed into the soft plush seat and began to concentrate on the film herself. She became so involved in it that towards the end, when a fearsome Red Indian warrior, tomahawk in hand, suddenly hurtled down from a tree and on to the hero's back, she yelped and jumped. To her horror, the sweets still left in the box she held shot out of it and all over the floor, rattling against the seats in front. A few heads turned, and there was a low ripple of amusement.

'Oh!' She tried to duck down so that she could scoop up some of the sweets, which were rolling around the carpeted floor, but Kenneth's hand came out of nowhere to stop her.

'Just leave them.' He didn't take his hand away again; it felt warm and comfortable and not in the least threatening. Under its touch, she relaxed again, and they sat companionably together for the rest of the film. When it ended with the hero-ine running into the hero's arms and resting her trusting head on his manly shoulder, it felt quite nice to be holding – or being held by – a man's hand. Elspeth felt a sisterly bond between herself and the heroine, who now had THE END running across the face lifted for the hero's kiss.

But when the lights went up again she was brought back to the present with a bump. 'Oh, look—' She stared in dismay at the sweets dotted about their feet, then squeezed down into the narrow space between the rows of seats and started gathering them up.

'Don't bother,' Kenneth said above her head. 'We can't eat them now.'

'I can't leave the place looking like this!'

'They've got folk who come in and clean it.'

'But they'll think I'm an awful slitter, leaving such a mess!'

'They won't know who did it.' He drew her to her feet. 'Mind you, we'd better get out quickly, before they come in and catch us at the scene of the crime.'

Her face was burning. 'You're laughing at me!'

'Mebbe just a wee bit. But I like your sense of what's right.' He glanced beyond her, and added, 'We'd better go, there's folk wanting out.'

Turning, she saw that there were indeed some people waiting patiently for her to get out of their way. Scarlet now with embarrassment, she snatched up her coat and moved on, feeling a liquorice allsort squash beneath her foot as she went.

'It was a terrible waste of good sweeties, after you spending your money on them,' she lamented as they stepped out on to the street.

'We'd eaten most of them anyway.' He took her arm and steered her round two drunken men who were staggering along the middle of the pavement. Again, he maintained the contact.

It was dusk when they reached Mearns Street. Elspeth wondered if he expected to be invited up to the flat, but he stopped at the close-mouth, touching her pebble brooch lightly with the tip of a finger. 'I like your brooch.'

'It was a birthday present from my brother Thomas, during the war. We used to collect pebbles together by the river, and he bought this to remind me about that.'

'I like the river. Mebbe we could take a walk down there some night?' Kenneth looked down the hill to where the Clyde could be glimpsed between tenements. The lamplighter came into sight, using his long pole to open the gas lamps. Just a touch of the pole against the wicks within turned them into soft golden globes of light.

'This is a lovely time of the evening,' Kenneth said quietly, looking down at her. 'Your eyes are like very deep, dark pools in this light.'

'Are they?' Nobody had ever talked to her like that before; she hoped that he couldn't see the colour warming her face.

'In daylight, they're so blue. You've got beautiful eyes,' he said, then, 'Before the lamplighter gets this far—'

With an unexpected movement he whisked her up the step and into the dim close. A hand beneath her chin tipped her face to his and he kissed her, his lips first brushing hers, then claiming them, just like the couple on the cinema screen.

'Goodnight, Elspeth,' he said a few moments later. 'Mebbe

we could go out for a walk tomorrow evening?'

'I'll look into the shop on my way home,' she promised, then she was alone, breathless with happiness at the realisation that in spite of the liquorice allsorts, he wanted to see her again. She leaned against the close wall, her mouth soft and a great sense of wellbeing flooding through her, and smiled dreamily at the opposite wall until the lamplighter suddenly invaded the close.

'Aye, lassie,' he said heartily, brushing past her on his way to the lamp at the foot of the stairs. 'A grand night for it, eh?'

'For what?' she asked, still dazed.

Soft gas light filled the close. The lighter, an elderly man, turned and winked at her.

'For bein' alive,' he said, and went on his way, while Elspeth fled upstairs, her mouth still tasting Kenneth's lips, her nostrils filled with the fresh soapy smell of him.

Kenneth was returning soon to Glasgow, but he and Elspeth made the most of the time that was left, seeing each other every day. Because he couldn't afford the cinema or the theatre often, they walked along by the river, or over the hills at the back of the town, sometimes talking, sometimes silently enjoying being together.

Like Elspeth, Kenneth was ambitious. He didn't find her yearning to work in an office at all strange, and with him, she felt that she could be herself, saying whatever she wanted without being laughed at, or accused of trying to get above herself.

He took her to his home in Gourock for tea, and his parents made her welcome. She plucked up the courage to invite him to Mearns Street, where, to her delight, he fitted in well. They all liked him, even Flora, once she had recovered from the shock of realising that Elspeth was walking out with a young man who was clever enough to become a doctor.

He and Granjan took to each other at once, and even

Grandmother approved. 'A civil young man,' she told Elspeth in the kitchen when she took Kenneth with her on her monthly visit. Then, delivering the highest accolade, 'Your grandfather would have been pleased.'

The best part of it was that Kenneth understood about Lachlan. He knew about shell shock, and admired the way Thomas was working to rebuild his brother's confidence.

'It'll take time,' he told Elspeth, 'just as it would if he had broken his leg badly. The hard thing is that in Lachlan's case the damage doesn't show, so folk don't know how to deal with it.'

Lachlan continued to improve. The drawings of Thomas being hurt and killed were a thing of the past; now he sketched the views from the windows, covering page after page with drawings of cranes and ships in construction, and the water and hills beyond. The nightmares that had plagued him, and the entire family, night after night were easing. He nerved himself to go out more, especially down to the shore, where he could sit for hours on end looking at the water.

'The river's not afraid of anything,' he explained to Elspeth. 'It just goes its own way, and it takes its own time, and it always gets where it wants to be. The river knows what's best for it.'

A week before Kenneth was due to leave, he and Elspeth went on an afternoon picnic with Mattie, Thomas and Lachlan. Because the shore at Greenock was lined with ship-yards, they took a short bus ride along the coastline to Largs, a handsome residential town popular with holiday-makers. It was the first time Lachlan had been in a bus since the war; sitting behind him, Elspeth saw his thin shoulders tense with the effort of keeping his nerves under control as the vehicle rattled along. Kenneth, beside her, leaned forward.

'Look at the water, Lachlan,' she heard him say. 'Just keep watching it and we'll soon be there.'

Lachlan's fair head immediately craned to the right, and the tension eased from his back. When they descended at Largs Pier, his eyes were bright with triumph at having broken through another barrier.

They found a sheltered pebble beach beyond the town, with rocks scattered here and there, useful as seats or back-rests. The long, low green shape of the Greater Cumbrae, one of the Clyde islands, lay across the water. Its small town, Millport, was also popular with holiday-makers and day-trippers, and passenger steamers were to be seen regularly plying between the island and Largs.

They paddled in the cold clear water, then ate the sandwiches and ginger beer they had brought with them. Afterwards, Mattie wandered off along the beach in search of shells and Lachlan perched on a rock, his eyes on the river. Thomas tossed pebbles into the water while Kenneth propped his back comfortably against a rock and opened a book he had brought with him.

Elspeth waded into the river again, braving the agony of walking without shoes over the pebbles, gasping as the water enfolded her feet in its cold grip. Her long brown plait swung over her shoulder, the golden hairs glinting in the sunlight. She found a half-submerged rock and leaned against it, watching her bare toes shimmering beneath the surface, then looking up as a passenger steamer passed quite close, tiny arms waving from the crowded rails. A gust of wind almost dislodged her straw hat; she pinned it down with one hand and waved back with the other, then as a slightly larger wavelet broke against her calves, she kilted her skirt higher and made her way back to the beach.

'I've been thinking,' Kenneth said lazily, watching her drying her feet, which were as scarlet as lobsters from the water. 'Why should that typewriter be sitting in the back shop, when you could be using it?'

'But I've not finished paying for it yet.' She handed back the clean handkerchief he had loaned her. Thomas flipped a round, flat pebble into the water and it bounced twice before disappearing beneath the surface.

'I know, but I've got work to do for the beginning of the university year. You could type it out for me if you had the machine – I'd pay you for it.'

'I couldn't take your money!'

'Of course you can,' Thomas said shortly. 'The very best money is the money you can get out of other folk's pockets and into your own. Or so I'm told.'

Kenneth looked puzzled, and Thomas grinned back at him, cold-eyed.

'What I mean is, Kenneth, we all need money, don't we?'

'That's what life's about.'

'I thought your life was going to be about making sick folk well,' Thomas said at once, and Kenneth flushed.

'It is, but I'll have to get paid for it. How else can I live?'

'There's your answer, Ellie.' Thomas sent another pebble into the air with a flick of the thumb. This time it bounced four times, and was quite far out before it sank. 'Folk need money to live, and you've as much right to live as anyone.'

'You earn a wage yourself,' Kenneth's voice was defensive, and Thomas laughed.

'Aye, but I'm only paid enough to enable me to exist.' He started to prise a large stone out of the ground. 'While the man that employs me lives very comfortably because he has a lot more money than me.'

The stone came free, and he held it up, gesturing around the beach with his other hand. 'Suppose this big stone's that man, and the rock our Lachie's sitting on's a man with even more wealth. But when you look all around, what d'ye see?'

His free hand dropped, to indicate the beach around them. 'Wee pebbles, all over the place. These pebbles are us, and all the folk like us. They're necessary, because without them there's no beach, but most folk don't realise that. Most folk think the pebbles don't matter, 'cos there's so many of them, and they're only wee.'

He scooped a handful of pebbles up and tossed them towards the water. They hit the surface with a series of soft plops. Then he hurled the stone viciously after them. It crashed into the river noisily, throwing up spray.

'Pebbles don't make enough noise tae be noticed, but the big stones do, because they're important – important enough to throw their weight around,' said Thomas, then scrambled to his feet, rubbing moisture from his hands.

'So take the lad's money, Ellie. Take all the money you can get. The more you earn, the bigger the pebble you'll be – and the more folk'll take notice of you, and see you as a person,' he said, then strode off along the beach, leaving them to gape after his retreating back.

'What's bothering him?' Kenneth asked, his voice subdued.

'I don't know. He's been like this for weeks. It's not like Thomas at all,' Elspeth fretted.

Kenneth shrugged. 'Whatever it is, it's not our worry. What I was saying is, I've been working in the pawn shop to earn money to help me through university. And it would help me if you'd type some of the papers for me.'

'What would your uncle say?'

'I've spoken to him about it, and he agrees. He's a businessman – he realises that if I pay you to do work for me, you can pay him what you owe on the typewriter sooner than you expected. And that suits him.'

18

Kenneth brought the typewriter to Mearns Street the next evening, trundling it through the streets on a handcart, then carrying it up the stairs to arrive, red-faced and breathless, at the McDonalds' door.

They all crowded into the small bedroom to watch as the typewriter was settled carefully on to a sturdy little table that he had brought from the pawn shop.

'A present from the management,' he explained casually.

Elspeth, shaking with excitement, settled herself on the side of the bed, because there was no room for a chair, and sent her fingers flying deftly across the keys. Listening to their admiring exclamations as she explained the workings of the machine, she glowed. Perhaps she wasn't going to be a teacher, like Mattie, or a doctor, like Kenneth, but this was something that she, and nobody else in the room, could do. She felt important, and gifted.

Kenneth, hunkered down on his heels by the table, his elbows on its edge, caught her eye, and gave her a warm, conspiratorial smile. She beamed back at him, remembering that she owed it all to him. If he hadn't coaxed his uncle to trust her, she might not have got the typewriter, her most precious possession.

Flora had wanted her younger daughter to continue living at home while studying at teacher-training college, travelling by train to Glasgow each morning and returning in the evenings.

But Mattie, suddenly ready to spread her wings, had argued that this was quite impossible; as well as being costly, it would give her little time to study.

To her relief her mother finally gave in. The headmistress of the school Mattie and Elspeth had attended was consulted, letters – typed by Elspeth – were sent out and replies received, and Flora and Mattie spent a nerve-racking day in the city, inspecting a recommended hostel for young women. When they arrived home, Flora flustered and Mattie giddy with excitement, it had all been arranged.

On Mattie's final evening at home, neighbours and friends flocked to the flat to wish the fledgling teacher well. Even Bob, who didn't often visit now, came with Rachel, who wore the dress that had been made for her wedding. It would soon have to be put aside, Elspeth thought, noticing how the skirt, which had hung so neatly back in May, was now tight over the girl's swelling pregnancy.

'Have you noticed the bold Bob?' Thomas murmured to her during the evening. 'That's never ginger he's drinking.'

'Of course it is. Bob's temperance.'

'I'm not so sure.'

It was true that Bob had changed. He was restless, and louder than usual, and she noticed that he had developed a habit of passing a hand over his lips, as though they were parched, although he had a glass in his hand every time Elspeth saw him.

She didn't have time to wonder at Thomas's words, because just then Kenneth, who was also leaving for Glasgow the following day, sought her out.

'It's too crowded in here, I'm going out for a breath of fresh air. Come with me.'

'You'll look out for Mattie, won't you?' she asked as they went through the close to the back yard. 'She'll mebbe feel lost in such a big city on her own.'

'I'm going to be busy, but I'll do what I can. Elspeth, Uncle

George was wondering if you'd look in at the shop tomorrow to have a word with him. I've told him that you might be willing to look after his books.'

'Me?'

'You've been taking book-keeping at night school, haven't you? It'd be good for you get some practice at it.' He put an arm about her. 'You're shivering. Here—' He drew her to where the wash house used by all the women in the tenement bulked against the tenement wall. The door was never locked; the interior smelled of bleach and soda, soap and wet clothes, but at least they were out of the chill night wind.

Kenneth was a silhouette against the small window, his breath warm on her cheek. 'I've done what I can with his books during the summer, but he needs someone to see to things properly. And he'll pay you fairly, I've seen to that too. Will you do it?'

'I'll have a word with him about it.'

'Good,' he said, then he kissed her, and suddenly she felt quite tearful at the thought of being without him. She clung to him in the soap-smelling gloom. 'I'm going to miss you!'

'I'll be home for the New Year.'

'But that's months away yet!'

Kenneth kissed her again, and she returned the kiss with passion, running her fingers through his hair and over the nape of his neck. She knew that he liked that.

'Oh – Elspeth!' he whispered, nuzzling at her neck then her shoulder, his mouth hot through the barricade of her woollen jumper.

Whether it was because of the darkness, or the small space they were enclosed in together, or because his kisses were more passionate than usual, she couldn't tell; she only knew that her stomach was churning, her knees so weak that she was grateful for the support of the big brick boiler against her back. She had heard from Lena and the other girls in the sewing room about love and passion, and had seen it on the cinema screen, but nothing had prepared her for such a sense of elation. She wanted to blend right into Kenneth, to be part of him and for him to be part of her . . .

For a long moment it was wonderful, then the sudden waft of cold air against her stomach when he began to unfasten her blouse brought her back to earth. His hands were sliding over her bare shoulders, his fingers slipping under her bodice to touch her breasts, his body shuddering against her. A strange, pleasant thrill was running through her own body, but at the same time a tingle of doubt flared in her mind.

'Kenneth—'

He didn't hear her, and she had to struggle inelegantly to push his hands down to the comparative respectability of her skirt waistband.

'What is it?' He sounded strange, as if he had just wakened from a sound sleep. 'Oh, Elspeth, please!'

Please, her aroused body begged along with him, but her brain, which had started to function again, said otherwise. Mind and body, longing and common sense – it was like being in a whirlpool. She wanted whatever was happening between herself and Kenneth to go on, but at the same time she knew that it was wrong.

'We'd better not,' she said, squirming away from him, pulling the edges of her blouse together, pushing buttons through buttonholes with nervous haste.

'But I'm going away – can we not just love each other a wee bit so that we've got something to remember?'

'Not like this.' Now that the heat was slowly draining from her, she knew that this wasn't the way she had imagined it would be. Not in the wash house, with the smell of soda and harsh yellow soap.

'Come on, Elspeth—' As he reached for her, light from the small window glinted off the whites of his eyes, and she suddenly realised that in the dark, he could be anybody. For all she knew, Kenneth might have been spirited away somehow, and his place taken by someone – or something – else. Memories flooded back of the man who had dragged her into the shop doorway during the street celebrations at the end of the war.

'Leave me be!' Spurred on by her over-strong imagination, she squirmed away from him, pushing at him frantically, then ran to the door. Her sense of direction had gone, and she panicked when her outstretched hands came up against the brick wall instead of the rough wooden door. She fumbled to her right, found planks beneath her fingers, and burst out of the wash house into the chill darkness.

'Elspeth!' Kenneth caught at her arm and turned her round. And there he was, clearly seen in the light spilling through a ground-floor window; Kenneth, her Kenneth, with his hair tousled and his round face perplexed.

She fell against him, half laughing. 'Kenneth, it's you!'

'Of course it's me, who else could it be? What's wrong with you?'

She sucked in a deep breath, smoothing his jacket with her hands. 'I'm sorry, Kenneth, I just – I had to get out into the fresh air.'

He said nothing, but moved back slightly, so that her hands dropped away from him.

'I have to go, I told my parents I'd not be late home.'

'Kenneth, don't be angry with me—' she began, then jumped away from him, startled, as Thomas spoke from the darkness of the close.

'Elspeth, it's time you were back in the house.'

'I'm just going.' Kenneth brushed past him without another glance at Elspeth.

'What was going on?' Thomas asked as Kenneth's footsteps disappeared along the close.

'Nothing was going on! What did you have to go creeping about like that for?'

'I saw you from the landing window, bursting out of the washhouse. What were the two of you up to?'

'Doing the washing, what d'you think?' She flung the words at him, pushing past him to reach the stairs. He had ruined everything. Because of him, Kenneth had gone, without giving her a chance to explain. She was so angry that she could have hit him.

He caught up with her on the first landing, stopping her and spinning her towards him with his hands on her shoulders. 'Ellie, you're still only a bairn.'

'I'm old enough to look out for myself!'

'You're not. No harm to Kenneth, he's a decent lad, but he's older than you, and he knows more about the world. Don't try to grow up too soon, Ellie,' he said, 'There are bad things as well as good things in it, and once you've taken the final step you can't change your mind and go back to being a bairn.'

'Leave me be!' She pulled free and ran up the stairs, away from him.

In bed later, Mattie clung to her, her tears on Elspeth's neck just where Kenneth's mouth had been, and just as hot. 'What if I don't like it, Ellie? What if I'm a dunce after all, and nobody wants to be my friend, and I'm all alone?'

'You'll be fine. You're clever, and of course folk'll like you. If you get too homesick, we're only a train ride away. You'll be fine,' Elspeth said again. 'Anyway, what about me, left here while you and Kenneth are in Glasgow? I'm going to be lonely without you.'

'But you've got Mam and Dad and Lachlan and Thomas.' Mattie sniffed. 'I'll not have anyone I know!'

By the time Mattie was soothed into sleep, Elspeth was wide awake, her mind filled with the scene in the washhouse. In the safety of her bed, her body tormented by the memory of Kenneth's touch, she wished that she hadn't pushed him away. She moaned softly as she recollected how his fingertips had brushed against her breasts. Would he forgive her for the way she had treated him?

Then she imagined herself having to tell Aunt Flora that a

bairn was on the way. The very thought of such a scene cooled and calmed her burning, restless body. Maybe she had done the right thing after all. Maybe one day she would be glad that she had done the right thing, hard though it had been.

With that thought held firmly in her mind, she fell asleep at last.

George Monteith was standing behind the counter when Elspeth went into the pawn shop after work the following evening. His presence more than anything else brought it home to her that Kenneth was far away in Glasgow now, and for a moment she knew a great sense of loss.

The pawnbroker invited her upstairs to his kitchen, a room furnished with a fireplace, gas cooker, table, chairs and sideboard, but with shelves holding a wide variety of items, all sporting pawn tickets, lining the walls. He laid the books before her on the kitchen table, together with an old tin biscuit box adorned on the lid with a splotched and faded picture of a basketful of kittens, and crammed with pawn tickets and scraps of paper. Each time the bell jangled in the shop below he scurried off, leaving her to find her way through the maze of paperwork.

Elspeth was appalled at the size of the task she had been asked to take on. George Monteith's idea of financial dealings was to scribble all his transactions down on scraps of paper and toss them into the biscuit box. His ledger was shamefully bare and neglected, with nothing balancing.

At first, she was inclined to make some excuse and get out of the place as quickly as she could, but on the other hand, the challenge interested her, and she had some idea in her head that by helping his uncle, she could make up for her childish behaviour towards Kenneth the night before. By the time she returned home, she and the pawnbroker had come to an agreement.

Flora was horrified when she heard that Elspeth was to do

Mr Monteith's books. 'I don't care if he is Kenneth's uncle, he's still a pawnbroker,' she said in outrage, 'and I'll not have you standing behind the counter of that pawn shop. As tae what your grandmother'd have to say if she heard – I've no wish tae have her round here again, makin' more accusations against me!'

'Aunt Flora, it's not going to be like that at all. I'll call in at the shop every Friday evening to collect the books, then bring them back here and work on them over the weekend. I'll hand them back in on Monday morning on my way to work. There's no shame in it,' Elspeth coaxed, horrified at the prospect of having to admit to Mr Monteith that her aunt had forbidden her to do his books. That was no way for a book-keeper to behave!

'Well, ye can give it a try,' Flora said at last, grudgingly. 'But if anyone talks about seein' you goin' intae a pawn shop, it stops at once, d'ye hear me? I've no wish to have folks thinkin' we're havin' tae pawn things in order tae eat.'

From then on, Elspeth was so busy with the task of organising Mr Monteith's books at the weekends and letter-writing in the evenings that she had very little time to miss Kenneth.

She wrote to him, apologising for her behaviour on his last evening at home. His reply was somewhat cool, but she kept writing, and gradually his own letters, never very frequent or very long, took on more warmth, and she felt that she had been forgiven.

Thanks to her work for Mr Monteith, the typewriter was fully paid for by October, and each morning when she woke and saw it sitting by the bed, she glowed with the pride of full ownership. Her bank account, sorely depleted by the money she had had to pay for the typewriter, began to flourish once more.

By the time Mr and Mrs Bruce and their daughter returned from their holiday in the south of France, Thomas, who had tormented himself during their absence with thoughts of

Aileen laughing and talking and dancing with other men, had resigned himself to the fact that he had lost her.

When she came home, he told himself during sleepless nights, he would learn that she had been promised to some handsome, confident, wealthy man. After all, that was what her parents wanted and expected. That was what she had been born to, and the sooner he accepted the truth the better. At least, he tried to tell himself, he had known more happiness with her than he had ever dreamed of. He would always have that to remember. But such thoughts were cold comfort. Aileen was the woman he wanted, and there could never be anyone else.

Ian Bruce, who had returned to Scotland before his parents and sister because of business commitments, went with Thomas to collect them from the station, travelling in state in the back of the car because it wouldn't have occurred to him to sit beside the chauffeur.

When the train came in, Thomas went directly to the guard's van to collect the luggage. By the time he emerged from the station with a porter and began packing the cases into the trunk the family were seated.

After making arrangements to have the rest of the luggage brought to the house in a hired cab, together with the valet and lady's maid who had accompanied their master and mistress on holiday, he took his place behind the wheel and drove from the station, his ears straining to catch Aileen's voice. Every laugh, every word she spoke, squeezed at his heart. Opening the car door at the house, he stared stiffly ahead like a sentry on duty, then glanced at her, startled, as she paused and said, 'Hello, Thomas.'

'Welcome home, Miss Aileen.' He tore his eyes away from her almost at once, afraid of staring, almost choking with anger as he heard her brother say clearly as he accompanied her up the steps to the front door, 'If you must chat with a servant, Aileen, at least use his surname.'

Although he had glanced at her only briefly, the image of her, cool and slender in a lemon jacket and skirt that emphasised her perfect golden tan burned in his mind's eye for the rest of that day and all through the night. He woke up the next morning with it strong and clear in his brain.

She came into the garage that morning when he was polishing the car, touching his shoulder lightly and making him jump.

'Miss Aileen—' One glance over her shoulder showed that she was alone, and he added, low-voiced, 'You're not supposed to be in here—'

She was dressed for riding, in a green shirt that emphasised the colour of her eyes. 'I had to see you.' The words sent a jolt of astonished joy through his entire body. 'I've missed you so much, Thomas. I wrote every night, then tore up the letters because I had no way of sending them to you.'

He swallowed hard, scarcely able to believe her. He had worked so hard at convincing himself that her feelings for him would have died by now. 'I – I thought you'd have found someone else.'

'How could you think that?' Her eyes caressed his face. 'How could you doubt me?'

'I – you must have met so many men while you were away.'

'I did, but I wasn't interested in them. I don't want anyone else, surely you know that by now? Oh, Thomas—'

She reached up to touch his cheek, her fingers sending the blood racing round in his veins. He wanted to pull her into his arms and hold her and never let her go; instead, he put his own hand up to cover hers, trapping it against his face for a few joyous seconds before lifting it away.

'You must go. What if someone comes in?'

'Where are you going to be later?'

'I'm taking your father to Glasgow. We'll not be back till late afternoon.'

'Tonight, then.'

'There's a dinner party tonight.'

'After dinner. I'll pretend to have a headache and meet you in the summerhouse.'

Someone walked past the slightly open garage door. 'You must go,' Thomas said again, in a panic.

'Nine o'clock,' she whispered, and left, not bothering to peer out first to see if the coast was clear, but leaving confidently, as befitted someone who had legitimate reasons for going into her own father's garage.

A few minutes later, Thomas, weak with relief at the knowledge that she still cared, heard her horse's hooves clattering on the cobbles outside. Hungering for another sight of her, he left the car and moved to the door to see her go by, straight-backed as ever, her small hands confident on the reins. He watched until she had ridden round the corner of the house and out of sight, then, about to turn back into the garage's gloom, he saw Ina standing by the kitchen door opposite, a basket of washing on its way to the drying green balanced on one hip.

He had put a stop to his meetings with Ina after he first kissed Aileen in the summerhouse, suddenly unable to bear the housemaid's kisses and caresses. It hadn't been easy, for since Rachel's wedding the girl had become very possessive, constantly urging him to agree to marriage, and Thomas couldn't explain to her why he no longer wanted to walk out with her. Finally, he had precipitated a quarrel over nothing, and told her that they were finished. Ina had taken it badly, and hadn't spoken to him since.

Now, she gave him a long, bold, cold look, then her eyes narrowed and she swung away with a toss of the head.

Thomas returned to his work, his joy over the meeting with Aileen suddenly tempered with apprehension. There had been something about Ina's calculating, knowing look that chilled him to the bone.

19

Although Elspeth missed Mattie, having the bedroom to herself meant that she could type without disturbing anyone. Lachlan took to coming in to watch her at work and to marvel at her skill. He was still quiet and withdrawn, but much more independent than he had been since coming home from the army. His father had hoped to get him back to his old job, but the continual noise in the shipyards still panicked him.

When, in the middle of September, Elspeth heard that there was a vacancy for someone in the packing office at Brodie's, she suggested it to Lachlan.

'It's not much, just packing up things that customers have ordered, ready for the carters. But it'd be a start. What d'you think?'

Lachlan, sitting on her bed, plucked nervously at the corner of the quilt, thinking for a while.

'I cannae go on like this all my life, can I?'

'It would be good for you to get out and about again. There's not many in the packing room, and I'd be near to hand. We could go to work together, and walk home together too.'

He looked up at her, fear in his eyes, but determination in the set of his mouth.

'I'll try.'

As luck would have it, Miss Arnold was off with toothache the next day, and Miss Buchanan busy with a client, so Elspeth was able to slip out of the sewing room and go to the office, where Theresa McCabe rattled efficiently at the type-writer and Wilma and Graham worked at the big desk.

Wilma raised her brows when Elspeth asked if Mr James was free. 'What d'you want to see him about?'

'I'll tell him that.'

Wilma gave an offended sniff, but got down from her stool and tapped on the office door, closing it behind her when Mr James called to her to go in. She returned in a few minutes and said sulkily, 'He'll see you.'

James Brodie's greeting was more welcoming. He shook Elspeth's hand, and waved her to a chair before asking, 'What can I do for you?'

She told him about Lachlan's shell shock and how he couldn't return to the shipyard because of the noise and the bustle of the place. Then, twisting her fingers nervously in her lap, she ventured, 'I've heard there's a position free in the packing department. I think he could do that.'

'Do you? And what does he think?'

'He'd like to try for it. He needs to do something, Mr James, before it's too late,' she added, trying hard not to beg.

He pursed his lips for a moment, then to her great relief he said, 'Bring him with you tomorrow morning and I'll have a word with him.'

She fretted half the night in case Lachlan's nerve failed him at the last moment, but the following morning, pale and tense, dressed in his best, he walked with her into the store. She took him to the office but then had to go to the sewing room. It wasn't until after work, when she got home, that she found out that he had been given a month's trial.

After all they had been through with Lachlan, it was as if he had gained a place at Glasgow University. Flora and Henry could scarcely conceal their elation, and Thomas, who had finally emerged from the moodiness that had dogged him for a full month and reverted to his usual cheerful self, slapped his brother on the back and insisted on taking him out for a drink.

When they returned, he tapped on Elspeth's door.

'You did well.'

She twisted round from the typewriter to look up at him. 'D'you think he'll be all right?'

'I don't know – it's up to him now. But at least you've got him this far,' he said, then let her get back to her typing.

As well as the letters she was commissioned to write, Mattie and Kenneth were correspondents now, just as Thomas and Lachlan had been during the war. Mattie's letters were long and enthusiastic; she was settling in well at college and in the hostel, making friends and enjoying her studies. Kenneth's letters were usually brief reports on the subjects he had studied that week.

To his family's relief, Lachlan settled into the packing department quite well. At first, going to work was a daily trial, but having made the initial effort, he refused to let himself give in and stay at home.

'If I give up now, I'll not go back,' he told Elspeth tersely one morning when he looked so strained that she tried to persuade him to stay at home. As the days grew into weeks she saw the tension easing from his mouth and eyes, and knew that he had broken through yet another barrier.

Night classes had started again, and thanks to her own typewriter and her work with Mr Monteith's books, her typing and book-keeping abilities had improved. She was even allowed, in the typewriting class, to take over the beginners now and then while the harassed teacher dealt with the more advanced pupils.

'You're good at helping them to understand,' the woman commented one evening. 'Have you thought of teaching typewriting yourself, once you get your diploma?'

'Oh, no.' Elspeth was taken aback by the very idea, but the teacher was serious. 'I think you should. You have the right approach.'

Elspeth almost danced her way home that night. She was still set on working in an office, but if nothing came of that, there was now teaching to consider. Gradually, her ambitions were coming closer to being realised.

In October, a few weeks after Elspeth's sixteenth birthday, Thomas came home, grim-faced, and told his parents that he had lost his job.

'You can't have!' Flora's lips were suddenly ashen, and one hand clutched at her chest. Because her own father had been unable to support his wife and child due to poor health, Flora, who had had a harsh childhood despite all her mother's efforts to be the breadwinner, had grown up with a terror of unemployment. 'What did ye do wrong?'

'I did nothing wrong. There was a difference of opinion between me and Mr Ian. He's an arrogant bastard, that one,' Thomas added bitterly.

'What d'ye mean, a difference of opinion? What was it about?'

'Nothing that concerns you, Mam.'

Flora gave an animal-like whimper. 'For God's sake, man, ye lose yer job and say it's none of our concern? D'ye know how many men are bein' turned off these days?' Her voice began to rise. 'D'ye know how hard it is tae find work?'

'I'll manage.' Thomas, Elspeth saw with concern, looked grey and ill. 'I'll find another place.'

'How d'ye expect tae find another position just like that when ye werenae able tae stay in the one ye already had?' Flora almost shouted at him. 'Are ye goin' tae get a good reference from Mr Bruce?'

Thomas looked away from her searching glance. He was her favourite, and there was little he could hide from her.

'Well – are ye?'

'No.'

'No – and how can ye, if ye quarrelled with his son! Can ye no' keep yer tongue quiet when ye're around yer betters, ye daft fool?'

Thomas was stung into rounding on her. 'A man like Ian Bruce isn't my better!'

'Is he no'? Whatever sort of man he is, he's got money, and what d'you have, tell me that? Not even a job!'

'Don't get yerself all upset, Flora.' Henry put a hand on her arm. 'The laddie's got a good head on his shoulders, he'll find somethin' else.'

'Ye think so?' Flora shrugged his hand from her arm and whirled back to Thomas.

'It's her fault, isn't it? That lassie ye brought home with ye – Bruce's daughter?'

His eyes blazed at her. 'Leave it, Mam – I'm going out.' He turned to the door, but before he could open it Flora was on him, clutching at his jacket, hauling him round to face her. 'Don't you walk away from me! It was her, wasn't it?'

'Who?' Henry asked, bemused.

'That Bruce girl – that lassie he brought here tae my house!' She flailed at Thomas with her fists, forcing him to duck and wrap his arms about his head in self-protection.

Elspeth and Lachlan and Henry watched open-mouthed, too stunned by the suddenness of the attack to intervene. They had never seen Flora in such a state before; her face was crimson, her eyes wild, her hair escaping from its pins. Her voice was a harridan's shriek, the words pouring from it as she belaboured her son.

'Dirty, filthy midden that ye are, runnin' after yer master's daughter,' she screeched. 'An' she's no better, flauntin' herself before decent folk! I saw the way ye looked at her that day! I told ye, didn't I? I told ye she'd bring harm on ye!'

'That's enough, Mam!' Thomas had been forced back against the door; now he straightened up, suffering the blows, grappling with her until he managed to catch her wrists. His own face was distorted with rage. 'I'll not have ye foul-mouthin' her!'

Henry, coming to his senses, caught his wife round the waist and dragged her away from Thomas. 'For God's sake, woman, d'ye want the neighbours tae call the polis? Leave the laddie be!'

'Look at the guilt in his face. Ask him if I'm no' right,' Flora panted. 'It was her that cost him his place – let him try tae deny it!'

'I'm not denying it,' Thomas said steadily. 'I love her – and she loves me.'

'Oh aye – it's love that made her stand by and let ye lose yer place, is it?'

'She knows nothing yet about what's happened,' Thomas flared back at his mother. 'She's away for a few days. It was Ina – she found out and told Mr Ian, and he went to his father.'

'Godsake's, man,' Henry groaned. 'Have ye no sense at all? You and Mr Bruce's daughter – how could ye think there was any future in that?'

'I knew there was no future to it, Da, but I cannae help my feelin's—'

'Can ye no'?' Flora stormed. 'Look at the shame yer precious feelin's've brought on us, ye—' Henry's grip on her had relaxed, and all at once she lunged forward, one arm lifting above her head, then swinging down to deliver a hefty open-handed slap across Thomas's cheek. The sharp crack of it rang through the room, then Flora, her rage spent, slumped back against her husband, sobbing, while Thomas put a hand to his reddening cheek. He stared in disbelief at his mother, then turned to the door.

'Come back here, Thomas, and let's get this business sorted out,' his father said.

'I'll come back when I get work, and not before. I'll not be a burden on anyone.' Thomas flung the words over his shoulder, just before the door closed behind him. A moment later, the outer door slammed.

Flora's knees gave way and she would have slid to the floor if Henry hadn't caught her and bundled her into a chair. 'What's goin' tae become of him now?' she whimpered, raising a face that was wet with tears, and aflame with angry red blotches now, as though she herself had been hit repeatedly.

'He'll survive, the way we all have tae.' Henry's voice was old and bleak. 'Ellie, ye'd best make yer auntie a cup of tea.'

Turning in a daze to do as she was told, she saw Lachlan standing in one corner, stooped over as though in pain. Elspeth's heart seemed to drop down through her ribs; this was the way Lachlan had been just after the war, before Thomas started dragging him out of his trauma.

Henry had noticed him too. 'Come on, son, sit over here,' he said, his voice gentle as he eased his son to a chair. 'It's nothin' tae get upset about.'

'How could Thomas do it?' Flora wailed as Elspeth made tea. 'Upsettin' his own brother, too, with never a thought of what he's been through already.'

Elspeth's blood boiled along with the kettle on the stove. If anyone had upset Lachlan it was Flora herself, with her venomous attack on Thomas. She bit the accusation back with an effort, saying instead, as she put a mug of strong, sweet tea into the older woman's icy hands, 'It's over now, Aunt Flora. Don't upset yourself.'

Flora glared up at her, looking like a witch with her untidy hair and narrowed eyes and blotched face. 'What d'ye mean, it's over? There's our Thomas out of work and the whole town'll be tattling tomorrow about what he's been up to with his employer's daughter—'

'He's not been up to anything,' Elspeth was stung into protesting. 'He said he loved her, but that doesn't mean that they've – they've—' She bit her lip, remembering that although she had been earning a wage for two years now, in Flora's eyes she was too young to know anything about what could happen between men and women.

'Love?' Flora gave a contemptuous laugh. 'Ordinary folk like us were never meant tae fall in love! Yer poor mother found that out the hard way – and it was me that was left tae raise the result. I'm not havin' my Thomas goin' along that road!'

'Flora, that's enough,' Henry barked from where he stood over Lachlan.

Despite the warmth of the room, a chill descended over Elspeth, as if someone had just dropped a flexible sheet of ice on her from above. Without a word, she poured out tea for Henry and Lachlan.

Thomas didn't come home that night. Flora, distraught, sent Henry out to look for him, and he came back at midnight to report that Thomas was staying with his grandmother.

'He says he'll come back when he's got a job, and not before.'

'Now look what's become of us.' Worry and exhaustion had taken their toll on Flora, dimming her anger to a feeble spark. 'That lassie's cursed this house!'

'For pity's sake, Flora,' her husband said wearily, 'She's done nothing of the sort. Now let's get tae our beds – we've got work tae see tae in the mornin'.'

On the following evening Elspeth and Lachlan hurried along to Granjan's little flat as soon as they could get away without rousing Flora's suspicions.

'Thomas isnae in,' the old woman said as soon as she opened the door. 'Come on in, the two of ye.'

'How is he?' Lachlan asked anxiously as they followed her into the kitchen.

'In a right state when he arrived here. He'd a good drink in him, and he's still in a right takin'. He cannae see past that Bruce lassie.'

Elspeth looked round the little room. 'Where did he sleep?' There was only the wall-bed, where Granjan slept.

'On the floor, wrapped in a quilt an' with a cushion under his head. He'll sleep there again tonight, for he's determined not tae go back home without a wage packet. Flora's in a terrible takin'.'

'She's been here?'

'Oh aye, most of the day. She's torn between wantin' Thomas home an' wantin' him dead. Ach, she doesnae mean it, though. She dotes on that laddie – on all her bairns,' she added hurriedly, a hand on Lachlan's fair head. 'The trouble with Flora is that she's never learned how tae love folk. She punishes them instead.' Janet Docherty sighed. 'I don't know how that came about, for she had plenty love herself as a bairn. Never be scared tae tell someone if ye love them, Elspeth, even if they let on they don't want tae know. It's the greatest compliment ye can give tae another human bein'.' Then, as the outer door opened, 'Mind what ye say, he's feelin' as tender as if he's been run over by the horse as well as the cart.'

Thomas, pale and drawn, stopped in the doorway when he saw the two of them. 'What are you doing here?'

'We came to see how you are.'

'I'm fine.'

'There's a pot of soup waitin' for ye.' Granjan bustled to the cooker. 'I got a nice bit of flank mutton tae taste it, so there's a good mutton stew as well.'

'I don't want anything to eat.'

'Of course ye do. Ye cannae seek work on an empty stomach.'

'Plenty have to,' Thomas said shortly.

'Aye, poor souls, but I've no intention of lettin' my own grandwean do that – not while I'm alive. Ye'll have a drop of soup too?' she asked Elspeth and Lachlan, who both hesitated. They had already eaten, but the broth smelled good.

'Come on,' Janet coaxed. 'Lachie can do with a bit more fat on his bones, and I'm sure you could manage a wee taste, Elspeth.'

As they squeezed round her little table, Elspeth marvelled at the difference between mother and daughter. Flora was always jumpy and on edge, while Janet was so serene. It would be better for Thomas, she thought, to spend time with his grandmother while his unseen wounds healed. When Lachlan tried to persuade his brother to return home with them, she said firmly, 'I think Thomas is fine here, for the time being.'

He smiled gratefully at her. 'I'll come back when I've got another job, Lachie.'

'When'll that be?'

'Soon, I can promise you that.'

When they rose to go, Granjan announced that she would go with them to visit Flora. As she and Lachlan set out along the road, Thomas detained Elspeth at the close-mouth.

'I've made a terrible mess of it all, Ellie,' he said wretchedly. 'I should never have let it come tae this!'

Elspeth thought of Aileen Bruce as she had seen her in the fitting room at Brodie's and at her sister's wedding. 'She's very bonny.'

'Aye,' Thomas said huskily. 'Why did Ina have to show such malice? Ian Bruce was fair pleased to find out something against me. He was there, in his father's study when I was sent for – I could see the gloating in his eyes.'

'Are you sure it was Ina?'

'She saw us talking once, not long ago. She must have been watching ever since, following one or the other of us. I should have ended it long since, but I kept wanting just one more meeting. Mam's right, I was a fool!'

'Will you try to see her again?'

'No. The damage is done, best leave it at that and not make things worse.' He rubbed his hand hard over his face. 'You'd best go.'

Hurrying along the darkening road after the two figures, one dumpy, the other tall, ahead of her, Elspeth wished that she could have stayed with Thomas. He was strong for others, but vulnerable in his own grief. She wanted to comfort him, but knew at the same time that the comfort he really needed could never be his.

20

It wasn't an easy time to find work. Men were being laid off everywhere, and there was always a crowd waiting down at the docks in the hope of finding even a few hours' paid employment.

Thomas went out every morning and came back every evening, worn out from trudging round the streets. His ability to drive and his skill with engines stood him in good stead; a week after being turned away by Mr Bruce he found work in a small garage run by Forbes Cameron, a man with a deep interest in motorcars and enough money to set up his own business.

Even though he was bringing a pay packet home again, things weren't the same between Thomas and his mother. In the past, he had been the only member of the family able to tease Flora without giving offence; she usually wrangled with him amiably, or, if she could think of nothing to say, reached up and boxed his ears. Now, mother and son were civil to each other, but too much had happened for forgiveness on either side, and the special bond between them had vanished.

Nor could Elspeth forget what Flora had said to her that night. She had always known that she wasn't really part of the McDonald family, but it had never been made so cruelly clear before. She wished that she could find some way of striking out on her own instead of being beholden to the McDonalds.

Early in November, Brodie's typist had to take time off work because of illness in the family, and to her delight, Elspeth was

PEBBLES ON THE BEACH

asked back into the office. This time she took over the task confidently, impressing Mr Brodie with her ability to rattle away on the typewriter instead of pecking nervously at the keys.

She was more confident, too, in the way she handled Graham Adams when he started pestering her to go out with him.

'I've got a young man,' she told him loftily. His face dropped, and dropped even further when he discovered that Kenneth was studying to be a doctor. He made one more feeble try: 'If he's away in Glasgow studying, there's no harm in you finding someone to keep you company in the meantime.'

Elspeth whisked a sheet of paper out of the typewriter and rolled another in. 'I couldn't do that. He's very jealous,' she lied, and he said no more.

Rain rattled against the windows as the hands of the clock on the kitchen mantel shelf reached nine o'clock. Flora, who had been throwing surreptitious glances at the clock for the past half-hour, put her darning down. 'Where's that laddie got tae?'

'He'll be working on an engine, Aunt Flora,' Elspeth said, though she herself was becoming concerned over Thomas's absence.

Flora got up and opened the oven, letting the smell of overheated food into the room. 'He'll be more able tae heel his boots with this than eat it, the time it's been waitin' for him!'

Thomas's new job meant erratic hours. He had thrown himself into it feverishly, often working past his official stopping time.

Flora's complaints about the number of times she had to reheat his evening meal only met with a cool gaze and an indifferent, 'I'm not bothered whether the food's burned or cold, Mam – I'm not even bothered whether you make it or not,' that frustrated and frightened her.

'He's never as late as this,' she said now, picking up the sock she was darning, then tossing it down and giving her husband a firm dig in the ribs. He woke with a start from his comfortable doze.

'Henry, that laddie's never back yet – away tae the garage tae see if he's still there.'

Henry McDonald stretched and yawned. 'He'll have stopped in at a pub tae have a drink with some of his pals.'

'Not without comin' home first tae change out of his workin' dungarees. Our Thomas'd never stand in a pub covered with oil and filth. Not like some I could name,' she added with a sniff and a meaningful look at her husband.

'I'll go,' Lachlan offered, just as the knocker rattled.

Elspeth reached the door first, to find a policeman standing on the mat.

'Is yer daddy in, hen?'

The door across the landing had opened a crack; respectable tenements were never visited by the police, and there would probably be an ear pressed to every door the man had passed on his way up.

'Come in,' she started to say, but Flora was already pushing past her to scoop the officer in and shut the door against eavesdroppers. Henry, alerted by hearing a strange voice, appeared at the kitchen door, his shirt open to show his semmit, his braces looped at his waist.

'What's amiss?'

The constable drew his helmet off and tucked it under his arm as he made his way along the short, narrow hall into the kitchen. 'Mr McDonald? I've got some bad news for ye,' he said ponderously. 'It's yer lad, Thomas. We found him an hour since, in a back court. Someone's given him a right beatin'.'

Flora sagged heavily against her husband, just as she had done on the night she and Thomas had had their bitter quarrel. 'Is he – will he—'

'He's been taken tae the Infirmary, missus,' the man told her. 'They'll be able tae tell ye more when ye get there.'

'I'm going too,' Elspeth and Lachlan both said as soon as the policeman had left, but Flora shook her head.

'We cannae all rush there – they'll no' let a crowd of us in.

202

Better for you two tae stay here and we'll go on our own.'

They had two long hours of waiting before Flora and Henry returned with the news that Thomas was going to be all right.

'There's no bones broken, but he'll be kept in for a few days, just so's they can keep an eye on him. He's in a terrible state, the poor laddie.' Flora's face was streaked with tears, her eyes red.

'Someone gave him a right hidin',' Henry confirmed.

Elspeth opened her mouth to speak, but the words wouldn't come out. It was Lachlan who said, 'But who'd do that to our Thomas? Was it money they were after?'

'And him in his dungarees and covered with oil? Even in the gaslight anyone could see that he'd no' have money on him,' Flora snapped. 'The polis think he was mebbe mistaken for someone else.' Then, wringing her hands, 'What a thing tae happen – a polisman at our door! What'll the neighbours think?'

When Elspeth went to the Infirmary the following evening she didn't recognise any of the men in the beds at each side of the long ward. It was only when he called her name that she found Thomas.

Tears came to her eyes as she reached the bed where he was propped against pillows, with one arm strapped against his chest. His face was a mass of bruises, and both eyes were half shut. 'Oh, Thomas!'

'Now don't start greetin', Ellie,' he said with difficulty through swollen lips. 'Mam's done enough for the whole town. She cried so hard they almost had to change the bed when she left last night, and she was at it again this afternoon.'

Elspeth blinked rapidly to hold the tears back. 'Your face looks like the map of Europe that used to hang on our class-room wall.'

Thomas started to laugh, then winced and stopped abruptly. 'You should see my ribs – they're a world map; but it's not as bad as it looks. My arm's strapped because they put the shoul-der out of place.'

She took his left hand in hers. 'There was more than one man?'

There had been two men at least, one stepping out of a close right in front of Thomas, another moving swiftly up behind him. After beating him unconscious they had apparently dragged him through a nearby close and into a neglected back court.

'I'm just lucky someone happened to come into the court and find me, else I'd have lain all night,' he finished.

Elspeth's palms stung; looking down she realised that she had doubled her hands into such tight fists as she listened that her nails were digging into the tender skin, leaving angry red crescents. 'Who would do such a thing?'

Thomas, exhausted with telling the story, slumped back against the supporting pillows. 'Ian Bruce might have the answer to that. I've seen him passing the garage a few times. I think he wanted me to know he was keeping an eye on me.'

'But you've not seen his sister since you lost your job.'

He began to shrug, then stopped as pain flickered across his face. 'He must think I'm still a threat to the family. He'd not find it hard to get men to do his work for him.'

'Did you tell the police?'

'Can you see them accusing Ian Bruce of having an ex-employee beaten?' Thomas asked drily. 'There's no sense in telling them anything.'

'If his sister knew—'

'Leave, it, Ellie. How's Lachlan?'

'He wanted to come with me, but as soon as we walked in the hospital door he started shaking. He'd to turn and go out again – he was awful vexed about it.'

'Tell him I'd not want him to force himself. I'll be home in a day or two. And don't you fret yourself, Ellie, I probably deserved what I got, playing with fire the way I did.'

'Nobody deserves to look like that.'

The words rang in her mind for the rest of the night, and

were still with her in the morning as she walked to work. Just because the Bruce family had money, it didn't give them the right to hurt folk.

The typewriter rattled ferociously that morning as she fumed over the injustice of what had happened to Thomas. Aileen Bruce was surely as responsible as he was for the love that had grown between them, and to Elspeth's mind, Aileen should know just what her brother had done in her name.

She thought of going to the Bruce estate and confronting the girl, but common sense prevailed. If she went to the door and asked to see Aileen she would almost certainly be refused admittance. If the girl's brother happened to be there, she might even put herself into danger. Anyone who could pay people to do what had been done to Thomas would think nothing of hurting a woman. A letter would have a better chance of reaching Aileen.

She had never before done her own work during office hours, but this was an emergency, she told herself, putting a blank sheet of paper into the typewriter. It didn't take long to do, for her fingers flew over the keys, and it was finished and in an envelope without anyone noticing. During the midday break she used some of her precious letter-writing money to bribe one of the messenger boys to deliver it during his rounds.

That evening, Flora came back from the Infirmary in a towering rage that spilled out in a flow of words as soon as the outer door closed behind her. Elspeth and Lachlan heard her squawking in the hall even before the door flew open and she stormed in, with Henry at her back, trying to placate her.

'The lassie was just visitin', Flora.'

'Visitin', d'ye call it? Well, I call it humiliatin'!'

'Miss Bruce came tae the hospital tae see our Thomas,' Henry explained to Lachlan and Elspeth as his wife paused to draw breath.

She wrenched the long pin from her hat. 'She'd no right! Walkin' intae the ward with a bunch of flowers that must have cost a month's wages! Everyone in the place stopped talkin'.' She whipped her hat off and stabbed the pin back into it fiercely for safekeeping. 'It was the silence and the look on our Thomas's face that made me turn round. And there she was, marchin' right past us as if we werenae there, lettin' the flowers fall over the bed and on tae the floor, and takin' his hand for all the world tae see—'

'She was cryin', poor wee lass,' Henry put in.

Flora glared at him. 'I was near cryin' myself. I've never seen such an exhibition! If one of my lassies ever behaved like that in public she'd feel the back of my hand, I can tell ye.' The witch-like, venomous look that Elspeth had seen on the night Thomas lost his job blotched the woman's face again. 'I didnae know where tae look—' All at once, she started to weep.

'Come on, hen,' Henry soothed, easing his wife into her chair. 'Best leave her,' he said over her head to the other two. 'It's Thomas bein' hurt an' all.'

It was more than that, Elspeth thought as she and Lachlan crept from the room. It was the realisation that Thomas was lost to her, now and for ever.

When Thomas came home a few days later, his face still bruised and swollen, Flora's wrath had not abated.

As a result, mother and son had another quarrel, even more vicious than the last, and again it ended with Thomas leaving home. His employer, who already thought highly of his abilities as a mechanic, let him sleep on a cot in the garage office. Ian Bruce found out, too late, that far from keeping Thomas away from his sister, his actions had forced Aileen to choose between Thomas and her own family. She chose Thomas, braving her family's wrath, accepting without flinching her father's refusal to help her in any way.

She ignored Thomas's protests too, and when he found a two-roomed flat to rent, she insisted on selling her personal jewellery in order to buy furniture for their new home.

Flora, just as proud and determined as Mr Bruce, also refused to forgive them, mainly because the story had gone through the town like wildfire and the gossips had had a wonderful time discussing it all.

'She's a snob in her own way, is our Flora,' Janet Docherty told Elspeth. Janet herself had infuriated her daughter by taking a liking to Aileen and refusing to turn her back on the young couple.

When they married at the end of November, only Elspeth and Lachlan and Janet were present. Watching Thomas and his bride standing before the minister in the empty, echoing church, Elspeth thought of Catherine Bruce's fine wedding at the end of the war. Aileen could have had a wedding day like that, with no expense spared, but the happiness on her lovely face as she turned to leave the church, her hand tucked under her husband's elbow, showed that in her own eyes she had made the right choice. Despite the fading yellow and blue and purple bruises still discolouring his face, Thomas, too, was glowing with joy.

It was very hard for Aileen, used as she was to servants seeing to her every need, to settle to such a different life, but she was determined to make her marriage work, turning to her husband's grandmother for help in learning the basic skills of running her new, tiny home.

'It's no' the lassie's fault that she's been brought up tae money and servants,' Janet said. 'As long as her and Thomas make each other happy, what does it matter where they were born and raised? Mind yer hair, pet, it's too bonny tae burn.'

The two of them were in Janet's little kitchen a week after the wedding. Elspeth, making toast at the fire, obediently pushed her long plait back over one shoulder. She always put it up for work, but let it hang free at other times. She had been considering having her hair cut short, but Flora still refused to allow it. Turning the slice of bread on the long toasting fork and thrusting it back towards the glowing coals, she said, 'They say in the sewing room that Mrs Bruce has taken to her bed with the shock of what's happened.'

'Ach, that's just a ploy rich women use tae hide away from folk till the fuss dies down. I daresay poor Flora'd enjoy doin' the same, but she'll just have tae thole it till the gossips get tired. It's a strange world, right enough – the rich don't like tae see their bairns marryin' the poor, and a lot of ordinary folk like Flora don't like tae see the poor marryin' the rich.'

Janet put the teapot on the table and covered it with the woollen cosy Elspeth had crocheted at school, then came to sit by the fire, turning up the hem of her skirt so that her plump legs, richly decorated with varicose veins, could bask in the heat. 'Folk have short memories where scandal's concerned. Another week and they'll have found somethin' else tae whisper about.'

She was right, as usual. With no more fuel to keep it going, the gossip about Thomas McDonald and his new bride died down as the year drew to its close. When Mattie returned home for Christmas and New Year she had blossomed and matured, put on some much-needed weight and gained an air of confidence that startled her family. Contrary to Flora's conviction that her younger daughter would die of asthma within weeks of arriving in smoky, industrial Glasgow, the childhood ailment didn't bother Mattie as often now.

Warned by Elspeth's letters, she said nothing about Thomas and Aileen. Neither did Flora, and the others knew better than to mention Thomas's name. But as soon as she and Elspeth were in their bedroom on Mattie's first night home, propped, as usual, at either end of the bed, she asked, 'What's happening with Thomas? There's a new pinched look about Mam – I didn't dare say his name.'

'They're both fine, and very happy. You must go and see them.'

'I'll go tomorrow. Will they not be coming to see the new year in with the rest of us?'

'I don't think Aunt Flora'll allow it,' Elspeth said, and Mattie's eyes clouded.

'But it's Ne'erday! Everybody's with their own folk at Ne'erday, to start the new year off!'

'She's set her face against accepting Aileen.'

'I never thought she'd turn away from Thomas,' Mattie said wonderingly, then, 'Well, you and me and Lachlan'll just have to go and see them after the bells, for I'm not going to leave my own brother without his family at a time like that, whatever she says. She'll be busy with all the neighbours then anyway.'

'Tell me about Glasgow, and college.'

Mattie's eyes brightened. 'It's grand, Ellie! Teaching's the right thing for me – the only thing. I was born to it.' She adjusted her pillow, which had started sliding down. 'Kenneth's been kind, he kept an eye on me at the beginning, and I see him now and again, but I'd have managed anyway. He said to let you know he's coming home tomorrow. Studying's not as hard as I thought it would be, and I can't wait to get into the class-rooms.'

She talked for a while about her life in Glasgow, and Elspeth drank it all in, wishing that she, too, could have had the opportunity to go to the city.

Mattie's yawns became more and more frequent, and finally she stretched her arms, then slipped beneath the blankets. 'I'm getting sleepy – I'll tell you more tomorrow. Lachlan's looking much better – that work you found for him's doing him good.'

'It's not much, but it's a start. He's been helping out with painting some of the departments, too, and Mr Brodie's talking about giving him more responsibility.'

'All we need now,' Mattie said drowsily, 'is for Mam to stop being so silly about Thomas and Aileen, and everything'll be all right.'

Kenneth was waiting outside the department store when Elspeth left work the following evening. She wanted to run to him, but hesitated, recalling their last meeting, and its sudden end when Thomas came across the two of them in the back court.

He, too, looked awkward; he held out his hand, and Elspeth shook it, aware that Graham Adams and Lena and some of the other girls from the sewing room were nearby. Lachlan, who usually walked home with her, had prudently disappeared.

To her relief, Kenneth drew her hand through his arm as they walked away. 'You've done a grand job with Uncle George's books. He's fair delighted.'

'It was good practice for me.'

He laughed. 'A challenge, more like. Anyone who can get *his* affairs into order must be clever.'

Pride and pleasure warmed her, and she relaxed a little.

That evening he took her to the cinema, and kissed her on the way home.

'I've been thinking, while I was away, about that last time – in the wash house,' he said awkwardly. It was as well that it was dark in the corner where they stood, for Elspeth felt her face burn at the memory. 'It was wrong of me, to try to—'

'I shouldn't have made such a fuss.'

'I shouldn't have—' He stopped, then said, 'I forgot that you're still very young. It'll not happen again.'

'Never?' She tried to get a teasing note into her voice in an effort to lighten the situation. She had missed him, and now she wasn't entirely sure whether she was relieved or disappointed at his words.

'Well – not till you're older, and I'm further on with my studies,' he said firmly, then put an arm about her and turned her towards the lighted street. 'Come on, it's too cold to be standing here. D'you think your Aunt Flora would be willing to offer me a cup of tea?'

21

Despite her family's arguments and pleas Flora obstinately refused to invite Thomas and Aileen to Mearns Street for New Year, so after midnight on Hogmanay, Lachlan and Mattie and Elspeth and Janet left the house shortly after the church bells and the ships' sirens out on the river had noisily welcomed 1920.

'I don't like leaving Mam on her own at New Year,' Lachlan said as they gained the street at last, having been stopped all the way down the stairs by neighbours wishing them a happy new year. As, traditionally, first-footers couldn't go into anyone's home empty-handed, he was armed with a bottle of whisky.

'It's her own choice,' said Mattie, who was carrying a lump of coal, denoting good wishes to the house they were going to enter, and wrapped in newspaper to save marking her hands or her coat. Elspeth's gift was a black bun – a rich fruit cake – that she had baked herself. When Thomas and Aileen came to the door their callers were arguing over who should go into the house first.

'It has to be you, Ellie,' Mattie was saying as the door opened. 'Your hair's not all that dark, but it's darker than ours.'

Thomas, his face split by a huge grin, put one arm about Aileen and reached his free hand out to draw them into the house. 'I've got my own luck-bringer,' he said, 'and nobody here's got hair as dark as hers, so come in, the lot of you. And welcome!'

•

To mark the new year, Lena had persuaded Elspeth to accompany her and her latest young man to the music hall at the Hippodrome Theatre.

'D'you not want to go on your own with Drew?' Elspeth had asked doubtfully when the outing was first proposed.

'I do not,' Lena said bluntly. George, the naval sweetheart Lena had been writing to when Elspeth first met her, had vanished from the scene almost as soon as the war was over, and since then Lena had changed escorts several times. 'I'm tired of lookin' at Drew, but he's too thick tae take a hint. That's why I want you tae come too, so's I'm not stuck with him all evening. I can scarce get tae the privy in our back court without him trailin' along at my back. Bring yer sweetheart, and Mattie and that nice shy brother of yours that works in the packin' room. He's got bonny eyes.'

'Bonny eyes or not, he's too quiet for you.'

Lena winked. 'I can be quiet and shy when I want tae be. Go on and ask him. Ye neednae fret, I'll not affront ye.'

Mattie agreed enthusiastically, and to Elspeth's surprise, both Kenneth and Lachlan accepted the invitation. When Thomas and Aileen heard what was afoot they announced that they wanted to go too, so there were eight of them in the third row that night, much to Drew's annoyance.

Lachlan, who insisted on sitting at the end of the row in case it all got too much for him and he had to leave hurriedly, glanced frequently and nervously round at the crowded auditorium and up at the boxes flanking the stage. Once or twice Elspeth, sitting next to him, thought that he was going to lose his nerve and make a bolt for the exit, but he stayed where he was, and when the lights went down and the crimson plush curtains swept open to reveal the three lines of chorus girls ready to sweep into 'Put on your Ta-ta, Little Girlie', she felt him relaxing in his seat.

It was an enjoyable evening. The comedians were exceptionally funny, the dancers and acrobats exceptionally lithe, the soprano and baritone of an exceptionally fine quality. The problem came towards the end of the evening, when it was announced that Miss Dolly Burnett, the popular soloist, had had to cancel her appearance because of illness, and someone else was taking over her spot in the programme. An ageing lady in a flouncy pink shepherdess costume then appeared onstage, and the orchestra struck up.

Almost as soon as the substitute raised her wavering voice in song the audience became restless. Murmurs rippled from all directions, and to her horror Elspeth heard Lena say clearly from further along the row, 'That reminds me, Drew, I forgot tae put the cat out before I left home.'

The applause at the end of the first song was sparse, and when the poor woman launched into a second melody, trying to achieve notes that her voice couldn't possibly reach, catcalls and jeers began to be heard from the gallery. The noise grew until the orchestra wavered into nervous silence, and the singer, crimson with mortification and anger, was forced to stop. The Master of Ceremonies rushed on to the stage to appeal for order.

'Ladies and gentlemen, this lady has very kindly agreed to step in at short notice. The least you can do is to give her a hearing.'

'We have,' Lena bawled back at him, bouncing to her feet and ignoring Drew's attempts to pull her back into her seat. 'Now the least she could do's tae stop givin' us an earache!'

The audience applauded, and Elspeth cringed back against her seat as the Master of Ceremonies glared down at the row where they sat.

'If you can do better, miss,' he said crushingly, 'you're welcome to try.'

Lena needed no further invitation. 'Right,' she yelled back, 'I will!' and jumping to her feet she started to push her way along the row towards the aisle.

The man's jaw dropped. 'This is a music hall, not a street

party. Please return to your seat, miss!' He danced at the edge of the stage, his arms making distracted, shooing motions.

'Away with ye, man,' someone bellowed back from right behind Elspeth and Lachlan, making them both jump. 'Ye asked if the lassie could dae better – let her have a try at it!'

The call was taken up across the auditorium and in the gallery as Lena continued to forge towards the aisle. When she reached it, she stopped and turned, taking Lachlan's face in her hands and smacking a hearty kiss on his astonished mouth.

'Wish me luck,' Elspeth heard her say beneath the audience's applause, then she was on her way up the steps to the stage. Glancing down the row, Elspeth could see Drew, red-faced with rage, leaning forward to glare at Lachlan, who was too dazed to notice.

Seemingly undaunted by the lights and egged on by the crowd's noisy encouragement, Lena marched to the centre of the stage. As she knelt to have a brief discussion with the orchestra conductor, the Master of Ceremonies hustled the bewildered shepherdess into the wings, shrugging and murmuring in her ear.

'I expect he's telling her that they might as well let Lena make a fool of herself,' Kenneth said, applauding vigorously with the rest of the audience as the conductor had a quick conference with his musicians, and Lena straightened up to face the auditorium, whipping off her felt hat and loosening the ribbon that kept her long red hair under control.

As it fell in curls over her shoulders the spotlights caught it, turning it into a burst of brilliant colour that distracted attention away from her plain dark coat and heavy practical shoes. Then the music started, the applause died down, and Lena began to sing.

She had chosen a song that began with a serious verse; as the introduction was played she stood alone in the centre of the large stage, head up and face solemn, her hands meekly before her, one holding her hat, the other her ribbon. Her voice was clear and sweet, reaching the high notes without effort. At the end of the verse, she held the final note for several beats, then paused, her eyes sweeping boldly over the waiting audience, before suddenly swinging into a saucy chorus, deepening her voice as she slapped the plain felt hat back on her head, this time at a cheeky angle, and began to dance along the front of the stage.

'My darling daddy never ever puts sugar in his tea,' she sang, then, winking at her listeners, ''cos my sugar daddy says his only sugar's me—'

As cheers and whistles broke out around her, Elspeth stared, dumbfounded, at this new Lena, who was behaving as if going on to a stage was a common occurrence. It was as though she had been born to it.

The applause at the end of the song was tumultuous, and when Lena made to leave the stage, the audience roared for more. This time she sang, 'Poor Butterfly', standing straight and still, her hands clasped before her; her voice, sweet and pure, bringing a lump to Elspeth's throat. She wasn't the only one to be moved – the noisy audience had fallen into attentive silence as soon as the first notes rose from Lena's throat, and now there were a few sniffs from somewhere behind Elspeth, and the occasional gruff clearing of a throat. She glanced at Lachlan, and saw that he was totally absorbed in the lone figure on the stage, his lips parted and his eyes shining.

The applause was again deafening when the last wistful notes faded away, with some members of the audience on their feet. Lena beamed at them, knelt to whisper to the conductor, then announced with a cheeky grin, 'One more song and that's all ye're gettin'!' For the final song, she completely changed her style again, swinging into a pert rendering of 'I Can't Find My Way Home'.

When the song ended, she blew kisses to every part of the theatre, then to the orchestra, before picking up her hat and hair ribbon and walking demurely to the steps. The Master of

Ceremonies appeared as she got there, and they spoke briefly before she continued back down to her seat.

'Thanks for the luck,' Elspeth heard her say to Lachlan, putting a hand on his arm as he stumbled to his feet to let her brush past him.

As the party made their way to the exit after the show they were halted time and again by people crowding round to speak to Lena. She shrugged off their praise modestly, but her pretty face glowed.

'I've always wanted tae dae that,' she said when they finally grouped together on the pavement.

'You were wonderful!' Mattie's voice was awed. 'I could never do what you did tonight.'

'Och, it's easy. Ye don't pay any heed tae the audience, ye just think about the songs and enjoy singin' them.'

'An' make a right exhibition of yerself,' Drew said sourly, glaring at Lachlan, who hadn't said a word but couldn't take his eyes off Lena. 'Come on, it's time we were gettin' home.'

'I've tae go round tae the stage door first. That man wants a word with me.'

'Aye, an' I can imagine what it is,' Drew snarled. 'I'm goin' tae no stage door. I've had enough of a showin'-up tonight as it is!'

'I never said you were goin' with me,' Lena snapped back at him. 'I can manage fine on my own.'

He stared at her wordlessly, then turned on his heel and stamped away. Watching him go, Lena shrugged.

'Good riddance tae bad rubbish.'

'D'you want us to go with you?' Thomas offered as she turned away.

'No, I'll be fine.' She tossed the words over her shoulder as she headed for the side street where the stage door was located.

On Monday morning, she arrived at Brodie's department store to give in her notice. That night she went onstage again at the Hippodrome, and a week later, when the company finished its Greenock booking, Lena left town with them, telling

Elspeth before she went that both Miss Buchanan and Miss Arnold had prophesied a terrible future for her.

'They seem tae think I'll either end up as a white slave or starvin' in a garret,' she said, amused. 'I told them that any- thin's better than dyin' of boredom in a sewin' room.'

'It's like a fairy story,' Elspeth marvelled, and Lena shrugged.

'It's just a matter of doin' what ye want tae do. Mind that when yer own time comes. Anyway – it was your Lachlan that gave me the good luck.'

She winked, just as she had winked on the Hippodrome stage. 'He might be quiet, but he's a lovely laddie,' she added, then she was gone.

As Lena's sudden decision to go on the stage meant that the sewing room was short-handed, Miss Buchanan demanded Elspeth's return from the office.

'As it happens, I'm expecting Miss McCabe back next week,' James Brodie said when he broke the news to Elspeth, 'so you would have been returning to the sewing room then in any case. But Miss Buchanan tells me there's a fairly large order in, so she can't wait.'

'I could do some work for you in the evenings, if I can take it home with me,' Elspeth offered, astonished by her own audacity. 'I've got my own typewriter there.'

His brows shot up. 'Your own typewriter? How did that come about?' She felt colour rise to her face as she explained, finishing with, 'It's old, but it's in good order.'

'But you shouldn't have to work in the evenings as well, my dear.'

'I don't mind. I don't go out much anyway,' she told him truthfully. Kenneth and Mattie had returned to Glasgow, and time was hanging on her hands.

He agreed, and each evening after that she went along to the office to collect the evening's work before going home. She was able to fit it in because the demand for her letter-writing skills had finally begun to ease off, though there were still several requests each week.

The work she had to do for Mr Brodie was easy compared to making sense of Mr Monteith's erratic book-keeping on crumpled scraps of paper. That task had seemed at first sight to be quite impossible, but Elspeth, determined not to let it defeat her, had worked hard, thankful, as the little bits of paper spread over the typing table, then the bed, and finally the floor, that she now had the room to herself and there was nobody there to complain.

Mr Monteith's writing was deplorable, his methods haphazard, but as time went by she had begun to read and decipher the scribbles more easily, and to grasp his strange logic. Gradually, the muddle had been transferred from torn-off scraps of papers and used envelopes into the large ledger. She had bought a smaller book and tethered it to the counter, persuading Mr Monteith to enter each transaction in it, rather than using bits of paper. He grumbled at first, but finally gave in.

It had occurred to Elspeth that most local folk took their most precious possessions into Mr Monteith's shop on a Monday morning, redeemed them on Friday, and pawned them again on the following Monday. Once James Brodie's typist had returned to work and Elspeth had more time in the evenings, she drew up a list of the items going through the pawnbroker's hands each week. When it was completed to her satisfaction she started listing the unclaimed or longer-term items stored in the back shop and the flat above, sneezing as the dust tickled her nose.

The listing meant that she spent far more time in the pawn shop than Aunt Flora would have allowed, had she known about it, but fortunately Flora was too wrapped up in her new grandchild to notice what Elspeth was up to.

Rachel's little girl, named Mary, after Mary Pickford the film star, was born less than two weeks after New Year. Once she was back on her feet, Rachel seemed to spend almost as much time in her old home as she had before she was married. Flora had no objection, for it meant that she could spend hours with her little granddaughter on her lap, cuddling her and crooning to her.

'Who's gran's best wee dumplin'?' she would say with a gentleness that amazed her family. 'Who loves her old granny?' Watching her joy in the baby, Elspeth saw another side to the woman she always thought of as sharp-tongued and difficult to please. Clearly, Aunt Flora loved babies, and it was easy to see, now, why she had taken her friend's orphaned child in with no thought to the cost of another mouth to feed.

'Mr James sent for me.' It was strange, Elspeth thought, to be visiting the office she had come to think of as her own work-place. Her eyes strayed to the typewriter, now under Theresa McCabe's control.

'I'll tell him you're here.' Wilma squirmed down from her high stool, saying as she went to the inner office, 'This is the lassie that did the typing while you were off, Theresa.'

'Oh aye?' The typist looked Elspeth up and down, then sniffed, clearly finding her wanting. It was a relief when Wilma reappeared, holding the office door open for Elspeth then closing it behind her.

To her astonishment, James Brodie reached over the desk and shook her hand. 'I wanted to thank you for the work you did in the office, and at home. And' – he held out an enve-lope – 'to give you this.'

Puzzled, she opened it, and her eyes widened as she saw that it held two crisp one-pound notes.

'But – I'm not due any wages till the end of the week.'

'That's from me, to express my appreciation.'

'Mr James, I can't take money I've not earned.'

'Of course you've earned it,' he said firmly, ignoring her outstretched hand. 'You'll have to learn to value your own skills – that's what business is all about.'

She didn't dare show the money to Aunt Flora, who had always warned the three girls about taking gifts from men. According to her, that was the swiftest way to hell. Surely, Elspeth thought as she left the office, Mr Brodie wasn't that sort of man. But Aunt Flora might not agree.

On the following day, she put the money into the bank.

At the end of January, a postcard arrived from Lena, addressed to Lachlan and bearing a view of Glasgow's George Square. According to the few words scrawled on the other side, Lena was appearing onstage in one of the city's theatres. Flushed with excitement, for he never received any post, Lachlan read it again and again, studying the photograph until Flora told him tartly that he'd wear it away with his eyes.

'I don't know what that lassie's thinkin' of anyway, sendin' cards tae a respectable house,' she added sourly. 'I don't like a son of mine gettin' messages from a woman who flaunts hersel' on the stage in front of goodness knows who.'

'There's nothin' wrong with goin' on the stage,' Lachlan retorted sharply, reducing his mother to open-mouthed astonishment. It was unheard of, even before the war, for him to answer her back.

When another card arrived a month later, this time from Aberdeen, he seized it and bore it off to his bedroom, refusing to discuss it with anyone, though he reported proudly to Elspeth later, 'She says she's doin' fine, and she's askin' after you. They're off to Dundee soon; she says she'll send me a card from there.'

But there were no more cards. As the weeks passed and Lachlan's eager anticipation turned to disappointment, Elspeth became furious with Lena for letting him down. There was nothing she herself could do about it, though, other than deciding that if Lena ever returned to Greenock she would have a few things to say to her.

22

Thomas, wearing trousers and a vest, opened the door to Elspeth.

'I've just arrived home,' he explained hurriedly, 'Aileen's cut herself, and I'm washing the dirt from the garage off my hands so that I can see to her.'

In the kitchen, fragrant with the smell of simmering broth mingled with an undercurrent of stew from the oven, Aileen was sitting on a chair by the stove, one hand nursing the other, a clumsy bandage wrapped about one of her fingers.

'I'll see to it,' Elspeth offered, but Thomas, already back at the tiny sink, shook his head.

'I can manage.'

Aileen smiled apologetically. 'It's just a wee cut where the knife slipped when I was peeling potatoes. I'm so clumsy – it's nothing to fret over.'

'You never know with cuts,' her husband insisted, reaching for the towel while Elspeth picked up the knife that Aileen had dropped and got on with the work of peeling the potatoes, noticing that the girl had cut the peel thick, taking a fair portion of the potato with it. Flora McDonald would have been mortified if she or any of the girls she had raised had indulged in such wastefulness.

Elspeth liked spending time in the little flat, and called in often. Although Thomas and Aileen couldn't afford much in the way of furniture, their love and joy in each other

221

permeated their home, turning it into a warm, welcoming place. Aileen, determined to be as good a wife as she could, worked hard at learning how to look after her new home; the small room was neat and bright and welcoming, the table set, the fireplace swept, the fire well tended.

The only untidiness was unavoidable – Thomas's oily working dungarees, which were lying on a sheet of newspaper in the corner. He himself washed them every Saturday, Elspeth knew, refusing to allow Aileen to take on the heavy, daunting task.

'How's Lachlan doing?' he asked as he tossed the towel down and knelt before his wife, carefully unwrapping the bandage.

'He's working late at the store this evening, helping with some painting.' Elspeth noticed that although Aileen had filled a pot with water in readiness for the potatoes, she hadn't yet put it on to the stove to heat, thus slowing down the cooking process.

'I want to do everything right for Thomas. He's given up so much for me,' Aileen had told Elspeth once, ignoring the fact that she herself had given up even more. She hated to let Thomas see the mistakes she made, although he never found fault.

Now, Elspeth signalled silently to Aileen with the pot before putting it on the stove, and the girl, understanding, gave an imperceptible nod, her green eyes flashing her gratitude. Just then Thomas's fair head dipped swiftly to let his lips brush the tiny cut on Aileen's work-roughened hand. Elspeth looked away quickly, feeling that it was wrong to spy on such special moments between man and wife.

Aileen was showing signs of strain, she thought as she began to cut the potatoes into quarters. A little worried frown was settling in between her brows, and there was an air of tension about her. It couldn't be easy for someone from her background to have to deal with the daily grind of trying to make a small wage stretch as far as possible.

'You'll stay for your dinner?' Aileen invited when the bandage was firmly in place and Thomas had freed her to join Elspeth at the stove.

'I'm expected at home. I just looked in to see how you were.'

'We're both fine,' Thomas said cheerfully, replacing the towel he had been using on its nail beside the window. He hesitated, sniffing the air, then pulled back a corner of the window curtain. Elspeth heard an intake of breath from Aileen as he turned, holding out a small bowl containing a deep blue hyacinth. Its delicate, haunting fragrance began to spread over the room.

'Aileen, pet, I told you we cannae afford to spend money on—'

'I didn't buy it,' Aileen interrupted, fingers twisting nervously at her apron. 'It was a gift. Ian brought it.'

Thomas's jaw dropped and his brown eyes widened. 'Your brother was here?'

'Just for a minute, to see how I was. He brought the wee plant.'

'From the greenhouses,' Thomas said, then swallowed hard. 'To remind you of everything you've turned your back on.'

'It isn't like that at all.' She stepped forward and put her hands over his, so that they were both cradling the bowl. 'He came because he just wanted to see me.'

'And he saw you in this tiny room that's all I can give you.' His shoulders slumped, and his voice was bleak with humiliation. 'Did he ask you to go back home with him?'

'I am home! He's my brother, Thomas, you're surely not going to forbid me to see him now and then, are you?'

'I'd never forbid you to do anything, you surely know that.' Then, with a visible effort, he forced a smile. 'I'm not complaining, lass, of course your brother'll want to see you. It was just – a surprise, that's all.'

'I wish Ian Bruce hadnae come back into our lives,' he told

Elspeth, low-voiced, as he accompanied her to the close-mouth a few minutes later. 'I'd never deny her, but I don't trust the man.'

'He can't come between you and Aileen,' she tried to reassure him. 'You're man and wife, and she'd not turn her back on you now.'

'I know, but—' Thomas sighed, then said, 'The man's a troublemaker.'

Ian Bruce visited his sister regularly from then on, though never when Thomas was home. Elspeth herself found him lounging in his sister's flat when she called one day. She slowed as she saw the smart sports car outside the close, circled enviously by a group of wide-eyed children giggling at their reflections in the gleaming scarlet paintwork. On the nearby street corner loitered the inevitable group of men unable to find regular work. They stared enviously at the handsome automobile that had cost more than a year's wages and muttered amongst themselves, hawking into the gutter.

Elspeth hesitated. She would have turned and hurried away, but she had promised to buy some meat for Aileen on her way home from work, and she had no option but to deliver it.

The girl looked worried when she came to the door, then smiled when she saw Elspeth waiting in the close. 'Come in and meet my brother,' she said, and Elspeth, who had intended to hand the parcel over then leave, was drawn into the kitchen.

She had only glimpsed Ian Bruce, in full uniform at his elder sister's wedding, and had thought then that he was the most handsome man she had ever set eyes on. Close to, out of uniform and in an open-necked white shirt, dark blazer and white trousers, he was like a Greek god. As he rose to his feet and took her hand in his cool, firm grip, his closeness set her pulse fluttering. He knew it – she could tell by the lazy amusement in the green eyes gazing down on her.

'You'll have some tea, Elspeth?' Aileen asked.

She recalled the reason for her visit, and withdrew her fingers hurriedly from Ian's. 'I can't stop, I'm just handing this in.'

Aileen unfolded the parcel and studied the piece of flank mutton, her brow wrinkled. 'How did you say I should cook it?'

'Wash it, then put it into the soup, to get the flavour,' Elspeth gabbled, aware of Ian Bruce's presence only inches away. 'Then take it out before you serve the soup, and put it on two plates with boiled potatoes and some carrots. That way you'll get full use from it.'

Aileen's hand flew to her mouth. 'The soup! I was doing the vegetables when Ian arrived.'

They lay in a small pile on a chopping board, onions and carrots, turnip and potatoes and a halved leek.

'There's still time. I'll see to the meat while you finish the vegetables.'

'How delightfully domesticated,' Ian Bruce drawled, as the two of them set to work.

'Oh, I've learned a lot,' Aileen told him proudly. When the vegetables were in the pot she dried her hands and reached for her purse. 'I'll pay for the meat now, Elspeth, before I forget.'

Glancing at the young man, Elspeth saw his mouth tighten as he watched his sister scrabbling in the small purse, then counting coppers carefully out on to the table. As Elspeth scooped them up and straightened, his gaze moved away, travelling round the room that was so unlike the grand house he and his sister were used to. His lip curled, and suddenly despising him for his dislike of the home Thomas had provided for Aileen, Elspeth stuffed the money into her pocket.

'I must go. Don't bother to see me out,' she added as Aileen moved towards the door.

'I'm sure your friend can manage to find her own way,' Ian agreed, detaining his sister with a hand on her arm. 'Sit down and have a rest. I hate to see you working like a skivvy.'

Outside again, Elspeth almost ran along the street, wondering how she could have been charmed, even for a moment, by the man who had had Thomas beaten unconscious as punishment for loving his sister. She, too, wished that Ian Bruce hadn't come back into Aileen's life.

But Aileen welcomed his visits. 'We were always close, and I've missed him more than I've missed my parents,' she confided to Elspeth the next time she called.

'After what he did to Thomas?' Elspeth's voice was sharper than she intended, and Aileen flushed.

'He knows he did wrong, and he's sorry about it. He even went to the garage to apologise, but Thomas wouldn't speak to him. But mebbe one of these days' – her face brightened – 'I'll get the two of them together. And Ian's trying to persuade my parents to change their minds. One day everything'll be all right.'

'I can't see your parents being happy about the sort of life you lead now.' Elspeth hated to throw cold water on the girl's hopes, but she felt that Aileen was expecting too much.

'They might, and so might Thomas's mother, now that—' Aileen stopped, a hand flying up to her mouth, and said guiltily from between spread fingers, 'Thomas wanted to tell you when we were all together. I'm going to have a child.'

'Oh, Aileen!' Elspeth hugged her. 'I'm pleased for you – for both of you.'

'So are we, and now I've spoiled it for Thomas. You'll not let on, will you?'

'I won't,' Elspeth promised, and managed to be convincingly surprised and delighted when she heard the news officially a week later. Thomas was almost bursting with happiness and pride.

'I'm going to work every hour I can to get somewhere better than this before the bairn comes,' he said exultantly, and when Aileen protested, 'There's nothing wrong with it, we'll manage fine,' he shook his head, hugging her tightly to him.

'I want to do more than manage.'

'And all I want is for our families to be happy for us, and for that to happen soon.' As she rested her head against her husband's chest, Aileen's lovely face was determined.

Outside, it was May; great clumps of golden broom splashed across the hills above the town and the sun's rays sparkled on the river beyond the dockyards, turning the water into a vast treasure chest filled with diamonds. But inside the Infirmary the long ward looked drab and dreary. Here and there, where the sunlight managed to squeeze through the tall, narrow windows, small pools of light dappled a locker top or a sheet.

Celia Bremner lay very still, as she had since being admitted, her bony hands folded on the stiff coverlet, her grey head scarcely denting the snowy pillow. Her eyes were closed and her mouth slightly open, the breath rattling unevenly in and out of her lungs. She hadn't fully recovered consciousness since being brought into the Infirmary after a neglected cold turned to pneumonia. Occasionally she moved, or muttered something unintelligible; once or twice she had opened her eyes and gazed vacantly around before lapsing back into her coma.

During the ten days her grandmother had been in the Infirmary, Elspeth had visited every evening and on Saturday and Sunday afternoons as well. Flora had accompanied her on one occasion, but this was the ward she had lain in during her influenza attack, and the memory of it made her fidget restlessly, anxious to get back home. Lachlan still had a morbid fear of hospitals, but both Thomas and Aileen had gone with her once or twice; as had Mattie and Kenneth during brief visits home at Easter, but preoccupied as they were with the thought of approaching exams they had both been poor company.

Granjan, who had declared from the first that visiting the

sick was no task for a young lassie to tackle on her own, was Elspeth's favourite companion, sitting patiently and calmly by the bed, occasionally reaching out to pat Celia's hand.

'Poor soul,' she murmured now from the opposite side of the bed, 'She'd hate tae know she's been brought tae this.'

A bell tolled in the corridor beyond the ward, and all down its length visitors began to get up and file out. Elspeth, with one last look at the grey, stern face on the pillow, rose and followed Granjan, guilty at the feeling of relief that always came over her as she stepped through the ward doors.

'Best go afore me, for I'm slow on stairs,' the old woman advised the people just behind her on the landing, adding carefully as the two of them waited for the flow of visitors to ease to a trickle, 'Have ye given any thought, pet, about yer grandma mebbe not gettin' better?'

'I know she's very poorly,' Elspeth said doubtfully. She couldn't imagine a world without Grandmother, couldn't imagine the still figure they had just left allowing herself to die.

'She is, poor woman. Best tae be prepared, just in case.' The stairs were clearing now, and Granjan gripped the rail firmly, taking the steps one at a time. When they reached the foyer she headed towards a nearby bench, as she always did. 'I'll just sit here for a wee minute tae catch my breath.'

Someone called Elspeth's name and she turned to see a girl who had attended the typewriting and shorthand classes with her.

'Peggy, what are you doing here?'

'Visiting my dad, he's had a bad turn again.' The girl looked tired and tense, and Elspeth recalled that she kept house for her father, who had a weak heart. 'He'll be all right, they say. Home again next week. What about you?'

'My grandmother's got pneumonia. How are you? Are you working?'

Peggy, who had been one of the star pupils in the typing

class, shrugged. 'Just in the early mornings, in a bakery. It's the only way I can bring in some money and see to Da as well. He can't be left on his own all day, so there's no hope of working in an office. They all want someone who can be there all the time.'

'I did some typing in Brodie's accounts office, but I'm back in the sewing room again.'

Peggy sighed. 'It's a terrible waste of all that learning we did, isn't it? I keep tellin' myself that mebbe one day I'll get to use a typewriter again, if my fingers are still up to it by then . . .'

Walking home with Granjan, Elspeth felt guilty about the typewriter sitting in her bedroom. At least she had her own machine, and some work to do on it, unlike poor Peggy.

Celia Bremner died a few days later, without regaining consciousness, and was buried in the same lair as her daughter. Flora, Henry, Granjan and Lachlan attended the funeral, and so did Thomas and Aileen. When she heard about the coming baby, Flora had finally given in and admitted her elder son and his wife into the family circle, though she was still somewhat stiff and formal with them both. Life was too short to bear grudges, Elspeth thought as she watched her grandmother's coffin being lowered into the ground.

As the undertaker's men withdrew the cords and stepped back, she suddenly felt completely alone. Cold and grim though she had always been, Grandmother had at least been of her own flesh and blood. For all Elspeth knew, her father and grandfather had both died long ago. She shivered, wishing that Kenneth could have been beside her. He, at least, was hers in some measure. She tried to console herself, as the minister's voice droned out the final words of the service, with the thought that he would be home for the summer in only two months' time.

23

A few days later she turned the key in the door and stepped nervously into Grandmother's flat, Rachel crowding in behind her.

'It's lovely!' the older girl breathed, staring at the carpeted floor and the large walnut coat-stand with its carved panels and decorative mirror. Celia Bremner's everyday coat and hat still hung on their usual hooks, and a long umbrella, neatly furled, waited in the stand for a hand that would never again lift it.

The flat was filled with her grandmother's presence, and she wouldn't have been at all surprised if the old lady had suddenly appeared at the parlour door. Crossing the hall and reaching out to open it, she was glad that she had thought of asking Rachel to help her to start clearing the place.

'I'm afraid that there is very little money involved,' the lawyer had said, sitting at his paper-littered desk and peering at Elspeth over the top of his half-moon spectacles. 'Your grandmother had a little money of her own, and used it frugally, but there's not much left. The proceeds of the sale of the furnishings will go to you, Miss Bremner, as sole surviving relative – that is, after my legal fees have been settled.'

'Sole survivor? Are you certain of that?'

'Of course,' the man said abruptly, and Elspeth swallowed hard, the nails of one hand digging into the palm. It had to be said. Everything had to be above board.

She swallowed again, then said, her voice little more than a whisper, 'My grandfather—'

The lawyer's bushy eyebrows shot up. 'You know of your grandparents' – er – situation?'

'I had heard something—'

He looked at her as though she had just shouted his own innermost secrets to the whole town, then said stiffly, 'Your grandfather died several years ago, Miss Bremner. As the family lawyer, I can assure you that you are indeed your grandmother's sole surviving relative.' Then he had changed the subject, and she didn't dare ask him for further details.

Elspeth had put the emptying of the flat off for as long as possible, but now time was running out and it had to be done so that the factor could rent the place to new tenants. Granjan would have helped, but stairs made her breathless, and Flora had made it clear that she had no wish to become involved.

'Never mind that nonsense about no' speakin' ill of the dead – I didnae like the woman and she didnae like me, so I want nothin' tae dae with her possessions,' she had said bluntly. 'I cannae abide that house anyway, it was always cold and unforgivin'.'

Rachel, on the other hand, seized the chance eagerly when asked to help, confessing that she loved seeing other folks' homes. Flora had agreed to take wee Mary off her daughter's hands for a few hours, and had borne the baby off to visit Granjan.

Although Elspeth had called at the house once a month for years, she had only seen the hall and kitchen and bathroom and parlour, and had never set foot in her grandmother's bed-room, with its vast wardrobe and double bed and marble-topped washstand complete with floral ewer and basin, or in the smaller bedroom that had once belonged to her mother. While Rachel exclaimed over the large sideboard and the slippery buttoned-leather *chaise-longue* in the parlour, Elspeth tiptoed into the smaller room, holding her breath, hoping desperately that she would come across something that had belonged to her mother.

But to her disappointment the small bed had been stripped bare and the single wardrobe was empty and smelled strongly of mothballs. The plain yellow ewer and basin on the washstand were bone dry, and the tallboy drawers only held spare blankets which also reeked of mothballs. Every trace of her mother had been swept away. It was as if she had never existed.

'I wish I'd a room like this for wee Mary,' Rachel said wistfully from the doorway, then, briskly unfastening her jacket, 'Well, we'd best get on with it.'

The grandmother clock in the living room chimed the half-hour just as she spoke, underlining the shortage of time available, and Elspeth reluctantly stripped her own jacket and hat off and donned the apron she had brought with her.

They worked hard all morning, opening drawers and cupboards, clearing shelves, sorting some forty years of Celia Bremner's life into various piles. The flat had been rented, and Elspeth was pleased about that, for she herself could never have lived in it. But once piles of clothes and sheets and towels and boxes filled with old-fashioned underwear and clothes and shawls and gloves and ornaments and cutlery and dishes and pots and pans began to litter the floor space, blurring the edges of the flat's former identity, she changed her mind. If it had been left to her, she could have given it to Thomas as a fitting home for his wife and coming baby.

The clock chimed again, and she closed the bottom drawer she had been emptying and went through to the kitchen, where Rachel was clearing out cupboards.

'We'll have a wee cup of—' she began, then stopped, staring. 'Rachel, where did you get that?'

Rachel, stretching up to a high cupboard, looked blankly at her over one shoulder. 'What?'

'That bruise on your arm.'

Rachel immediately dropped her arms and stepped away from the cupboard, tugging one sleeve down. 'I don't know what you're talking about.'

'Yes you do.' Elspeth caught at the other girl's wrist, and after a brief struggle managed to push the sleeve up to reveal a nasty yellowing bruise on Rachel's upper arm. 'There.'

'Och, that? I banged my arm against the close wall.' Rachel put her free hand nervously to her throat, and Elspeth's eyes followed the movement.

'Did you bang your chest against it too?' Before Rachel could move, Elspeth drew the neck of her blouse aside to reveal another bruise marring the creamy skin.

'I just – I—' Rachel pulled back. 'It's nothing.'

'Rachel—'

'I deserved it,' Rachel said defensively, then, sudden tears filling her eyes. 'Let it be, Ellie!'

'I'll do nothing of the sort. Does Aunt Flora know about this – and Uncle Henry?'

Rachel flew into a panic at mention of her father's name. 'Don't tell him, Ellie, for God's sake! He'll go for Bob, then Bob'll go for me and—'

Elspeth picked up the kettle. 'Sit down, I'm going to make some tea.'

'But there's still a lot of work to do!'

'Never mind the work, just sit down. We'll have some tea, and then,' she added over her shoulder as she wrenched at the tap and began to fill the kettle, 'I want to know what's going on – all of it, Rachel.'

Half an hour later, when Grandmother's teapot, which for the first time in its existence had been filled to the brim with strong dark tea instead of the pale liquid it had normally held, had been emptied, the whole sorry story of Bob Cochran's brutality had been spilled out.

'He doesnae mean it,' Rachel said for the fourth or fifth

233

time, her face puffy and wet with the tears she had shed. 'It's the drink – he's not used to it.'

'But Bob's teetotal.'

'He used to be.' Rachel took a moment to blow her nose and dab at her eyes. 'It was the war – it changed Bob just as much as it changed Lachie, only nobody knew it at the time because there was nothing to see. He worries about things – whether he's goin' to be turned away from his work, and what'd become of us if he was. He even worries in case there's ever another war and he has to go away again. And then he has to have a drink to stop the worrying, then another. And when he comes home wee Mary's crying bothers him, though she can't help it, poor lamb, and one thing leads to another.'

'What about his parents? Do they know he's drinking?'

Rachel's body quivered. 'They found out. Now they'll have nothing to do with him, or me. They won't even look at my poor wee M-mary . . .' The tears began to flow again.

'You have to tell Uncle Henry, Rachel. He'd not let this happen to you if he knew.'

'I daren't, because of what he'd do to Bob. And Mam says—'

'You've told Aunt Flora?' Elspeth asked, astonished. 'She knows about this?'

'I had to tell someone.' Rachel had worked her way through both her own handkerchief and Elspeth's. As more tears streamed down her face Elspeth delved into a drawer and found a tray cloth.

'Here, take this.'

'I can't,' Rachel protested, trying to push it away. 'It's far too bonny – look at the nice stitching!'

'Go on – Grandmother'll never know the difference now. What were you saying about Aunt Flora?'

Rachel mopped at her face. 'She says I have to deal with it myself.'

'What?'

Rachel sprang to her mother's defence. 'She's had enough to worry about with Lachlan, then Thomas and Aileen. And she's right – Bob's my husband, and I married him for better or worse. It's up to me to stop him from drinking and h-hitting me.'

'How?'

'Well—' The tears welled again, and Rachel refolded the tray cloth to find a dry spot. 'If I was a better wife to him, he'd not hit me.'

'Did she say that?' Elspeth asked, outraged, then, as Rachel nodded, 'That's terrible!'

Rachel reached across the table and clutched at her hand. 'Promise me you'll say nothing to anybody!'

'But Rachel—'

'Promise!' the girl insisted, and Elspeth chewed her lower lip for a moment, then said reluctantly, 'If that's what you want.'

'It is.' Rachel gave her nose a final blow, and got up to splash cold water on her face. 'It's helped, just talking about it – now, let's get on with the work.'

It took two weeks to clear the house, working at weekends and in the evenings. Every time Elspeth thought she had finished at last, she discovered another drawer stuffed with half-finished knitting or sewing or boxes of buttons.

When it was done, she gave all the bed linen and napery to Rachel, urging her to sell what she didn't want, and spend the money on herself and Mary.

'Don't let Bob take it for drink.'

'I can't stop him,' Rachel said listlessly. She had lost all her confidence, Elspeth realised, and wondered why she and the rest of the family hadn't noticed the change in the girl before. 'If he sees me buyin' stuff we can't afford on his wages he'll want to know where the money's coming from.'

'Then put it aside, to use when you need it.'

'He'll only find it,' Rachel said, and in the end Elspeth sold the linen and napery herself to the owner of a small second-hand shop, and banked the money for Rachel.

Granjan and Aileen also benefited from the flat clearance, but Flora refused to accept anything. Celia Bremner's clothes, together with the small household items left, were collected by a charity happy to get them, and Elspeth called in an auctioneer to take the furniture and carpets off her hands.

Taking a final look round on the day the furniture was to be removed, she discovered that a small drawer tucked away in her grandmother's large mothball-smelling wardrobe refused to shut flush with its framework. After struggling with it for a few moments, she pulled it clear and knelt to feel in the space behind it. The blockage had been caused by a few letters without envelopes, tied together with a piece of string.

Replacing the drawer, which now slid smoothly into place, she sat back on her heels and loosened the string, which had been tied in a neat bow. The pages, released, fell across her lap like dead leaves, and she gasped as the word 'Whore!' seemed to fly up at her from among them. It was scrawled across one of the sheets in a large, angular hand, written so viciously that here and there the pen had broken through the paper. It was repeated on every sheet, almost obliterating the cramped copperplate writing beneath.

The doorknocker crashed on to its brass plate in a way that would have set Grandmother's eyes flashing. Elspeth jumped, then hurriedly gathered the pages up and thrust them into her pocket as she went to let the auctioneer's men in.

Their loud voices and the tramp of their feet across wood and linoleum banished the last trace of Celia Bremner from the house she had lived in for so long. When they had gone, taking the furniture with them and leaving only its imprint on the papered walls, the flat was large and echoing, a place that Elspeth had never been in before.

She closed the door behind the last man and took the letters out of her pocket, moving into the parlour to hold a sheet up to the light from the window, squinting at it until she managed to make out the words, 'My dearest Robert.'

Her eyes flew automatically to the mantel shelf where her grandparents' photograph had stood. Now it was packed into a box under her bed in Mearns Street, together with the few pieces of jewellery she had come across. It was only then that she realised that there had been no trace of her grandfather in the flat either, apart from the photograph. Celia Bremner had wiped both daughter and husband from her life. Everything apart from a few letters written to her grandfather, Elspeth discovered as she strained to decipher the faded writing on the pages in her hand, and even they had been defaced until it was almost impossible to make much out.

As she grew accustomed to the writing, she realised that she was looking at love letters, signed with the name 'Ann'.

Time was passing; she pushed the letters into her pocket and got on with the task of sweeping the floors and making sure that everything was clean and neat for the new tenants.

Leaving the flat for the last time, she walked to the factor's office in Port Glasgow to hand the key in, then squandered a few pennies on a tram ride back to Greenock, too tired for once to walk home.

There was nobody in the flat when she got back. Flora would no doubt be at Rachel's, Lachlan often visited Thomas and Aileen on a Saturday afternoon, and Henry would be at the bowling green with his cronies. In the kitchen, she pulled the letters from her pocket, recalling the story Granjan had revealed about Robert Bremner leaving his wife, eloping with a colleague. At the time Elspeth had struggled to put the tale out of her mind, fearful that Grandmother's sharp eyes might bore right into her skull and discover what she knew. She had succeeded so well that she had almost forgotten it, until reminded by the letters.

Somehow, her grandmother had got hold of them, and had kept them hidden away, perhaps taking them out to read now

237

and then, tormenting herself, stoking the flames of bitterness, nursing her hatred and keeping it alive. Even when the man was dead – and surely the lawyer must have informed her that she was then, truly, widowed – she had kept the letters, refusing to let the matter end.

This, Elspeth thought with horror, was the woman whose blood ran in her own veins. She vowed there and then that she herself would never, ever bear a grudge, or allow bitterness to warp her life as it had warped Celia Bremner's. She lost all desire to decipher the letters further; even lying in her hand they seemed to radiate a pain that she couldn't bear.

Instead, she crumpled them into the empty grate, then took the big box of matches that always stood on the mantel shelf and struck one. Afterwards, she crushed the ashes into powder which she swept up and took down to the midden in the back court, watching with relief the last grains fall from the shovel.

Now the letters were where they belonged, out of harm's way at last.

As Elspeth went back upstairs, she paused on the final landing where the colours from the stained-glass window lay like a spilled rainbow on the stone floor. The letters Celia had kept hidden all those years had suddenly become linked in her mind with the present; a thought occurred to her that surely couldn't be right. And yet . . .

She ran up the last flight of stairs, anxious to make the most of the little time she had left to herself in the empty flat. In the kitchen, she drew aside the curtains hiding the wall-bed and went down on her knees to scrabble in the space beneath the bed. Flora McDonald kept a large biscuit box there, right at the back, a box that nobody, including Henry, was permitted to touch.

Elspeth's groping fingers found it, and she drew it out into the open, prising the lid up and riffling hurriedly through Flora's most precious possessions – her marriage certificate, her children's birth certificates, letters written by Thomas and Lachlan during the war. She had reached the bottom of the box and begun to think, with relief, that she had been mistaken, when her fingers touched a slim bundle.

For the second time that afternoon, Elspeth drew a well-kept secret from its hiding place. This one, like the letters in Celia Bremner's flat, was tied with string; she had no need to unfasten it, for one glance showed that it held half a dozen postcards, bearing pictures of various Scottish towns and addressed to Lachlan.

Flora was the first of the family to return home, arriving just after Elspeth had returned the box to its proper place and closed the curtains. She retained the small package of postcards, and as soon as her aunt came in she silently laid them on the table.

Flora's eyes almost bulged as they took in the postcards, and her mouth worked silently for a few moments before she managed to speak.

'Where did ye get these?'

Elspeth swallowed hard. She had done a terrible thing, but surely right was on her side. 'I went looking for them and I found them. They belong to Lachlan, Aunt Flora, not to you.'

Again, Flora McDonald's mouth worked for a second or two before she said, 'I'll not have any son of mine gettin' involved with a woman that earns her livin' on the stage!'

'There's no harm in the postcards – you saw how pleased he was to get the first two.'

'Oh, I saw all right – why d'ye think I held the others back? He's had enough hurt, without her givin' him more.'

'Hiding the cards didn't save him any pain – he was hurt at the thought that Lena had forgotten about him.' Elspeth pushed the postcards across the table. 'Give them back, Aunt Flora. Tell him they must have been held up somewhere and they all arrived today.'

'I should've put them in the fire when they first came!'

'If you burn them now I'll tell him about them.'

'So this is what it's come tae? After all I've done for ye, this is the thanks I get?' Flora pulled her hat off and thrust the hatpin through it savagely, then attacked her jacket, wrenching buttons from buttonholes. 'Have I not had tae suffer enough shame over Thomas as it is? I'm not lettin' our Lachie go the same way. This is a respectable family!'

Exasperation flared beyond caution. 'It'll not be a family for much longer if all you worry about is what the neighbours think. Thomas and Aileen are happy together – surely that's all that matters!'

'She's not the right woman for our Thomas.'

'You thought Bob Cochran was the right man for Rachel, and look what's happened to her.'

'There's nothing wrong with Rachel's marriage,' Flora flared.

'I've seen Rachel's bruises, Aunt Flora, and heard about Bob's drinking and the way he treats her. She's told me that you know all about it, yet you've done nothing to help her.'

'Mind yer own business!' Flora McDonald slammed both hands down hard on the table. Seeing the rage in the woman's face, Elspeth thought she had gone too far. She took a step back, clutching at a chair for support.

'Ye've been nothin' but a troublemaker since ye left the school,' Flora hissed into the space between them. 'Sidin' with Thomas when he came between me and Lachlan, sendin' that girl tae the Infirmary when Thomas was hurt – oh, I knew your hand was in it somewhere, madam, for ye cannae keep out of other folk's business, can ye?'

She hauled open a drawer in the dresser, and fumbled through it, then extracted an opened letter and tossed it on to the table.

'Here's another thing ye can poke yer neb intae. This came yesterday, and I was tryin' tae find the right time tae tell ye about it, but ye might as well read it for yerself,' she said coldly. 'Go on – read it!'

Slowly, Elspeth drew the letter from its envelope. It was from Mattie, and ran along the lines of the letters Elspeth herself received from the girl, telling about her progress at a school she was teaching in as part of her training. Puzzled, Elspeth looked up at her aunt, who stood watching her closely. Her face was hard and unforgiving.

'Try the next page,' she ordered.

At first, Elspeth's eyes ran along the close-packed lines without taking in the words, then she blinked, focused, and started again.

'There's something you should know, Mam,' Mattie had written. 'I need to tell someone before I come home for the summer, because I don't know what to do about it. Kenneth and I—'

Elspeth read to the end, a paralysing chill descending on her and numbing her body until she had no physical sense of her feet on the floor or her fingers holding the letter. Just as she finished, the outer door opened and Henry's tuneless whistle was heard in the hall. Flora scooped up the postcards with one hand, reaching the other across the table to pluck the letter from Elspeth's unresisting fingers.

'One word from you about Rachel,' she hissed, 'and you're out on the pavement – d'ye understand?'

Then Henry was in the room, filling it with noise and movement as usual, quite unaware of the tension between his wife and their foster child.

It was easy enough for Elspeth to slip out of the kitchen and out of the flat without arousing comment. She sped down the stairs; once outside she started to walk quickly, not thinking of where she was going.

Sickened by the ugly scene in the kitchen, she wished that she had never thought of looking for Lachlan's postcards. Then, remembering the sudden radiance in his face after Lena had kissed him at the theatre, and when he received the first postcard, she knew that he had been cruelly wronged, and deserved her help. Lena's fondness for him was probably too fragile to last, but Lachlan was entitled to know that at least she had cared enough to keep in contact, and hadn't forgotten him so soon.

But she had had to pay a bitter price for defending him. 'Kenneth and I—' The words sang mockingly in her head as she walked. Kenneth and Mattie. Kenneth being kind to Mattie at Elspeth's request, helping her to settle into her new life in Glasgow.

Their meetings must have continued, first of all by chance, then by arrangement and choice. Kenneth and Mattie, falling in love, planning to marry when he had gained his degree, and at a loss as to how to break the news to poor Elspeth.

'Could you tell her for me, Mam?' Mattie had written. 'Do it as gently as you can. I don't know how I'll face her. Kenneth's working in Glasgow for most of the summer, so he'll not be home for long. I won't either, I'm coming back early to be with him.'

Aunt Flora had certainly found a way of breaking the news, and at the same time had found a way of punishing her foster daughter for having dared to interfere in family business.

Elspeth wondered if Kenneth had tried to go further than kisses and cuddles with Mattie. If so, how had Mattie responded? She was older than Elspeth, and probably more worldly-wise since moving to Glasgow. Instead of panicking as she, Elspeth, had done in the wash house that night, Mattie might have given Kenneth what he wanted, and given it gladly.

Turning a corner, Elspeth was astonished to see the garage where Thomas worked only yards along the street. She looked round, down over the rooftops to the sun-blessed river below. Without noticing, she had climbed almost to the inland edge of the town.

Thomas was working on a car in the yard. Alerted by her footsteps on the cobbles, he looked up. 'Ellie?' At once, his expression changed. 'Has something happened to Aileen?'

'No, of course not. Why should it?'

'You looked so serious.' He reached for a rag and wiped his oily fingers, then glanced at her again. 'If it's not Aileen, what is it?'

'Nothing, I was just passing.'

'Nobody just passes along this street.' Thomas came round the bulk of the car he was working on. 'What's wrong?'

The concern in his voice was her undoing. She felt her face melt as though it was made of candle grease, and Thomas's figure, as he came towards her, shimmered as tears filled her eyes and began to spill over.

'Come on, I'll make us a cup of tea.' He put a firm hand beneath her elbow.

'Your work—' she protested as he began to lead her over the cobbles towards a door.

'I can take a few minutes off, and Mr Cameron's not here this afternoon, so you don't need to worry about him.'

He urged her through the door and she stopped in her tracks, staring round at the small, filthy kitchen.

'This is terrible!'

'It serves its purpose,' Thomas said blithely, pulling a chair forward and filling the kettle at a squeaky old tap. 'We only use the place for making tea now and again.' Then, as she continued to stare round in horror, 'Never mind the state of the place – sit down and tell me what's bothering you.'

At his reminder, her misery came flooding back. She collapsed into the chair, not caring about her skirt, and poured out the story of Kenneth and Mattie while salty tears trickled, one after another, down her cheeks.

'Well, well – Mattie and Kenneth.' Thomas pushed a mug of tea into her hand. 'Drink that down, now.'

She did as he was told. The tea was very sweet and very hot. The first tentative sip burned its way down into her stomach, and the second set up a glow that began to thaw out the numbed feeling. She looked gratefully at Thomas, who was propped against the sink, cradling his own mug in both hands. Dirty and oily though it was, his face was kind and concerned and his sympathy was so obvious that she felt that if she had reached out a hand she could have touched it.

'How do you really feel about it?' he asked, taking her by

surprise. She opened her mouth to reply, then sipped at her tea instead, giving herself time to think about the question.

Kenneth had never said much in his letters, and he had certainly not made any declarations of love. The letters had eased off over the past month or so, but she had been too busy visiting Grandmother in hospital then clearing out her house, to notice. She had assumed that in the summer, when he came back from the university, everything would go on as before.

'I want him to be mine, not Mattie's,' she said at last, slowly. Then, tipping her head back to look up at Thomas, 'But mebbe I only want him because now he's Mattie's.'

'D'you want to spend the rest of your life with him?' Thomas probed, and smiled when she replied, irritably, 'I don't know – I'm too young to think of the rest of my life.'

'You're right there – you're still far too young to tie yourself down. And no matter what age you are when the right one comes along, you know about it when it happens. Take my word for it – and let Mattie have Kenneth, if she wants him so badly.'

'I'd not want to keep him against his will – but it hurts,' she admitted candidly, 'knowing that he prefers someone else to me.'

A smile pulled at the corners of his mouth, and was quickly subdued. 'I know, Ellie. It's happened to me too, and it always hurts. But that's the way life is sometimes.' Then a frown puckered his brow. 'But I don't understand why Mam let you read the letter without giving you any warning. She didnae need to be so cruel.'

Again, Elspeth opened her mouth then closed it. She had promised Rachel that she would say nothing about Bob's ill-treatment, and if she was to tell Thomas about Lachlan's postcards being kept from him, it would probably do the new and fragile relationship that he and his mother had started to build no good at all.

'What is it?' He was watching her closely. 'You're gasping

like a baggy minnow that's just been scooped out of a pond.'

She got up and eased him aside so that she could rinse out the empty mug. 'I was cheeky to Aunt Flora, so she gave me the letter to punish me.'

'You must have been awful cheeky to deserve what you got.'

'I was,' she said shortly, and he had the sense to leave it at that.

As they left the kitchen, Elspeth to return to Mearns Street, Thomas to get back to his work, she put her arms about him and hugged him closely. He smelled of cars and oil and, faintly, of the soap Aileen kept by her kitchen sink.

'Here—' he protested, surprised and embarrassed.

'I don't know what I'd do without you, Thomas.'

'Ach, away ye go and let me get on with my work,' he said gruffly. Even so, he returned the hug for a moment before opening the door and shooing her out into the yard.

Going back down the hill, she felt warmed and healed by that moment of contact with another person. The coming baby was very fortunate to have such loving parents as Thomas and Aileen, she thought, then pushed the thought away hurriedly because it reminded her of her own situation, orphaned and, as far as she knew, without kith or kin.

When she got back to the flat Elspeth went straight to her own room and peered into the small mirror on the wall. The tea, the talk with Thomas, and the walk home had cleared all traces of tears, though her mouth had a downward twist. She forced a smile at her reflection, pulling a comb through her hair at the same time, and vowed to herself that she would never let Flora McDonald know how much Mattie's letter had hurt her.

When Lachlan tapped at the door a few minutes later she was ready to face him, her hair neat and her smile pinned firmly in place.

'Look!' He was almost incoherent with pleasure. 'Postcards

from Lena, lots of them from all over.' He began to spread them across the bed, reciting, 'Dundee, Inverness, Fort William, Perth, Paisley, Ayr. They must have been stuck somewhere, then they all arrived together. You can read them,' he offered magnanimously.

Although she felt that she had had more than her share that day of reading other people's letters, Elspeth did as she was bid. Lena's spelling left much to be desired, but her enthusiasm spilled across the small space allowed for messages. She seemed to be having a wonderful time, and pleasing audiences everywhere the troupe went. Each card, Elspeth noted, ended with a casual, 'Love, Lena.'

'They're lovely, but Lachlan, Lena's always been a bit' – she searched for the right phrase, but could only think of – 'generous towards folk. She treats everyone the same way.'

'You're worried in case I believe it when she sends her love,' he said in a surprisingly matter-of-fact voice, gathering the cards into a neat stack. 'I don't, but it's great tae have a friend. For a wee while there I was so shy and scared that I was like a wean again. I thought I'd never feel comfortable with anyone outside this house. Now I feel differently, and Lena's helped.' He gave her a slightly embarrassed smile. 'When the cards stopped I was a bit hurt because it was so sudden, but I got over that. If they stop again, it won't bother me.'

Flora was unusually quiet that evening. Throughout the evening meal, she slid sidelong glances at Elspeth, who was deliberately cheerful and carefree. It was, she thought later when she had escaped to her room, a performance that would surely have won her a place in the troupe that Lena worked with.

25

By unspoken agreement, a truce was decided between Elspeth and Flora, with neither making any further reference to the ugly quarrel they had had. But as far as Elspeth was concerned, the harm had been done, and the animosity she had sensed in her foster mother, even in babyhood, had been brought into the open. Nothing, she thought, absently fingering the little pebble brooch pinned to her blouse, would ever be the same again.

Mattie and Kenneth both wrote to her, their letters arriving on the following Saturday morning. They lay unopened in her pocket until the afternoon; she finally opened them on the beach where she and Kenneth had often picnicked with the others, and where she was free to settle her back against a rock and read with only the seagulls for company.

Both were short and apologetic, both spoke of fighting against their growing feelings for each other, and losing. They both expressed a hope that Elspeth would be able to understand, and to forgive.

She stared out across the water, seeing the two of them in her mind's eye, writing their letters together, comparing words and phrases. The waves washing almost to her feet echoed their sighs of relief when they finally signed their names, folded the single sheets of paper, and sealed them into envelopes. She pictured them walking together to a postbox, slipping the letters into its waiting mouth, then hurrying away, fingers entwined, thankful that the difficult task was over, and free, now that they had confessed, to enjoy their love.

She wanted to cry, but there were no tears left. Instead, she tore the letters up, tossing the shreds of paper to the breeze, which then committed them to the water. She had had enough of letters that had been kept and agonised over – the past was past, and only the future mattered.

As the time for Mattie's return from Glasgow drew near, Elspeth sought for ways and means of keeping herself too busy to think about the summer she had once looked forward to. Mr Monteith, well pleased with the work she had done for him, had told her several weeks earlier about a friend of his, a second-hand furniture dealer in Port Glasgow, who could do with some help with his paperwork. Elspeth put on her best hat and coat and paid a visit to the man, coming home with an armful of books to work on.

Lachlan offered to take Elspeth to the pictures on the day of Mattie's arrival, and was surprised when she refused.

'But Kenneth'll be coming as well, for his tea, and Mam'll probably make a fuss of them both. You'll not want to be there when that's going on.'

'I have to be there. I have to face the two of them sometime, Lachie, and it might as well be now.' Even to her own ears she sounded very cool and grown-up, although her stomach was full of butterflies.

He scowled. 'I think our Mattie's got a cheek, parading him in front of you.'

'She's got every right to bring her fiancé to her own home.'

'Are you telling me that you don't mind?'

Elspeth had never lied to Lachlan or Thomas, and wasn't going to start now. 'I minded a lot when I first heard, but I've got used to the idea now. I'd not have wanted Kenneth to stay with me against his will. And I'm going to be here when Mattie brings him home.'

'Oh, all right – but if you feel that you want to get out of the place, tip me the wink and I'll think of something.'

When the moment came, it was hard for her to see the happiness in Mattie and Kenneth's faces and to hear Flora making such a fuss of the two of them. But Elspeth had worked hard to prepare for the ordeal, and she managed to deal with it calmly, congratulating them both and admiring the engagement ring Kenneth had given Mattie. That made it official, she thought, gazing down at the small diamond. There was no chance now of Kenneth changing his mind and asking her to take him back.

Lachlan hovered around Elspeth protectively all afternoon, giving Kenneth a curt nod when he arrived, then eyeing him coldly across the table during the meal. Henry, too, tended to sympathise with her, but Kenneth and Mattie both looked so guilty each time they caught Elspeth's eye that she found herself making a point of being nice to them both.

As the rest of the family were there as well – Granjan and Thomas and Aileen, Rachel and wee Mary – things were easier for Elspeth. The kitchen was so crowded that it was easy for her to avoid the happy couple after greeting them.

Flora, glowing with pleasure and triumph at the good marriage her younger daughter was making, found herself eclipsed somewhat when Thomas announced at the table that his employer, Forbes Cameron, had decided to buy a partnership in a larger garage in Gourock.

'He's going to spend most of his time there, and I'm to run the Greenock garage for him,' he said proudly. 'I've not been there long, but he's pleased with my work and says he couldn't find a better man for the job. I'm to get in another mechanic to work under me. And it means more money, so' – he put an arm round Aileen, sitting by his side – 'we'll be able to afford a better flat before the bairn arrives.'

As the two girls were going to bed that night, Mattie tried to explain, as she had in her letter, that she and Kenneth hadn't intended to fall in love. Elspeth, who couldn't face the prospect of another discussion about the matter, broke in almost at once.

'Mattie, Kenneth and me were just friends, nothing more. I don't mind about what's happened.' She wasn't sure whether that was a lie or not. She was still hurt, but at the same time she was aware of a faint sense of freedom. 'He cares more for you than he ever did for me, and there's nothing else to be said about it.'

Mattie's eyes, which had been sliding away from Elspeth ever since she arrived, brightened. 'You're awful generous, Ellie.'

'I'm just being sensible,' Elspeth told her briskly, then, longing to change the subject, 'It's good news about Thomas, isn't it?'

Celia Bremner's furniture was sold not long after Mattie and Kenneth returned to Glasgow, raising more money than Elspeth had expected. She would have liked to spend it on the others, but realised that in view of the tension between herself and Flora, that would not be wise. Instead, she bought small gifts for Granjan and Rachel and wee Mary, and a pretty scarf in different shades of green to match Aileen's eyes.

'I'm so glad to see you!' the girl welcomed her when she called with the gift. 'Thomas is working late again, and I'm tired of my own company.'

The note of complaint in her voice, unusual for Aileen, put Elspeth on the defensive. 'He's trying to make a success of running the garage on his own, so that he can earn enough to give you and the bairn a good life.'

'I know, but—' Aileen hesitated, then said slowly, 'Has he told you that Ian's offered to give us a loan until things get better?'

'Your brother? Thomas would never agree to that!'

'Thomas,' his wife said shortly, 'has more pride than he can

251

afford. I don't see why we shouldn't accept – Ian's my brother, after all, and he only wants to help. It would make such a difference to us, yet Thomas refused to even discuss it.'

'Can you blame him, after what happened?'

Aileen flushed. 'That was ages ago, and Ian's done everything he can since then to make up for it. It's Thomas who's being difficult now. You'd think he'd want what's best for both of us. For a start, we could move out of this place and into something with more room.' She threw her hands out to indicate the small kitchen that she had so lovingly painted and furnished less than a year ago, then said with sudden hope, 'Would you speak to him, Elspeth? He thinks highly of you, and he'd listen to you. You could explain to him that Ian only wants to help us.'

'But I couldn't interfere in Thomas's life,' Elspeth said wretchedly, then, as Aileen opened her mouth to argue, she held out the small package. 'Grandmother's furniture's been sold, so I brought you a wee gift to celebrate.'

To her relief, Aileen brightened at once, exclaiming with delight over the scarf then tying it round her neck and admiring herself in the small wall mirror.

Thomas arrived just then, his eyes suddenly wary as he stepped into the room and saw the pretty green scarf about his wife's throat.

'Is this another of your brother's wee presents? Aileen, I've told you—'

'Elspeth gave it to me. I suppose that's acceptable, since she's a member of your family, not mine?' There was a sharpness in Aileen's voice that Elspeth had never heard before, and she wished that she had left before Thomas's arrival.

He flushed scarlet beneath the streaks of dirt and oil from the garage. 'I'm sorry, Ellie, I didn't realise,' he said, then as he looked again at his wife, the wariness fled and he smiled. 'The colour matches your eyes. You look lovely.' He moved to hug her, but she backed away.

'Don't get oil all over it. I wish you'd wash at the garage, Thomas, and not walk through the streets looking like that.'

'I told you, if I take the time to heat water on the gas ring, a customer's sure to arrive while I'm doing it, then I'm trapped for another half-hour.' He poured hot water from the kettle on the range into a basin and snapped open the metal fastenings holding the shoulder straps of his dirty dungarees. 'It's best to just lock up and go while the place is empty. As for walking home like this, a wee bit of dirt's a badge of honour. There's plenty of poor souls in this town that'd give anything they had for the chance to get their hands dirty from work.'

He stepped out of the overalls and tossed them on to the newspaper waiting in the corner for them, then reached for the harsh yellow soap by the sink and began to wash.

'I'd best go and let you have your meal in peace,' Elspeth said, but Thomas, dousing his face, spluttered through a veil of water, 'Wait a bit, Ellie, I want to ask you about something.'

'What did you buy for yourself?' Aileen wanted to know.

'A new pair of gloves.' Now that the angry flush had left the other girl's cheeks, Elspeth saw that there were shadows beneath her slightly slanted eyes, and the corners of her mouth were drawn down. The baby was showing now and increasing weight had robbed Aileen of her usual grace; as she picked up a jug and went to rinse Thomas's hair she put her feet down heavily, moving with the sway-backed walk of pregnancy.

Her blouse and skirt strained tightly over her rounded belly, so that the hem at the front of the skirt was dragged up, giving the garment an uneven look.

Elspeth felt a stab of pity for the girl. If she had married her own class, she would have been pampered throughout this pregnancy, not allowed to lift even a finger. She would have worn clothes specially made for the occasion, cut skilfully to conceal her swelling figure. Instead, she was denied the luxury that was hers by birthright, forced to cope as best she could. It was little wonder that she was tired and irritable.

'How would you like me to make you a new dress?' she offered impulsively. 'Something loose and more comfortable.'

Aileen handed Thomas a towel and he buried his head and face in it. 'Could you?' Her eyes lit up, the weariness and stress vanishing. For a moment she was pretty and carefree again, then her eyes clouded. 'How much would the material cost?'

'Whatever it is, we'll find the money,' Thomas put in quickly from the folds of the towel. 'It's well past time you had a new dress.'

'Don't worry about the cost – we get remnants for nothing at work, and there's a lovely piece of silky material lying in the sewing room just now, a nice bluey-green that would suit you.'

It wasn't true. Miss Arnold didn't allow the girls in the sewing room to take even the smallest scraps that were left over from their work. As Lena used to say, the overseer wouldn't have given her nail-clippings away free. But Elspeth had been admiring the piece of blue-green material on the remnants counter at Brodie's that very day. It wouldn't cost much, and she could use some of Grandmother's money.

'I'll bring the material in tomorrow, on my way home from work,' she promised. 'We can decide on the style once you've had a look at it.'

Aileen nodded eagerly, her face radiant, as Thomas turned from the sink, running his fingers through his wet hair. 'I'm looking for a favour from you as well, Ellie.' He looked embarrassed. 'With me being in charge of the garage now, it means that I've to balance the books and send out the accounts. I've never in my life had to see to that side of things – I just handed my pay packet to Mam and she handed back my spending money. It was much the same in the army. And Aileen here has no more idea of working with money than I have, though' – he shot a proud look at his wife – 'I've never seen anyone make a few coppers go further than she can.'

Aileen coloured, and said quickly, 'I'm learning, but I can't deal with ledgers and payments and all that sort of thing. I'm still finding out about the cost of vegetables and washing soap.'

'So I thought mebbe you could show me how to do the books,' Thomas went on. 'I'll try to learn from you so that I can take them over myself soon.'

He was running a comb through his hair now; it clung to his skull, combining with his newly scrubbed face to take years off his age. He and Aileen, Elspeth thought as she looked from one to the other, both looked too young to shoulder all the responsibilities and worries that crowded in on them. At that moment, she felt older than either of them, though she was several years their junior.

'Of course I will. Can you bring them home with you tomorrow? I'll have a look at them after I've measured Aileen for the dress.'

Studying the ledgers and cash-books spread before her, Elspeth could see that although Forbes Cameron had known what he was about, Thomas didn't. His financial dealings since taking over the garage reminded her of Mr Monteith's book-keeping.

'I've not got the time to do it all properly as well as getting on with my own work,' he explained anxiously, watching as she riffled through the notes he had made. By his side, Aileen caressed the dress material Elspeth had bought that morning from the remnants counter.

'To tell the truth, it would take too long to sit down and teach you how to keep your own books, but I could see to them for you if you want, and teach you what I can when you've got the time. I could type out your bills properly while I'm at it.'

His eyes lit up. 'That would be grand! How much will you want for it?'

She thought fast, guessing that any money he paid her would have to come from his own wages.

'You've got an office at the garage, haven't you?'

'It's not much – a room with a desk and a gas ring and a paraffin heater.'

'Could I move my typewriter in and work there? I think Aunt Flora's getting tired of the noise the typewriter makes,' she hurried on as Thomas raised his eyebrows. 'If I could use your office I'd do your books in place of paying rent – unless you think Mr Cameron would object.'

'He'll not bother his head about it. But it's not a very cosy room, Ellie.'

'That'll make me work faster, so that I can get away to somewhere more comfortable.'

'In that case, you've got a deal.' Thomas took her hand and shook it vigorously. 'I'll collect the typewriter from Mearns Street tomorrow.'

26

The garage workshop had at one time been the stable and carriage-house of a sturdy Georgian family home on the hill above Greenock. As the town expanded the garden had disappeared beneath cobbled streets and small factories, but the house still remained, its brickwork badly in need of repointing, its high, wide windows either boarded up or so dirty that it was impossible to see through them, its once-handsome front door dingy and permanently sealed.

The only usable entrance to the old building was the kitchen door, which opened from a cobbled yard where horses had once been led out to be yoked to carriages. The upper floor and the attic had been closed off, and only the front two ground rooms were in use, one as a storeroom, the other an office of sorts.

Thomas was right, Elspeth discovered at first sight of the room. It was the most cheerless place she had ever seen. Large and high-ceilinged, it had once been a drawing room, but now the timbered floor was scuffed and scored, faded paper hung dismally from the walls, and the mouldings on the ceiling could scarcely be seen in the dim light from a filthy window. The enormous fireplace lurked against one wall like the mouth of a dark and dismal cave, and the furniture consisted of a few chairs, a paraffin stove, a large sideboard piled with books and papers, a sagging *chaise-longue* that looked as though it had crept into the house to die, and a dusty table where Thomas set down her typewriter. The bulky machine, which had dominated her little bedroom, suddenly seemed small and quite forlorn in the middle of the long table.

'I told you it was cheerless,' Thomas said from behind her as she gazed round. 'Are you sure you want to work here?'

'I'm quite sure. At least I can make as much noise as I like without disturbing anyone,' she added wryly as a loud crash came from the direction of the yard.

'I'd better go and see what Joe's up to,' Thomas said hurriedly, and left.

Now that she was alone, Elspeth took time to study the place more closely, noting the dust that lay everywhere, and the grime on the windows, cutting down considerably on the amount of light in the room. At least something could be done about that. Tiptoeing across the hall, a square, gloomy place with a curved stairway leading up into total darkness, she found that the room at the other side was filled with bits of machinery. She hurriedly closed the door after one brief glance and returned to the office, wiping her dusty hands on her handkerchief.

'I hope you're not going to start fussing,' Thomas said anxiously when he returned to find her rubbing hard at the table with a rag she had located. 'It's only an office, mind.'

'I know, but nobody could work in there the way it is. All that dust'll ruin the typewriter. Don't worry, I'm not going to expect you or Joe to start painting and papering.'

Rachel willingly agreed to help, and the two of them spent the following weekend scrubbing and sweeping and climbing precariously on to chairs in order to knock down spiders' webs with mops lashed to broom handles. They wrapped themselves in huge aprons and swathed their heads in scarves to protect their hair against the dust. Baby Mary slumbered in her perambulator in a safe corner of the yard.

'It's been a bonny house,' Rachel said breathlessly, balancing on the windowsill and rubbing hard at the glass. 'Imagine living in a place like this, with nice furniture, and flowers outside the windows instead of just the street and folk passing by.'

'And a servant to come and turn the pages of your book for you,' Elspeth agreed from the sideboard, where she was sorting through the books, shaking each one vigorously to clear the dust from it. She was enjoying Rachel's company. They had never really known each other before, for Mattie was nearer Elspeth's age and Rachel had always been the older sister, contemptuous of the two younger girls. Now, Elspeth discovered that Rachel was a good companion, with a sense of fun she had never demonstrated before.

As the other girl stretched up to the top of the window, Elspeth noticed a few bruises on her arms. Clearly, Bob was still ill-treating his wife. But she had the wit to say nothing, taking her frustration and anger out instead on a fragment of wallpaper dangling above the sideboard, wrenching it savagely from the wall. It came away with a satisfactory ripping sound, showering her with grit.

'Ellie, what're you doing?'

'It might as well be off as hanging there.' Elspeth stepped back to look at her handiwork, refastening the scarf round her head. 'If we brush over the plaster it'll look better than the way it was.'

'Let me.' Rachel deftly stepped from the sill to a chair, then caught at another drooping piece of wallpaper and tore it free. 'It feels good, doesn't it?' she said with enthusiasm. When she laughed, Elspeth noticed, she looked years younger.

Half an hour later, when Thomas glanced in to see how they were getting on, there was a small pile of paper in the middle of the floor.

'You don't mind, do you?' Elspeth asked, noting Rachel swiftly tugging her sleeves down to ensure that the finger-shaped blue marks on her arms were hidden. 'The walls looked worse with the paper than they do without it.'

He shrugged, and handed over two mugs of strong tea. 'As long as you get my books into order I don't care what you do.'

Their throats were clogged with dust, so they went out into the yard to drink their tea, Rachel going at once to the perambulator to look at her daughter. Six-month-old Mary, oblivious to the noise from the workshop, was sound asleep on her back, one arm thrown above her head, long dark lashes brushing her plump cheeks.

Joe, the man Thomas had hired when he took over the running of the garage, came over to admire the baby. He was a cheerful man in his forties, a marine engineer who had lost his job as a seaman after an accident damaged one leg. Although he could no longer shin up and down the narrow metal ladders of an engine room he was well able to cope with garage work, and enjoyed dealing with cars and motor bicycles instead of ships' engines.

He touched the baby's half-open hand very gently with the tip of one finger, taking care not to dirty her white skin. 'That's a right bonny wee lassie ye've got there, hen.'

Rachel smiled shyly, then said when the man had gone back to work, 'I wish she'd been a laddie.'

'Why?'

'Women don't have much of a time – not women like us, anyway.'

'Are things still bad?' Elspeth ventured, and the older girl shrugged.

'They're no worse, and I suppose I ought to be grateful for that. Never marry for love, Ellie, it doesnae buy food or pay the rent, and it only makes folks bitter in the end.' She bent to draw the blanket gently round her slumbering daughter. 'I'm going to try to teach her that when she's older.' Then, straightening, she said suddenly, bleakly, 'I'm expecting again, Ellie, but don't say a word to anyone till I tell Mam. She'll want to be the first to know.'

'What does Bob say?'

'It's not something I'm in a hurry to tell him. I'll have to pick my time.'

'He'll be pleased, surely.' And surely, Elspeth thought, he'd be kinder to Rachel when she was carrying his child.

Rachel's mouth twisted wryly. 'I was daft enough to think he'd be pleased when I fell with Mary, but that's when the trouble started. To him a bairn's just another mouth to feed and one less drink. That's why I'm hoping this'll be a wee laddie – he might take that a bit better.'

'Why don't you do sewing for folk to make more money, since Bob's drinking most of his wages?'

'I couldn't,' Rachel said at once, startled.

'Yes you could. You earned your living by sewing before you married, and you're good at it. Look at the bonny wee clothes you've made for Mary. There must be neighbours who can't sew – you could offer to help them.'

'They'd not be able to pay me.'

'Money's not the only way to pay for things. They could look after Mary for an hour and let you get some time to yourself, or mebbe give you a few scones, or – there are lots of ways folk can help each other,' Elspeth pointed out. 'If any of your neighbours does cleaning for someone with money, she could mebbe mention your name, then you might get work from people who can afford to pay.'

'I'll think about it. We'd best get back to work.'

'You should have told me about the bairn,' Elspeth said as they rinsed their mugs in the kitchen. 'I'd not have let you climb up on the windowsill or the chairs.'

Rachel threw her a sidelong look from the corner of her eye. 'Why else did you think I was so keen to do it?' she asked, and went back to work.

With the layers of dust removed and daylight filtering in through the cleaned windows, the office, while still shabby and neglected, was at least usable. Elspeth started working there the following weekend, relishing the space she now had.

In her bedroom, papers had been strewn over the bed and

261

the floor, but here the table was large enough to accommodate them all. It was satisfying, too, to hear the crisp tapping of the typewriter keys and the crash of the returning carriage echo in the large room, knowing that Flora wasn't going to bang on the door to tell her to stop the noise.

It didn't take her long to put the garage books into order. She did Mr Monteith's work there too, as well as Mr Leslie's, the shopkeeper who had heard of her skills from Mr Monteith. Normally, she would only have been able to work in the office on a Saturday morning, but Thomas, in his eagerness to do his best for Aileen and their coming child, often worked into the evenings from Monday to Saturday, and always spent part of every Sunday at the garage, making it possible for Elspeth to put in longer hours than she had expected.

He was driving himself too hard, but her attempts to tell him that were brushed aside.

'It's only rich folk who deal with stocks and shares that make money without getting off their backsides,' he said contemptuously. 'And I'd not want to earn my bread that way, by the sweat of other men's foreheads. If I don't make this place a success Mr Cameron'll close it down, then where'll we be – me and Aileen and the bairn?'

'And where'll Aileen and the baby be if you make yourself ill?'

'Stop girnin' at me, Ellie,' he said, irritated. 'I've got enough on my mind as it is.'

She held her tongue after that, though she continued to worry about him, and about Aileen. She was busy in her spare time making the new dress she had promised Aileen, and she had met Ian Bruce more than once at the flat. Aileen was always animated when her brother was there, and it was clear that he adored her. Surely, Elspeth told herself, it was only natural for Aileen to want to keep in touch with the only member of her family who, at the moment, would have anything to do with her. But at the same time she had the uncomfortable

feeling that Ian Bruce was encouraging Aileen's growing dis-
satisfaction with her surroundings.

Once, rounding the corner on her way to visit, she was in
time to see Ian Bruce handing his sister into his car. It was a
cool, breezy day and the green scarf Elspeth had given Aileen
was tied around her head. Her thickening figure was enveloped
in a warm fur coat that Elspeth had never seen before – presumably a garment brought from the wardrobe she had had to
leave behind when she walked out of her parents' mansion to
marry Thomas.

Neither of them noticed Elspeth; as the red car roared past
her, she saw that all Aileen's attention was fixed on her
brother.

'I love Thomas, and I'd not want to be away from him,' she
said to Elspeth a few days later. The new dress was almost
completed, and Elspeth was kneeling at her feet, pinning up
the hem. 'But I'm so tired of having to do without and count
the pennies. If he'd just let Ian help us, things would be much
easier, and we'd have more time together. Ian's sure that once
the baby's born Mother and Father will come round. And
there's no reason why Father shouldn't buy Thomas a garage
of his own.'

'Thomas would never allow that, Aileen,' Elspeth said carefully, and the skirt twitched in her hand as the other girl
shrugged.

'He could, if he'd give up this stubborn pride of his.'

When the dress had been taken off, Aileen opened a drawer
and showed her a lovely pair of gloves, soft and beautifully
made. 'Ian gave them to me, to wear at the baby's christening.'
Her eyes shone as she stroked the material with work-reddened
hands. 'Don't tell Thomas – I'm going to hide them away until
the time comes.'

She had asked Elspeth to buy some mince on her way to the
flat; when she opened her purse to pay for it, Elspeth saw that
there was more money in it than usual. Remembering Thomas's

boast about his wife's ability to make a pound note go a long way, she wondered if Ian Bruce was giving his sister money.

There was nobody she could talk to about her suspicions, not even Granjan, in case she inadvertently let a word slip out in Flora's hearing. So Elspeth held her tongue and tried to assure herself that once the baby arrived Aileen would revert back to her former self.

The garage books gave an impressive picture of Thomas's ability to run the place. Once she managed to sort out the paperwork she found that business was brisk, although she already knew that from the number of people who called in at the garage every day, and from the telephone calls.

Before her arrival, Thomas had dealt with the telephone, which stood in the kitchen. Now it was Elspeth's job to answer it when she was in the office. At first, unused to the machine, she had been nervous.

'Ellie, I've got enough to do without running in here every time the telephone rings. It's only a machine,' Thomas told her impatiently. 'Machines are made for folk's convenience – no need to be afraid of them!'

Stung by his words, she had made herself master the instrument, and within a week had become used to it, though she was thrown into alarm when one of the callers barked, 'Tell McDonald to come to the phone,' as soon as she answered.

There was so much authority in the voice that she obeyed, and had reached the kitchen door before realising that nobody had the right to order her around like that. She returned to the machine.

'Please.'

'What?'

'C-courtesy costs nothing,' she said, then tried to force the nervous quiver from her voice. 'You could have said please.'

There was an exasperated sigh, then the man at the other end of the line asked, 'Will that bring McDonald to the phone any faster?'

'It will.'

'In that case – please.'

'If you'll just hold on, I'll go and get him,' Elspeth said primly, and went to call Thomas from the workshop.

He came into the office a few minutes later. 'What did you say to that man?'

Elspeth finished the entry she was making before looking up. 'The man on the phone? He was impertinent, so I made him say please, that's all.'

'Ah. I don't think anyone's ever made him say that before.'

'I wasn't impertinent back to him. If he says I was, he's lying.'

'He didn't,' Thomas said, and turned to go.

'Who is he?'

'Forbes Cameron, the owner of this place,' Thomas said, and returned to his work.

Forbes Cameron strolled into the office the following weekend to introduce himself.

'And to apologise for my boorishness on the telephone,' he added, and Elspeth flushed.

'I didn't realise it was you.'

'That shouldn't make any difference. You were quite right, I behaved badly. My only excuse is that I'm so used to working among men that I've lost my manners. I'm sure my mother would wholeheartedly agree with you that it was time someone pulled me up about it.'

He was a stocky, broad-shouldered man, a few years older than Thomas. Dark hair that looked as though it had been brushed that morning, but had then found a way of breaking free, topped a square, tanned face. His eyes were grey, and his mouth wide above a determined chin. She knew from what Thomas had said that Forbes Cameron had been born into money and had travelled extensively. He was a racing-car driver and yachtsman.

He glanced around the room, then back at her. 'I never realised what good lines this room has before.'

'It just needed cleaning.'

'It needs more than that.' He looked at the wall behind her, covered here and there by wallpaper, but mainly showing the bare plaster. 'It needs re-papering, for a start.'

'It's not worth papering an office.'

'Painting, then. What colour would you like?'

'There's no need to—'

'Blue? Yellow? Purple? Tell me what you think.'

Elspeth studied the walls. 'If I was doing it, I'd choose a soft shade, mebbe a parchment colour, mebbe a bit lighter than that.'

He strode over to where her coat hung on a nail. 'Come into the town with me and choose something. We'll get a decent coat-stand while we're at it.'

'But I'm in the middle of some work.'

'Give yourself an hour off to choose paint.'

'The room's fine as it is.'

'It's my room, and I say it needs painting. So—' She was scooped from her seat and being helped into her coat before she knew what was happening. Ten minutes later the two of them were choosing paint.

'What about the doors and skirting boards and window frames?' Forbes Cameron asked when she had opted for a pale fawn shade.

'It's too beautiful to be covered, even though it's all marked.'

'Varnish, then, with some treatment first,' he decided briskly. 'Now come and have a cup of tea, and tell me about yourself.'

'This is ridiculous,' she protested as they sipped tea in a small tearoom.

'Not at all; you deserve a proper office, especially after you've done such excellent work on our books.'

'You've seen them?'

'I call in every week to keep an eye on things. McDonald tells me you've refused to take any money for the work.'

'Thomas has enough to do with his wages. He lets me keep my typewriter in the office, and do work for other people there in return for what I do for the garage.'

'Nevertheless, it's me who should be paying you, not McDonald. I've been very lax about that. We'll arrange proper payment on the way back, and I'll see that the room's painted during the week, so that it's all ready for you by next Saturday.'

But by the following Saturday a freshly painted office was the last thing on Elspeth's mind. Three days after she met Forbes Cameron, Ian Bruce's handsome red car spun out of control on the hill road to the Loch Thom reservoir, smashing into a stone wall.

Ian and his passenger, his sister Aileen, both died immediately.

27

A clerk from Mr Bruce's lawyer's firm called at Mearns Street, where Thomas was staying with his parents, to inform him of the arrangements Aileen's father had made for the double funeral.

The family, at their evening meal, sat in awkward silence as the man, his bowler hat tucked beneath one arm, talked to Thomas. When he had finished he left, politely refusing Flora's flustered offer of a wee cup of tea.

'Ye'd've thought they'd've had the decency tae call at a better time – and to consult ye,' she raged when the man had gone. 'They've not even invited ye tae the house, and you their son-in-law!'

'Leave it, Mam,' Thomas told her brusquely. He had scarcely spoken since hearing the news.

'But she was your wife, an' carryin' your bairn—'

'The lassie I was married to's gone, and so's the bairn that never was. No point in quarrelin' over what's left. Anyway, she was a Bruce more than a McDonald.' He got up from the table, pushing his chair back noisily, and left the kitchen. A moment later the outer door shut.

'Now where's he goin'?' Flora wailed.

'Probably back to the garage, Mam,' Lachlan said.

'But he's already put in his day's work, and scarcely touched his food. If he's goin' tae insist on workin' every hour of the day an' night he'll have tae eat tae keep his strength up!'

'Leave it be, Flora, the laddie needs tae go through this in

268

his own way,' Henry said with a rarely heard ring of authority in his voice. 'Don't fuss him.'

She glared, then went over to the sink, leaving her own plate half-full, and began to crash dishes about. 'I don't know – ye'd think he'd talk tae us about it, or even cry if it takes him that way. But this is no' like our Thomas at all.'

'He'll be all right,' Elspeth tried to assure her, though she too was worried about the way Thomas had completely withdrawn from everything and everyone since his wife's death.

'Come and eat yer own food,' Henry added.

'I don't want it.'

'Sit down and eat, woman!' He all but shouted the words. Elspeth and Lachlan glanced at each other, then dipped their heads over their own plates. Although there was nothing wrong with the food, it was as interesting as cardboard to Elspeth, and she was sure that Lachlan felt the same way. They were both making a show of minding their own business in order to avoid the confrontation that seemed inevitable. Henry McDonald, Lachlan had once told Elspeth, could be a feared dictator at work, but he had always been content to let his wife rule the house, until now.

The confrontation didn't come. Flora flounced away from the sink and sat down, picking up her fork and knife.

'It's as if he doesnae care,' she muttered to the cooling, congealing mince and potatoes and carrots.

'Of course he cares – can ye no' see it in his eyes? He cares so much that he cannae speak for the pain of it.'

'Then why doesnae he let his own folk comfort him?' Flora asked, a tremor in her voice, 'When I think of that bonny wee thing, no more than a child hersel' – and how could he say she wasnae a McDonald, when they were wed in front of a minister and her own family's had nothin' tae dae with her since? It's us should be buryin' her, not them!'

'Flora—' Henry said quietly, with real steel in his voice this time. To Elspeth's relief the woman subsided.

Thomas hadn't set foot in the flat he shared with Aileen since hearing about the accident. He had moved into his parents' house at once, unable to return to his home, sending his father to collect clothes for him. He had insisted on working at the garage as usual, and when he was at Mearns Street he sat alone in the tiny room he once more shared with Lachlan, or in the kitchen making a pretence of reading the newspaper. He had aged overnight, and his brown eyes, normally lively and bright, were dull pebbles set in bony hollows.

Neighbours calling to express their sympathies were met with a set, withdrawn expression, and he usually left the kitchen or even the flat when outsiders called, letting his mother do the talking for him.

As a result of this, Elspeth knew, the neighbours were muttering to each other that he was too stuck-up for his own good and no longer interested in his own folk after marrying one of the gentry. She wanted to shout at them that it wasn't true, that Thomas should be left in peace to grieve in his own way, but she couldn't. That would only have incensed Aunt Flora, and made matters worse.

The funeral service was held in the grand church Catherine Bruce had been married in not long before the end of the war. Aileen's flower-bedecked coffin lay beside that of her brother, almost exactly where she must have stood on that long-past wedding day in her pretty yellow bridesmaid's dress.

As Thomas led his family in, an usher scurried up to tell him in a discreet murmur that there was a place for him in 'the family pew'.

'I wasn't welcome in their company when she was alive, and I see no reason to sit with them now,' Thomas said in a low, clear voice and ushered his family into a row halfway up the church while the man retreated, red-faced.

Flora wanted to sit by her bereaved son, but he had paid no heed, and as church was no place for an argument, she had to submit to his wishes, following Janet Docherty to the end of the empty row while the others huddled nervously in the aisle, anxious to be seated as quickly as possible and out of the view of the rest of the congregation.

Thomas chose the seat by the aisle for himself, looking straight ahead and seemingly oblivious to the stares and murmurs as the mourners coming down the aisle recognised him as Aileen's husband. He seated Lachlan beside him, then came Elspeth and Mattie, who had arrived that morning from Glasgow to attend the funeral. Rachel, who was having an uncomfortable pregnancy and looked pale and drawn in her borrowed black coat and a hat that didn't suit her, sat between Mattie and Bob.

As they waited for the service to begin, Flora fretted about Thomas's refusal to sit at the front of the church. 'They'll think he's snubbin' them,' Elspeth heard her say in an agitated whisper, loud enough to set heads in her vicinity turning.

'It doesnae matter any more what they think, does it?' Henry retorted gruffly, and Elspeth could positively hear Flora's withering glare as she subsided.

Many of the people pouring into the church were young, presumably Ian's friends – and former friends of Aileen's, thought Elspeth, though not one of them had visited her after her marriage. Forbes Cameron paused by Thomas, who got to his feet and shook hands with his employer and with the elderly couple by his side before the trio moved on to take their places elsewhere in the church.

The sombre organ music and the heavy scent of the massed funeral flowers had given Elspeth the beginnings of a headache by the time Mr Bruce and his daughter and son-in-law arrived, Catherine's face hidden by heavy veiling. She was the Bruces' only surviving child, Elspeth realised as the three of them walked down the long aisle, and she pitied these people who in their arrogance and insensitivity had turned their backs on Aileen in the final year of her life. For all their money and all their pride, the Bruces were still parents, and this must be a terrible day for them.

As soon as the family was seated the minister began to speak at length about the tragedy of two premature deaths. He talked about Aileen without once making reference to her marriage, her husband or her unborn child. Slipping a glance at Thomas, Elspeth saw that his profile could have been carved out of stone. Not a muscle twitched, not an eyelid flickered, even when the service finally ended and his wife's coffin was carried out, so near to him as it went by that he could have reached out and touched it. Mr Bruce and his daughter and son-in-law, walking behind the coffins, passed Thomas without a glance.

As she rose to make her way out of the church Elspeth saw some of their neighbours from Mearns Street sitting at the back, together with others who were probably Bruce servants.

Outside, the sun was shining, oblivious to the fact that today of all days the sky should have been overcast and weeping cold rain. As the McDonalds hesitated on the gravel drive, clustered in a knot for mutual comfort, Forbes Cameron brought over the elderly couple he had escorted into church, introducing them as his parents. They, at least, were friendly, and Elspeth, who had noticed with concern that Flora had begun to look pinched and shrunken and was clinging to Henry's arm for support, was relieved to see the woman expand a little under Mrs Cameron's kindly warmth. Just like a little Japanese flower, she thought, remembering her childhood, when she had loved to watch tiny dried-up flakes of apparently colourless paper blossom into bright flowers when dropped into a cup of water.

The usher who had spoken to Thomas in the church arrived by his elbow again to inform him that there was a place for him in one of the leading cars.

'Thank Mr Bruce,' Forbes Cameron told him blandly, 'and explain that Mr McDonald and his family are travelling with us.' Then he swept them off to where three handsome black limousines, each with a uniformed chauffeur, waited in the long line of cars.

In the cemetery, Thomas took hold of Elspeth's arm as she stepped out of the car. 'Stay with me,' he said; startled, for it was the first thing he had said to her since hearing of Aileen's death, she allowed herself to be drawn along with him through the crowd of mourners to where the two coffins waited beside the open graves.

In death, as in life, the Bruce family believed in their right to own land. An elaborate wrought-iron fence defended the considerable area set aside solely for their dead; each well-tended grave was watched over by a handsome headstone, and in the middle of the lair a marble memorial soared above the heads of the gathered mourners, the names of all those buried within the fence inscribed on its four smooth sides.

'Hold your head high, Ellie,' Thomas murmured as they took their places on the opposite side of the graves from Mr Bruce and his daughter. She did as she was bid, raising her head, topped by a wide-brimmed, high-crowned black straw hat, on the long stem of her neck, proud to be standing by Thomas, who, although his black suit hadn't cost a fraction of the money that most of the mourners had clearly paid for their funeral clothes, seemed to her to be the most elegantly dressed man there. Aileen, she thought with tears aching in her throat, would have been proud of him.

Arm against arm, they stood motionless during the short-ened version of the church service, separating only when Thomas stepped forward to take hold of one of the cords to help lower his young wife and their unborn child into their final resting place.

Ian Bruce had been buried first, his father and brother-in-law throwing handfuls of earth in on top of his coffin. As the undertaker's men took over the cords, smoothly lowering Aileen to the bottom of the grave, Thomas stooped and gathered a firm fistful of soil from the pile nearby, then held his arm out over the void, opening his fingers to let the earth patter down in a final salute to his wife.

It was hard not to gape when the funeral party went into the Bruce house. Although she had known that the place would be sumptuous, Elspeth was unprepared for the massive hallway they passed through after entering the house.

'It's almost big enough to hold our entire tenement,' Mattie murmured at her side as they stepped through the front door, staring at the huge staircase rising to the next floor. The fireplace in the vast drawing room was as broad as one of the kitchen walls at Mearns Street. Looking around at the paintings, the furniture, the wide, high windows opening on to a terrace where flower-filled stone urns stood, Elspeth felt her heart break for Aileen.

No wonder the girl had been suffocated in the tiny flat that was all Thomas could provide. No wonder she had been so pleased to make contact with her brother, and so eager to urge Thomas to take advantage of an offer that would have given them a larger home.

Mrs Bruce, her face grey and old against her black dress, her eyes filled with a sorrow that would never leave her, put in a brief appearance once the mourners were gathered. Supported by a uniformed nurse, she spoke to a few people, but neither she nor her husband or daughter came near Thomas. If it hadn't been for the kindness of Forbes Cameron and his parents, the McDonalds would have been completely isolated.

The Camerons fussed over Flora in particular, making certain that she had enough to eat, seeing to it that her cup was refilled, although Elspeth could tell by the flickering of Flora's lashes as she sipped carefully at the fragile china cup that the weak tea it held wasn't to her liking.

Standing close to her mother as though for protection, Rachel kept an anxious eye on Bob, who had eagerly accepted a glass of whisky and drunk it swiftly. Flora hadn't noticed, but Henry did, frowning in puzzled disbelief. Now Bob's eyes thirstily watched the silver trays of glasses being carried round the room by immaculately uniformed maids. His face was flushed, and he continually plucked with one finger at the collar of his shirt, or tugged his jacket down. Like Rachel, he must have borrowed his funeral clothes from a more affluent neighbour, for they were too tight for him. When one of the trays moved in his direction his fingers trembled and the tip of his tongue flicked across his lower lip, but somehow Henry, clearly realising that his son-in-law had broken the teetotal pledge made as a child, managed to step between Bob and the crystal glasses half filled with amber liquid.

Watching Bob's suffering, Rachel's misery, Flora's discomfort and Thomas's stoic indifference to his surroundings, Elspeth longed to sweep them all away from the magnificent house which had been the cause of so much heartache. None of them deserved to be treated like this. It was a relief when Forbes Cameron suggested leaving.

'We've been here for an acceptable length of time, and I see that some other people are preparing to go. My mother's tired, and I'm sure that you are too, Mrs Docherty.'

Janet was the only member of the group to have been at her ease, taking in her surroundings and the fine clothes of the women in the room with swift, birdlike glances that carried not a sign of envy. 'I'm f—' she began, then, with a look at her daughter, who was beginning to wilt again, she amended it to, 'I'm fair exhausted, tae tell ye the truth. Would ye mind if we went home, Flora?'

Mrs Bruce had long since retreated from the room. They made their farewells to Mr Bruce, who held each hand limply for a second and made murmuring noises, gazing past their heads, then Cameron saw them into the limousines, which were magically waiting before the door when they went out on to the steps.

Elspeth rode with Rachel and Bob, who were taken straight

home because Rachel was worried about wee Mary, being cared for by a neighbour. She arrived back at Mearns Street in time to see the garage owner assist Flora on to the pavement, under the interested stare of half the street, and bow over her hand before she summoned up the last of her strength and swept regally into the close.

'Such a nice man,' she said when they had gained the kitchen, stripping her hat and gloves off. 'A real gentleman. Elspeth, for pity's sake put that kettle on, I'm parched for a decent cup of tea. That was nothin' but coloured water they were pourin' out of they silver teapots.'

'They're a right gutless lot,' Henry grunted, sinking into a chair and easing his shoes off. 'I'd like tae see them try tae manage a decent day's work in the yards – it'd kill them off before they got properly started. Here – what was Bob Cochran doin', drinkin' whisky?'

'He wasn't,' Flora said at once.

'I'm no' daft, woman, I know whisky when I see it. He'd have had more if I hadnae worked it so that we both got lemonade the second time.' He wrinkled his face up. 'It meant I'd tae do without more whisky mysel', and it was the best I've ever tasted, tae.'

'The lemonade was made from real lemons,' Elspeth said in an attempt to make peace.

'Lemonade?' Henry snorted. 'The only decent drink in this country's the one made with grain and good Scottish water, and I'd tae miss out on my share because of that eejit our Rachel married.' Mention of Bob reminded him of his earlier question. 'And what happened tae the pledge he signed?' he demanded to know.

'Where's our Thomas?' Flora jumped up from her chair and her husband waved a carefully polished black shoe at her.

'Will ye stop jumpin' about like a flea on a dog?'

'He didn't come upstairs,' Lachlan reported. 'He said he wanted a bit of a walk.'

'There ye are, then, he's fine.' Henry relaxed into his chair, wriggling and stretching his stockinged toes. 'An' there's Elspeth made yer precious tea for ye. Now for pity's sake will ye put yer backside down on that chair and drink the stuff?'

Flora, having achieved her main aim and taken his mind off Bob, did as she was told, for once.

28

'Never bother with me, lassie,' Janet Docherty said that evening, poking the coals in her grate into a blaze. 'I've been tae more funerals than you've had hot dinners, and though this was one of the hardest tae thole, I'm old enough tae accept whatever the good Lord chooses tae throw at us. It's Thomas that's needin' a friend tonight, poor soul.'

'He doesn't want anyone.' Elspeth had gone round to Janet's flat to keep the old woman company.

'Aye he does, it's just that he hasnae realised it. His mother's nae comfort, for she fusses too much, and we all know she never wanted that marriage in the first place. With all the goodwill in the world, Flora'll no' be able tae stop hersel' from remindin' him time and again that she's been proved right after all. But you're different, lassie. It was you he chose tae stand by him at her grave. Seek him out, Elspeth. Don't push intae his grief, but let him know ye're there if he needs someone.'

When Elspeth knocked on the door of the flat Thomas had lived in with Aileen, there was an empty, desolate echo to the sound. Convinced that he wasn't sitting inside, refusing to answer, she went back out to the pavement, thinking hard. It wouldn't be his way to seek solace in the noisy, smoky atmosphere of the town's pubs, and if he had gone walking in the country above the town or along by the river, there was no

hope of locating him. There was only one place she could try
before conceding defeat.

To her disappointment, the garage and workshops were
dark and silent. Without hope, she threaded her way round the
hulking shadows of vehicles parked in the yard, sliding her feet
cautiously along the cobbles at each step, wary of banging her
shins or ankles on the pieces of machinery that usually littered
the place.

The back door to the house was unlocked, creaking open
eerily to reveal a pitch-black cave beyond. Elspeth hesitated.
There was a box of matches on the gas stove only a few steps
to her left, and candles on the shelf above, but the thought of
reaching out into the dark, fumbling for the shape of the
cooker and perhaps encountering something else – a hand, a
face – was unnerving. Forcing her imagination under control,
she proceeded as best she could without seeking light that
might attract attention from a policeman passing by on his
patrol, and cause further bother.

Gritting her teeth, she inched forward, her outstretched
fingers identifying the back of a wooden chair, the corner of a
cupboard. Her eyes had become accustomed to the darkness
now, and by the time she reached the door leading to the hall
she could just make out the outline of the kitchen furniture in
the very faint grey light from the window behind her.

The hall was a deep black well. She stood still for a while
until her eyes again became accustomed to her surroundings,
breathing in the smell of damp and dust and metal and oil that
permeated the house. There was a new, sharper smell too,
which she puzzled over briefly before identifying it as the
smell of paint from the newly decorated office. When her
straining eyes finally found the fan-shaped wedge of grey that
was the window above the sealed front door, she began the
perilous journey across the hall towards the office, lifting each
foot elaborately high, then putting it down gently, quietly, on
the wooden floor she couldn't see.

She was halfway across, by her own reckoning, when she heard sudden movement from above. She had been trying hard not to think about the staircase to her right, leading up into unknown territory, but now she spun round to face it, her heart leaping into her mouth.

'Thomas?' Her voice, squeaky and trembling, startled her, and she clapped a hand to her mouth. There was no reply, and she didn't dare call again. She wanted desperately to run back through the kitchen and out into the comparative safety of the yard, but she knew that if she panicked now she would lose all sense of direction, with little chance of finding the back door quickly, so she made herself stand still, breathing deeply to calm her racing heart, refusing to accept the sudden picture that had flown into her mind of Thomas on the upper floor, swinging from some hook in the ceiling.

Mice, she told herself – the noise would just be mice, making free of the abandoned rooms. She had seen their droppings on the ground floor, and some of the paperwork piled on the old desk when she first came to the office had been nibbled by tiny teeth. There were rats, too, about the yard.

She was no stranger to rats and mice and cockroaches, for the working class and the poor always shared their lives with such creatures. She had little fear of them, apart from a dislike of their way of appearing suddenly, without warning, and on the whole she accepted their right to exist. But now, alone in the dark, she felt that their presence was menacing. This was their time of day, their territory rather than hers.

All had fallen quiet upstairs, and she told herself firmly that now she had come this far it was better to continue rather than to retreat.

At last she gained the office door and opened it, wrapped in the smell of fresh paint as she stepped inside. Mercifully, the moon was shining on the front of the building, and there was more light in here, enough for her to make out the comforting shape of the desk she worked at, and the smaller hump that was her covered typewriter. She started towards them, then spun round, giving a muffled yelp, as Thomas said from behind her, 'Who is it?'

'Oh – Thomas!' He was sitting on the sagging old couch that stood against the wall opposite her desk. In her relief she wanted to rush into his arms, but managed to hold herself back.

'I came looking for you.' Her voice was still weak and shaky. 'We were worried – nobody knew where you'd gone.'

'You surely knew I'd be all right – or did you think I was going to kill myself?'

'Of course not,' she lied.

He moved, and the *chaise-longue* creaked. 'I'd not do that,' his disembodied voice said. 'It'd be too easy. I just needed to be on my own, to think about things.'

She waited, letting the silence between them gather, then at last he said, 'I was going to ask you. Ellie – would you see to the house for me? I can't bring myself to go into it, and I'd not want to ask any of the others.'

'Of course I will. What d'you want me to do with—'

'Get rid of it all,' he interrupted harshly. 'Everything. I don't want anything from it. The rent's paid up for another two weeks, that should give you enough time. Here's the key.'

She could see well enough now to cross the room quite easily. His hand was cool and dry, the metal key warm as it passed from his fingers to hers. She slipped it into her pocket and retreated to the desk, sensing his need to be on his own.

After another long silence he spoke again, bleakly. 'I did a terrible thing, marrying Aileen. If it hadn't been for me she'd be alive today, probably wed to some man who could have given her everything she deserved.'

'Don't be daft, Thomas McDonald!' The words rushed hotly to her lips. 'Aileen came to you of her own free will, and she didn't regret one minute of it.'

'Ellie, you saw that house today – the servants, the comfort of it all. Who'd willingly walk away from that?'

'It was when I saw the house that I knew how much she must have loved you, to give it up for you. And I understood why,' Elspeth said passionately. 'There wasn't an ounce of warmth in that place, while your wee house was brimming over with love and happiness. As for the folk I saw today – they didn't deserve someone like Aileen. There was no – no joy in them.'

'Would you expect them to be joyful on a day like this?' he asked sarcastically.

'You know fine what I mean. They were all wrapped up in themselves. What sort of folk would turn their backs on a lovely lassie like your Aileen just because she insisted on going her own way?'

'Mam did.'

She swatted the words impatiently into the dark shadows of the room. 'Aunt Flora's always like that when she's defied. Anyway, she'd come round to accepting your marriage. Don't be hard on her, Thomas – she's suffering torments over the way she treated the two of you when you first married. I doubt if Mr and Mrs Bruce feel as bad as she does.'

There was a pause before he spoke again. 'Mr Bruce's lawyer offered me money. I got the letter yesterday. One thousand pounds, he'll pay me, if I'll sign a bit of paper promising I'll make no claim on the Bruce family.'

Elspeth almost choked with outrage. 'That's insulting!'

'It's the only way they know. They think that even people can be bought, especially people like us.'

'Pebbles on the beach.'

'What?'

'That's what you said, one day when we were all on the beach at Largs. You said that ordinary folk are like pebbles, too many and too small to be noticed.'

'I don't mind saying it, but it's true. I went to the office and told the man that I'd not take a penny from the likes of the Bruces, not even if I was starving in the gutter. The only way to get respect from folk like that is to show them that you're as good as they are. That's what I'm going to do, Ellie. I'm going to work even harder for Aileen than I did when she was here. I'm going to show the Bruces and the whole town that given time I could have provided her with everything she wanted.' His voice was low and level, but intense. 'I'll make my own thousand, then another thousand, and another. I'll make them admit that they were wrong about me, even if I have to ram bundles of notes down their throats to do it!'

Elspeth shivered though the room wasn't cold. She felt as though someone had just walked over her grave.

'Don't become bitter, Thomas.'

'Of course I'm bitter! Can you blame me? If I hadnae been so opposed to her seeing her brother she wouldnae have gone off with him in his car. We'd had words about it just the day before.'

She thought of the day she herself had seen Aileen drive away in Ian Bruce's car. There had probably been other times that neither she nor Thomas knew about.

'But she must have been in her brother's car hundreds of times before she met you. The accident could have happened at any time.'

'You're talking nonsense.'

'I know,' she said wretchedly, confused by her own clumsy attempts to reason with him. 'It's hard to find the right words. I'd do better if I was putting them down in a letter.'

He laughed, an unexpected barking sound. 'Mebbe you should write to me, then,' he said, his voice suddenly weary, 'Come to me, Ellie.'

When she did as she was told he drew her down on to the couch, putting an arm about her and holding her close. 'Are you cold?'

'No, it's warm enough.'

'You don't need to find the words.' His breath was warm against her ear. 'Just wheesht for a wee while, and let me listen to them for myself.'

Timidly, she put her own arms around him. He was so tense that it was like wrapping her arms round the trunk of a tree. They sat in silence for a long time, long enough for his body to relax gradually, until he was leaning quite heavily against her. She wondered if he had fallen asleep. The couch was lumpy and uncomfortable, thrusting small hard fists into the softness of her buttocks, but she didn't want to move in case she disturbed him. Instead she stayed still, inhaling the clean soapy smell from his hair, listening to his breathing, feeling the slow steady thump of his heart echoing against her own ribs. The street outside was silent, for this was an industrial area and not many people had occasion to pass through it at night. Once, she heard a scampering above her head, but with Thomas close beside her there was no need, now, to be afraid.

Finally, when she was almost asleep herself, he stirred and straightened and sat upright. 'You'd best go home, Ellie. Mam'll be wondering where you are.'

Her arms were stiff and numbed. She moved her fingers surreptitiously. 'Come back with me.'

He was still so close that disturbed air brushed her cheek when he shook his head.

'I'm staying here tonight.'

'But—'

'I'll be fine. Come on, now.' He rose and pulled her up from the couch. The life was just beginning to come back to her hands, and they felt as though they were clad in thick woollen gloves. Thomas led the way, sure-footed, through the hall and kitchen with Elspeth clinging as best she could to the back of his jacket. In the street he said, 'Tell Mam I'm fine, and I'll look in on her tomorrow. You'll manage home all right?'

'Yes.'

His hands cupped her shoulders, his lips touched her cheek. 'Thanks, Ellie,' he said 'You're a grand sister.' Then, turning her about to face the empty street, he gave her a little shove. 'Go on, now.'

Pins and needles danced all the way up and down her arms. She welcomed the sensation, because it promised eventual normality, something that had been lacking in her life ever since Aileen's death.

At the corner she stopped and looked back. Thomas's hand was a tiny pale movement against the darkness of the building behind him as he waved.

She waved back, and set off for Mearns Street.

Elspeth walked in through the main entrance of Brodie's department store and across the carpeted floor to the elegant lift provided for those paying customers who declined to use the staircases. Patrick, the lift operator, gaped as she stepped in and said, 'The top floor, please.'

'Lassie, what're ye doin'?'

'I'm going to see Mr James.'

Patrick peered out, glancing furtively from right to left. 'But ye cannae use the lift. It's for the gentry!'

'I can do as I please. Will you get on with it, or do I have to see to the buttons myself?'

Alarm flared into his eyes. 'Don't you touch they buttons, Elspeth Bremner! This is my lift and I'll be the one tae—' He broke off as two well-dressed women stepped into the silk-lined lift, and asked, with a noticeable change of accent, 'Which floor, moddom?'

'The third,' the older woman ordered curtly.

'The top,' Elspeth said just as curtly, adding after a pause, 'Please.'

The woman glared, and settled her fox-fur more comfortably on her shoulders, while Patrick, shrugging helplessly, slid the door shut and set the lift in motion.

'Are ye sure?' he asked plaintively as the two women stepped out at the third floor, leaving behind them the powerful scent of expensive perfume too lavishly applied, and an undertone of perspiration. It was May, and too hot for fox-furs.

'I'm sure.'

'It's mair than yer job's worth, lassie, usin' the customers' lift.'

'I'm not bothered.' She had been awake half the night, fretting over the news she had heard that evening, and by morning she had decided on a course of action. It was too late, now, to change her mind. She had already used the main entrance, and the lift. She might as well go the whole way.

It had been over a year since she had worked in the accounts office, but little had changed. Wilma and Graham still laboured over huge ledgers at the sloping desk, and Theresa McCabe typed busily in her corner, though the brisk clatter of keys slowed and stopped at Elspeth's entrance.

'I want to talk to Mr James,' she told Wilma.

'He didn't ask to see you.'

'I know that. It's me that wants to see him.'

The typewriter keys stopped altogether. Graham gaped and Wilma bristled. 'He's dealing with this morning's post. Try again in an hour.'

'I must see him now. It's very important.' The anger that had been burning in Elspeth for the past fifteen hours or so gave her voice a crisp edge. Wilma hesitated, then slipped down from the high stool.

'I'll see what he says.'

'You're looking well, Elspeth.' Graham's eyes travelled slowly down her body.

'Am I?' She had decided not to wear her usual working skirt and blouse today; instead, she had on her best blouse, striped in different shades of brown, and a fawn pleated skirt beneath a smart brown jacket she had made herself. The pebble brooch was pinned to the jacket's lapel, and beneath the blouse's high collar her lucky silver threepenny piece nestled against the hollow of her throat.

The typewriter keys rattled again as James Brodie himself opened his office door and ushered Wilma out.

'Miss Bremner – come in. Take a seat,' he invited, closing the door behind her.

She shook her head. 'I'll only be a minute. I believe you've taken on a new typist?'

'That's right, Theresa's leaving to get married. I was surprised you didn't apply for the job yourself,' he went on, taking the wind out of her sails. She stared, then rallied.

'I would have, if I'd known. I only heard about it last night, when I met a girl I knew from my typing class and she said she'd applied and been unsuccessful.'

It was Brodie's turn to be taken aback. 'But you were the first person I thought of when Theresa said she was going. Miss Arnold told me that you'd decided to stay on in the sewing room.'

Elspeth's knees suddenly went weak, and she sank into the chair she had just declined. 'She told you that?'

They stared at each other for a moment, then James Brodie said slowly, 'It seems that you've been deceived. I'm very sorry, my dear. I would have been happy to give you the position, but unfortunately it has already been filled.'

'Elspeth Bremner, d'you know what time it is?' Miss Arnold squawked as soon as Elspeth went into the sewing room. 'And just what d'you think you're wearing? You know that you girls aren't allowed to—'

'I'm late because I've just been along to see Mr James about the typist's position, Miss Arnold.'

The woman flushed, then rallied. 'Without asking me to arrange an appointment for you? You'd no right to burst in on Mr James like that!'

'And you'd no right to tell him that I wanted to stay in the sewing room instead of applying for the typist's job without consulting me first.'

There was a concerted gasp from the listening women round the large table, and the usual muted roar of sewing machines in operation faltered, then died.

Miss Arnold's face was almost purple. 'Miss Buchanan and I discussed the matter fully and agreed that you're of more value to Brodie's in this department. You're a good seamstress, and a lot of work's gone into training you. In a few years you could mebbe even become supervisor.'

'I won't be here in a few years, Miss Arnold, or even a few minutes,' Elspeth told her, and turned towards the door.

'Stop,' the woman shrieked. 'I'll not have such insubordination!' Then, as Elspeth put a hand on the handle, 'If you persist in this nonsense, Elspeth Bremner, you needn't think you'll get a reference from Miss Buchanan!'

'I won't require one. I'm going to set up in business for myself,' Elspeth said, and walked out of the sewing room for the last time, closing the door on a babble of excited voices.

Flora McDonald was beside herself with rage when she heard the news. 'After all the trouble I went to tae get ye that position! How could ye dae it? Ye'll never get work as a seamstress in the town again once word of this gets out. What have I done tae deserve this?'

The cold anger that had seized Elspeth when she first heard of the position she had lost through deceit still held her in its grip.

'It was you that wanted me to be a seamstress, Aunt Flora, not me. I'm seventeen now, old enough to make up my own mind. I've been thinking about it all, and I'm going to set up my own business, doing typing and book-keeping for folk like Mr Monteith who can't afford to employ someone all the time.'

'Are ye wandered in yer head, lassie? How could the likes of you manage that? Ye're too young, for a start!'

'I don't think I am.'

'And where would ye go? Not in my bedroom, I'll tell ye that!'

'I think I already know of somewhere,' said Elspeth, refusing to let anything her aunt said affect her. She had burned her boats, and now the only way to go was forward.

At Christmas Forbes Cameron, stammering like a schoolboy, had invited Elspeth to dinner at the large house where he still lived with his parents. Surprised, but somewhat flattered, she had accepted, and had enjoyed herself. Mr and Mrs Cameron were kindly people, as she had discovered at Aileen's funeral, and Forbes himself was an entertaining and considerate companion. They had been meeting each other ever since, a relationship that had almost caused a quarrel between her and Thomas.

'I've nothing against the man – he pays my wages – but he's a good ten years older than you are,' he said baldly.

'Does that mean that he's not to be trusted?'

'No, but—'

'Mebbe it's me you don't trust?'

'Don't be daft,' Thomas said, exasperated.

'I'm not a child, so don't treat me like one.'

'I know you're not, but even so, you'd be better with someone more your own age.'

'Like Kenneth?' she asked sarcastically.

'Oh – go your own way, you'll do that anyway. There's no reasoning with you, Elspeth Bremner,' he snapped, and stormed out of the garage office.

As it happened, she and Forbes were going to the theatre in Largs the day she left Brodie's for good, then having supper in a small restaurant.

Prudently, she waited until the meal was almost over before putting her plan to him.

'The old house? My dear girl, it's in a terrible state – you couldn't set up this business of yours in a place like that.'

'It's neglected, but the building's still sturdy. At least let me have a look at it. Please, Forbes – I've got to find some way of earning my living quickly, and this is my chance to do what I've always wanted.'

'Have you really thought about this idea of yours, Elspeth? You're young to start up in business, and it's not that easy.'

'Why does everyone keep going on about my age? Seventeen isn't all that young, and there are times when I feel much older than that. I know of two girls from the typing and book-keeping class who'd probably be glad to come in with me. Neither of them has been able to find work in an office.'

'Do they have money to invest in the idea?'

'No, but they've got office skills, and that's what I need. Peggy has a sick father who can't be left on his own for too long at a time, and Kirsty's got a baby to care for. I could offer them working hours to suit their domestic responsibilities, and there must be a lot of small businessmen like Mr Monteith who could do with typists and book-keepers but can't afford to employ somebody. With two more typists, I could go out to look for new clients. I'll need to buy another two typewriters and some office furniture, but I got my own machine in a pawn shop – I might find others there. And there are good second-hand furniture shops.'

'What about financial support while all this is happening?'

'I've still got the money from the sale of my grandmother's furniture, and I've been saving what I've made working for Mr Monteith and Mr Leslie.'

'And if this venture of yours fails?'

'Then I'll have to admit defeat and look for other employment for myself. I know enough about keeping accounts by now to put an end to it before I run myself into trouble. But it will work – I know it will.' She leaned across the table in her urgency to convey the strength of her feelings for this new venture. 'I want this too much to let it fail.'

'You're taking on an awful lot, Elspeth,' said Forbes

Cameron, who had always relied on his parents' financial support in any venture he attempted.

'I'm not afraid of hard work. Please, Forbes?'

'You look so beautiful when you're enthused about something that it's very difficult to deny you anything,' he said wryly. 'I suppose there's no harm in having a proper look at the place.'

'Oh, thank you! I'll go tomorrow morning – I'm trying to keep out of Aunt Flora's way anyway, in case she starts on about finding another job for me.' she said happily.

It wasn't until she was getting ready for bed that night that she recalled his exact words. At the time she had been too intent on persuading him to let her explore the old house to pay much attention. Now, she peered wide-eyed into the mirror in an attempt to find out why he had described her as beautiful.

The ends of her long brown hair, freed from its plait and fresh from a good brushing, caught the gaslight as it swung about her face. Her blue eyes were clear, but quite ordinary, and her nose and mouth weren't too large or too small. She smiled at her own reflection, and decided that, again, her smile was ordinary.

'You're certainly not beautiful, miss,' she told her mirrored self. 'But you'll do. You'll have to – you're all I've got.'

True to his vow, Thomas had devoted himself to making the garage a success after his young wife's death. Under his single-minded supervision, it had already gained a reputation for excellent service and fair dealings.

Business had done so well that Joe, Thomas's assistant, had been promoted to the position of foreman, and two more mechanics taken on to enable Thomas to concentrate on the sales side. At his suggestion, Forbes had agreed to move into the area of car sales, and to this end the workshops had been expanded and improved and the original garage frontage removed to add a forecourt. During the work, Forbes had had the outside of the old house refurbished and painted.

Car engines were still dear to Thomas's heart, and when Elspeth arrived at the garage on the following morning she found him in his dungarees, working on an engine. She waited, trying to curb her impatience, until he was free, then explained her new plan to him.

His first reaction was a scowl. 'Is this going to mean a bunch of women traipsing through my yard and getting in the way?'

'The front door could be opened up for our use.'

Thomas grunted, then wiped his hands on a rag. 'I suppose you wound Cameron round your little finger?'

'I just asked him if I could have a good look at the house, and he agreed.'

'It's his house,' Thomas said, and called to one of the mechanics to take over.

'The keys to the upper rooms are here somewhere,' he said vaguely, rummaging in a kitchen drawer while Elspeth hovered, trying not to fidget. She had been waiting for so long to realise her dream, and now it was so close that every second's delay was unbearable.

She looked around the kitchen in an attempt to take her mind off her own impatience. She had managed to improve it, scraping years of grease from the gas stove, replacing the cracked linoleum with a remnant piece, clearing and cleaning the cupboards. Now that the garage covered car sales as well, the other downstairs room had been cleared and painted and turned into a proper office where Thomas, in a smart suit, could deal with possible buyers.

He had changed a lot since Aileen's death. Long, bitter months of grief had aged him, but not altogether unkindly. Though his first youth had gone he had taken on a new maturity that suited his lean features. The laughter in his eyes had given way to solemnity, and his body, used now to long hours of hard work and little rest, had a whip-like strength.

In recent months Elspeth had noticed sudden interest flickering into the gaze of more than one woman accompanying a husband or sweetheart to the garage to buy a new car from Thomas McDonald. A few of them had even found ways of making opening advances, but Thomas, steadfastly following his vow to show the Bruces that he was as good as they were, paid them no heed. He had moved his possessions into the old office in the garage house, refusing to give in to his mother and move back to Mearns Street permanently.

'Mam would expect everything to go back to the way it was before,' he told Elspeth. 'She can't understand that life can never go back, only forwards. I couldn't abide her fussing, anyway.'

Because she understood what he meant, and never fussed over him, Elspeth was one of the few people Thomas trusted now, and the affection that had been between them since she was a baby had strengthened.

'Here they are.' He waved a bunch of keys at her, then made for the inner door. 'Let's get this nonsense over with, then I can get back to my work.'

Elspeth kept close behind him as he led the way upstairs to a large, dark landing and unlocked the first of the three doors.

'Hold on.' He paused at the threshold and stamped hard on the floor. There was a scuttling, rustling sound, then silence.

'Mice – mebbe rats.' He crossed the room to wrench at the wooden shutters nailed across the windows.

'I'll get a cat – or a dog, if necessary,' she told him lightly, though she paused on the threshold for a moment before venturing in.

'What about the cockroaches?'

'Jeyes fluid and a scrubbing brush.'

Thomas grunted something, and pulled once more at the shutters, which gave way, dust and grit showering to the floor like a hail storm. The room was revealed, large and handsome and empty.

'It's just like the downstairs rooms. Once the windows are cleaned and the walls painted—'

'And the spider's webs cleared away,' Thomas put in, moving to the other window.

'—and some furniture installed,' she went on, ignoring the interruption, 'it'll make a fine office.'

The second room held the sagging remains of a metal bedstead and the third door, situated above the kitchen, led to a bathroom complete with a huge, stained claw-footed bath.

'Oh, look at this!' Elspeth, brought up in a house with a privy on the landing, was delighted. She tried to turn one of the taps in the cracked hand-basin, but it was too tight for her. After a brief struggle Thomas managed to loosen it, and a trickle of rusty water emerged. Elspeth pulled experimentally at the chain hanging above the privy, and it came away in her hand.

'It'd need a lot of work.' Thomas's voice was heavy with disapproval.

'But it would be worth it.'

'Ellie, you're daft!'

Standing in the ruins of the bathroom, dust streaking her face, cobwebs in her hair, the rusty cistern chain dangling from her fingers, she laughed. 'Mebbe I am, but it'll all work out – just you wait and see.'

It was the busiest summer Elspeth had ever known. Kenneth and Mattie came back to Greenock for the summer holidays, which meant that Kenneth spent a lot of time in the Mearns Street flat. Seeing the two of them together didn't trouble Elspeth a bit. She was too involved in her own life to mourn any further over what might have been.

When she wasn't at the garage, working on books for the clients she already had or chivvying the workmen upstairs, she was tramping the streets, calling in at every small business she could find – not only in Greenock, but in the neighbouring towns of Gourock and Port Glasgow. By the time the building was ready for scrubbing brush and broom she had invested some of her savings in two more second-hand typewriters and found a dozen employers, enough to get her new business off to a start.

When the time came to prepare the upper floor before furnishing it, Peggy and Kirsty, her future employees, arrived to help with the cleaning. So did Rachel, who had given birth to a second daughter, Pearl, in February. This time Elspeth insisted on paying her for the hours she put in.

'But I'm already making something from my sewing,' Rachel protested.

'That's got nothing to do with what you're doing for me.'

'It's thanks to you, for it was your idea in the first place, and you're looking after it for me.' They had agreed that the safest thing was for Rachel to admit to Bob that she was earning a certain amount – most of which he took from her to spend on drink – while she handed over the rest to Elspeth, who banked it along with the money from the sale of Celia Bremner's napery and bed linen.

'I'm still going to pay you for the work you do here. I just wish you could use a typewriter, for I could have taken you on in the office,' Elspeth said, struck to the heart by the older girl's wan, tired face.

'Even if I could type, it wouldnae work, not with the bairns still so wee,' Rachel said wistfully. 'It'd be nice to have something different to do with my life, though.' Then, squaring her shoulders and taking up a broom, she added, 'But Mam's right – I've made my bed and I must lie in it.'

The two of them were alone in the big room that was going to be the office. Kirsty and Peggy were scrubbing out the smaller room, and Mary was playing in the hallway with Sandra, Kirsty's little girl. Pearl, the baby, had been fed, and settled down in a blanket-filled box in a corner.

'It depends who's lying beside you,' Elspeth said, though

she wished she could say much more, and to Thomas and his father. Bob was still violent towards his wife, and Flora still refused to acknowledge what was happening, let alone tell Henry.

'Ellie! Don't be coarse! And mind your tongue in front of the weans,' Rachel added as Mary and Sandra scampered through the room.

'I'm just saying what I think.'

Forbes Cameron followed Elspeth's progress with keen interest.

'Let me start you off with a loan,' he suggested one day, finding her at the downstairs desk frowning over columns of figures and chewing the end of her pencil.

'I wouldn't dream of it. This is my idea, and I'll not risk anyone else's money.'

'Does that mean that you think there's a danger of failure?'

'Of course not.'

'Make it an investment, then. Call me a shareholder and start paying me dividends at the end of your first year.' Then, when she still hesitated, he suggested, 'If you don't like that idea, I could offer a reduced rent for the first year instead,' and went on to name a very low sum.

She squinted at him suspiciously. 'What benefit would you get out of that?' In her opinion, the suggestion smacked of charity.

'The pleasure of helping you to get started, for one. And for another,' he went on hurriedly as she opened her mouth to refuse, 'I'd insist on a more realistic rent after that, to make up what I lost in the first year. And I'd want the chance to get first refusal if or when you decided to sell shares to raise more money.'

'But you've already put a lot into getting the house put to rights. You shouldn't be thinking of spending even more on me.'

'But I've already made an investment of my own. If your business should fail, you'd get nothing back, while I'd still have the house, in better condition than ever before. I could recoup all my outlay by renting the upper floor to someone else.'

Elspeth studied the page before her. Her savings had dwindled quite frighteningly, and soon there would be wages for Peggy and Kirsty to take into consideration. She couldn't afford to be too proud.

'I accept,' she said at last, and he beamed.

By the time she celebrated her eighteenth birthday the upper floor was ready. Three sturdy desks, made for her by Peggy's brother, a carpenter, had been set up in the larger of the two upper rooms to hold the typewriters. Two cupboards bought from a second-hand shop were ranged along one wall, and a polished brass sign – Forbes' birthday gift to Elspeth – engraved with the words 'Bremner Office Agency, First Floor' had been fastened by the front door, which was now in use again.

Forbes held a party to celebrate the opening, inviting a number of guests, including all Elspeth's clients. His parents were there, as were the McDonalds – Lachlan and Henry bursting with pride at Elspeth's achievement, Flora torn between possessive pride and embarrassment. She had been shocked at first by Elspeth's 'walking out', as she put it, with Forbes, agreeing with Thomas that the garage-owner was too old for her, but he had soon charmed her doubts away.

'You know what she's hoping for, don't you?' Lachlan said now, nodding at his mother, deep in conversation with Mrs Cameron. 'You wed to a wealthy man and Mattie wed to a doctor. That'd give the folk in Mearns Street somethin' tae talk about.'

She laughed, and shook her head. 'If that's true, she'll have a long wait on my part. I'll be too busy with my business to think of marriage for a good long while.'

Lachlan himself was doing well in the maintenance department at Brodie's store, and still corresponding with Lena. It was his hope that soon she would appear onstage in Greenock.

'Come on, Elspeth, time to declare the agency open.' Forbes called from the hall, and the crowd of guests parted to let her through. Dazed with the sudden realisation that she had achieved her ambition, she walked between them to the foot of the stairs.

The scissors crunched through the ribbon, it fluttered away on both sides, and the dream she had held close to her heart for the past four years had come true.

30

In January, almost exactly two years after leaving Greenock, Lena Stewart returned to appear for a week in the King's Theatre.

Lachlan was beside himself with excitement when he received the news. At the family's traditional New Year's Day dinner his happiness helped to mask the fact that the annual meal, once a landmark in the McDonald calendar, was quieter than usual. Janet was there, but Thomas had refused to join them, and Mattie was spending the day with Kenneth's parents, much to her mother's disappointment. Rachel had brought her daughters to Mearns Street, but Bob wasn't with her, to Henry's surprise. Flora and Rachel had both had a difficult time fobbing off his questions. Between that, and Lachlan's constant talk about Lena's return, Flora was noticeably irritable before they even sat down at the table.

'Ye'll mebbe get a surprise,' she informed her son crustily. 'She'll have got too high-and-mighty for the likes of you. Ye'll not likely see hide nor hair of her off the stage.'

'You're wrong there, Mam,' he told her breezily, helping himself to another slice of bread and winking at wee Mary, who doted on him. 'I'll see quite a lot of Lena, for she's arranged for me to work as a stage hand in the theatre during her week there.'

Soup spoons clattered against Flora's best china bowls all

round the table, and he smirked as everyone stared at him, enjoying the sensation he had caused.

'She's what? Well, ye can forget that, for no son of mine—' Flora began, but he interrupted her.

'It's already arranged, Mam, and I've said I'm doin' it. I've been to see the stage manager at the theatre and it's all agreed.' Lachlan dunked his bread in his soup, something Flora abhorred, and took a mouthful.

'And not a word tae us about it?'

'Leave it, Flora,' Henry advised quietly. 'Lachie's a man now, old enough tae join a circus as the elephant trainer if he chooses. Now – take yer soup before it gets cold. You too, Rachel.'

Rachel had been staring down at her bowl, the spoon drooping from her hand. She jumped, and began eating again, while her father watched her, his brows knotted with concern.

'Are ye ailin', hen?'

'Of course she's not ailin',' Flora snapped.

'She looks awful pale,' Henry said, and Janet nodded.

'I think so too.'

'And so would you look pale if ye'd two weans under yer feet day and night. I'd as soon do a day's labourin' in the shipyards as look after weans.'

'Will ye give the lassie the chance tae answer for hersel'?' Henry asked in a rare burst of impatience, then, as Flora's mouth clamped into an offended line, and she got up and collected in the plates that had been emptied, 'Ye're no sickenin' for somethin', pet, are ye?'

Rachel shot a sidelong look at her mother, then said, 'I'm fine, Da. It's this weather, I've never liked the winter.'

'It's not the winter, you've been looking poorly for a while now.' Elspeth was unable to keep silent any longer.

Despite the fact that not everybody had finished the first course, Flora banged a huge bowl of potatoes down so hard on the table that the cutlery jumped and jangled, and Mary, sitting on a pile of cushions to enable her small face to peep over the table, and tied into her chair for safety, burst into tears. Her sister, on Rachel's lap, immediately followed suit.

'Now look what ye've done!' Flora accused her husband, while in the ensuing rush to comfort the children Rachel whispered to Elspeth, 'Leave it be, for pity's sake!'

By the time the little girls had been calmed, Henry, waiting impatiently for the main course, was too hungry to remember what had caused all the fuss.

Forbes had tried to persuade Elspeth to spend the day at his parents' home, to meet some friends of theirs.

'My mother will be disappointed if you don't. You know how much she enjoys your company.'

'I can't let Aunt Flora and Uncle Henry down, not when Mattie and Thomas are both staying away.'

'But it's not as if they're really your family, is it? Not your own flesh and blood,' he added as she stared at him, puzzled.

'For goodness' sake, Forbes, they're the only family I've ever known!' On occasion, she thought with irritation, Forbes was capable of displaying a grating insensitivity towards others. 'If it comes to that, you and your parents aren't my family either.'

'Mebbe that'll change by next New Year,' he murmured, drawing her into his arms, his mouth seeking and finding hers. The anger ebbed as she closed her eyes and let her body blend with his, parting her lips against the moist warmth of his mouth.

She was very fond of Forbes, she thought, returning kiss for kiss. He had done so much for her, and had become a dear friend as well as a pleasant companion. He had never tried to force himself on her as Kenneth had, so long ago in the wash house, but his kisses and caresses were exciting and desirable, and Elspeth felt that one day quite soon she would want more from him than this chaste loving.

She hadn't as yet decided what she would do when that day

came, but the thought of it warmed her. She was a woman now, no longer a naive girl.

Although she wasn't the star of the music hall her company staged in Greenock, it was Lena that most of the folk in the audiences came to see. When the Master of Ceremonies introduced her as Greenock's own songbird, the storm of applause made the chandeliers high above the auditorium tremble and tinkle.

Elspeth gripped Forbes' arm as the curtains parted and Lena stepped forward, hands outstretched to receive the adulation of her public. The gasp that greeted her appearance could be heard even above the applause. She wore a sea-green gown, cut low in front to reveal her smooth white throat and the shaded hollow between her full breasts. Skilful draping along the top of the bodice enhanced the swell of her bosom, while below the tiny waist the skirt hugged her hips and thighs, then swirled into deep frills. The sleeves were long and tight, and hundreds of sequins caught the light with every movement she made, so that her entire body shimmered. Her red hair was caught up in an intricate pile of curls, with a large bejewelled Spanish comb thrust into them at the back.

Graciously, she acknowledged the applause from every corner of the theatre, then waited, still and erect, until it had ebbed away completely before giving the orchestra conductor a nod.

She had come a long way since her first impromptu appearance on the stage two years before. The voice that filled the theatre was stronger now, clearer and more confident. As before, she slid from one mood to another without effort, singing a ballad then swooping to the wings to collect a cloak and umbrella before launching into a comedy number that was greeted with howls of approval. Then came a slow, sad song that brought a catch to her listeners' throats.

'Didn't I tell you she was good?' Elspeth asked Forbes,

clapping until her hands stung as Lena finally left the stage, blowing expansive kisses to her ecstatic audience.

'You did, and you're right. She'll go a long way,' he predicted.

When she and Lachlan finally arrived in the hotel where they had arranged to meet for supper, Lena walked the length of the dining room like royalty, halted at almost every table by people who had been at the theatre earlier and wanted to congratulate her. She had changed into a narrow, ankle-length deep brown velvet dress, sleeveless, with a silvery silk-chiffon cape floating from beaded shoulder straps. Her hair was still up, and her only ornament was a beaded sash around her hips. Lachlan, in an evening suit, followed closely behind her, glowing as he basked in her success.

Arriving at last at the table Forbes had booked for the four of them, Lena shook his hand, hugged Elspeth, then collapsed into a chair. 'My feet are killing me!'

Forbes was enchanted by her, but it was Lachlan who absorbed all Elspeth's attention at first. 'Lachie, where did you get those clothes?'

He grinned self-consciously, and put a hand up to the bow tie at the collar of his dazzlingly white shirt. 'D'ye like it? Lena made me borrow it from the wardrobe department.'

'I like it very much.' The formal clothes had transformed him from the Lachie she knew into a stylish young man. 'You look so handsome!'

'He is handsome,' Lena said. 'You've just been too used to looking on him as a brother.' She flicked a teasing sidelong glance at Lachlan, and he beamed back at her, comfortable in her presence. 'I saw him as he really is the first time I clapped eyes on him in that big room at Brodie's store where we all ate our dinners. He was a poor wee thin creature then, in an overall that was far too big for him, but I knew what he'd look like in different clothes – and I was right.' Then she leaned across the table, her eyes brimming over with laughter. 'D'ye mind those days, Ellie?'

Clearly, although the sewing room rebel had become a sophisticated and elegant artiste, Lena's zest for life hadn't changed. She entertained them all throughout the meal with her memories of the sewing room, followed by a string of stories about her life in the theatre, each one more outrageous than the last. Diners at the other tables glanced across enviously at the four young people rocking with laughter, so obviously enjoying their evening out. Finally Lena announced that she had said more than enough, and demanded to know all Elspeth's news.

'I knew you were wasted in that dreary wee sewing room,' she said when she had heard something of the new business. 'You wrote such lovely letters. Wait and see – we're both going to become very famous and earn lots of money.' Then, with a wicked gleam in her eyes, 'And we'll have our clothes made at Brodie's, and criticise every stitch, and drive Miss Buchanan and Miss Arnold mad.'

'Miss Arnold's in charge now. Miss Buchanan retired a month or so ago.'

'Then we'll invite ourselves to Miss Buchanan's for tea as well, and criticise her taste in crockery,' said Lena.

She called in at the office two days later, all work coming to an abrupt halt when she swept into the room in a loose-fitting calf-length black woollen coat with a wide collar and deep cuffs at the wrists. Her red hair was tucked under a small black hat with a wide brim turned up all round and trimmed with jet beads. A large white satin bow was pinned at one side.

'I admire you,' she said as the two of them stood in the smaller of the two upper rooms where, Elspeth had explained, she hoped eventually to install more typewriters. 'You've done so much in such a short time.'

'Not as much as you, travelling all over the place and appearing in front of hundreds of people.'

Lena shrugged, smoothing her black gloves. 'The life's not as romantic as it looks. There are a lot of nasty little boarding houses I'd not put a cat into, and a lot of audiences more interested in throwing insults than flowers. Anyway, I was lucky – I got the chance to climb up on to a stage and sing. My voice did the rest. Now you – you've changed your life right here in your home town, and that's far more difficult. I can be anyone I like when I'm far away from the folk who knew me before.'

'Your father must be pleased to see you home for a wee while.'

Lena threw her head back and laughed. 'Him? I'm not so sure. D'you mind old Miss Lambert that lived upstairs from us? The retired schoolteacher? It seems that she took to "keeping an eye on poor Mr Stewart when his daughter upped and left him"' – she imitated an elderly woman's dry, genteel voice to perfection – 'and now she's got her feet tucked very comfortably under his table. If you ask me, they'll be wed by the time I come back again.'

'At their age?'

'Love doesn't worry about birthdays,' Lena said blithely. 'She's not my choice as a stepmother, but if she's his as a wife, good luck to the two of them.' Then, her lovely turquoise eyes fixed on Elspeth, she said thoughtfully. 'Talking of marriage, Forbes seems a nice man.'

'He's helped me to set up the agency, and he's a good friend, but I'm not looking for marriage.'

'He is. I could tell by the way he looked at you. No need to put that face on, Ellie Bremner, you could do worse than marry money. I nearly fell over when he ordered champagne the other night!'

'I'd as soon earn my own fortune.'

'Then mebbe you should make that clear to Forbes before it's too late,' Lena advised, moving to the window to look down on the windswept cobbled street below. 'It's a grey old town this, isn't it? But I'm still fond of it.'

As Elspeth escorted her down to the door Lena said casually, 'Lachlan's working well in the theatre, you'd think he'd done it for years. The rest of the crew like him. He's fairly come on since I went away.'

'Your cards and letters helped.' Elspeth thought of Flora, hiding the cards, then decided to say nothing of that to her friend. 'It was kind of you.'

'Away with you – I've never been kind in my life. I did it because I like Lachlan. I always have and I always will,' Lena said, and left, her feet seeming to skim over the cobbles.

The local people, proud to know that one of their own had become a public performer, flocked to see Lena and the company played to packed houses throughout the week. Each night after the show there were crowds waiting at the stage door to speak to her, and by mid-week her photograph was on the billboards at each side of the theatre entrance.

'Dolly Costello's not pleased,' she reported gleefully to the girls in the agency. 'She's had star billing since before I was born – so mebbe it's time she got used to the idea of moving over for someone younger.'

'It must be hard for her, though,' Elspeth said, and Lena retorted, 'It's life. One day the same thing'll happen to me.'

She called in almost every day, perching on a stool in the corner, enthralling Peggy and Kirsty with her stories about theatrical life. Delighted though she was to see Lena again, Elspeth was secretly glad to know that she was only in town for a week. If it had been longer, she thought ruefully, reminding the other two yet again that there was work to be done, she might go out of business.

Despite the fact that Lena arranged free tickets for all the family, Flora steadfastly refused to attend the music hall. 'I've never approved of women flaunting themselves on a stage, and I never will,' she said coldly when Lachlan tried to coax her.

He reddened with suppressed anger. 'Lena doesn't flaunt herself. She's got a beautiful voice and folk love to hear it. Where's the harm in that?' he argued, but got nowhere.

Thomas refused as well, but civilly, and to Lena's face when she met him in the garage.

'I'm pleased for you, lassie, but I'm not ready yet for enjoyment.'

For once, Lena's pretty face was solemn. 'I can understand that, but would your Aileen want you to shut yourself away from the rest of the world and work yourself to death?' she asked bluntly.

Thomas didn't take offence. 'I've asked myself that, and the answer's no, she wouldn't. Nor would I have wanted her to mourn for ever if it had been me killed instead of her. But something inside me says I'm not ready to face things yet. Mebbe I will be, the next time you perform in Greenock.'

'I hope so,' she agreed, then put a hand on his arm. 'Don't punish yourself forever over something that wasn't your doing, Thomas.'

As they walked out on to the street, she said to Elspeth, 'When you see a decent man like your Thomas with all the life taken out of him, then look at some of the folk walking around that the world could do without, you wonder what God's thinking of at times.'

Janet Docherty and her neighbour, Mrs Begg, spent an enjoyable night at the theatre, and even Bob and Rachel took advantage of Lena's generosity. Elspeth looked after the little girls for them that evening. She was rarely in Rachel's home, and now that she had the time and the freedom to study her surroundings properly, she was struck by the dreariness of the place.

Everything was spotlessly clean, but the linoleum and the fireside rug were badly worn and the furniture cheap and uncomfortable. Mary and Pearl tended to be shy, though at the garage they usually blossomed in the warmth of Joe's kindness. But here, in their own home, both little girls seemed very withdrawn. Given the bleak atmosphere of the small flat, Elspeth could understand why.

Rachel and Bob didn't come home until about an hour after the show ended. When they did arrive Bob smelled of drink and Rachel's eyes were anxious despite the pretty flush that the chill night air had brought to her cheeks.

'I'm sorry we're late,' she burst out as soon as they arrived. 'We met some folks and got talking.'

'I'm in no hurry,' Elspeth assured her, although she had been nodding over the book in her lap for the past half-hour. 'Did you enjoy the theatre?'

'Oh, it was bonny! All those lovely clothes, and the music – and Lena was beautiful!'

Bob said nothing, but Elspeth was aware of his eyes on her as she fetched her coat. 'I'll walk ye home,' he offered.

'I'll manage fine on my own.'

He tried to insist, then lapsed into a huffy silence when she finally told him sharply that she could manage. Rachel accompanied her to the close-mouth. Someone had shattered the gas mantle, and the close behind them was pitch black.

'Don't mind Bob,' Rachel whispered as soon as they left the flat. 'He's tired.'

'How much did he have to drink on the way home?'

'Just the one wee glass, to keep the cold out. Just the one. You'll not say to—'

When Bob spoke his wife's name from just behind her, both women jumped and gasped.

'What're ye whisperin' about?' he wanted to know suspiciously, sliding an arm about Rachel's hips and glaring at Elspeth. In the dim light from the street, he looked menacing, and Elspeth edged towards the pavement as Rachel, chattering nervously, 'I'm comin' – just comin',' was drawn back into the close.

Once out on the pavement Elspeth broke into a run, and raced all the way to Mearns Street as though a pack of devils were at her heels.

*

309

Despite his mother's open dislike of Lena, Lachlan insisted on bringing her to Mearns Street for the midday meal on Saturday, the day of her final appearance at the King's Theatre. Out of deference to Flora the girl dressed demurely in a plain jersey and skirt, scrubbed her face clean of make-up, and tied her glorious hair back with a ribbon.

'Mrs McDonald, it's lovely to see you again,' she flattered as soon as Lachlan ushered her proudly into the kitchen. Flora murmured something unintelligible.

'And Mr McDonald. Did I not see you in the audience on Thursday night?' Lena asked, shaking Henry's hand.

'What?' Flora barked, while her husband's face drained of colour.

'No, no, lassie, it was never me – I've a union meetin' on Thursday nights.'

'If ye were at yer precious meeting last Thursday, how did the lassie come tae see ye in the theatre?' Flora asked ominously.

'I must have been mistaken,' Lena said before Henry could speak. 'With the lights shining on us it's difficult to see the audience – we just get wee glimpses sometimes.'

'But ye saw Henry clear enough.'

'I thought I saw someone like him. But now I look at you, Mr McDonald, the man was nothing like you at all. It was a right noisy audience that night—' Lena chattered on until Flora finally turned back to her cooking. Henry, relaxing visibly behind her back, winked at Lena, who winked back.

She did her best to dampen down her natural vitality during her short visit, but even so Flora's disapproval hung in the air like the smell of burned cabbage. She studiously ignored the angry looks Lachlan gave her from time to time, and by the time he and Lena left for the Saturday matinée his face was tight with suppressed rage.

Elspeth walked downstairs with them. 'Pay no heed to Aunt Flora, Lena, you know what she's like.'

'Stop makin' excuses for her, Ellie,' Lachlan burst out. 'She'd no right to be so cold!'

'Ach, don't fret, she doesnae bother me,' Lena assured him, then hugged Elspeth. 'Mebbe next time I'm back in Greenock you'll be a married woman with a bundle of weans round your knees.'

'And you'll be the top of the bill.'

'I will that,' Lena said, and left for the theatre, Lachlan in attendance.

Upstairs, Flora was already washing the dishes vigorously, as though trying to erase every sign of the recent visitor. 'Thank goodness the week's over,' she said as soon as Elspeth went into the kitchen. 'She'll be out of the town tomorrow and we can get back tae normal.'

Lachlan hadn't returned from the theatre by the time they went to bed that night.

'They'll be clearin' everythin' away, ready tae move on tomorrow,' Henry said placidly when Flora looked at the clock for the hundredth time. 'Mebbe havin' a bit of a party. He'll come home when he's ready.'

Elspeth was roused some time later by the sound of the outer door closing softly, and when she slid back into sleep a few minutes later Lachlan was still moving about his room.

When he came into the kitchen the next morning, shaved and dressed in his best clothes, Henry raised his brows.

'I thought ye'd be too tired tae go tae the church today.' The McDonalds weren't regular churchgoers, but since recovering from the effects of his shell shock Lachlan had taken to attending the Sunday service almost every week.

'No, I'm—' Lachlan hesitated, then said, looking at his mother, 'I'm off to Ayr, with the company. I've taken up a position with them.'

Henry, still tousled from a night's sleep, his unshaven chin black with stubble, gaped, while Elspeth almost dropped the

311

large teapot she was carrying from the cooker to the table.

'Don't be stupid,' Flora said crisply. 'Ye've got a good job here. There'll be no goin' off tae Ayr or anywhere else.'

'Mam, the train leaves in an hour's time and I'll be on it. I'd have told you two days ago, when they first asked me, but I knew you'd only start on at me to turn it down, so I kept my mouth shut.'

Flora spun away from the cooker, porridge ladle in hand. 'It's her – that woman. I knew she'd try tae entice ye away from us!'

'It's not Lena, Mam, not altogether.' Although he had had very little sleep Lachlan looked rested and confident. It was clear to Elspeth, at any rate, that he meant what he said and wouldn't be swayed from the path he had decided to take. 'Mebbe she's part of it, but it's mostly the work. I've enjoyed this week, and I like the thought of the travellin', too.'

'Ye're not goin'!'

'I am. I'll write to you, every week, and I'll send what I can afford—'

'Ye're not goin'!' his mother repeated, dropping the ladle, oblivious of the porridge spraying from it. She advanced on Lachlan and caught at the lapels of his coat. 'D'ye hear me? Ye're not goin' – I won't let ye go!'

Her voice began to rise, out of control. Henry pushed his chair back and got up, taking his wife by the shoulders. 'Flora, sit down and let's talk about it.'

She ignored him, and Lachlan himself had to loosen her grip on his coat, finger by finger. 'Mam, will you listen to me, just for once? I want to do this. I want to get on with my life!'

'He's got the right tae dae as he pleases, Flora.' Henry's voice was gruff as he drew his wife back against his own body, wrapping his arms about her in an attempt to confine her struggles. 'I don't want tae see him go any more than you, but it's his decision and we have tae abide by it.'

'We don't have tae do anythin' of the sort! She'll desert ye when she's done with ye, d'ye not have the sense tae realise that?' Flora spat the words at her son. 'She'll laugh at ye an' send ye crawlin' back home!'

'I told you, Mam, it's not Lena I'm doing this for, it's me.' Lachlan's face was pale but determined. 'Mebbe we'll end up together, mebbe we'll part, but that doesnae matter. What matters is me doin' what I want to do.'

'Ye've already got a job here! And ye've got family, and a home!'

'Ye'll tell Mr Brodie for me, Elspeth? Explain things tae him?' Lachlan said, and she nodded.

'I will. Write to us.'

'Every week.' He hugged her tightly, then glanced at his father.

'I've packed my clothes, they're waitin' at the door.'

Henry was still holding Flora. 'Best just go now, lad. And I hope everythin' goes right for ye.'

'It will, I'll see tae that,' Lachlan said, then, with a faint tremor in his voice, 'Take care of Mam for me.'

He went without a backward glance. Flora, fighting hard against her husband's iron arms, screamed out her son's name, but there was no answer.

The outer door closed, and Lachlan had gone.

31

Pausing on the landing to shift the weighted shopping bag from one hand to the other, Flora McDonald cast a sidelong glance at the smooth brown hair lying against Elspeth's cheek.

'Every time I look at ye I think ye're a stranger.' Her voice was heavy with disapproval. 'I don't know why ye did it – ye'd such bonny hair. Thinkin' of it on someone else's head gives me the shivers. It's like wearin' someone else's dentures.'

'There's plenty that do that, Aunt Flora.' Since taking over Mr Monteith's pawn shop books, Elspeth had seen and heard of many things.

'Aye, well, nob'dy in my family's ever done it, or ever will!'

'The braid was too heavy, and it took so much looking after,' Elspeth explained for the umpteenth time, 'And the money I got for selling it came in useful.'

'Ye'll be sellin' yer soul next.' Flora gave her familiar, last-word sniff, a sniff that indicated that Flora McDonald knew best and there was no sense in further discussion, then set off up the final flight.

When the shopping had been unpacked and stored away, Elspeth went into her own small room to change from her everyday skirt and blouse into a lemon cotton dress with brown trim on the crossover bodice and on the cuffs, for she was calling on a prospective client that afternoon. Glancing in the mirror as she fluffed out her bobbed hair she decided that whatever Flora might say, she herself liked the new style. It made her look older, more like the professional woman she had become.

Returning to the kitchen, she found Flora, who always made tea her priority after being out, filling two cups from the teapot.

'Aunt Flora, I've not got much time—'

'Time enough for a cup of tea and a scone.' It was waiting on a plate, already buttered. 'Ye don't eat enough these days. Too eager tae look smart for yer precious clients' – Flora said the word with contempt – 'and that Forbes Cameron.'

The accusation was unjustified. Elspeth's weight and shape were the same as two years before, when she had worked in Brodie's sewing room. It was true that the clothes she wore now were more fashionable and flattered her slim figure, but there was no sense in explaining that to Flora, for Elspeth knew very well that there was another reason behind the woman's carping.

After years of dominating her family, Flora McDonald had lost her main purpose in life now that they had all flown the nest, and was finding it very hard to come to terms with the situation she now found herself in.

Lachlan had been gone for six months, and despite his mother's dire predictions at the time, the letters that arrived every week were written by a man who had finally found his proper place in life, and was supremely happy. Flora always left it to Henry to open the letters, and looked as though she was sucking lemons as he proudly read each one aloud.

'You'd think she'd be pleased for Lachlan,' Elspeth had said to Rachel, who replied flatly, 'I sometimes think Mam can only be pleased for folk if they're doing what she wants them to do.'

Mattie and Kenneth had married at Easter, and had settled in Glasgow, where Kenneth was working in the Southern General Hospital. Thomas still drove himself on relentlessly, and had done so well that Forbes Cameron had made him his partner and there was talk of buying another garage. He had long since cut his mother's apron strings, and even Rachel's visits weren't so frequent now that she had her sewing to occupy her time.

Only Elspeth, the child Flora had taken in and never loved, remained. As she sat down at the table she flicked a swift glance at the clock on the mantel shelf. She and Peggy and Kirsty organised their work round the needs of their clients and their own domestic duties, each taking time off in turn when the office was quiet. Elspeth saw to it that the other two were always free on Saturday afternoons and Sundays, but she herself often worked at the weekends, enjoying the peace and quiet of the office when nobody else was there.

As she glanced at the clock again, someone knocked on the outer door. Flora, tutting, put her hands flat on the table and started to lever herself up. 'That'll be Annie from across the landing. That nose of hers can smell fresh-made tea through stone walls.'

Elspeth was already on her feet. 'I'll go.'

As she opened the door her eyes moved to the spot where she expected to find wee fat Mrs McGlashan's face, and saw instead the buttons on a smart grey morning coat. Startled, she lifted her gaze and saw a tall, elegantly dressed man in the act of raising his bowler hat.

'Good afternoon, is Mrs McDonald—' His voice faltered and his polite smile faded as their eyes met. Elspeth's knees suddenly started to tremble, forcing her to tighten her grip on the edge of the door in order to stay upright. The man was a stranger to her, and yet she recognised him after just one glance at the clear blue eyes set in a handsome, middle-aged face. She knew those eyes so well; she should, for she saw them every time she looked into a mirror.

'Elspeth,' Flora said impatiently from behind her, 'there's a terrible draught comin' intae the house. Who is it?'

The man on the landing tore his gaze from Elspeth's face to look beyond her shoulder. 'Good afternoon, Flora,' he said through pale lips, and Flora's hand clutched at Elspeth's arm, her fingers digging in painfully.

'Oh my God!' Her voice came out in a strange croak. 'You?'

'Yes, it's me.'

'What d'ye want?'

'I've come to see my daughter,' he said, then, throwing a glance over his shoulder as Mrs McGlashan's door gave a slight creak, 'Would it not be better if I came in?'

'I thought you were still a child,' Duncan Crombie said in the kitchen a few minutes later. 'Time passes so quickly.'

'Aye, 'specially when ye've turned yer back on yer responsibilities,' Flora said harshly. She hadn't mentioned the cup of tea that was always offered to visitors as soon as they stepped into any West of Scotland home. Instead, she sat on the edge of an upright chair, her face pinched, her hands clasped tightly in her lap.

'I'm not proud of what I did, Flora.' His voice was pleasant to the ear, his accent anglicised Scots. 'I can only say in my own defence that I was very young – mebbe too young to face up to my responsibilities.'

Although he was answering Flora, he spoke directly across the table to Elspeth. Since his arrival they had been unable to take their eyes off each other. 'And Maisie's parents didn't make things any easier. They were against me from the first.'

'With good reason – look what ye did tae her,' Flora said bitterly, and he flinched.

'Aunt Flora—' Elspeth, embarrassed, put a hand on the woman's arm but it was twitched off.

'This is my house, I'll say what I please!'

'You never liked me either, did you, Flora? Between you and Maisie's mother we never had a chance.'

'I didnae trust ye, and I was proved right – ye cannae deny that.'

He shrugged, then got to his feet and reached for his hat

and cane. 'I'd best go. I've no wish to upset anyone.' Dipping into a breast pocket he removed a small flat case and opened it to extract a slip of pasteboard. 'Here's my card, Elspeth. The address of my hotel's on the back. I hope you'll call on me there.' Then, as Flora got to her feet, clearly determined not to let him have a moment alone with Elspeth, 'I'll see myself out.'

'Let me see that wee bit of paper,' Flora demanded as soon as the outer door closed behind him.

Elspeth, knowing that it would be thrown into the fire immediately, curled her fingers about the card. 'It's mine, Aunt Flora.'

'Ye're surely no' goin' tae see him?'

'I have to. I can't just let him walk out of my life again.'

'Of course ye can, and ye must, if ye've got any sense at all. That man's no use tae anyone, you take my word for it. He's a sleekit, deceitful devil – look what he did tae yer poor wee mother!'

'He meant a lot to her, once.'

'Aye – and she died hatin' him. She'd no' want ye tae have anythin' tae dae with him!' Flora's eyes were slits, her lips drawn back in a snarl. Elspeth jumped up, suddenly desperate to get out of the place. 'I must go, I'm late as it is.'

'If ye see that man again ye'll be turnin' yer back on me and all I've done for ye.' Flora followed her out on to the landing to throw the words at her departing back, then, as Elspeth started down the stairs, she leaned over the wrought-iron railing that edged the landing. 'I'm tellin' ye,' she called down as Elspeth started down the stairs, 'ye'll be turnin' against me if ye as much as set eyes on him!'

Thomas McDonald, leaning against the door of the car he had been working on, took a large swallow of tea from the mug Elspeth had brought him, then wiped the back of his hand across his mouth. 'So – what are you going to do?'

'I don't know. What d'you think would be best?'

'You're a woman, Ellie, not a bairn,' he said implacably. 'You have to make your own decisions.'

She clenched her fists, longing to batter them on his chest. 'Thomas, this is important – help me!'

He emptied the mug and handed it over before turning back to the car that stood with bonnet raised, like a fledgling waiting in the nest to be fed by the parent bird. 'Don't bring me or anyone else into it, Ellie.' He tossed the words over his shoulder, his hands already on the engine. 'I've told you, it's your decision.'

Going back into the house, she met Rachel settling little Pearl in her perambulator while Mary and Sandra, Kirsty's little girl, bounded around the hall like little rubber balls.

'We're going to the park,' Mary announced, rushing to hug Elspeth's knees as she always did.

'Mind your Aunt Elspeth's nice dress,' Rachel ordered, tucking a blanket round the baby's waist.

'It's only a dress, and I've got my smock on anyway.' Rachel had made loose smocks for herself and the typists to wear over their clothes as a protection against oil and grime. With the garage yard so close, they frequently got stains on their clothes.

'I'd best get this lot out of your way. We'll be back by the time Kirsty's ready to go home.'

Rachel had been working for Elspeth for the past two months, ever since Kirsty, her face white with misery, had handed in her notice.

'I don't want to leave, for I've loved working with you, but it's the wee one.'

Sandra, a toddler with dark curly hair and a dimpled smile, was the reason why Kirsty had been unable to apply for full-time work after completing her typing course. Deserted by the child's father before Sandra was born, Kirsty had refused to consider giving her baby up for adoption, and the two of them lived with Kirsty's parents. When Elspeth had first set up her agency nine months before, Kirsty's mother, delighted at her daughter finally getting the chance to earn her own living, had agreed to care for the little girl.

But the woman had recently had a bad bout of pleurisy, and as there was nobody else to care for Sandra, Kirsty had no option but to leave.

Elspeth, distressed at losing a good worker as well as a friend, had had the idea of turning the room she had intended one day as a second office into a nursery, and asking Rachel to spend time at the garage every day, caring for Sandra and her own two.

'I'd pay you,' she told Rachel. 'And it would only be for the afternoons, because Kirsty doesn't work in the mornings.'

'Folk don't get paid to look after bairns,' Rachel protested.

'Nannies and nurserymaids do.'

'That's different. Anyway, why should you put out more money just for the one wee girl? Would it not be easier just to let Kirsty go and find someone else?'

'Kirsty's my friend,' Elspeth said firmly, 'and she's a good worker. She needs the little I can afford to pay her.'

Rachel's eyes brightened, and a touch of colour came to her pale face. 'It's a bonny room, right enough, and there's so much space for the bairns to play.'

'What about Bob? What would he say about it?' He had been getting moodier lately, and had lost his job after arguing with the foreman. Henry had managed to find a place for him in the shipyard where he himself worked. Elspeth didn't want to cause even more trouble for Rachel by crossing Bob.

'He'll not care as long as his dinner's on the table when he comes home from work – if he comes home instead of going to the public house,' Rachel added with contempt.

Elspeth had scoured the second-hand shops and pawn shops for furniture for the empty room, gaining two new clients in the process, and Sandra had quickly settled down with Rachel, who loved children and got a lot of pleasure herself out of the new arrangement.

'It's such an easy room to keep nice,' she told Elspeth. 'Not like home, where everything's packed in like sardines in a tin. It minds me of the times we had, you and me and Mattie, playing at wee houses.'

She insisted on taking over responsibility for cleaning the whole upper floor, and keeping everyone – Thomas and his staff as well as the typists – supplied with tea. She organised the kitchen and even baked scones occasionally in the large old cooker, brushing Thomas's mild grumbles aside.

'This is a garage, not a restaurant,' he pointed out when the first plate of scones, light as feathers and smelling delicious, came from the oven.

'I've not set foot in your yard, nor do I intend to,' Rachel retorted, her face flushed with the heat, her curly fair hair escaping in wisps from the pins that were supposed to keep it in place. 'But there's surely no harm in a wee bit of baking now and then.'

'No harm at all,' Joe agreed enthusiastically, his voice muffled by a mouthful of scone. 'I've never tasted anythin' as good as this!'

Rachel slapped at Thomas's hand as it reached out towards the plate. 'Wash that first – I'm not having good food smothered in oil before it gets to your mouth.'

He gave her an exasperated look tinged with amusement, and did as he was told. From then on, Rachel ruled the kitchen. She had blossomed since starting work, Elspeth thought now as she helped her to lift the perambulator down the front steps, though she still tended to keep her sleeves rolled down, to hide her forearms.

Elspeth saw the little group off, then, glancing up to make sure that Rachel's back was turned, rubbed at an imaginary speck of dirt on the nameplate, 'Bremner Office Agency, First Floor', with a corner of her smock. Rachel polished the plate every day, but now and again Elspeth liked to find an excuse to touch it, just to make sure that it was real, and not a dream.

Later, she tried to concentrate on the long list she was typing, the rattle of Peggy's and Kirsty's typewriters providing a pleasant background as she painstakingly transferred scribbled notes on crumpled scraps of paper into neat, clear columns on a fresh white sheet. But her mind kept returning to Duncan Crombie. Discovering that she had typed 'father' on the list instead of 'feather', she ripped the half-finished page free with an exclamation of disgust.

'Something wrong?' Peggy asked cheerfully.

'I wasn't concentrating properly.' Elspeth glanced at the clock and pushed her chair back. 'It'll have to wait until later, I'm due to call in at that new bookseller's soon.'

As it happened, the bookseller's shop was almost directly across the road from the hotel where Duncan Crombie was staying. From where she stood explaining the services the agency offered, Elspeth could see the corner of the building; by the time the business meeting had come to a mutually satisfying conclusion her mind was made up.

When she left the shop, she crossed the road and stepped into the hotel.

32

'You're so like Maisie,' Duncan Crombie marvelled an hour later, as they faced each other across a small tea table in the hotel lounge.

'But I've got your eyes.'

He smiled. 'You have indeed. Maisie's were like trees in the autumn, golden brown – something like the colour of your own hair.' His face softened with memories. 'They were long-lashed and always laughing. She was so unlike her parents that I used to tell her she must have been a changeling, left in her crib by the little folk.' Then, returning to the present, 'I understand that her parents have both died.'

'My grandmother died two years ago. She'd been' – Elspeth hesitated, then said carefully, reluctant to entrust Celia Bremner's bitter betrayal to this man who was her own flesh and blood, yet a complete stranger – 'on her own for years, since I was very small. I never knew my grandfather.'

'I liked him well enough, but his wife ruled the roost,' Crombie recalled. 'Poor man, he must have been stifled, living with that woman year in and year out. As for me – Maisie's mother was convinced that I'd never come to anything. She wanted better for her daughter. I don't think anyone other than royalty would have pleased her.'

Two middle-aged women passing their table glanced back at him with interest. He was still a good-looking man; in his youth he must have been very handsome. Elspeth could understand why her young mother had fallen in love with him.

'Tell me about my mother. There was nothing of hers in Grandmother's flat, not even a picture.'

He looked down at his cup, taking the teaspoon from the saucer and stirring his cooling tea slowly. 'She was beautiful, and loving, and I treated her badly. I was an orphan, living with my uncle, a man with no time for human weakness. I took fright when she told me she was carrying my child, and I ran away. My uncle had apprenticed me to a legal office, and I wasn't earning enough to keep the two of us. I couldn't face him – or Maisie's parents.'

He put the spoon down and took a sip of tea. 'I thought that if I was out of the way her mother and father would help her. If I'd only known how wrong I was!'

They talked the afternoon away without noticing time passing. Crombie told of his life in England, where he had found a position in another lawyer's office, working his way up and eventually marrying his employer's daughter.

'My wife's health broke down and we moved to the Isle of Man. I've been very lonely since she died a year ago, and finally I thought of trying to discover what had happened to Maisie and to our child. I'd always assumed that she had married, and that you had probably been raised by her husband as his own. I knew that I'd already caused her great unhappiness – I didn't want to do so again. Then I discovered that she died all those years ago, and that you'd been raised by Flora and her husband.'

His mouth twisted wryly. 'Flora never had any time for me either, because I worked in an office. In her opinion the only real men are those who work with their hands.'

'She was opposed to me taking up office work.' Elspeth told him about her struggle to achieve her ambitions, and he listened with interest.

'I'd like to see this office of yours.'

'You will, on Monday,' she promised, then, her heart

quickening at the thought of half-brothers and sisters, 'Did you and your wife have a family?'

To her disappointment he shook his head. 'We would have liked children, but there were none – until now.' He reached out and covered her hand briefly with his, his eyes sparkling. 'And now I have a beautiful daughter – I can't believe that we're finally together.'

Smiling at him, Elspeth relished the thought of introducing this man to people with the words, 'This is my father.'

At last she belonged to someone who was truly her own flesh and blood.

Everyone who met Duncan Crombie took a liking to him, apart from Flora and, to Elspeth's surprise, Forbes.

'I hope he doesn't intend to try to interfere with your life.' He took her hands in his. 'You've got your own business, and folk who cared for you long before he came along. He's left it too late to start making demands on you.'

'For goodness' sake, Forbes, he has no intention of making demands. Even if he did I wouldn't give in to them.'

She had cause to remember his words a short week later, when Duncan Crombie rented a small but comfortable house in Greenock, hired a housekeeper, and asked Elspeth to live there with him.

'We've been apart for so long, my dear, and now I want to be with my daughter. We need to get to know each other.'

When she refused, as gently as possible, hurt flooded into his expressive face. She tried to explain, choosing her words carefully in order to avoid causing further pain. 'I've just begun to control my own life. I need to be free at the moment to get the business established.'

'But you know I would never stand in your way! I'm very proud of what you've achieved already.'

'I know you are, but in any case I can't leave Aunt Flora and Uncle Henry just now.'

'Now that,' he said explosively, 'is ridiculous! You've just been talking about controlling your own life, and now you tell me that you can't live where you choose.'

'Their own family's gone now and I know that Aunt Flora's missing them. If I left I'd feel that I was deserting the two of them.'

'You're too soft, Elspeth. How d'you expect to run a successful business when you're worried about hurting people?'

They were in the drawing room of his new home, facing each other across the fireplace after enjoying an excellent meal.

'Aunt Flora's not a client. I owe a great deal to her, and caring about her feelings is entirely different from doing business.'

He bit his lip. 'You're right, and I apologise. It's just that—' He got up and paced the floor for a moment, then turned. 'We've lost so much time, you and I.'

'It may take more time for us to get to know each other.' With an effort, she managed to rise fairly gracefully from the deep, soft armchair. 'I must go. Give me a little while yet.'

He put his hands on her shoulders and kissed her forehead. 'I won't mention the matter again. I'm just fortunate to have found you at all.'

As the summer passed, Duncan Crombie moved with ease into the town's social life, drawing Elspeth with him. Without quite knowing how it had happened, she found herself attending concerts and soirées and dinner parties, even acting as his hostess when he invited people to his new home.

She gained a few more clients at these social occasions, for Duncan, proud of his new-found daughter, bragged to all and sundry about her talents as a businesswoman.

Once, when the two of them attended a performance by the Carl Rosa Opera Company at the King's Theatre with Forbes and his parents, she came face to face with James Brodie and his wife.

The store owner looked at her, puzzled, as they were introduced. 'I've met you before, Miss Bremner.'

'I used to work in Brodie's sewing room, and did some typing in the accounts office when Theresa McCabe was ill.'

His jaw dropped. 'Good heavens, so you did. And you left because you didn't get the position when it fell vacant. I always regretted that – I felt that we had let you down.'

'On the contrary, I'm grateful to you. I set up my own agency after I left Brodie's,' she explained as the puzzled look came back. 'And the bonus you paid me for doing your typing came in useful.'

'I'm very glad to hear it, and to see you looking so prosperous.'

Mrs Brodie, an elegant woman, had been studying Elspeth with interest, taking in her smooth, shining cap of hair and her elegant, simply cut crimson dress.

'Tell me, Miss Bremner,' she asked carefully, 'did you buy your gown in Glasgow?'

'I made it myself.' She had bought the material only the day before, and had persuaded Flora to let her use her old heavy sewing machine. With Rachel's help she had made the gown in an evening.

The woman's eyebrows rose. 'To your own design?'

'I copied it from a sketch in a magazine.'

'Indeed?' Envy flickered across Mrs Brodie's face. 'You have more than one talent,' she observed, and Duncan and Forbes, flanking Elspeth, both glowed with pride.

'You can look better in a home-made gown than all the other women in the clothes that cost them a fortune,' Duncan murmured as they left the Brodies and returned to their seats for the second part of the opera.

Hurrying along Hamilton Street with a thick envelope of completed work under her arm, Elspeth noticed a 'For Sale' sign on the opposite side of the street. She hesitated, then crossed over during a break in the traffic to look more closely at the property – a double-fronted shop. Pressing her nose against the glass and holding the bulky envelope up to block the reflection from the street behind, she made out a spacious interior with a counter, and a door in the rear wall. Further investigation through the close by the side of the shop revealed a walled back yard.

Elspeth returned to the street and took another look at the empty property. Then, thinking hard, she went on her way.

During dinner that evening at the Camerons' – a frequent occurrence, since Mrs Cameron had taken to Duncan from their first meeting – Elspeth announced that she was thinking of moving the agency to new premises. She could tell by the way his brows drew together that Forbes disapproved.

'There would be more space for us in that shop than at the garage,' she hurried on before he had a chance to object. 'I was asked only a few weeks ago to supply a temporary typist to work in an office in Port Glasgow, but none of the three of us can be spared for that sort of thing, and I've not got the space to bring anyone else in.'

'That's because you gave the extra room over to a child minder,' Forbes pointed out curtly.

'If I hadn't done that I would've lost Kirsty, and she's a good worker. Now that I've got Rachel I could mebbe employ another young mother looking for part-time work. I've been thinking of going back to letter-writing as well – I'm sure there's still a demand for that. It would help to be nearer the centre of the town, too. As things are, the three of us have to walk quite a distance each time we deliver work to our customers. If I took over that ground-floor shop the clients could come to us.'

'I think it's a good idea,' Duncan Crombie said. 'Perhaps it's time for you to expand your business.'

She turned to him gratefully. 'The shop itself would make

a good-sized office and I'd not need to do much more than have it painted. The big windows would give us more light – I'd put some net curtaining over them to prevent folk gawping in at us from the pavement. And there's a back room with a cooker and a sink.'

'You sound as though you've already decided.' Forbes sounded hurt, and she turned to him apologetically.

'I know you've done a lot to the old house for my sake, Forbes, but you did say at the beginning that if I failed you could let the upper floor out to someone else.'

'If you ask me, it's too early for you to consider moving, Elspeth. You should harvest your resources for at least a year before making changes.'

'I don't agree,' Duncan Crombie said at once. 'There's nobody else in the area with a typing agency. If Elspeth expands now folk'll take that as an indication that she's doing well. Success builds on success – you should know that as well as I do.'

Forbes said nothing, but looking from his closed face to her father's bland, handsome features, Elspeth felt, not for the first time, like a bone being fought over by two dogs. The coolness between the two men and the way they tended to vie for her attention made her uneasy. She was quite sure that if Forbes had shown enthusiasm for her new plans, her father would then have opposed them.

On the following afternoon Duncan Crombie arrived at the garage when Elspeth was working on her own. He took a turn about the room, stared out of the window for a few minutes, then said, 'I've had a look at that property you mentioned last night.'

She felt a tingle of annoyance at his interference, but curbed it, asking mildly, 'What do you think of it?'

'I notice that there's a small upstairs flat included. Are you thinking of living there?'

She was, but knowing of Duncan's desire to have her living

under his roof, she avoided a direct answer to his question, 'If I take on the property, Rachel'll need somewhere to care for the children.'

'Ah.' There was relief in his voice. 'You don't want to pay too much attention to what young Cameron says, Elspeth. He's never had to worry about money. It's folk like you and me who've pulled themselves up by their bootstraps who know when to take our chances. What d'you plan to do about financing the move?'

'I've already seen the bank manager and I think I can get a loan large enough to set up the place and compensate Forbes for the move. He let me have these rooms for a low rent for the first year, and I'd like to reimburse him for that if I leave,' she explained as her father gave her a questioning look.

'I don't see why you should, if he made the offer of his own free will.'

'I'd prefer to set things straight. After all, he was very kind to me when I first decided to start the agency. I could never have done it without his help.'

'I'm sure,' Crombie said drily, 'that he had his reasons. The man's besotted with you, Elspeth, you must know that. It would only be natural for him to want to help you and place you under an obligation so that he could turn things to his own advantage.'

She felt herself tense with anger. Why did her father and Forbes always have to use her as an excuse to criticise each other? Why couldn't they be more like Thomas, who believed in giving others the right to do as they pleased, and had merely said when told of her new plans, 'You could do well with anything you tackled, Ellie. You've got the courage to fight your own battles.'

'I think you're being unnecessarily hard on Forbes,' she said. 'He's a good friend, and I'm very fond of him.'

'Fond enough to agree to marry him? That's what he's after, my dear. Make no mistake about it.'

'As to that, he hasn't proposed marriage – and if he does,' she said, letting a little of her growing irritation reveal itself, 'I'll be the one to decide what to say.'

He lifted his hands in swift apology. 'Of course you will. Forgive me if I'm interfering, my dear. I'm still learning how to be a father. In any case, I didn't come here to criticise Cameron. I came to say that I'd like to give you a personal loan for the new premises, instead of you having to go cap in hand to the bank. My terms would be more advantageous.'

'I can't let you risk your own money. What if something went wrong?'

'It won't. I have faith in you, and I want to show it in more than words. Please consider it, at least.'

Forbes, Elspeth thought, might say that now it was the older man who wanted to place her under an obligation. On the other hand, she had already hurt her father's feelings by turning down his invitation to move into his home. She owed him something.

'I accept. Thank you,' she said at last, and his face lit up.

'I'm so glad, my dear! I wish your mother could have known that we're together at last. It would have made her happy, I'm sure.'

33

Elspeth and Forbes almost fell out over her decision to lease the shop and the flat above with a loan from Duncan Crombie.

'You should have let me lend you the money!' he argued, his lower lip pushed out like a sulky child's.

'You've done more than enough for me as it is.'

'And how d'you repay me? By moving out of the garage house.'

They were down on the beach, still one of Elspeth's favourite places. She sat on a rock, while Forbes, sprawling on the ground, threw pebbles into the water, one after another. He had none of Thomas's expertise, she noticed, but on the other hand Forbes wasn't attempting to skim the stones across the water's surface, he was hurling them as though trying to punish the waves, which took no notice, but continued to break in lacy froth on the beach, absorbing the thrown pebbles effortlessly.

'I need more space.'

'I could have given you the other downstairs room.'

'You need it as an office – and I'd not put Thomas out of the only home he has.'

He tossed a final stone and sat up, linking his hands round his knees. 'Why expand the business anyway? You've proved your point – you've shown everyone that you can do it. Isn't that enough?'

'No, it's not. It's more important to me than that – it's my future.'

'I'm your future.' Forbes suddenly twisted round on to his knees, reaching out to take her hand. 'Marry me, Elspeth.'

'Forbes—'

'I'm serious. I want you to be my wife.'

She hadn't been prepared for such a sudden proposal. 'I'm too young for marriage,' she protested weakly.

'You're almost nineteen, the same age my mama was when I was born.'

'But I don't want to marry anyone just yet,' she said in a panic. Despite himself, he started to laugh, then gave a grimace of pain.

'Ouch! I wish I'd picked a better place to propose.' He got to his feet and bent to rub at his knees. 'I'm crippled – and you don't even have the decency to say yes and make it all worth the suffering.'

She rose and put a hand on his arm. 'I'm sorry, Forbes, but I really and truly don't want to think of marriage just now. Not yet.'

'It's not Crombie, is it? Is he turning you against the idea of marrying me?'

'Of course not!'

'He doesn't approve of me. I don't think he'd approve of any man who might come between you and him.'

Elspeth thought fleetingly of her father's comment that only royalty would have met with Celia Bremner's approval as far as her daughter was concerned. 'You're wrong, Forbes. I'm not the sort of spineless creature who would allow anyone to dominate her.'

'I know – that's why I love you, and why I'm going to keep on proposing until you say yes.' Then, as they turned together to walk back to where the car stood, 'You don't really know much about him, do you?'

'I know that he's my father, and he's a good man.'

'A wealthy man, too – yet he came from nothing. What d'you know about the way he earned his money?'

'He earned it honestly!' she snapped, breaking free of him and striding ahead to the road.

Hours later, lying in bed and staring up at the pattern thrown on the bedroom ceiling by the moonlight, she tried to understand why she hadn't accepted his proposal. Was it because of her father's attitude towards Forbes? she wondered, then decided that the reason lay in herself. She liked Forbes very much, and took great pleasure in their shared caresses. But surely there should be more than just a sense of pleasure between two people who genuinely loved each other?

On the following morning Rachel and her daughters were late arriving at the office. The children were unusually subdued when they got there, while Rachel, who claimed to have toothache, had tied a scarf over her head, half obscuring her face.

Once she had given her foster sister time to settle the children, Elspeth left her typewriter and went down to the yard. Thomas, in his dungarees, was working on a car and reluctant to leave it.

'If it's something that needs fixing upstairs, get one of the other men to see to it.'

'I doubt if you'd want any of the men to see to this problem,' she persisted, and finally, grumbling, he wiped his hands with a rag and followed her into the house and upstairs.

Leaving him in the corridor, she put her head round the playroom door and asked Rachel to come outside. When the other girl joined them her face was still wrapped in the scarf. At sight of Thomas she ducked away and tried to go back into the room, but Elspeth was too quick for her. She caught at the scarf and it fell away to reveal a livid black bruise covering most of the side of Rachel's face and puffing the tender flesh beneath one eye.

Thomas's breath caught in his throat. 'Good God, Rachel, what's happened to you?'

'I fell against a door.' His sister tried to turn her injured cheek into the shadows, but he forestalled her, putting one hand beneath her chin and turning her head so that the light from the window at the end of the hall showed up the ugly bruise.

'I think she fell against Bob's fist, and more than once by the look of it,' Elspeth told Thomas.

'Bob?' His voice cracked with disbelief. 'Did Bob do this to you?'

'He's been ill-treating her for a long time, but she wouldn't let me tell anyone.'

'You promised you wouldn't!' Rachel accused Elspeth, tears glistening in her eyes.

'I know I did, but I've held my tongue long enough, and so have you. He's never hurt you as badly as this, Rachel – what d'you think his next step'll be? You could end up in the hospital, or in a graveyard. And what about the bairns? When'll he start on them?'

'He won't – and he'll never touch my sister again,' Thomas said thickly, releasing Rachel and moving towards the stairs.

'Thomas!' She threw herself after him, clutching at the banisters. 'Where are you going?'

'To see Bob,' he said from the landing. 'He's not going to get away with what he's done!'

'No – please! Thomas!' Rachel tried to follow him, but Elspeth held her back.

'Rachel, he can't mark you like that and think that nobody'll see it. Sit down.' As Rachel's knees sagged, Elspeth eased her on to the top step and wrapped her arms about the banisters. 'I'll be back in a minute.'

She put her head round the office door and asked Kirsty to keep an eye on the children for a while. 'Rachel's toothache's worse and I'm going to make some tea for her,' she explained, then helped Rachel downstairs.

As there was a risk of Joe or the other men coming into the

kitchen and finding them, she led the distraught girl into the downstairs room that had once been the garage office, and was now Thomas's home.

'He'll not mind us sitting in here, I'm sure.' She settled Rachel in a chair and went to the kitchen, returning a few minutes later with two cups of strong tea.

'Bob'll kill me for this,' the girl said as Elspeth put a cup into her hand and folded the cold fingers of her other hand round it to hold it steady. Her voice was flat and listless and eerily certain of the truth of the words.

'He'll not.' Elspeth leaned forward and put her own hands round Rachel's. 'We'll see to that – Thomas and me.'

'I'm his wife, you can't stop him.'

'Yes we can. For a start, you're not going back to that house.'

'I have to – where else can I go? I'm not having my bairns sleeping in the gutter or the poors' hospital.'

'Aunt Flora and Uncle Henry'll take you in.'

Rachel laughed bleakly, then winced at the pain in her face. 'Mam? She's told me often enough that a woman's place is with her man, no matter what happens.'

'Uncle Henry wouldn't agree with that.'

'He's got little choice,' Rachel said wryly. 'I'll not be the cause of trouble between them – and I'll not live where I'm not wanted.'

She was right. If Flora McDonald was overruled, and forced to take Rachel and the children in, she would make their lives miserable. Elspeth thought briefly of her father, who had room enough in his rented house, but she couldn't see him agreeing to having two children he didn't know running round the place.

Searching for a solution, she glanced around the room Thomas had been living in for several months. It was immaculate and sparsely furnished, with nothing out of place. The chairs she and Rachel sat in flanked the fireplace, and the sagging old *chaise-longue* that she and Thomas had sat on, holding each other, on the night of Aileen's death had been replaced by a sturdier couch that acted as a seat by day and Thomas's bed by night. A marble-topped washstand in one corner of the room held a large basin and ewer, and a curtain had been hung across one corner as a makeshift wardrobe. The only other pieces of furniture in the room were a chest of drawers with a brush and comb and mirror on top, and a small bookcase.

The house had been designed and built to hold large, heavy Victorian furniture, and Thomas's few possessions scarcely began to use the available floor space. As a result, the room had a barren, cheerless air about it. Every time she went into it Elspeth longed to make it more comfortable, but knew that Thomas would resist such attempts. Since becoming a widower he had had no time for comfort and pleasure.

She sighed, cast a glance at Rachel, who was sipping her tea, then looked up at the ceiling and found the answer to their problems.

'You could live here, Rachel, you and the girls – in the playroom. It's big enough for the three of you, and there's the bathroom – and the kitchen downstairs, and Thomas here at nights, so you'd not be alone.' Now that the idea had occurred to her, Elspeth could see no barrier to it. 'We'll get some furniture easily enough, from second-hand shops. Mr Monteith might be able to help us, and some of my other clients.'

'It wouldn't work,' Rachel said, but there was a faint gleam of hope in her eyes. 'Thomas wouldn't agree – and what about Mr Cameron? It's his house.'

'Leave them to me. We could get something arranged today, then you'd not have to go back to Bob at all. And,' Elspeth added, regretfully relinquishing her secret hopes of moving out of Mearns Street, 'there's the flat above the shop. That'd be ideal for you once I move the office from here.' She got to her feet. 'Finish your tea and we'll see what we can do.'

*

Thomas was working in the yard when they returned, and at sight of him Rachel gave a squeal of horror.

'What happened to your mouth?'

Hampered by a cut lip and a blue knot on his jaw, he gave her a lopsided grin. 'I went to the shipyard and made it clear to Bob Cochran that the McDonalds don't take kindly to their womenfolk being ill-treated.' He looked at his bruised knuckles thoughtfully, then added, 'It took a bit of explaining, but I think he understood what I was trying to tell him.'

'You hit Bob?' Her eyes were dark with horror.

'It's the only language a man like that understands, Rachel. Don't fret – I'll mend, and so will he, for I let him off lightly.'

'And he'll not be able to take it out on you or the children, for you're not going back to the flat,' Elspeth put in, and explained to Thomas about the upstairs room.

He nodded. 'It's the best way, and I'll be here during the night to look after them. You'd mebbe better ask Mr Cameron's permission, though, since it's his property.'

'I've already done that, and he's agreed.'

Thomas gave her a look that Granjan would have described as 'old-fashioned'.

'He'd not deny you anything, would he?'

She flushed, but refused to rise to the bait. 'And I've arranged for some bits of furniture to be delivered, to tide Rachel over.'

'Bob'll not like this,' Rachel moaned. 'He'll mebbe come after us and make us go home.'

'He'll do nothing of the sort. Da was there when I went to the yard, and if I hadnae seen to Bob, he would've. He'll not let the man bother you again,' Thomas assured her.

'But my clothes, and all the bairns' things – they're still at the house.'

'Elspeth and me'll go down with you this evening to collect them. There'll be no more trouble, Rachel, I promise you. Men like Bob Cochran are cowards. They only hurt folk that can't hit back. Now that me and Da know about him, he'll keep well away from you.'

In spite of all their reassurances, Rachel was shaking with fear as the three of them walked to the flat that evening, and Elspeth herself, remembering the way Bob had looked at her in January when she had cared for the children while he and Rachel went to see Lena at the theatre, felt her stomach clenching as her foster sister turned the key in the door.

Thomas went in first, and the two girls stood quaking in the close, clutching at each other and ready to flee if necessary, until he reappeared, grim-faced.

'He's not here, but the place is in a bit of a mess, Rachel.'

'How can it be? I always clean it before I go to the gar—' Rachel, who had pushed past him as she spoke, stopped short, a hand flying to her mouth. Following close behind, Elspeth saw that the kitchen looked as though a whirlwind had passed through it, with drawers thrown to the floor, the curtains ripped from the window, and plates smashed. Clothes and the few toys that Mary and Pearl owned had been strewn everywhere, and a pretty little wall mirror, a wedding gift from Granjan, had been torn down and smashed.

Rachel fell to her knees, trying to gather everything up at once. 'Look at Mary's bonny wee dress that I made just last week!' She held it up to show them the great jagged rip where the skirt was almost torn away from the carefully smocked bodice. 'And Pearl's dolly—' The head had been wrenched off, and lay in a corner, half under a torn fragment of cloth that Elspeth recognised as part of Rachel's favourite skirt.

She knelt and took the other girl into her arms. 'Don't fret, Rachel, it'll all mend.'

Above their heads Thomas said grimly, 'We'd best just gather the lot up and take it all out of here. Then he can live on his lone in the pigsty he's created.'

34

They had to support Rachel between them back to Mearns Street, where Flora, tight-lipped, was looking after the children. To Elspeth's relief the little girls were sound asleep in the darkness of the curtained wall-bed, and were spared the sight of their mother's distress.

Granjan had arrived, and she immediately gathered Rachel into her plump arms and rocked her while Thomas upended the sack he carried and let the debris of Rachel's married life spill out on to the kitchen floor.

'There, there, pet, don't fret yersel', we're all here tae put everythin' right,' Janet Docherty soothed, while Henry, his shirtsleeves rolled up and his braces dangling round his hips, chimed in with, 'As tae that blaggard Bob Cochran, don't give him another thought, for he'll have more sense than tae come near ye after the lesson our Thomas taught him. By God, but it's been many a year since the yard saw such a fight!' He slapped his son on the back. 'Ye went at him as if he was responsible for all the ills o' the world.'

'He's been responsible for enough of them,' Thomas said shortly, his eyes on his sister.

'I didnae know ye were so handy with yer fists—'

'Bein' able tae hit a man hard's nothin' tae be proud of,' Flora broke in. 'And we'll have no more talk of fightin' in my kitchen. Elspeth, make some tea. Rachel, wash yer face and help me tae

340

sort out this mess that's been dumped on my clean floor.'

Henry prudently took his son out for a drink while the womenfolk sifted through the pile of toys and clothing that Thomas had brought from Rachel's flat.

On closer inspection, the damage wasn't as bad as they had first thought. In the throes of his mindless rage, Bob hadn't taken the time to destroy each item individually, so quite a few of the garments and toys had simply been thrown down and were still intact. Some were repairable, and only a small percentage was beyond redemption. The four women settled down with needle and thread, putting things to rights.

'I'm sorry, Mam,' Rachel said meekly as they stitched.

'Sorry doesnae pay for food tae put intae yer bairns' bellies and clothes on their backs. It's menfolk that dae that.' Flora's voice was hard and unforgiving, and Elspeth felt sudden anger against her. Not once had the woman comforted her distraught, bruised daughter.

'If this is what Bob does to his children's clothes,' she held up the tiny skirt she was trying to mend, 'his children are better off without him.'

'And what dae you know about husbands – or fathers, come to that?' Flora asked crushingly.

'I know that Rachel would be better off earning her own money. At least she'd get the use of it, instead of seeing it all go in drink.'

Bright spots of colour flamed on Flora's cheekbones. She had been proud of Bob's teetotal background when he and Rachel first married, and had bragged about it to the neighbours. Now she would have to eat humble pie, something that Flora McDonald hated doing. 'Ye think our Rachel's goin' tae manage on the few pence ye hand over tae her every week like Lady Muck?'

'It's not just what I earn at the garage, Mam.' Rachel rushed to Elspeth's defence. 'There's the money in the—' She caught Elspeth's warning glance and subsided.

'What money?' Flora asked at once. 'What're ye talkin' about?'

The two young women exchanged glances, then Rachel said carefully, 'I've been doing sewing for folk, and Elspeth put the money I earned into the bank for me.'

'Bank?' Flora spoke as though her daughter had just admitted that she had been working in a brothel. 'What are ye doin', havin' truck with banks?'

'It was the only way to keep Bob from taking it, Aunt Flora.'

To Elspeth's relief, the menfolk returned just then, Henry jovial and Thomas his usual quiet, controlled self. The children were coaxed awake and tucked into their coats, and while Henry set off to walk Granjan home, Elspeth accompanied the others to the garage to settle Rachel and the children into the playroom.

'I'm sorry, Mam,' Rachel said timidly as she was about to leave.

'Sorry?' Thomas echoed. 'It's not your fault that Bob Cochran turned out to be such a poor excuse for a man.'

Flora's face was still stony. 'What's done can't be undone,' she said enigmatically.

Thomas carried Mary, the older and heavier of the two little girls, while Elspeth hoisted Pearl's solid, warm little body into her arms and Rachel carried the sack with the salvaged clothes and toys. They walked uphill through the darkness in silence, past the lit windows of tenements. Pearl, light enough when they first set out, seemed to grow heavier with each uphill step. Her head rested on Elspeth's shoulder and her breath was hot and tickly. Elspeth longed to shift her burden to her other arm, but didn't dare for fear of wakening the little girl, who had fallen asleep again.

'Are you managing?' Thomas asked as they neared the garage.

'I'm fine.'

'I hope Bob's not come after us,' Rachel said nervously.

'He's got other things on his mind. It's not just the hiding he got from me – now that Da knows what he's been doing to you, he'll be keeping a close eye on Mr Bob Cochran too,' Thomas told her confidently.

After the day's turmoil it was soothing to be out in the night. Thomas walked between Elspeth and Rachel, and the three of them had fallen into step, their shoes tapping down on the pavement to the same beat. Now and again their arms touched and Elspeth took comfort from Thomas's reassuring nearness.

Despite the fact that the furniture had been acquired so hurriedly, the playroom looked quite comfortable. Joe had set a fire in the grate, and when Thomas put a match to it, the flames took hold at once. Elspeth drew the curtains as Rachel turned slowly, wide-eyed, to take everything in.

'It looks so – cosy!'

They helped her to tuck the children into bed, then left her. 'I'll walk you back home,' Thomas said as they reached the front door.

'And leave Rachel and the bairns here on their own? You'll do nothing of the sort – you know that she's nervous in case Bob's around.'

'Him? He'll be licking his wounds in some public house.'

'Did you really give him a thrashing?'

'Not as bad as Da says, and not as bad as he deserved.' His jaw tightened. 'I could have killed him, Ellie, and I wanted to. I wanted to just keep on hitting until there was nothing left of him but I held back because I knew it wasn't just Bob Cochran I was lashing out at, it was Ian Bruce as well. I've been needin' to hurt someone for a long time, and today I got my chance.'

'Mebbe now that you've got it out of your system you'll be able to get on with your life.'

Although he didn't move she sensed his instant withdrawal. 'I'm fine as I am.'

'You should take some time off.'

He gave her a level look from beneath his brows. 'What would I do with it?'

'Go further down the river and sit on the beach, or walk up over the braes to Loch Thom. I'll come with you, if you like.'

He smiled slightly. 'You've already got your hands full with Mr Cameron.'

She poked him in the ribs. 'Do you want another punch in the mouth?'

His smile widened to a grin, then he was serious again. 'Mam didn't have much to say for herself tonight, did she? I thought she'd have been ranting on about Bob.'

'She already knew about him,' Elspeth said, then, as he looked puzzled, 'Bob's been ill-treating Rachel since Mary was small.'

'And Mam knew? Why didn't she say anything?'

'She didn't want to admit that Rachel had made a bad marriage.'

The anger was back in his face and his voice. 'She stood by and let her own daughter suffer just because she didn't want the neighbours to talk? I'll never understand that woman!'

'There are a lot of folk like her in Greenock – probably in the rest of the world too.'

'Aye – folk that let everything crumble about their ears just so's they can go on pretending everything's fine.' His voice was thick with contempt.

'I'll have to go, it's getting late.'

'What'll happen to Rachel when you move?'

'She'll live in the wee flat above the shop.'

'I thought you'd want that for yourself.'

'I was thinking about it, but Rachel's need's greater than mine.'

Thomas ran a hand through his fair hair. 'She's my sister, and it should be my place to find somewhere for her to live – especially after the way Mam turned her back when Rachel needed her most.'

'She's my sister too, and you're doing enough. She can sleep safely at night knowing that you're downstairs.'

He tried again to insist on walking back to Mearns Street with her, but she was adamant.

'Rachel needs to know that you're downstairs and she's not alone in the house. I can look after myself.'

'I never doubted that, but even so—'

'I mean it. I'll be home in five minutes.'

He gave a resigned shrug and reached for the front door latch. Elspeth too had begun to reach for it, but Thomas was swifter, and as her hand landed on his knuckles she winced slightly.

'Let me see—' She took his hand and turned it over, palm on palm, drawing him towards the glow of the gas mantle. His knuckles were bruised and torn and painful-looking.

'I'll find something to put on them,' she said, but Thomas put a hand on her shoulder as she began to lead him to the kitchen, where she had gathered together a box of ointments and salves to treat any cuts or bruises the men might suffer during their workday.

'Don't fuss, it'll be healed by the morning.'

She glared up at him, exasperated. 'You're such a difficult man to help.'

'And you care too much about folk.'

'Only some folk,' Elspeth said. His hand was warm against hers and his other hand still gripped her shoulder. As she looked up at him she saw that the dim light from the gas mantles touched the ends of his rumpled fair hair and his eyelashes with pale gold and cast shadows over his face, emphasising its strong planes and angles. His hazel eyes glowed, and she could smell a hint of the drink he had had earlier on his breath, mingled with the fresh outdoor air on his clothes. She felt slightly dizzy and confused.

345

'Only special folk,' she heard herself say, then the words died away into silence. Something was happening; it was as if the hallway where they stood was changing, becoming a magic place she had never been in before. Thomas, and her feelings towards him, were also changing.

Suddenly embarrassed in his presence, she dipped her head and found herself looking at the square, strong hand still resting on her own. Although he scrubbed his hands thoroughly after each day's work his trade was etched on them in a faint, permanent tracery of oil around the knuckles and dark shadowing beneath the fingernails, cut short and straight across. The sight of his bruised, painful knuckles struck her to the heart; she laid the palm of her other hand gently over the broken skin as though trying by touch to make him whole again.

The hand on her shoulder moved, the fingers landing lightly on her neck, just below the smooth line of her bobbed hair. The unexpected caress sent a blaze of warmth through her. His thumb moved across her cheek so gently that she scarcely felt it, to touch the corner of her mouth. Giving way to impulse, she turned her head so that her lips brushed the hollow of his palm, tasting the faint mixture of oil and soap that was Thomas's physical signature.

She heard him make a tiny sound in his throat, and as if it was a signal she had been waiting for all her life, she let herself sway towards him. His arms received her, closing round her, gathering her body against his.

She lifted her face, seeking and welcoming his mouth with parted lips. His hair was soft and springy beneath her hands, his kisses urgent, his arms strong and possessive. This was surely what loving felt like. It was far greater than the mere pleasure she knew with Forbes; it was a fierce hunger that, for her, could only be sated by one man. And at last she had found him.

When they drew back from each other she looked up into

his eyes and for just one fleeting moment saw what she had been confidently looking for. Then it was gone. His lids dropped to hood his eyes, his face went blank, his hands put her gently but firmly away from him.

'You'd best go, Elspeth.'

'Go? How can I just go after what's happened?'

'Because it should never have happened. I – forgot myself.'

'It seems to me that we've just found ourselves.' She couldn't believe that he was sending her away. 'Thomas—' She put a hand on his arm, which was hard and unyielding. 'You've been alone for almost two years now. That's long enough.'

'Long enough to realise that happiness has to be paid for, and the price is too high. I'll not walk that road again.'

'Do my feelings not mean anything to you?'

'They mean a great deal – too much for me to let you throw yourself away on me. I failed Aileen and I couldn't bear to fail you too.'

'You didn't fail Aileen – she loved you, and you never let her down.'

'Talk sense, Ellie,' he blazed down at her. 'I took her away from all she'd ever known and put her into a – a box! If I hadn't let her down she'd never have been in that car. She'd be alive today!'

There was no reasoning with him, she thought in despair. No way of convincing him that the blame for Aileen's death shouldn't be lying on his conscience. 'So you're going to punish yourself – and me – for the rest of our lives over what happened to Aileen?'

'You'll thank me, one day. Leave it, Ellie,' he ordered as she began to protest. 'I'll not discuss it again. Are you certain that you don't want me to walk down with you?'

She did, so much. She wanted to be alone with him in the dark night, just the two of them, but she knew by the set of his jaw and the steely note in his voice that he meant what he had said. She had found him and lost him in the space of five minutes.

All that was left to her now was her dignity – tattered, but still there. She gathered it around herself like a shield. 'I'll manage fine,' she said, and stepped out on to the pavement, feeling more alone than ever before.

35

When Elspeth told Joe about what had happened to Rachel he made no secret of his disgust and anger.

'How can anyone treat a bonny wee family like that so badly?'

'There are plenty around like Bob Cochran.'

'I hope I never come across them.' His big fists clenched. 'I'm glad tae hear that Thomas taught the man a thing or two.'

'You'll not say a word in front of Rachel? She's so ashamed of what's happened.'

'What's she got tae be ashamed about?' Joe demanded to know. 'We're all responsible for our own sins, but not for other folk's. Ye neednae fear, lassie, she'll no' hear a word about it from me. Mind you, I thought there was somethin' goin' on. The bairns were too quiet at times – wee ones shouldnae ever look worried, but there were days when Mary and Pearl seemed tae have the cares of the world on their wee shoulders. I can see the difference in them already.'

'Now you come to mention it, so can I. Why didn't I notice it before?'

'You were too close tae them,' he told her. 'We tend tae see what we expect tae see, an' it never occurs tae us tae take a fresh look at folk now and again.'

'I wish I had your understanding, Joe.'

'I learned the hard way.' His face took on a grim look. 'I lost a mate once, at sea. He deliberately put himself overboard,

349

with his pockets weighted down so's we couldnae save him. A right cheery fellow he was, tae. It wasnae until he died that I discovered that he'd been nursin' all sorts of problems and never sayin' a word. I never forgave mysel' for not seein' the truth and doin' somethin' about it in time tae save him. How's Ra – yer sister goin' tae manage?'

'There's the wee bit I pay her, and she'll not be without a roof over her head. She does sewing for people, and that'll help.'

'I'll pass the word around our street,' said Joe. 'She'll probably be glad of some extra work.'

They were in the kitchen. The other mechanics had returned to the yard, but Elspeth had kept Joe back to tell him about Rachel. Now he glanced out of the window and moved away from the sink, where he had been rinsing his cup.

'There's the gaffer – I'd best get back tae work.'

A sense of loss swept over Elspeth as she stood by the window, watching Thomas stride across the yard and disappear into the garage. The night before he had talked of the heavy price he had to pay for Aileen's death, and now Elspeth felt that she herself was paying for the few moments she had spent in his arms. The closeness they had always shared had vanished, possibly for ever. She didn't know whether the ache of bereavement in her heart was due to losing the old Thomas, a dear and trusted friend, or the Thomas she had just discovered and known so briefly. The only thing she was certain of was that the pain of her loss was more than she could bear.

Drearily, dragging her feet, she went back upstairs and tried to get on with her work.

In the afternoon she walked down to Hamilton Street, where she had arranged to meet a local painter to discuss work to be carried out on her new premises.

It took an hour to agree on colours and terms for the work on the flat as well as the office; Elspeth had been looking forward to the task of redecorating the former dress shop to suit her own tastes, but now that the moment had come, she found herself unable to concentrate, and ended up agreeing to the painter's suggestions.

'Aye, ye've got yersel' a nice wee property here,' he said as they returned downstairs after going through the flat. 'Well placed, too.'

'Yes.' Elspeth looked round the spacious area that was to be the office, and wondered if she had done the right thing in renting it. She suddenly realised that the painter was looking at her as though expecting an answer to some question.

'Did you say something?'

'Twice, lassie. I wanted tae know about your name above the door.'

She looked at him blankly for a moment, then remembered that that had been one of the first things she had written at the top of her list – a list she had left lying on her desk at the garage.

'I'd forgotten about that.'

'I thought ye had,' the man said drily. 'Now – what sort of letterin', and what d'ye want it tae say?'

All the pleasure had gone out of the move, Elspeth thought when the man had departed after agreeing to start work the following day, and to call in someone he knew to put the back yard to rights. Rachel and the little girls would be happy in the snug flat, Kirsty and Peggy would enjoy the spaciousness of their new workplace, and now there would be room for another desk and another typist. Thanks to her father's generosity she had a loan large enough to accommodate her plans for expansion.

She looked out at the busy street, so unlike the quiet area where the garage was located, and knew why she had suddenly lost interest in the move. In Hamilton Street she might go for days or even weeks without seeing Thomas. She would have no reason to go to the garage, and that would probably suit him, for he hadn't as much as glanced at her since the previous night.

A church clock chimed as she was locking the door. She had stayed longer than she had intended, and it was too late to return to the garage. She might as well go back to Mearns Street.

Flora was crashing pots about in the kitchen, her features gathered into a tight knot, her body almost throwing off sparks. As soon as Elspeth went in, the woman rounded on her.

'You've got a nerve, walkin' in here as if ye owned the place!'

'What?'

'Don't play the innocent with me, miss. I can see through ye, even if others can't – breakin' up our Rachel's marriage and makin' her the laughin' stock of the town!'

'Aunt Flora, you saw the mess her face was in. Everyone saw it. You surely don't want her to stay with a man who'd treat her like that?'

'A marriage should only concern the two folk that's wed tae each other. "For better or for worse." Rachel made the vows, and it's her duty tae keep them.'

'Bob made vows as well. He vowed to care for her,' Elspeth pointed out, and her aunt glared.

'Bob Cochran was a decent enough man when our Rachel married him. If anythin's gone wrong between them she's tae blame as much as him.'

'Bob Cochran,' said Elspeth clearly, 'is a weakling who needs drink and a woman to bully before he can pretend to be a man.'

'Ye know an awful lot for someone who couldnae even keep her own sweetheart. Ye've never forgiven our Mattie for takin' Kenneth away from ye, have ye? Ye've been spoilin' tae cause trouble in this family ever since.'

'Aunt Flora, that's not true and you know it. I've never wished Mattie and Kenneth anything but well.'

Flora had worked herself up into a frenzy. 'Sniffin' round

that Forbes Cameron just because he's got money! I don't know what yer mother would say if she could see what ye've turned intae! She was an angel, and God knows I did my best tae raise ye tae be like her, but it's been an uphill battle all these years. And how dae ye show yer gratitude for all me and Henry's done for ye? Ye talk Rachel intae makin' fools of us in front of the whole town!'

'I'm grateful to you for taking me in, and I've always done my best to please you, Aunt Flora. But I've always known that you didn't want me.'

'That's what I mean – ingratitude!' Flora shrieked, her rage going out of control. 'It's that wastrel of a father of yours – he's turned yer head altogether since he's come here. Not that it was hard tae dae, for ye've always been his daughter, rotten tae the core!'

Years of resentment had broken through, and now her hatred filled the room, pushing against the walls and stifling the breath in Elspeth's lungs, so that she could only stare at the older woman in stunned silence.

'An' look at what's happened tae our Lachlan, runnin' off after that whore that flaunts hersel' on the stage for all tae see – it was you that encouraged him, and you that got the two of them together—'

At last Elspeth found the energy to turn and stumble from the room. Ranting on, Flora followed. Elspeth shut the bedroom door on the older woman's crimson face, then pushed the one and only chair beneath the door handle which twisted back and forth. Thwarted, Flora McDonald banged on the closed door, screaming abuse, the words running into each other. As Elspeth began to gather up her belongings with shaking hands and push them into the battered old case which one of the boys had used when they went off to the army, she heard the outer door open, then Henry asking, 'Flora? What's amiss?'

To Elspeth's relief Flora McDonald stopped banging on the

door. 'She's amiss – that ungrateful besom I took in when nobody else wanted her!' One single blow on the door made Elspeth jump nervously. 'Get her out of my house – tell her tae go!'

'Who are ye talkin' about? What besom?'

'That daughter of Satan that's destroyed my family,' Flora screamed.

There was a tentative tap on the door. 'Hullo?'

Elspeth's knees were shaking. She leaned against the door panels. 'Uncle Henry—'

'Don't you talk tae her!'

There was the sound of a scuffle, then Flora started to cry with loud, harsh tearing sobs. Beneath the noise, Elspeth heard Henry murmuring soothingly and coaxing her along to the kitchen. The door closed but Elspeth waited, afraid to venture out in case Flora came back.

Five minutes later knuckles tapped gently on the door. 'Ellie?' Henry McDonald whispered. 'Let me in, hen.' She had never been so glad to see his sturdy, stolid bulk. His hair was tousled, his face almost grey. 'Are ye all right, lass?'

'I'm fine,' she told him through chattering teeth. 'How's Aunt Flora?'

'I've never seen her like this – but I knew somethin' was comin' on her, for she's not been hersel' for a while. She's quietened down now.' His eyes fell on the bag in her arms. 'Ye're leavin'?'

'I can't stay here, can I?'

'Where'll ye go?'

If the quarrel had happened a few days earlier she would have gone straight to Thomas, but now that avenue of escape was closed. Nor could she involve Granjan – that would only force the old woman to take sides between her daughter and Elspeth.

'My father's got a spare room I can use. What'll you do?'

'I'll send a neighbour's bairn tae fetch Flora's ma. She'll

354

know what's best.' As Elspeth opened the main door he put a hand on her shoulder. 'Take care, lass.'

'It's you that needs to do that, Uncle Henry.'

'I'll be fine – and so will she,' he said sturdily.

Duncan Crombie himself opened the door, his eyebrows rising as he saw his daughter standing in the tiny porch, a battered old suitcase clutched in both arms, her face white as a sheet.

'My dear girl, what's happened?'

'I've come to live with you,' said Elspeth, and burst into tears.

Although her father and his housekeeper did all they could to make Elspeth feel at home, she found it hard to settle down. Her new room was bright and spacious and comfortable, but she couldn't forget that if things had gone as she had originally planned she would have been able to live alone in the flat above the shop. Now that the flat was earmarked for Rachel and her children, Elspeth had no option but to stay with her father for the time being, much to his delight.

After her outburst, Flora had alarmed the entire family by taking to her bed for the first time in her life. Janet Docherty moved into Elspeth's former bedroom to nurse her daughter, who lay flat on her back in the wall-bed, staring at the ceiling and taking no interest in life.

The doctor was called in and prescribed an iron tonic to build up her strength, and the removal of all her remaining teeth.

'He says they might be poisonin' her system,' Janet reported to Elspeth. 'But our Flora just gave him one of her looks, then shut her mouth tight and stared back at the ceiling. It'll take a better man than Dr McKee tae open that mouth and take the teeth from it.'

Lachlan, who was working near Glasgow that week, was contacted, and travelled to Greenock with Kenneth and Mattie for a family consultation. He bounded into Thomas's garage room and gave Rachel and Elspeth hugs that almost crushed them.

'It's good to see you both again – and to see Greenock, though I've got no regrets about leaving the place.' He had put on weight, most of it muscle, and had regained all his pre-war vigour, but now it was tempered with maturity and a purposeful air. Studying him, Elspeth saw that Lachlan looked as though he fitted perfectly into his own skin and his own personality, with none of the boneless gawkiness of his youth, or the heartbreaking timidity the war had stamped on him.

'Is Lena with you?'

'She wasn't able to get away – she's almost top of the bill now,' he reported proudly. 'I can only stay for two days myself, for we're moving to Edinburgh at the weekend and I'll be needed.'

'Have you seen Mam?' Rachel asked anxiously.

'We all went straight to the house from the station.' Mattie, bulky in the sixth month of pregnancy, cast an envious sidelong glance at Elspeth's royal-blue hip-length jacket over a slim-fitting cream dress.

The excitement and pleasure vanished from Lachlan's face, leaving it still and shadowed. 'Poor wee Mam – I never thought to see her looking so pathetic and helpless, lying in her bed in the middle of the day.'

Henry and Janet arrived just then, having left Flora in a neighbour's care so that they could join in the family conference, and the excitement of meeting up again abated as they settled down to discuss the reason for their gathering.

Rachel had taken her mother's illness badly. 'It's my fault,' she told the others wretchedly. 'It's me leaving Bob and defying her when she told me to go back to him that did it.'

'From what I hear, you did the right thing,' Lachlan said at once, while Mattie chimed in, 'The only thing. No man should be allowed to strike his own wife!'

Henry, his normally cheerful face suddenly old, put an arm about his elder daughter's shoulders. 'It's not your fault, hen. Ye were quite right tae leave him. If I'd only known about this sooner ye'd have left him long since.' He looked around the group. 'Bob's goin' from bad tae worse, drinkin' most of the time. If he doesnae watch out he'll be turned off from his job. I've tried tae get him tae see sense, but there's no talkin' tae him.'

'If anyone's to blame for Aunt Flora's condition it's me,' Elspeth pointed out. 'I'm the one she quarrelled with just before she fell ill.'

She found an unexpected ally in Thomas. 'I'd say that it's her own temper that's finally turned in on her. Mam's always been used to ruling our lives, and now that we've grown and gone our own ways she misses being able to dominate us. She's brought this on herself.'

'Thomas!' Mattie was shocked. 'It's your own mother you're talking about!'

'I know, but I'm only speaking my mind.' His glance at his father was half apologetic, half defiant. 'This is mebbe hard for you to hear, Da, but it's the way I see it.'

Henry nodded his grey head. 'I cannae deny that yer mam has a temper. It's somethin' I've always accepted, for it's just part of the way she is. It's mebbe the only way she has of showin' she cares. But I know it was hard at times on the rest of ye.' He looked round the circle of faces. 'Especially you, Thomas. I'll always regret that, but it's too late now tae do anythin' about it.'

'Far too late,' Thomas agreed, his face suddenly grim with bitter memories. There was an awkward silence, then Kenneth did his best to bring a note of optimism to the meeting.

'As far as I can gather from Dr McKee there's little physically wrong with her. What she needs most is a good rest.'

'I think she's on her way back to her old self already.' The mischievous smile that had been missing for so many years

357

began to break through Lachlan's solemnity. 'She managed to rouse herself enough to tell me that it was time I settled down and got back to the shipyards.'

'Kenneth's right,' Granjan said briskly. 'All she needs is rest and looking after for a wee while. And some plain, nourishing food.'

Henry looked hurt. 'When did I ever deny her the money tae buy good food?'

'It's nothin' tae do with that,' his mother-in-law told him briskly. 'Women who raise families never eat properly – they're more inclined tae feed themselves from what's left on other folk's plates. They're like rubbish tips, but it's all part of bein' a wife and mother.'

'Are you all right, Da?' Thomas suddenly asked, reaching across the table to put a hand on his father's arm. 'There's nothing to worry about. Kenneth's right – she needs a rest, and once she's had that she'll be right as rain.'

'I know that. Don't worry about us, laddie, ye've got enough tae do with keeping this place goin'.' Henry looked at those who had been away for a while, and added proudly, 'Our Thomas has done a grand job. He'll be owner of his own garage afore he's finished.'

After that, the business over and everyone more at ease about Flora, they settled down to the serious work of catching up on each other's news.

Tomorrow, far too soon, Lachlan and Mattie and Kenneth would return to their own lives, but they would all, those who left and those who stayed, retain a little of the rekindled warmth of their relationships with each other, Elspeth thought, looking at their animated faces.

Flora McDonald's breakdown had served one very useful purpose – it had brought her family together again.

36

Two days after Lachlan and Kenneth and Mattie left Greenock, a horse-drawn wagon clattered to a standstill in front of the garage house to be loaded with furniture for Hamilton Street.

'I never realised we'd gathered up so much stuff,' Peggy lamented, opening yet another drawer to find it filled with papers and notebooks.

'Folk are like magpies,' Kirsty told her. 'Put it all into different boxes, so that it doesn't get mixed up.'

With Thomas's permission, Joe was pressed into carrying boxes downstairs to the waiting cart. Kirsty's daughter and Rachel's little girls, excited by all the activity, tried to accompany him, weaving dangerously round his legs, and Rachel was forced to round them up and remove them from under his feet.

'They're no trouble,' Joe assured her breathlessly, staggering out of the office under the weight of a pile of boxes. 'I'm just worried about their own safety, for I'd not like tae see them trip and fall down the stairs.'

'If you ask me,' Peggy remarked to Elspeth when Joe and Rachel were both safely out of the way, 'Joe's got a fancy for your Rachel – and she likes him too.' She tossed her head. 'After what she's been through she's entitled to some happiness with someone else.'

'But she's married. D'you mean she should get a divorce?'

359

Kirsty asked, wide-eyed. Not many people in Greenock got divorced.

'She's still young, and Joe's a good man. He dotes on those bairns too—' Kirsty swiftly changed the subject as Rachel returned, her eyes shining with excited anticipation. Even with her hair tied up in a scarf she looked pretty, Elspeth thought. It was understandable that Joe was attracted to her. And Peggy was right – surely Rachel deserved some happiness after what she'd been through. Mebbe a divorce wasn't out of the question.

Carrying down a box filled with pens and pencils and ink bottles and paper a few moments later she almost bumped into Thomas, who was ushering out a client.

'I'll take these.'

'I can manage. You don't want to get your good suit all dusty,' she pointed out, but he took the box from her arms.

As he stowed it on the wagon, she lingered in the doorway, using her handkerchief to remove a slight smear from the brass plate, which was to be unscrewed in the morning. There was no need for it in Hamilton Street, where her name was painted above the door, but she intended to keep it safe forever.

'A car sale?' she asked as Thomas returned.

'I hope so. How's the move going?'

'We'll finish it tomorrow.'

'The place'll be quiet without the lot of you running in and out.'

'I wish we weren't going, Thomas,' Elspeth said impulsively, and for a brief moment their eyes met. Then his were veiled.

'I think it's for the best,' he said quietly.

'I don't—'

He held a hand up. 'Ellie, I don't want to lose your friendship. Leave it at that,' he said, and after a long, difficult moment she bit back the rebellious words flooding to her lips and nodded.

'Neither do I.'

Then they went their separate ways, Thomas to his room to change into his working clothes, Elspeth to climb the stairs, the now-familiar ache, lodged uncomfortably somewhere near her heart, worse than ever.

The opening of the new office was marked with a party on the premises, followed in the evening by a dinner held in Elspeth's honour by Forbes' parents, and attended by Duncan and several of the area's businessmen.

'Forbes and his father thought of inviting them for your benefit, my dear,' Mrs Cameron murmured confidentially as she led Elspeth to a bedroom to take off her coat and brush her hair. 'They're all influential people – they may well bring business your way.'

'I hope so.' Elspeth sat down at the dressing table and studied her face critically. She had learned to use make-up discreetly – a very thin film of powder, a touch of pale pink lipstick to highlight her mouth.

'That's such a pretty dress. I like periwinkle blue – and it matches your eyes perfectly. I can't tell you how pleased my husband and I are about you and Forbes, my dear,' Mrs Cameron went on. 'Every mother likes to see her son settled.' Then, with an arch twinkle in her eyes, she added, 'As you'll find out for yourself one day.'

'Forbes and I are good friends, Mrs Cameron, nothing more.'

'There I go again, jumping to conclusions! I know nothing's been decided, Elspeth, but perhaps one day . . .?'

Elspeth smiled and murmured something noncommittal as she ran a comb through her hair, which now clung to the shape of her head and fell in soft feathers round her face.

As she and her hostess walked into the drawing room, Forbes came forward to meet them, his eyes signalling his approval of her simple tubular dress and its silver lace over-bodice.

'The best-dressed woman in the room,' he murmured. 'And without doubt the most successful. Come and meet everyone.'

The dinner was superb, but only part of Elspeth's mind was on the food she ate and the conversation around her. The other part was looking ahead to the following day, the first in the new office. She had advertised for another typist, and hoped that there would be at least a few applications.

While listening with apparent interest to someone enthusing over a play that had recently been staged in Greenock, she ran over the list of things that had been done that day. Everything was in order for the morning, and Rachel and the children were comfortably settled in their new home. As the dinner party prevented Elspeth herself from looking in on them that evening, Joe had promised to call on his way home from the garage to make sure that they had everything they needed. Not that Hamilton Street was on his way, but that wouldn't worry Joe, who lived alone and had little to go home to.

She glanced up the length of the table and saw her father talking animatedly to an attractive woman by his side, who hung on his every word. Duncan Crombie adored social events. He had so much energy and such enthusiasm for life that sometimes Elspeth wondered how long it would be before he tired of Greenock and wanted to move on. He had indicated to her several times his desire to travel, suggesting that she should accompany him.

'See something of the world before you settle down,' he had advised.

'I have settled down. I'm quite content here.'

'Nonsense,' he had retorted. 'How can you know you're settled until you've tried other places and met other people?'

Once, he had spoken like that in front of Forbes, who had flown into a panic in case Elspeth gave in to her father and went off with him. The gulf between the two men was gradually widening, and Elspeth was uncomfortably aware that she herself stood in the middle, courted by both of them.

After the meal the guests roamed the downstairs rooms freely, their voices rising and falling. Forbes escorted Elspeth round the drawing room to make what he called useful introductions.

The warmth and the wine she had had during dinner, coupled with the day's excitement, had made her sleepy. The curtains hadn't yet been drawn over the long drawing room windows and it was dark outside, the glass reflecting movement and colour from within the room. She smothered a yawn and glanced at a clock. It was almost ten o'clock. In another hour, she decided, she would make her excuses and leave.

Forbes was making his way over to her, a prosperous-looking man by his side. Elspeth pinned a polite smile to her lips, but before the two men reached her a maidservant touched Forbes on the arm, murmuring to him. He halted, frowned, asked a question. The woman shook her head and pointed to the hallway, and with a brief word to his companion Forbes turned away.

Elspeth followed, her curiosity roused. At sight of the police constable standing in the hall her blood froze and memories of the night the policeman had called at Mearns Street to tell them that Thomas had been beaten unconscious flooded her mind. This constable, like the other, looked solemn and carried his high helmet beneath one arm. She hurried across the carpet and caught at Forbes' elbow.

'What's happened?'

His face was dazed with disbelief. 'This fellow says the garage is on fire—'

'Thomas! Is Thomas there? Is he all right?' She let Forbes go and clutched at the policeman, who shook his head.

'I don't know any names, miss, but I b'lieve there was someone found on the premises.'

'I must go,' Forbes said. The maidservant was already on her way back from the cloakroom with his coat. 'Tell my parents that—'

363

'I'm coming with you.'

'Elspeth, you can't do anything to help!'

She was already running to the cloakroom, for there was no time to go upstairs to fetch her own coat. She took the nearest garment from its hook and struggled into it as she hurried outside. Forbes was already getting into his car while the policeman pedalled off down the driveway on his bicycle. Hampered a little by the borrowed coat, which was far too large for her and smelled of cigars, Elspeth reached the car and climbed in just as the engine roared into life.

A cloud of oily smoke shot through with streaks of fire hung above the garage. The red glow of flames nearer ground level flickered and danced over the street and the buildings beyond. A fair-sized crowd had gathered, and a fire wagon stood at the kerb.

'The house is standing – it's the garage itself that's burning,' Elspeth heard Forbes say as the car came to a standstill. She threw herself from it and pushed through the gawping people, her muscles and bones strangely lethargic, as though she was struggling through deep water.

'You can't come any closer, miss.' A policeman barred her way. 'It's too dangerous.'

'I'm the owner,' Forbes said breathlessly from her side.

'In that case, follow me, sir.' The man turned, and Elspeth hooked a hand into Forbes' coat pocket to make sure that she wouldn't be left behind. His own hand slid into the pocket to close over hers.

'It'll be all right,' she heard him say reassuringly, but in the red glow from the flames she saw that he was as apprehensive as she was.

They were led across the road to where a group of men huddled together a safe distance from the blaze. Elspeth glimpsed a fireman, axe in hand, running round the side of the house, and others handling a hose. From this vantage point she could also see an ambulance wagon waiting further down the street, well away from the conflagration.

'I'm afraid we're not going to be able to save your garage, sir, or any of the vehicles in it,' someone was saying to Forbes, 'not with all that petrol about. But the house is all right and the fire's beginning to come under control.'

'Damn the garage, man, my manager was in the house,' Forbes said impatiently. 'Is he safe?'

'My men searched the house, but there wasn't anyone there. They've found two men in the garage, though. I can't tell you yet what condition they're in. The medical people are with them now.'

Fear caught at Elspeth's throat and her grip on Forbes' hand tightened. 'Two?' she heard him ask, then his face, stained crimson by the flames, as though covered with blood, swung round towards her. 'Who—?'

'Joe.' To her own ears her voice sounded strange, as though someone else was speaking. 'He must have stayed later than he meant.'

'Oh my God!' Forbes said, just as a group of men appeared through the smoke, two stretchers being handled among them.

'Thomas!' Elspeth tried to run across the street, but some-one held her back. 'Best to leave them to get on with their work, miss,' a voice told her, while Forbes said swiftly, 'We'll go to the hospital.'

As she followed him back to the car she realised that the fingers of one hand were scrabbling at the lapel of the thick leather coat she had dragged on during her rush from the Camerons' house. For a moment she couldn't understand why, then she remembered the pebble brooch, pinned to the collar of her own coat.

She had been trying to clutch at it for comfort, as she always did in moments of stress. But this time, the brooch wasn't there to reassure her that all would be well.

*

It turned out that when the fire started Joe was sitting in the flat above the Hamilton Street office, chatting comfortably to Rachel. Thomas McDonald, found in the yard where the blast from an explosion within the workshop had thrown him, had been badly burned. Bob Cochran, inside the workshop at the time, had died when it blew up.

Elspeth would gladly have spent all her time sitting by Thomas's bed in the hospital, but Flora, who had recovered with startling suddenness on hearing that one of her own had been hurt, was there each time Elspeth went into the ward, straight-backed and stony-faced in an upright chair. Uncomfortable in her presence, Elspeth was forced to cut her own visits back. There was plenty for her to do, but she went about all her tasks feeling as though she had been split into two people. One of them was in the hospital with Thomas, the other dealt with the office and with Rachel, shattered by sudden widowhood. Mrs Cameron, who loved children and had told Elspeth frequently that although she herself had not been blessed with the large family she had desired, she hoped to have a lot of grandchildren, took Mary and Pearl over to let Rachel cope with the suddenness of Bob's death.

'I never thought he'd – mebbe if I'd stayed,' she said to Elspeth and Granjan, her face blotched with tears. 'I should never have left him!'

'It was the only thing ye could have done, lassie,' Janet Docherty told her. 'Ye've heard what the polis said – the man was so drunk that he didnae know what he was doin'. An' he'd just been turned away from the shipyard. Ye might as well say that they were tae blame for takin' his work away from him. If that had happened, an' you were still with him, there's no knowing what he'd have done tae ye.' She shivered, holding Rachel close. 'It might be you and the bairns bein' buried at the end of the week, and not Bob, God rest him.'

Bob's drunken rage and his thirst for revenge had centred instead on Thomas, who had given him such a humiliating beating at the shipyard. Venturing into the ward on the day after Bob's funeral, Elspeth was startled to see Thomas's bed unattended, the bedside chair empty. He was lying back on the pillows, eyes closed, bandaged hands lying limply on the bedspread. She perched on the edge of the chair supplied for visitors, anxious not to disturb him. When he was first taken in almost all of his face had been swathed in bandages; now, only one side was covered, and the bandages had been removed from his neck and chest, revealing red but healing skin.

It was the first chance she had had to study him, and now her eyes devoured him as though trying to imprint the memory of him forever in her mind. His fair curly hair had, amazingly, been spared by the flames though his lashes and part of his eyebrows had been burned off, giving what could be seen of his face a strangely naked look.

With a twist of the heart she recalled the night he had kissed her in the garage house. Gaslight from the street outside had caught the tips of his lashes then, making them sparkle with gold light.

In repose he looked vulnerable against the crisp white of the hospital pillows. She desperately wanted to touch him, to brush her fingertips or, better still, her lips over his sleeping face, but she held the yearning in check. Which was just as well, since she found, on transferring her gaze from his mouth to his eyes, that they, in turn, were studying her.

'Did I wake you?'

'I wasn't asleep. I heard you coming and I thought it was Mam. She sits and stares and won't answer any questions. I'll be glad to get out of here.'

'When'll that be?'

'Next week, they say. I'll mebbe have a bit of scarring on my face and on the back of my hands, but I'll be fine.' A shadow came into his eyes. 'It was Bob's funeral yesterday, wasn't it?'

'Yes.' It had been a sorry affair, with only Rachel and Forbes and herself sharing the graveside with Bob's parents and his sister and brother-in-law. There had been no gathering afterwards; each group had gone silently away, with nothing to say to the other.

'How's Rachel?'

'She's taken Bob's death badly. Granjan's been staying with her.'

'It's a terrible thing to say about a man who's dead, but she's better off with him out of her life once and for all.'

'What happened?'

He wrinkled his brow. 'I don't mind much about it – I was in my room and I heard a noise round the back. When I went into the workshop Bob was splashing petrol around the place. I went for him, and he threw the can at me and knocked me off my feet. I must have hit my head when I fell, for the next thing I knew there was fire all round and someone was dragging me along the ground.' He shook his head. 'You'd have thought the man would at least have had the sense to get clear before he started the fire.'

'He was very drunk, seemingly. Mebbe he didn't know what was happening.'

'If so, it would be for the best, poor creature.'

She shivered, and changed the subject. 'Forbes says he's going ahead and buying that other garage he's thinking of, and you'll manage it.'

'Aye, I know. He looked in this morning to tell me.'

She began to say something else, but the words seemed to clump together into a large ball that stuck in her throat. Thomas's face misted then shimmered.

'What's amiss? Is there something they haven't told me yet?'

She swiped at her eyes with one hand. 'It's you. You could have died.'

'But I didn't.'

'You could have! And then I'd not have had the chance to tell you—'

'Ellie,' he said wearily. 'Nothing's changed, and nothing will change.'

'Of course things have changed.' Tears gave way to anger. 'Everything's changed. You almost died! Does that not make you give some thought to your future – our future?'

'My future lies in getting another garage started. Yours is with your agency, and mebbe with Forbes Cameron.' For a moment their eyes locked and to her despair she saw the same stubborn determination in his as before. Then his gaze slid past her and he gave a muffled groan then went limp, his lids closing as Flora McDonald arrived at the other side of the bed.

'I thought you'd be busy with yer fancy new office.'

'I just looked in. He's sleeping.'

'He's always sleepin',' Flora said with a sniff. 'It's this place – it doesnae agree with him.'

She looked pointedly at the chair, and Elspeth relinquished it and left.

37

To Flora's annoyance Thomas refused to convalesce at Mearns Street when he was discharged from hospital. He went straight back to his own home, beside the blackened ruins of the garage he had worked so hard to build up, and he and Forbes immediately became absorbed in plans for the new garage, on the shore road between Greenock and Port Glasgow.

Elspeth rarely saw him. She too had thrown herself into her work, taking on another typist earmarked for temporary work in offices. Her belief that the agency would do well in the heart of the town proved to be correct and her decision to return to letter-writing brought in a fairly steady stream of clients. Peggy, a good letter-writer, shared the task with her.

The rivalry between Forbes Cameron and Duncan Crombie continued as Duncan became increasingly bored with life in Greenock, and pressed Elspeth to sell the business and travel with him.

'Can't you see what he's up to, Elspeth?' Forbes asked. 'He wants you all to himself, and he doesn't care what sort of sacrifice you might have to make. You wouldn't be allowed to be your own person.'

'And could I be my own person if I stayed here and married you?' she asked drily, and he flushed.

'That's different – you know that I'd do anything to make you happy. And you've known me longer – I'm not a fly-by-night who's scarcely been here long enough to take my hat off.'

Often in the evenings she escaped from them both to Granjan's placid little flat, where there were no demands made on her other than making toast or buttering hot home-made pancakes. A month after the fire she found Thomas there one evening; the skin on one side of his face was still red and tender-looking and although the backs of his hands would always be scarred he had retained full use of them.

He didn't stay for long after she arrived. 'He's lookin' well, our Thomas,' Janet said as she returned from seeing him out. 'Havin' that new garage tae hold his interest has helped.'

Elspeth, staring into the fire and wrapped in her own thoughts, said nothing, and Janet lowered herself into her chair with a grunt of relief, turning her skirts back to let the fire warm her knees.

'The nights are fair drawin' in – the bairns'll be round the doors lookin' for their Hallowe'en next week.' Then, with a sidelong look, 'When are ye goin' tae stop pinin' for the man, lassie, an' do somethin' about it?'

'What?' Elspeth was startled out of her reverie. 'D'you mean Forbes?'

Janet Docherty tutted. 'Of course not! Oh, he's a nice enough laddie, but he's not for you. I'm talkin' about Thomas – an' don't try tae tell me I'm haverin', for I've seen the way of it ever since he came back from the army.'

'That's nonsense!'

'I mebbe talk a lot of rubbish at times, but never nonsense. I did think when he met Aileen, rest her soul, that that was an end tae it for you and him, but as it turned out I was wrong there.'

'Thomas has told me that he won't marry again. He means it.'

'So ye've discussed it?'

'No, we—' Elspeth stopped short and felt her face warm. She knew that it wasn't caused by the fire.

'He always was stubborn. So are you – that's what makes

the two of ye so suited.' Janet Docherty leaned across the rag rug and put a swollen-veined, work-roughened hand on Elspeth's knee. 'But it seems tae me that you've been short on yer usual stubbornness over this business. Lassie, if something's worth the havin', it's worth fightin' for.'

'I've tried.'

'Tuts – if ye havenae won it means ye've no' tried all that hard. You're the only person that can get ye what ye want. Nob'dy'll dae it for ye.'

Elspeth stared into the flames. 'Mebbe I'd be as well marrying Forbes, or giving in to my father and going away from here.'

'Have I not already told ye that he's no' the right one for ye? Oh, he'd make ye happy enough, and so would Duncan Crombie, for they both care for ye in their own ways and they've both got the money tae spend on ye. But will either one of them bring ye contentment? That's what ye've got tae ask yersel'. Contentment's gettin' what's right for ye, no' just gettin' by.'

Elspeth snuggled into her warm coat and watched the moonlight tracing a path across the dark, almost still river. On the opposite shore, houses and streetlights looked like jewels strewn over the black velvet of the hills. It was a clear, cold night in early December, and Forbes was driving her home along the coast road after an evening spent with friends of his.

As they drew up at the house and she moved to open the door he put a hand out to stop her. 'Let's just sit here for a minute.'

'D'you not want to come in for a cup of tea? My father'll be expecting us.'

'I want to say something, and it's not for his ears.'

Her stomach fluttered, then tensed. She had been expecting another marriage proposal from him, but had thought that he would choose Christmas or possibly the New Year. She hadn't been prepared for it to be so soon.

He sensed the slight withdrawal. 'What's the matter? Are you cold? There's a rug in the back. Or, even better—' He drew her towards him and kissed her, his mouth moving gently on hers, the moustache he had recently grown rough on her upper lip. The scent of the hair oil he used mingled with cigarette smoke and the car's leather upholstery to produce a familiar, pleasant, essentially secure aroma. Security, Elspeth thought, could be very important. Not that Granjan would agree.

When they finally drew apart he shifted slightly in his seat, clearing his throat and staring out through the windscreen. 'Elspeth, I've – heard something about your father.'

'Heard?'

'If you must know, I've been making enquiries. I know I'd no business to do so,' he added hurriedly as she started to speak. 'But he's only just come into your life and I felt it was right that somebody should look after your interests. I discussed it with my father, and he agreed.'

'But you didn't discuss it with me.' She was furious with him for interfering, and for broaching the subject in a voice so serious that it caused her flesh to cringe with apprehension and anxiety.

'You're still very young—'

'I'm old enough to run my own business, old enough to look after my own life!'

'D'you want to hear what I have to say?'

She didn't. She wanted to get out of the car and walk away from him and from Greenock and from everyone. She wanted to put her head under the blankets then wake up to find that the world had been set to rights. She reached up to touch the pebble brooch; she wanted to go back to the day Thomas had given it to her, the day of her thirteenth birthday dumpling.

Instead, reluctantly, she listened to what Forbes had to say, then crept quietly into the hall in the vain hope that Duncan Crombie might have decided, for once, not to stay up for her return.

He appeared from the drawing room as she eased the front door shut. 'Is young Cameron not with you?'

'Not tonight.'

'Come and tell me all about your evening.'

'I'd rather just go to bed. I've got a bit of a headache.' It wasn't a lie; there was a tight metal band round her temples.

'Do you want something for it?'

'I just need my bed.'

'Elspeth,' Duncan Crombie asked with an edge to his voice as she started to climb the stairs, 'Cameron hasn't upset you, has he?'

'No, I'm just tired. Goodnight.' She escaped to the privacy of her room, closing the door with relief. She had a great deal to think about before morning.

Crombie's handsome face wore a worried frown when the two of them met at the breakfast table.

'You don't look at all well. You'd better go back to bed and I'll call a doctor.'

'I'm fine, please don't fuss.'

He looked more closely, and his face darkened. 'Cameron did upset you last night. What happened?'

Elspeth poured herself a cup of tea with a steady hand. 'He asked me to marry him.' Then, as his eyes went blank, 'And I turned him down, once and for all, because he told me that he'd been making enquiries about you.'

'He did what? The young pup!' he exploded, half rising from the table.

'Sit down please, Father.'

He did as she asked. 'What did he tell you?'

'That when your uncle died six months after you went away he left you quite a lot of money in spite of what happened between you and my mother. In fact, it was because you went away – because you did as he told you – that he kept you in his will. Forbes says' – she set the teapot down gently –

'that you inherited enough to support my mother and me. But in spite of that you didn't come back to Greenock.'

The colour drained from his face and the piece of toast he was about to butter was put back on to his plate. 'I – I wrote to Maisie, at her parents' home, asking her to come to England. When she didn't reply I thought—'

'You must have known that her mother would intercept the letter and probably destroy it. You should have come back for her.' Elspeth fisted her hands on the table. 'For us.'

'I – you have to understand that I was very young, Elspeth, younger than you are now. I had no way of knowing if Maisie would take me back. I had no choice but to leave – my uncle held the purse strings, and he arranged the job in England for me with a lawyer he knew.' He swallowed hard, then went on, 'I don't suppose Cameron told you that my uncle had already arranged with the lawyer to buy a junior partnership for me once I'd served my time. The money left to me in his will was part of the arrangement. If I'd returned to Greenock I would have lost it all. I still wouldn't have been able to support you and Maisie.'

'So you put yourself first and kept the money, and left my mother to cope as best she could.'

'I told you – I thought that her parents would look after her – and you – if I was out of the way. And I did come back to look for you, to atone for what I'd done to the two of you all those years ago.'

He leaned across the table earnestly. 'Elspeth, we've only just found each other. Now's the time for us to start again, together. Don't let Cameron's mischief-making come between us – that's what he wants. Once he gets me out of your life, he'll marry you. That's what he plans. You deserve better than him, my dear. Sell the agency and come away with me.'

Elspeth had been making a pretence of drinking her tea. Now she put the cup down gently and got to her feet. 'I'm not my mother. She's dead, and nothing you can do for me will make up for the wrong you did her.'

375

'Elspeth—'

'I'll come and collect my things when I've found somewhere to stay,' she said steadily from the doorway. 'As for the loan you made me to rent the shop and the flat—'

All his confident charm had gone. He looked old and defeated. It would have been easy to pity him, but Elspeth knew of the dangers that lay in that direction. 'I don't want it back!'

'I wasn't going to offer it. I'm going to do as you wanted in the first place and accept it as a gift – for my mother's sake,' she said, and went out of the house without a backward glance.

She attended to her office duties as usual throughout the day, glad that there were no prospective clients to see, and worked on into the evening, until she was sure that Thomas would be home.

He answered the door in shirt and trousers, blinking his surprise. 'What are you doing here?'

'I want to ask a favour.'

'Did you forget your key?' he asked over his shoulder as she followed him into his room.

'I gave it back to Forbes.'

The room was neat and clean, as usual. An empty plate with knife and fork on it stood on the table, together with a mug.

'I was just finishing my dinner,' Thomas said, following her glance. 'D'you want some tea?' He reached for his jacket, hanging over the back of his chair.

'No, I want you to come to my – to Duncan Crombie's house with me to collect my things.'

He paused in the act of slipping one arm into a jacket sleeve. 'You're moving out? Have you found somewhere else to stay?'

'I'm sharing with Rachel and the bairns for the time being.' She told him, in detail, what Forbes had found out about Duncan Crombie, and he heard her out in silence, then said,

'It takes all sorts of folk to make the world, Ellie.'

'I know that, and mebbe one day I'll forgive him for what he did to my mother. But I'll not stay under his roof.'

'What're you going to do? Marry Forbes?'

She looked him in the eye. 'D'you think I should?'

His gaze dropped. 'You could do worse. He'd be able to give you everything you want, not like—' He paused, then said carefully, 'Not like most men in this town.'

'Money's not everything.'

A muscle jumped in Thomas's jaw, just below the livid scar that now bisected one cheek. 'Mebbe not, but it can be very important.'

'Aileen didn't think so, and neither do I. I'm not going to marry Forbes, for I couldn't marry a man who thinks he has the right to pry into other folk's lives. But I can do business with him.' She glanced round the room. The house windows had shattered in the heat from the fire, but they had been replaced, and the old building still stood steady as a rock. 'I'm going to ask him to sell me this place.'

His jaw dropped. 'What on earth—?'

'I need to live somewhere, and I've always liked this house. It should be lived in, properly, by a family. I'm going to see the bank manager tomorrow, then I'll have a word with Forbes. He might be quite glad to get the place off his hands now that he's got a new garage to finance.'

'And what about me?'

'I'd never turn you out on the street. There's room enough for us both, though I'd really like to see this room going back to being a drawing room. I'm sure we could come to some arrangement,' she said sweetly, and understanding began to dawn in his face.

'Ellie, if this is a ploy to force me to—'

'I've no intention of forcing you to do anything, Thomas McDonald, but I've had enough of accepting what other folk say. Granjan told me that if I wanted something badly enough

I should fight for it. And that's what I'm going to do.'

She held his gaze with her own, while her fingers nimbly unfastened the pebble brooch from the lapel of her grey jacket. 'I can never take Aileen's place, but I can give you a different kind of happiness. I want you to think over what I'm saying, and when you get round to admitting that I'm right, I'm going to sell the agency and buy a wee garage where you can look after the motorcars and I can see to your books. We'll mebbe even rebuild this garage, if that's what you want. Here—'

She crossed to where he stood, going up on tiptoe to fasten the brooch to the inside of his lapel, feeling his chest warm and solid beneath her fingers as she did so. 'You can keep it for the next five years if necessary,' she told him, stepping back. 'When you're ready to see sense you don't have to say so, you only have to return the brooch. Now – come and help me to collect my things and take them to Hamilton Street.'

'You're daft, Elspeth Bremner,' he said, as she reached the door.

She smiled at him over her shoulder, and saw his lips twitch in reply.

'I know I am, but I see no reason to change,' she said, and went through the door and out into the dark street, knowing without having to look back that he was just behind her.

She doubted whether it would be another five years before the pebble brooch came back to her, but even if it was, she could afford to wait.

Five years was such a small price to pay for an entire future.